ASSAULT
ON CAMBRIOL

Cover Art and Design © 2014 by Bryan Rogers

Copyright © 2014 by Black Canyon Press

Copyright © 2014 by Jerry Borrowman

Printed in the United States of America

First Edition: April 2014

MILITARY SCIENCE FICTION

ASSAULT ON CAMBRIOL

JERRY BORROWMAN

Black Canyon Press

ACKNOWLEDGEMENTS

I owe a debt of gratitude to many people who have helped with this story, including Tina Foster and the many readers who shared their opinions. I particularly appreciate best-selling author Jeff Savage for taking time from his own writing to act as story editor. I'm also pleased to introduce Bryan Rogers, the terrific graphic artist who designed the outstanding original artwork for the cover. You can view Bryan's work at behance.net/bryanrogers and reach him at brdesignstudio@comcast.net. Special thanks goes to Mark Sorenson, my copyeditor who makes this publication possible by getting it in final form for e-books and printing. As you can see, it takes a lot of great people to publish a book, and I am grateful for all of them. I hope you enjoy the story of the Assault on Cambriol.

PROLOGUE: THE LEGEND OF THE LEXUS

"Prepare to fire a dazzle blast!"

"Weapons ready, Sir!"

Captain Pietr Jesik frowned as he studied the forward instruments display, then instructed the Helmsman to bring the ship to a new heading of 310 degrees west, 10 degrees elevation. "Blasted kids," he muttered under his breath, "it looks like one of those new Lexus space utility vehicles. What were their parents thinking, anyway?"

Lexus was the name given to a luxury brand of space runabouts that comfortably seated four people while zipping from one planetary system to another. No one really knew where the name came from, although it was generally thought that it dated back into antiquity when vehicles operated solely on a planet's surface. However, at this time a Lexus represented a particularly annoying problem since it carried four small missiles that could easily be fired at an asteroid or small moon from a distance of one to five thousand kilometers. The intent of the missiles was self-defense or to blast small meteors out of a flight path, but were often used for more mischievous purposes when in the hands of teenagers.

"They've started their approach to Cambriol, Sir and it looks like they're heading for the Zestrian Low Pools."

"Thank you Mr. Brighton," said Jesik with a scowl to his First Officer. "Close range, Mr. Wight!"

This was just what the young Ensign, currently acting as Helmsman, had been waiting for. After four boring weeks with nothing to do but intercept and register lumbering cargo ships, he finally had a chance to see what the old Lentissimo could do. Jamming the forward thrusters to maximum, he felt a satisfying lurch as the Aegis Class Boundary Patrol Cutter accelerated to his command. He turned around with a satisfied smile, only to see the Communications Officer, John Williams, picking himself up off the floor, looking anything but happy. Wight jerked his head forward and gulped. Fortunately, the drama was heating up enough that no one took time to chew him out. But of course that would come later.

"Estimated time to firing range?" inquired Jesik.

"Sixty-eight seconds, Sir."

"Fire the moment we come into range!"

Everyone held their breath. At precisely sixty-six seconds, the little cruiser launched two missiles at the surface of Cambriol. At sixty-eight-point-five seconds, the Fire Control Officer fired the dazzle blast.

"Damn!" shouted Jesik as he watched the exhaust trails of the missiles form a perfect trajectory towards the planet's surface. Thirty seconds later, two large explosions were clearly seen on the planet, followed by the blinding detonation of the Dazzle Blast some ten kilometers from the Lexus runabout.

"Nice shot," said the First Officer, smiling.

"Yes, nice shot indeed," growled the Captain, then added, "Close to the runabout, Mr. Wight. And take it a little easier this time!"

The Ensign cringed as he edged the ship in the direction of the disabled spacecraft now lying off their port side. Although the bridge officers had other duties to attend to, they couldn't resist watching the main viewer to see how the space cruisers' missiles had succeeded in stirring up a sulfuric plume from the moon's surface. There was an audible gasp when two magnificent reddish-orange explosions appeared, sparkling like a rain shower during a bright Cerelean star rise.

"Wow! They must have hit the black water pools perfectly to get that mix of water and powder," said the Navigator.

The unique coloring of the sulfur surface was perfect for stirring up dust towers that could be seen from the planet's surface. The system star, Kalenden, which shared the same name as its most prominent planet, was relatively young and provided brilliant illumination for the clouds.

"Spectacular," agreed the First Officer. "I bet those plumes can be seen from all three continents on Kalenden!"

"We'll know soon enough." Jesik sighed, then ordered the communications officer to tune into Sector Control short space.

"My bet is that we'll be hearing from them in three minutes or less."

It was actually less. Approximately ten seconds, for anyone keeping track. They knew they were really in for it when they saw the bloated face of Colonel Kensington shoving a young Corporal off the video monitor.

"Jesik!" the image shouted, "What in blazes is going on out there? Is the whole moon disintegrating and on its way to knocking us out of orbit?"

"Colonel?" Jesik answered in a puzzled voice, "it was only two small missiles from a Lexus mini-Cruiser. I know the plumes are rather spectacular, but certainly no threat."

"No threat!" Kensington shot back, "Then how do you explain this?"

The screen brightened with a video image that showed most of the southern sky of Kalenden filling with an expanding cloud of bright orange vapor that dimmed the sun and appeared to be rapidly swallowing the second moon that was sometimes visible in that hemisphere.

Jesik hit the mute button and turned to his Chief Engineer, Timothy O'Casey. "What is it, Chief? How can two plumes create such havoc on Kalenden?"

Chief Engineer Casey looked perplexed as he studied his instruments. Kensington was still shouting into the monitor, but no one paid attention. Finally, O'Casey looked up relieved and said, "It's just a dust storm Sir, passing between the planet and the moon. Because Kalenden is at apogee, the light reflecting off Cambriol has magnified the effect of the sulfur so that it looks like the whole sky is on fire. It should calm down in about twenty or thirty minutes."

First Officer Brighton tried to suppress the smile that would almost certainly provoke Kensington into a heart attack. Still, it was hard not to show some amusement at the havoc their little space marauders had caused. Hard for everyone but the Captain.

"Colonel Kensington, my Chief has an explanation for you. There's no danger, so I recommend you cancel all alerts."

After listening to the Engineer's report, Kensington told the assembled crew that there would be hell to pay and that it was disgraceful that a four-seater could get past a Sector Defense cutter and cause such a ruckus, particularly when the Quadrant Council was meeting on Kalenden.

When Jesik had heard enough, he gave a passable excuse and moved down to the docking bay where he expected to find three or four dazed cadets being dragged out of their runabout.

Entering the bay, Jesik rubbed his temples. *After six years on a battleship, what did I do to wind up transferring to a cutter to police truants who like to take potshots at a deserted sulfur moon,*. Of course the question was completely rhetorical, since Jesik knew perfectly well what he'd done to deserve such a backwater command. He looked at the pile of young space cadets at his feet with contempt.

Eventually one of the young men in the gaudy uniform of the Kalenden Arms Academy groaned and rubbed his eyes. He looked up at the stern face of Pietr Jesik, groaned again, then sat up with a start and said, "Sir, how did we do? You knocked us out before we got to see the impact."

Jesik tried, but couldn't suppress a smile. After all, he'd been a cadet once. However, he'd grown up in a second-class family, where kids had to worry about the damage they caused. Academy students came from the refined cream of Kalendan society, the top tier of the first-class, so they could go around blowing up asteroids and moons, secure in the knowledge that their parents would pay the damage and secretly smile at their sons' pranks.

The problem with firing on Cambriol, one of two moons orbiting the system's primary inhabited planet, is that the black water pools that made the columns sparkle so brilliantly also held a mineral-rich water rumored to have aphrodisiac qualities. That made it a favorite getaway for the beautiful people looking for a secluded weekend of love-making. The two competing interests of shooters and bathers kept the Boundary Patrol busy. "A very meaningful way to spend ones' professional career," muttered Jesik. He reflected on the fact that in spite of all the threats and dangers, the mineral rich pools still attracted people from the entire sector, even though Cambriol had been declared off limits to all human life years earlier because of the weak atmosphere, violently unpredictable weather patterns, and acrid rain that could cause allergic reactions.

Still, the bathers came, only to be fired on by thrill seeking teenagers on leave from the local space academies that populated this corner of the Kalenden Star Cluster. While this gave rise to some wonderfully tragic stories of lovers covered in slime and ash, while yet locked in a passionate embrace, every so often a bather would be killed. That's when the legends and lawsuits started, with everyone blaming the Boundary Patrol for not doing a better job of protecting people from their own stupidity.

"Sir, how'd we do!" Jesik's mind jerked back to the present and he found a slender young man with sandy hair and pale blue eyes standing at attention before him.

"What's your name, Cadet?"

"Cadet Travis Eaves of the Kalenden Arms Academy, Sir!"

"Well, Cadet Eaves, you scored a direct hit on the Zestrian Pools and now have two plumes over 8,000 kilometers in height, shimmering for the whole of the planet to see in the Kalenden star rise.

"8,000 kilometers—that's awesome!" A broad grin filling Eaves' well-sculpted face.

"Yes, I'm sure you'll be welcomed home as conquering heroes. By the way, although it probably never crossed your mind, our sensors indicate that there were no bathers at the pool, so you didn't maim or kill anyone." Jesik hoped for some kind of response, but neither Eaves nor his now-awake companions appeared very interested.

Youth, thought Jesik . *What do you expect from healthy young guys who are turbo-charged by hormones? All they're thinking about is the effect this will have on the local female population when they get home. Quadrant Councils and over-aged lovers are the last thing on their minds.*

"Speaking of home Sir, when do we get to leave?" asked the second occupant of the Lexus, a cadet who identified himself as Sean Magill.

"*If* you get to leave, not when," the Captain corrected him.

"What do you mean, *if,* Sir?" asked Eaves, with no trace of fear in his voice. He'd obviously been in trouble before.

"What I mean," said Jesik with the slightest hint of triumph, "is that while your timing was perfect to capture the best star rise in the past ten years, it also came while a dust trail was passing between Cambriol and Kalenden, which made it look like the moon itself had blown up down on the planet surface. It seems you boys have caused a major panic on the planet, just as the Quadrant Council was in session. If the images of mayhem in the streets are any indication, you're likely to make the news throughout the entire system! I'm not sure even your parents, who I assume are very wealthy, can afford to make restitution for an entire hemisphere's worth of damage."

Jesik was quite pleased with his effect on the boys. All of a sudden there were two very embarrassed young men in front of him, rather than the cocky swashbucklers of a few moments ago. To further sober them up, he added, "The truth is, your timing couldn't have been worse. The academy may expel you for political reasons." That made them so delightfully miserable that Jesik thought they were finally getting it.

"Take these young men to temporary quarters and see that they get something to eat," said Jesik to a nearby security officer. Then he walked over to the nearest communication port and said, "Lieutenant Williams, please request a flight plan to bring us to Sector Control Platform Five on Kalenden."

"Request being transmitted now, Sir," came the hollow reply through the overhead speaker system.

"Very good. Inform Helmsman Wight when orders are received and please ask Commander Brighton to come to my quarters."

"Right away, Sir,"

Turning to the boys one last time, he said, with a softer tone in his voice, "It really was great shooting. I hope they don't file criminal charges though, since that would keep the two of you from ever being eligible for military service. What a waste that would be."

As he was about to turn and make a dramatic exit, the ship's stabilizers temporarily failed, throwing everyone in the corridor against the walls. Then, as the ship returned to horizontal, Jesik realized the gravity sphere must have malfunctioned because they all began to drift in the air. It was always comical to see the negative effect on the dignified bearings of highly-disciplined military people when thrown unexpectedly into zero gravity. There was absolutely no way to be graceful.

Jesik shouted into his personal communicator, "Mr. Brighton, what's going on up there?"

"Trouble maintaining our orbit around the moon, Sir. Something seems to be pulling us away from the star!"

"Trouble maintaining orbit?" Jesik caught his breath. "I'll be right there." He then fought his way towards the nearest transport tube, using his feet to kick away from the wall. Flying through space has the appearance of swimming underwater, except without any resistance. One kick sets a person in motion until something stops him. Accordingly, Jesik stretched out his arms and grabbed the handrail in front of the tube, leaving himself floating prone, about five feet above the deck. But, just as he reached the tube, the gravity generator reasserted itself, causing him and all other objects and people in the room to crash to the deck. Jesik shook his head, rubbed his nose and pushed himself up to a standing position. He also concealed the pain he felt, for all public spaces were under constant surveillance and captains should show no pain.

Brushing off his trousers, he entered the tube which whisked him directly to the bridge. As he came on deck, he was startled to see the video monitor filled with dark, sinister-looking, rock fragments moving past the ship toward deep space.

"What are we doing in an asteroid belt?" he demanded. Fortunately he had the presence of mind to clamp his jaw shut tight when everyone turned to look at him.

The Chief Engineer responded, "It appears that all the space debris in the area is being drawn towards an unwelcome intruder from the Sendite Quadrant – a superlative-density ferrous metal fragment."

The Sendite quadrant was uninhabited since, by some unusual twist of fate, there were virtually no stars, planets, or even space debris there. When the first settlers arrived on Kalenden several hundred years earlier, they had been unnerved by the sight of one entire section of the night sky that was perfectly black. Yet, that's how it appeared from the planet.

"Why didn't we receive a warning about something as dangerous as this?"

"With no interplanetary traffic in that area, there's been no live patrols for at least several years," replied First Officer Brighton. "And, apparently the automatic sensors failed, perhaps from lack of maintenance, Sir."

"Thank you, Mr. Brighton." Jesik paused to ponder what he'd just heard. Even if all the sensors had failed, there's simply no way something as powerful as a remnant could get this far into the system undetected.

"How powerful is the fragment, Chief?"

"It's not a black hole, Sir. It's only the size of golf ball, but it's powerful enough to attract everything that can move in its direction, including us. Initial calculations indicate that its gravitational field may actually be powerful enough to warp the normal orbit of Cambriol. The attraction between the fragment and the Kalenden star is so overwhelming that it's likely to eventually distort the normal orbits of everything in the system."

"It seems to me that disruptions to orbits is the least of our worries," said Brighton. "There's no telling what kind of reaction will occur when the fragment collides with our star. If we live through the explosion, it will be interesting to see if the star absorbs the fragment, or the other way around."

Jesik sighed. *What a day. First, we're suckered by two kids with an expensive space utility vehicle and now we're about to mate with a fragment.*

"How long do we have, Mr. Wight?"

"With standard engines at maximum, about forty-five minutes before our resistance becomes futile, Sir."

"And what if we engage the vortex drive?" asked the Captain of his Chief Engineer. "Can we escape the asteroid field and gain some distance from this thing?"

"We've run the numbers, Sir and it looks like the magnetic-gravitational pull of the fragment is so strong at this point that we couldn't successfully create a vortex field, other than one in which the debris belt lies directly in our path. In other words, no hope of escape."

"Thank you, Chief."

It's times like this that Captains are supposed to pull some magic out of the air and initiate a bold, daring move that saves the ship and everyone onboard. Everybody expects it. Movies require it. Unfortunately, a Boundary Patrol Cutter just doesn't have the necessary horsepower to do a lot against the force of a star fragment. So, deciding to put protocol aside, Jesik turned to the assembled crew and asked, simply, "Any ideas, gentlemen?"

There are occasions on a military vessel that one wishes desperately for silence … some relief from the throbbing of the engines, the pinging noise of navigation and the meaningless chatter of shipmates. There are other times, like this one, when the last thing anyone wants is silence. Everyone wants to hear someone say, "Why, yes, Captain, I have a great idea! If my calculations are correct, we can just try such and such."

It just wasn't a good day for hope, unfortunately. The crew was deathly silent. Clearly, the next move was still up to Jesik.

Turning to the Communications Officer, he voiced, "Have you communicated our predicament to the authorities on Kalenden, Mr. Williams?" The look he got in reply announced things were even worse than he thought.

"We're unable to transmit anything through the magnetic disturbance, Sir. The last message I heard was the sound of Colonel Kensington giving a planet-wide stand-down to the alert, telling everyone there was nothing to worry about, other than a few harmless plumes on Cambriol magnified by a passing dust storm."

"That's great," muttered Commander Brighton under his breath. "We've managed to neutralize the planets' early warning systems."

"Do we have any Esper links onboard – certainly they could get past the interference?"

"Not presently, Sir, since our patrol has been confined to the solar system we haven't really needed one."

For a few moments Jesik was dazed. What could they do other than prepare for a sudden, crushing death, knowing that in less than five hours an entire planet would be drawn from its normal orbit into one certain to destroy its atmosphere? With an increasingly unstable planet, a full-scale evacuation was impossible. It was all so staggering that his mind almost failed to grasp its full meaning. The hopelessness of the ship being dragged to a crushing end seemed the perfect metaphor for his ill-fated career.

"I just don't see how this thing could suddenly appear out of thin space!"

All the other officers kept their gaze forward. There was no plausible explanation.

"If only there was a way to get a message out."

The ship lurched again, throwing Jesik off balance. At the moment, he had a fleeting image of the incident with the two cadets. He tried to dismiss it so he could concentrate on the problem at hand. But, then, slowly, an idea began to form itself in his mind. With the Lentisimmo's own death certain, he no longer had to worry about that, which freed his mind to think more clearly about how to help the planet. After a few moments in which everyone stood in expectant silence, the Captain shook his head, took a deep breath and made a decision.

The crew noticed his back stiffen as he turned to everyone and declared, "Gentlemen, we've got to warn the planet of their danger. If we give them enough time, perhaps they can launch some nuclear weapons that will divert the fragment from its collision course with Kalenden. Unfortunately, our present trajectory prevents us from properly placing our own missiles and we can't break free of the fragment's gravity to maneuver into proper firing position.

He noted that the navigator nodded to confirm his conclusion.

"To get a message out, we need to get a clear line at a communications corridor and since there's no way we can break free of the field, we're going to have to deploy a surrogate." That statement produced a sea of blank stares.

"Mr. Brighton, please order the two young men from the academy to join us in the shuttle bay."

"Yes, Sir."

Then the Captain asked Weapons, Navigation and Communications to join him for a brief, whispered conversation. The others looking on were somehow pleased to see the three of them start to shake their heads in the affirmative, though no one smiled. "What's the Captain have up his sleeve?" Ensign Wight whispered to the Navigator. It was a rhetorical question. The point is that the Captain had a plan and that's all the crew needed for the dark mood to disappear.

Down in the shuttle bay the two boys stood at attention as the Captain strode into the room.

Jesik didn't have any time to waste, so he said simply, "Gentlemen, there's been an unanticipated change in our condition. A high-density fragment has somehow slipped past system sensors and is attracting all the space debris in the area. It's pulling us in as well and will undoubtedly warp the orbit of the Cambriol moon if left unchecked. Kalenden itself is in grave danger unless we can get your ship out of harm's way to pass a message through to Sector Control. Quite simply, we're counting on you to send perhaps the most important message in the history of this planet."

One can only imagine what the cadets had imagined they'd hear from the Captain, but this clearly wasn't it. They were floored, and stood motionless with vacant stares. Jesik wanted to shout at them to get moving, but realized they needed time to process what they'd heard.

Finally, Cadet Eaves cleared his throat and said, "Excuse me, Sir, but if the Lentissimo can't pull clear of the gravitational pull of the fragment, how can our little four-seater possibly break out?"

"A good question, Mr. Eaves. Here's the plan. We're going to use our ship's Vortex drive to create an inverted cone from the Cambriol radiant. Because it won't be a completed vortex, it should simply have the effect of neutralizing gravity in the area, rather than creating a deep-space fissure. Think of it as a coral reef protecting the water in the lagoon from the wave actions of the ocean. You'll use full thrusters to clear the gravity field and then bring yourself into a neutral position with a clear shot to Kalenden where you'll send a high-speed coded transmission that will automatically launch a planetary alert. That should give Fleet Control enough warning to take countermeasures."

Jesik watched their faces to gauge whether or not they had the courage to do what he was requiring of them. If there was any hesitation he would have to send one of his own officers to command the mission. In some ways he'd prefer to spare one of his own men, but his first responsibility was to save civilians. Fortunately, he was reassured by what he saw in their eyes.

Eaves' companion, Sean Magill said, "Sir, may I ask what will happen to the Lentissimo if you divert enough energy to give us a clear path? It seems to me that you'll never be able to break away in time."

"An astute question, Mr. Magill. Honest questions deserve honest answers. You're exactly right. Instead of having 38 minutes of fuel, we'll have just ten. That's not your problem, though, it's ours."

"Sir, if I may also say, perhaps it's better for us to stay onboard. There must be an alternative to passing through a vortex field that is likely to crush our ship."

Jesik saw the growing fear in the young man's eyes and knew that he had to move decisively.

"Gentlemen," he spoke with firm authority, as Cadets at Kalenden Arms Academy you are subject to immediate impressment in the Sector Defense. You will each consider yourself so pressed as of this moment. You are now commissioned as acting Ensigns in Boundary Patrol, assigned to my command. Is that understood?"

"Yes Sir," they replied in unison, a hint of disbelief in their voices.

"Can I count on you to execute my orders with precision?"

Commander Brighton, who had been standing by during the conversation, noticed an almost instantaneous change in the boys. They assumed a military bearing and seemed to straighten to the task before them. Brighton could tell that all this was wearing on the Captain, so he said, "Gentlemen, the Captain has given you an order. There's no time to lose in meaningless discussion. Our engineers have reversed the effect of the dazzle blast on your ship. Please prepare for immediate departure."

The boys gave a crisp salute.

Turning to the Captain, Brighton said, "Sir, the Lexus Class minicruiser we commandeered for Sector Defense is ready for immediate departure."

"Very good." Turning to the cadets, he offered, "Gentlemen, good luck!"

With that Jesik turned and strode away as the newly minted ensigns scrambled into their tiny little craft. Once settled in, they found a sophisticated communications array strapped into the empty third seat.

When the Captain reached the bridge he asked the Helm if it was ready to create a vortex field on their next pass. Ensign Wight responded in the affirmative. The Captain then asked Communications if everything was ready to trigger the array once it was clear of the interference. Again he received a positive response.

"Very good, then. Chief, would you please divert energy from the standard engines to the Vortex Drive." It was an order, not a question. As the Chief Engineer began the process, the Captain switched on the public address system and addressed the entire crew.

"Gentlemen, fate has dealt us the opportunity to make a difference today. Our ship is lost, no matter what course we follow. By hastening our demise, however, we may save millions. Please join me in saluting the newest members of our crew and wishing them Godspeed as they begin what will be an extremely dangerous journey out of the grasp of the deep-density fragment!"

Jesik was gratified to hear the crew give three hurrahs in traditional military fashion as the Lexus fired its inertia engines. Suddenly the lights dimmed and the ship jerked wildly as Ensign Wight attempted to engage the vortex drive. The field was unstable, as they knew it would be. Still, they could see the debris field clear before them and then, in an instant, the little Lexus runabout rocketed out into the deep blackness of space. In three minutes all would either be well with them, or they'd be destroyed. And all the fuel in the Lentissimo would be gone, except for ten minutes of emergency standard drive. The Captain discovered he wasn't afraid of his own death, but mourned greatly the thought of losing his crew. As he watched the little craft disappear from the video monitor, he found himself wondering if there really was life after death.

Onboard the Lexus, Acting Ensigns Eaves and Magill were hanging on for their lives. The ride was wilder than anything they could imagine, the little vehicle being buffeted about in cascading waves of the vortex drive. Nothing in their experience had ever prepared them for such a thing. If it hadn't been so exhilarating, it probably would have been terrifying. For three minutes all they could think of was whether their ship would hold together until they reached safety. Fortunately, the Lexus was known as one of the finest crafted vehicles in the universe and it stood up to this challenge.

Once clear of the field, Travis Eaves deftly maneuvered the spacecraft to its pre-assigned position and Sean Magill initiated the emergency launch sequence of the communications array. The cabin divided into four airtight containers, one for each member of the crew and then jettisoned the communications buoy.

Even though they expected it, it was still startling to hear the radio burst into life with a system-wide emergency signal that they themselves had initiated.

"Warning, Warning, Warning … all military and civilian spacecraft … extreme danger in the Kalenden system … prepare for an emergency announcement from Sector Control!"

The boys smiled, knowing that Sector Defense was, at this moment, unscrambling the message and would, just as soon as possible, deploy all available spacecraft for an assault on the debris field and the errant fragment. They couldn't help but let out a cheer, even though they were now officially commissioned junior officers.

After the shout, a hollow silence settled in. Eaves turned to Magill, the best mathematician of the two and asked, "How much time does the Lentissimo have?" Magill did quick calculations on his slide rule and said, "About nine minutes."

Eaves then asked, "You're the expert on deep-space deployment – how long before the planet can launch effective countermeasures against the asteroid belt?"

Sean replied in a subdued voice, "At least twenty to thirty minutes before they can develop strategy and position themselves far enough out to avoid being trapped by the gravity field, while still in range to fire weapons."

The two boys found it hard to speak as they looked back in the direction of the belt they had just escaped. It was illuminated by strange and shifting light patterns created by the magnificent colors of the plumes they'd stirred up. Now they understood why their attack had created such an unusually spectacular display. But, the giant plumes were merging into one as they were drawn by the gravity of the fragment. The sulfur cloud would never settle down. It's like a whole section of the night sky was on fire with agate, amber and crimson. And it seemed unfair that the Lentissimo would die amid such overwhelming beauty.

It's strange how an unspoken resolve can begin to grow between two like-minded people. No one knows exactly what the other is thinking, yet somehow both know. So it happened this time. Eaves, who had grown up as a spoiled child of a patrician family was in superb physical condition, typical for boys of the ruling class. His training was impeccable, yet he'd never really learned to care for anyone but himself and his immediate friends. Through grade school and junior high he'd stirred up trouble wherever he could, always being bailed out by his parents.

Magill was from the third-class, with a different kind of toughness, but had joined Eaves and his group at the academy where he'd been accepted on a merit scholarship.

"You know," Eaves said, "when we first met Jesik I thought he was just a traditional military buffoon like our instructors. After all, why would any serious Commander his age be assigned to a Boundary Patrol Cutter? But he's actually a really decent guy and a capable leader."

"No kidding, did you see how cool he was when he ordered us to abandon the ship, knowing that everyone else aboard was going to die? That took real guts!"

They both agreed that he was obviously much more than the usual martinet they'd come to expect from the service. It'd been many centuries since the Fleet had faced any real threat and so leadership positions were usually given as a political reward, rather than recognition of talent and valor. Clearly, Jesik had somehow offended the military politicians. But, whatever his offense, he did have valor and now each of them felt his coming death deeply.

That's where the resolve came in. It was Eaves, the pilot and seemingly more natural leader, who broke the silence. "We can't just let them die without trying. There's got to be something we can do!"

That sort of talk was always a clue for Magill to come up with a plan. While Eaves played the role of cavalier daredevil, Magill was the more collected one. A quick thinker, his academy major was Geology and Physics.

Almost unconsciously, he switched on the sensors array, for the Lexus was well equipped with almost as much computational power as a small frigate. Scanning past the asteroid field, he quickly zeroed in on the tiny fragment of a collapsed star that was inexorably draining the life out of the Lentissimo.

"Look at it," Magill marveled as he magnified the view. "It looks impregnable." They watched as a huge remnant of an asteroid collapsed into seeming nothingness, adding an infinitesimal amount of mass to the one-inch fragment. Next they saw an old satellite collapse like a crushed soft drink can until it, too, disappeared from sight.

"That's what's going to happen to the Lentissimo," said Magill quietly.

"The fragment is so dense that there are no pock marks or even scratches on it, even though it's probably absorbed space debris at least ten or twenty million times through the eons!"

None of his sensor revealed anything that could give them even a remote opportunity to make a difference in the life and death struggle of the cutter.

Magill flipped some switches on the sensor panel and accidentally tripped the audio array, causing it to emit an ear piercing shriek. While the noise could be great fun when swooping down on an unsuspecting beach party at night, it was useless in deep-space, since there's no medium to transmit the sound. Which is why he and Eaves were startled out of their wits when their main console returned the shriek from deep in the debris field.

"What the hell was that!" shouted Magill. Eaves reached over and quickly flipped the switch off, then stared at Magill. Slowly the color returned to Sean Magill's face as he said, "Of course! The magnetic field is so strong around the fragment that it provided a medium for the sound to reach the field and return to us!"

"So," Eaves asked, with a hint of exasperation, "Who cares?"

"We do!" Magill replied quickly, "listen to the sound going out and coming back." He replayed the sequence and there was a distinct tonal difference in the returning waves.

"What does it mean?" Eaves inquired.

"It means that there's something unstable in that fragment. There must be a reaction taking place. And where there's instability, there's a chance to cause some damage."

Eaves was paying close attention now. This was the kind of information he was looking for, a weakness to exploit, an obstacle to conquer. He shouted, "We still have two torpedoes, will that shake it up?"

Magill quickly re-calibrated the audio to get precise information on the fragment's hidden flaw. Then, working together on the math, he and the ship's computer calculated the impact point that stood the best chance of aggravating the fragment's nuclear core. Because of its density, it was likely that a small explosion would take place, which would disturb the gravitational field of the entire area. It would certainly be enough for the Lentissimo to pull free and may even enough to reduce the pull on Cambriol and divert the fragment away from the system star. A lot of ifs, to be sure, but what else was there to try?

Eaves contemplated the plan. "Of course, if we miss the shot, we'll be sucked into the gravitational field ourselves and beat Jesik and the others to an early demise."

They looked at each other apprehensively, then said, almost in unison, "What the heck, let's go for it!" With the tension broken, Eaves placed his hands on the Forward Thrusters Control and confidently shoved it to maximum.

* * *

So it is, then, that the "Legend of the Lexus" was born. Not until hours later did the boys learn that because of bureaucratic maneuverings, nothing could be launched from the planet in time to avoid a disruption to the Kalenden orbit. Even if the planet lived through the fusion of the fragment with the star, the people would have to abandon their homes in a full planet evacuation as the fragment was clearly destined to end all biological life in this sector.

It was the boy's attack that prompted the crew of the Lentissimo to look on in stunned disbelief as the tiny mini-cruiser came shooting past their starboard bow on a direct collision course with the fragment. But when they launched their two tiny, dust-devil torpedoes, with an unusual explosive pattern set to destabilize the fragment, Jesik stared in awe. Then he did his very best to keep his head from being torn from his neck as the explosion of the fragment sent the Lentissimo hurling across two parsecs of space, end-over-end the whole way. The crew was ultimately disoriented and bruised when it was over, but, miraculously, everyone was still alive.

The success of the attack was the source of the legend of the two young truants who were dazzled twice in the same day; once by a dazzle blast and the second by the largest explosion ever recorded in the Kalenden Quadrant. After regaining consciousness, Ensign Magill was embarrassed to realize that, in the heat of the moment, he'd misplaced the decimal point when calculating the explosive power of an ultra-high density fragment de-stabilizing and disappearing into an alternate universe. In fact, the fragment's disappearance became an important part of the legend. Quantum analysis indicated the probability was extremely high that the unusual pattern of the fragment's flaw made it prone to bounce from one parallel universe to another with some regularity, which is why it had not been detected earlier. And "alternate universe" theories suggested it was even possible that two teenagers in an adjoining reality had used the very same ploy to send it into this universe.

In the end it was a very good thing that the fragment chose that exit route, rather than simply exploding in this universe. If the full force of the blast had been absorbed exclusively in this universe, they wouldn't have had to worry about saving the planet, or even the entire solar system, for that matter. They would simply have all been blasted into oblivion before anyone knew what hit them.

Adding to the mystique of this modest assault was the twisted wreckage of their mini-cruiser, which ended up looking like it had been sucked backwards through the wrong end of a black hole. It was put on permanent display at the Sector Control Military Museum, where children and their parent's marvel that anyone could survive in that tangled mass of once shiny metal.

It's often a short distance between rogue and hero and sometimes it takes just one event in a lifetime to turn an otherwise self-centered, insignificant individual into a great leader. Without their modest assault on Cambriol, the distinguished military, diplomatic and scientific careers of Travis Eaves and Sean Magill might never have been.

It was also the end of exile for Captain Pietr Jesik, who, by virtue of his "Valor and Honor," restored luster to the Boundary Patrol. Since politicians love heroes, his became one of the most recognized faces in the service.

Perhaps it wasn't such a bad day, after all.

1 - MATTER OF PATERNITY

"Thank you, Mr. Williams, I'll take it at the Science Station. Please invoke a privacy field."

Williams, the ship's Communications Officer, looked around the spacious bridge of the Allegro, the newest and most powerful battleship in the fleet. It still seemed miraculous that after the Cambriol incident the entire crew of the Lentissimo had been transferred as a single unit under the command of Captain Pietr Jesik. That was four years ago. *Our reward for saving the folks at Fleet Headquarters. Amazing what a little political favor can do for a crew's fortunes.*

The Lentissimo had been so badly damaged by the blast of the fragment and its subsequent tumble through space, that the instrument array was permanently scrambled, the hull pitted and dented like a brass tuba in a high school band, and the forward thrusters crippled beyond recognition. It made sense to de-commission the ship a few years early, rather than undertake the extensive repairs required to make her space worthy again.

Still, Williams thought, it was sad to watch her final departure out of the space dock at the official de-commissioning ceremony.

There had been two incredible results of the ship's final ordeal at Cambriol. The hull stresses had exceed maximum tolerances by more than 600% -- making it statistically impossible that anyone onboard could survive. Yet, aside from cuts, bruises, and broken limbs, not a single member of the crew had died. Little wonder they felt so attached to the ship. As a sign of respect for saving the Kalenden System, Fleet Command authorized the ancient practice of sending an honorably dented and bruised, but still operational ship, on a final voyage into the gravitational field of the Kalenden star itself. A more practical and usual procedure was to salvage all useable instruments and parts and then recycle the alinite hull for future use. Since alinite was such an expensive alloy and Fleet Command so uncommonly stingy, it really was a remarkable honor for the ship.

Williams leaned back in his chair and recalled the ceremony. Impressive and solemn, it was very moving when Captain Jesik pressed the remote control activator to start the ship on its final voyage while Commander Brighton read lines from an old star mariner poem, "Descent Into Eternity,"

> "What magnificent fate
> For a ship that dies,
> 'Mid nuclear fires and furnace seared
> A final plunge to the heart of a star,
> Where none return, or feel to mourn"
>
> (author unknown)

Williams smiled at the memory of the onboard video cameras returning vivid images until the monitor flared its brightest hue and went dark. The real show of the final voyage occurred in the eastern sky above Kalenden's main continent where the sparkling silver hull reflected the brilliant fires of the star with such radiance that people swore it blinded spectators who were foolish enough to look with unprotected eyes. Next came the explosion of the alinite hull, which disintegrated with an effect equal to a nuclear explosion. And since the ship exploded before its image merged with the star itself, for a brief moment it was like having two stars in the sky. After the initial flash, which lit the evening sky for nearly two minutes, the decaying cloud looked like a gaping, reddish wound radiating out from the star. It was both beautiful and terrible to think that humans could create an effect as brilliant.

As a deck officer he had been given a spot of honor on the reviewing stand, along with members of the Quadrant Council itself. "A fine day!" he reflected with satisfaction. His self-congratulatory revelry was disturbed by the Helmsman, Kevin Wight, who had been checking bearings against a nearby Interplanetary Positioning buoy. "Wow, I've never seen Commander Brighton's face so flushed – what do you think he's talking about?"

Williams glanced up in time to see the normally unflappable Brighton raise both hands to his forehead, cover his eyes, then slap them back down to his side. "That is unusual," he said. "All I know is that the call came from the Tatrion System, re-routed a couple of times to obscure its precise origin."

The privacy field blocked out any sound and actually created a visual blurring of Brighton's mouth movements to throw off any would-be lip readers. But, it couldn't block out the fact that he was agitated. Or, perhaps a better word would be angry.

The call ended abruptly and Brighton made a slicing motion across his neck. Williams immediately terminated the privacy field.

"Mr. Gentry, please stand forward as Officer of the Bridge. Lieutenant Commander Gentry was the Weapons officer and a formidable individual. "Lieutenant Williams, thank you for the communications-link. Follow protocol for a Level-6 message and destroy all record of this transmission, immediately."

"Yes, Sir!" The reminder was quite unnecessary, since Williams knew better than to hang on to a Level-6. It was a court-martial offense, for crying out loud.

"First Officer leaving the bridge," said Alec Gentry in his sonorous voice as he left the weapons console to sit in the Captain's chair.

"Wow, again," Williams muttered as the transport tube doors closed. "Whatever it is, it certainly has thrown the Commander off-horizon."

The Helmsman was about to respond, but his witty reply was cut short, falling victim to Gentry's terse, "Cut the banter, gentlemen and return to your duties!"

Those weapons guys have no sense of curiosity, Williams thought as he turned back to his console.

In his private quarters, Brighton ordered some anteberry tea which materialized a few moments later. "This can't be happening," he muttered into the cup, though it didn't seem to care. *How could she be so careless and how could I be so stupid?* He walked to his bed, slipped off his trousers and shirt and laid down on the cool bedspread. Addressing the ceiling, "Please display my personal file on Sondra Vivendel."

A three-dimensional image of Sondra appeared at the foot of his bed as the metallic voice of the computer intoned, "Sondra Vivendel, resident of Tatrius. Female age 32, a ceramics and metal alloy engineer. Graduate of the Tatrius Engineering Institute with a PhD. in metallurgy."

"Personal background on subject?"

"Subject is single, no children. She lives in the Coltrax district of the capitol city. Address and communications profile protected by privacy regulations."

"Display all photos in the file, three second delay."

The air was filled with various three-dimensional images of Sondra Vivendel that she had posted through the years, starting as a chubby baby, growing into a stocky teenager, turning into an attractive, well-muscled adult. *Cursed gravity on Tatrius. It's no wonder she could beat anyone on the Allegro in a leg wrestle. Why did I decide to go back to her apartment that night?* He rubbed his temples with the palms of his hands and closed his eyes. It didn't help though, for he still saw her in his mind. He also knew why he went home with her that night; she was available, he'd been drinking the local brew, and it seemed like such a great idea at the time. "Who'd have guessed we'd spend the next two days and nights in her apartment?" He opened his eyes, saw an image of Sondra in a bathing suit and moaned. He slumped back onto the pillow.

It's the stupid rules on Kalenden – they make me crazy. At least whenever I manage to escape their tentacles. Sondra wasn't the first woman he'd worked his charms with. In fact, he'd often been able to attract some breathtakingly beautiful women. Certainly not a Lothario, but accomplished nonetheless.

But, Sondra had been different. Her athleticism, good nature and, most of all, her completely non-judgmental attitudes had been truly attractive and made the days with her the best he'd ever had. She satisfied his spirit as well as his body. But, then it was over and he was gone. Their time together was great, but nothing more than a passing encounter of two people from different worlds who hoped to enjoy some companionship and create some pleasant memories.

Of all the planets to be born on, my parents chose Kalenden! The star system Brighton was born into was complex, occupied by former Earth residents who emigrated from Earth for various social and economic regions. The major players were Kalenden, which was inhabited by social conservatives who kept a tight lid on sexual mores, Tatrius, a small, but liberal trading post between major star systems, Alturus, a major planet that had been out-of-contact with Kalenden for nearly 100 years because of social divisions, and Keswick, a small planetoid on the border between Kalenden and Alturus that was unusually endowed with key minerals that were used to supply the fuel for interplanetary travel. Beyond that were dozens of other planets, all of which had to be monitored, but none that posed an immediate threat to Kalenden. When residents of Kalenden wanted to escape for a week or two of unmonitored fun (leading to debauchery) it was off to Tatrius they went.

Pleasant memories are fine, but who said anything about making a baby! He moaned again. How could she be pregnant? She seemed a woman of the world, so why wouldn't she be prepared? And what did she mean when she said "Don't worry, Tom, you won't have to be involved in our lives at all. It's acceptable to be a single parent on Tatrius – we're not like the people of

Kalenden." Her sarcasm was not becoming.

He rolled onto his side and felt the silky smoothness of the Ethereon bed sheet brush against his face. Ah, Kalenden, my home and nursemaid. The most conservative planet in the known universe, where boys and girls are chaste and men and women marry before starting a family. Actually, he liked the idea that people marry to have children. He looked at the nearly empty glass in his hand and said, "Kids need both a father and a mother, or something's missing from their lives." He smiled at the glass, which continued to listen patiently. "The thing that gets me into trouble is my belief that it's okay to practice, a little, before marriage."

Trouble. As an officer and gentlemen it was presumed that he would never degrade the honor of a woman by "cleaving to her" outside of marriage. Kalenden Fleet rules stated clearly that "an officer convicted of fornication or adultery is subject to severe penalties, including reduction of rank or dishonorable discharge from the service." The rules were seldom enforced, though, because no one really followed anyone around to see where they were going. But, a baby was pretty difficult to slip past the unofficial "Don't ask, don't tell" policy of the fleet.

He sat up in bed, pushed against the membrane of the Conformagel mattress and stood up to pace around the room.

Okay, you've gotta get hold of yourself, Thomas. Maybe a good way to start would be to stop talking to yourself.

It didn't work. This kind of conversation needed two voices and he didn't want anyone but his own brain and vocal chords to know what was going on. He strode silently across the room, turned and came back. *She's an alien from a society considered a moral rogue by the Kalenden Quadrant Council and that's good since it precludes a Courts Martial. You can only go to jail for getting a girl from the Kalenden System pregnant.* He'd always been careful on that score, saving his liaisons for trips out of the Quadrant into one of the neighboring systems. Of course a lot of starmen did that – it was probably one of the greatest enticements to enlist, (although the officer corps would deny it with all the righteous indignation they could muster if ever spoken publicly). *If anyone finds out about Sondra, it can still cause a mandatory freeze in grade for two years. Which means it will be at least two years before I'll be offered my own command anyway, so that's not so bad.*

His pacing slowed and he sat down in his easy chair. The heated gel membrane swelled up around his back, arms, and thighs so that he was supported perfectly at all points of contact. He settled back, the chair instantly adjusting to his new preference. He put his arms behind his head and thought, *If I can just figure how to keep this quiet, it'll have no effect at all on my career. After all, Sondra said she really doesn't want to marry me, so why should I press the matter?*

There was a reason, but this wasn't the time to think about it. It would only weaken his resolve to distance himself from the woman and her child.

He spoke up in the authoritative voice that told the ever-listening computer he was about to issue a command. "Please signal the Communications Officer." He pulled on sweatpants as William's face materialized. "Mr. Williams, I need to place a confidential contact, Security Level-6. Will you please arrange a privacy field for my quarters and connect a patch through to Tatrius?"

"Right away, Sir." Williams looked curious.

"Let me know when you're ready."

Williams face disappeared, obviously disappointed.

Biggest gossip on the ship and he's planted in Communications.

Oh, well, Brighton would be allowed to privately enter the local communications address line once the interstellar link was completed through to Tatrius.

The distance between star systems was so great that communication links were impossible to connect without the assistance of multiple operators spread across hundreds of light years. When the vortex drive was first discovered centuries earlier, humankind had been thrilled at the opportunity of escaping to distant stars where they could colonize and create new societies based on their preferred social conventions. It was calculated that the vortex drive could open one-one thousandth of the Milky Way Galaxy to exploration and still hold people within ten years travel time back to the home planet, Earth. For some reason, that proximity seemed really important to the early settlers. They'd imagined a great confederation of humans linked back to earth and the need for a single alliance was taken for granted since a belief in "Unidentified Flying Objects" convinced the majority that their new ability to travel to the stars would bring them in contact with alien races hostile to incursions from earth.

"Aliens and UFOs" Brighton muttered. "Little did they know just how empty space is. In four hundred years we've never encountered so much as a flint arrowhead on any of the thousand or so planets we've charted. It appears human evolution, or creation, was an isolated event, after all. Or, at least no other species in this corner of the galaxy have the means or interest to look for us."

In the absence of an external threat, the grand alliance never materialized and the vast distances effectively isolated each star system to its own government and laws. Adjoining systems formed Quadrants and adjoining quadrants promoted interstellar commerce, but few political contacts. Tatrion was a star system at the border of a neighboring quadrant and therefore immune to Kalenden laws. It wasn't allied with any Quadrant. Its home planet, Tatrius, was a reliable trading partner, but much too socially liberal for Kalenden taste.

Williams' voice announced, "We have six of seven links completed, Mr. Brighton, you should have Tatrius in approximately two minutes."

The tremendous distances required a new form of communication. At first, lasers were used, but even at the speed of light communications could take years to transmit a message, then years to receive a reply. Aside from providing historical news, it was useless for contemporary communication.

Then someone hit on the idea of studying Extra-Sensory Perception (ESP), that odd human ability to sense something is happening with another person even before traditional mechanical or electrical systems could respond. Unfortunately, researchers never succeeded in isolating how ESP worked, so they couldn't duplicate its effect electronically. But they did learn to train those who were sensitive to such impressions to act as carriers for voice, visual and limited file transmissions across the darkness of space. Amazingly, a string of Espers, scattered across the quadrants, could transmit volumes of data without ever invading the privacy of those sending it, unless they consciously tuned into the impressions. Acting as a communications link had become one of the highest paid professions throughout the entire Earth Descendencies and some families actually made it their legacy to raise their children for employment as Espers in "ComServe," where it was a matter of principle to strictly observe privacy protocols.

Even at that, the distance two Espers could communicate across was limited, so it often took numerous links to get a message through. Contemporaneous communication was available for up to ten links. Beyond that, a delay began to set in, which required the parties to pause while awaiting a response. The distance to Earth was so great that it took more than 150 links from Kalenden, making contemporaneous communication impossible. That's why nearly all messages were sent as text, which was less likely to deteriorate than a voice message and where a delayed response was acceptable. Still, Tatrius was close enough to Kalenden that contemporaneous voice was available, though expensive. A Code-6 Transmission meant that only the most reliable and experienced Espers were involved, with absolute privacy guaranteed. That's why it took really big coronas to pay for it.

"Final Link in progress, Sir!"

Brighton's heart rate increased at the thought of talking with Sondra again. He'd been very hard on her in their earlier conversation, even going so far as to question whether he was the child's father. Although she acted tough, like it didn't matter if he was willing to accept paternity, he knew that she was simply not one to make a false accusation. He suspected that he'd been the only man she'd been with, which added to his feeling of guilt.

So, why would she call me, if not to hope I'd take an interest in her and the child? He pursed his lips and unconsciously rubbed his thighs, which hurt from the suppressed tension.

"You have Tatrius, Sir," said Williams triumphantly.

"Terrific job, Mr. Williams, I doubt anyone's ever connected in less than ten minutes. You're the best."

"Thank you, Sir." Williams smiled, "I'll activate the privacy field now and you can enter the remaining numbers."

Williams face disappeared and a holographic keypad appeared in front of Brighton. He typed in Sondra's private communications address and felt his throat tighten as the audio indicator sounded its repetitive tone, indicating that the hail was being received at her residence. Of course he had no idea what time of day or night it might be on Tatrius, since he'd completely forgotten to have the computer check for the best time to call.

"Hello?" Sondra's voice sounded tense and tired.

"It's me again, Tom."

"Tom? I thought you'd said everything you wanted to say during our earlier call."

His face flushed with regret.

"No, not everything. I didn't tell you I'm sorry for reacting so badly. You deserved better." He heard her catch her breath, probably her indignation turning to confusion.

"The truth is, Sondra…" he struggled for breath. "The truth is that you took me so totally by surprise that my brain didn't register exactly what was going on until long after my mouth had made a fool of me."

She attempted a laugh, but didn't say anything.

"Sondra, if you want to raise a child, then I'm glad for you. I still can't entirely get my mind around the thought that I could be a father. For reasons I've never shared with anyone, I'd made up my mind to never have a child. But, that's changed."

"Tom." She worked hard to control her voice. "I'm … I'm sorry I dropped this on you, but I didn't know who else to tell. My mother's the only one I could count on to understand and she's visiting her family on Kalenden. It was just too big for me to keep to myself."

"I understand," he said, "you were right to call me. I think I'm better prepared to talk about it now. We're certainly not the first people this has happened to." He felt himself sweating, which annoyed him greatly. "We can work everything out." He tried to sound reassuring, yet not endearing.

Just as he was about to continue, a sudden, very cold dread started at the top of his head and worked its way down into his consciousness. When it reached his stomach, he felt like someone had slugged him.

"Did you say your mother was visiting relatives on Kalenden?"

"Yes, my grandmother and aunt."

Brighton gasped for air and mumbled weakly, "But, I thought your parents were Tatrians, that you're Tatrian."

"My father is, but my mom moved here from Kalenden as a teenager, when her dad accepted an appointment to an interplanetary engineering exchange program. What's wrong, you sound terrible again."

Brighton couldn't talk. He'd placed the call on an impulse after the thought struck him that he could create a trust fund for the child without ever formally accepting paternity. That would have protected him from prosecution by the Fleet Adjutant, even if the whole thing were ever discovered. But, if Sondra was half Kalenden, then he was open to criminal prosecution.

"Tom, what's wrong?" Sondra pleaded.

"It's just that I didn't know about your mom."

"Tom, nothing's changed. I still plan to raise the child by myself. No one ever needs to know about it. I just wanted you to." She sounded genuinely confused. How could she possibly understand the repercussions he would face? She'd grown up in a system that was so much more accepting of unusual situations that she simply had no way to understand his plight.

"Sondra, we need to find a way to talk this over, face-to-face. Perhaps we could meet on Stirium and spend a few days together?" Stirium was a privately owned planetoid located about half-way between Kalenden and Tatrius, notoriously secretive so that prominent people could slip in and out undetected.

"I'd like to see you," she said, "but I'm not showing any signs of the pregnancy. In fact, it's unlikely that I'll ever show – you know that a Tatrian woman's build helps keep private things private." She tried to laugh. "So, I don't see that there's a rush for us to get together. Why don't you visit me here on your ship's next regular visit? I know you'd be embarrassed to have people see us together, but Stirium frightens me for some reason?"

"It's nothing like that, Sondra. I'm not ashamed of you. It's just that I can't risk being seen inside the Quadrant." His mind raced. If he told her everything, she could blackmail him. But, if he didn't trust her with the situation she could make an innocent mistake that would ruin everything.

"Sondra, I could be arrested for getting a Kalenden pregnant. At the very least, my career will be over and I'll have to move out of the system." It was in her hands now.

"But, how will anyone ever know? I told you I'm prepared to raise the child by myself."

"Oh, they'll know. Believe me, they will." She sensed the anger in his voice – not directed at her, but at whoever "they" were.

"When the baby is born, they'll post his or her genetic tracer to the Interstellar Registry. The Kalenden Department of Genetics has pre-programmed their systems to automatically identify all children born with more than 50% Kalenden DNA patterns. I'll supply 50%, you'll supply 25% and so there will be a positive match. Then I'll receive a coded message to report to the nearest star base where they'll start the inquiry. And that will be that."

"Tom, I'm sorry." What more could she say? "This wasn't supposed to happen. I thought I'd protected against pregnancy. But, as you may have guessed, I didn't really have experience at that sort of thing and simply did it wrong. Being with you was great, but now it's ruined everything for you. I'm sorry."

Brighton rubbed his temples. "Me, too" he sighed.

Sorry, for myself, he thought savagely. But what about them, why don't you feel sorry for Sondra and your child?

"Sondra, we have to get together and talk. I need to think through all this."

"I'll go to Stirium, Tom. When do you want me there?"

"I'll have to arrange a Leave of Absence and come up with some excuse to travel in that vicinity. I could probably get there in…"

Brighton's room suddenly went red, the lights pulsing in a Code 1 Alert. The alert overrode the Privacy Field, interrupting their conversation with the order,

"All officers to the Bridge! All Officers to the Bridge!"

"What now?" Brighton sputtered. "Sondra, I'm sorry, I've got to go, something's happening. I'll be in touch as soon as I can."

"But, Tom, wait, when,…"

The connection was automatically broken by the fifteen-second pro-tocol initiated by a Code 1 Alert. He stood alone in the silence, the lights flashing menacingly around him.

It seemed an ideal metaphor for his life. A fifteen minute out-of-parsec communications link is going to cost a fortune. And now an alert. And a baby! Can't forget the baby. What else can go wrong?

2 - TROUBLED FRONTIER

Brighton entered the bridge conference room to find the other officers taking their seat. The color of the month was blue, with all furnishings in the room color-coordinated with the military artwork to create a sense of visual unity. Brighton particularly liked this scheme since the paintings all featured ancient sailing craft on white tipped ocean waves. "Much better than next month's theme," he thought, when all the fabrics and textures in the room would automatically shift to "Crimson Sunset," featuring desert warfare pictures. He shuddered at the thought.

Glancing at a painting of a 72-gun frigate with all sails run out, he wondered what it would be like to have lived on Earth in those ancient times, when a sailor's essential skills included navigating by the stars and figuring out how to beat against the wind to gain the advantage of an adversary in battle. Strategy was everything and men had to display a rare kind of personal bravery to engage in hand-to-hand combat once two ships grappled together in a life-and-death struggle. Of course the motivation was the promise of prize money – capture an enemy ship and everyone onboard got to share in the value of the ship and its contents. That was enough to motivate even the most cowering of seamen to throw caution to the wind. How different things were once the navies were automated and combat meant firing 2,000-pound shells across an expanse of twenty nautical kilometers, or, later, launching ballistic missiles that traveled upwards of a hundred kilometers. Then, when humans began to conquer space, deep-space torpedoes often traveled tens of thousands of kilometers before striking their targets. Battles became so impersonal you could kill people without ever seeing their face. *Perhaps the old battles were better because you had to measure the real cost in personal terms and the blood on your hands was literal, rather than abstract.*

"Gentlemen, we've just received a coded transmission from Fleet Command indicating a problem in the Keswick System. As the closest ship, we're instructed to proceed to the planetoid Keswick where a rebel force is threatening the Royal Family. Any trouble there can threaten the orchidite supply, which would cripple our economy. The Keswick Royal Family has sent out a general request for assistance and both Alturus and Kalenden have chosen to respond."

There was an audible gasp in the room, which forced Jesik to pause for a moment. "You heard right – Alturus is on their way. After 100 years our two militaries will be circling the same small planetoid. The risk couldn't be greater. Lieutenant Wight will now brief us on our approach."

The Lieutenant stepped forward a bit awkwardly and motioned for the computer to display a two-dimensional map of the Kalenden and Alturus Star Quadrants. "As you can see, the Keswick system lies on the historical boundary of Alturus and Kalenden. Since it consists of just two stars, with approximately 1000 asteroids in orbit and twenty planetoids, it fails to qualify as a member of either quadrant. Previous applications to join our Quadrant have been rejected since the only planetoid that can support life is Keswick, which orbits the primary star. There are approximately thirty million inhabitants on a single continent. The population has been in balance for at least 150 years."

He paused to give everyone a chance to study the charts and get oriented to the course before them. "The approach is tricky, because of the high number of asteroids that interfere with a clear shot for the vortex. Captain Jesik has requested a maximum vortex drift to the outer boundary of Kalenden, with a forced reduction to light drive to maneuver through the asteroid belt. At that rate it will take us two Kalenden-months to reach Keswick, one in vortex drive to cover ninety percent of the distance, one in light drive for the asteroids. We'll have a scheduled stop on Space Station Twelve for supplies and information when we come out of vortex drive."

"May I ask what our involvement will be, Sir?" asked Lieutenant Sean Magill, now grown up and appointed to serve. Both he and Travis Eaves had requested appointment to the Allegro because of their admiration for Pietr Jesik.

Jesik frowned and asked if there were any questions about the approach before proceeding to the political questions. It was all pretty straightforward, so no one really needed more information at that point, although Brighton seemed to take a more active interest when Space Station Twelve was mentioned.

"Alright, Mr. Magill, on to your question. I've asked our political offi-cer to fill you in on the situation, as we know it. Mr. Barrows, proceed."

First Lieutenant Keith Barrows stepped forward and shifted the map to a three dimensional image. Pointing to Alturus he began his briefing, "As you know, Alturus is an historical rival to the Kalenden System. In the first 50 years after separation, we fought three separate engagements that cost more than one million lives on each side. The final war was so devastating that it cost nearly 15 percent military casualties on Alturus and effectively decimated the Kalenden military structure. Both sides agreed to give up in exhaustion. The neutral area between the two systems has been observed ever since. Kalenden society was so dispirited by the war that the formal aristocracy was abandoned and the system became a Republic. Of course families in our system are still categorized by class, but membership in the first-class is not a formal pre-requisite for government service."

"May I ask, Sir, if any sort of unofficial contact exists between the two systems today?"

"A good question, Lieutenant Magill, with an unfortunate answer. While we maintain Space Station 12 to monitor any incursions into our space and to facilitate communications should Alturus wish to contact us, we now have more than a century under our belt with virtually no contact, until this past week. Our Espers occasionally detect communications ema-nating from the Alturian Quadrant, so we've known they're still out there. Plus, we can monitor their video broadcasts to neutral systems, which has given us some insight to their continuing development."

Brighton joined in and added, "We also have occasional face-to-face contact when competing with the Alturians for trading alliances outside our own systems, but their people are quite aloof. As far as I know there's never been even a casual conversation with any of their representatives."

"Doesn't sound very friendly," replied Magill.

Lieutenant Travis Eaves raised his hand. "In view of what you've just told us, I'm not entirely clear, Mr. Barrows, about the order of battle once we reach Keswick. Will we be fighting *with* Alturian troops, or in opposi-tion?"

"Both systems will be fighting as allies of the ruling family. The reason, quite simply, is that Keswick has an abundant supply of orchidite, which they sell to both sides. Their ore is particularly hot, so it's extremely effective in powering a vortex drive. The rebels have been agitating for Keswick to raise prices to enhance their standard of living, but the Loyalist government wants stability, so hasn't been willing to risk antagonizing their customers by a precipitous price increase. Of course neither Alturus nor Kalenden want the rebels to gain control of the mines, so we'll be fighting as reluctant allies. As to your unspoken question, we quite honestly don't know what this new contact with an ancient enemy is going to do. We can hope that it will give us the opportunity to establish civil relationships now that all the old combatants are gone. But, who knows, perhaps there are still some smoldering embers just waiting to be fanned back to life and we'll find that even as we act as allies in the immediate conflict, old wounds will be re-opened. This is new ground for everyone."

"Which is one of the reasons why, gentlemen, you will drill your troops in battlefield etiquette and provide extensive training on Alturian customs and manners." Jesik shifted his gaze to each officer in the room until he was satisfied they'd heard his threat. "Under no circumstances will this ship provide an excuse for hostilities between these two systems. Is that understood?" Each officer nodded assent. "Good. Thank you Mr. Barrows. Weapons, please continue the briefing about expected battlefield conditions."

Lieutenant Commander Gentry stepped forward and activated a panoramic viewer panel. High-resolution images of a moderate sized planetoid came into view, then zoomed to reveal details of the atmosphere and surface. "Over 80% of the surface is covered by a deep ocean that supports an unusually diverse marine ecology, one that easily supplies the nutritional needs of the inhabitants. Because of the planetoid's close proximity to its star the atmosphere is almost constantly at 90% humidity or greater, so the land vegetation is of a tropical rainforest quality."

He paused for a breath and questions, but none were raised, so he continued. "The capital city, Keston, is to the northern end of the single continent, probably because that is the least tropical area of the planetoid. Their land transportation is well developed between major cities because the single ocean would require greater distance for water transport. The fishing industry makes extensive use of specialty fishing watercraft, with a limited Coast Guard for search and rescue operations. Typhoons form the greatest natural threat to ships at sea. Wave action is so severe during storms that most cities have been located at least twenty kilometers inland."

Eaves raised his hand, again. "Do you have intelligence about rebel bases and where the fighting is most likely to occur?"

Jesik studied the young Lieutenant, Junior Grade. He was clearly aching to join the fight. After graduating from the academy he and acting Ensign Magill had made the unusual decision to join the fleet, rather than pursuing advanced studies at the academy. Politics had played a role, with their exploits on Cambriol elevating their status in the public eye. It only made sense that they would enter the branch of service where their commendations would lead to immediate promotion. Still, Jesik couldn't help but feel that Eaves would tire of the relatively clumsy star-fighters that were used to chase down pirates in favor of atmosphere launched aircraft that provided a decidedly more thrilling ride. Perhaps that's why he was taking such an interest in this operation, knowing that it would be fought primarily on the ground and in the air, rather than in near space orbit.

Commander Gentry responded to Eaves's question. "Information is sketchy, of course, but Fleet has managed to interrogate some merchant marine Captains who trade with Keswick and it's their opinion that the rebels are most likely sequestered in the almost impenetrable rain-forests of the southwest. Apparently the undergrowth is so thick that even electronic surveillance often fails to detect normal indicators of life and movement. They're also able to move their aircraft and low-space orbiters on mobile launch pads where they can initiate a strike and return to ground before the planetary defense system has time to respond with a counter-attack. Our intelligence indicates that they're extremely effective pirates, with the full cost of their operations paid by extortion extracted from the merchant ships. It's become so bad, of late, that trade with Keswick for other than orchidite, has fallen off precipitously. That's what prompted the move against the rebels. At first the government had some notable successes in their military campaign, but the rebels adapted and launched a number of terrorist attacks against Keston that has devastated public confidence. Now that they're gaining the upper hand, the ruling family is pleading for assistance."

It looked like Gentry had more to say, but Jesik was impatient to get underway. In spite of a number of raised hands, he cut the briefing short and announced, "Mr. Gentry will be in charge of both space launched and ship-to-ship weaponry, under direction of Commander Brighton. Surface aircraft will report to the Operations Chief and land-based operations will be under direction of the Marines. Lieutenant Eaves, you should prepare to lead one of the aircraft wings with Lieutenant Jason Carter as your navigator and Lieutenant Magill will be placed under temporary assignment to the Marines to assist in the land operations. Any questions?"

There were undoubtedly more questions, but everyone correctly guessed from the Captain's tone of voice that this wasn't the time to ask them. Jesik stood to leave, prompting the others to stand at attention. "One last thing – it's been over two hundred years since a ship of the fleet has faced a full-scale military operation of this nature. We have just two months to dust off the history books, study operations and drill the crew for battle. Even though these rebels come from a relatively insignificant planet, their guerilla activities have given them superb training in real-life combat. History has shown that highly motivated insurgents can wear out even the greatest of superpowers. Do not underestimate them." With that his officers stood at attention while Jesik made his exit, then dispersed into small groups to return to their functional areas.

* * *

"So, you're going to be a 'grunt' hacking your way through a rain forest," said Eaves to Magill as they walked back towards their assigned operations area. "You'll probably get to wear camouflaged fatigues and black face and look just like G.I. Joe on maneuvers."

Magill acknowledged his friends' sarcasm. "Yes and you'll be up in the sky scaring the guano out of high flying seagulls. Hope none of it lands on your window."

Eaves wasn't fazed. "Who would have thought that by passing on a posting to flight academy I'd actually get the chance to be in the first air-to-air combat against terrorists in the last two hundred years? I gotta tell you, Magill, blasting those pools on Cambriol was the luckiest thing we ever did."

Magill walked along in silence for a while. For some reason he thought of his parents. His adopted, parents, rather. Glancing at Eaves he couldn't help but remember how their friendship began. The Magill's were a third-class family living in a modest section of Kalenden's capital city. In junior high school Sean Magill and his other third-class friends had a number of run-ins with kids from the first-class schools until he'd developed a genuine prejudice against the upper class. They were such jerks. He was proud of the fact that he could hit harder than they could, but in spite of his physical toughness he never got over their insults and he hated the fact that he could never have the opportunities they did without first-class credentials. The more he pretended not to care, the angrier it made him. His dad was aware of this and tried to change his opinion by reminding him that even as a member of third-class he had applied himself in school and in his profession until he gained recognition as an accomplished chemist who now supervised a crew of thirty at a rocket propellant laboratory. It was his hope that Sean would grow up and follow in his footsteps. But Sean loved politics and soccer and thought he would die if he had to sit at a laboratory bench all day.

It had been the biggest surprise of his life when the prestigious Kalenden Arms Academy offered him a full ride scholarship – a privilege granted to just three third-class students per year. All the rest of the students were from the very best families. Sean had ranted that there was no way he was going to be a snob at Kalenden Arms, since those were the guys he hated the most. His dad agreed, saying that he should be content with his place in society, but his mother urged him to accept. "How can you ever hope to realize your dreams if you don't take a risk?" she asked.

"How can I spend four years with those guys; they'll all look down on me for being third-class," he pleaded in return.

"Sean, if you really want to be a leader, you'll have to learn to work with everybody, even the first-class. Besides, they're people, just like you. Perhaps they earned the right to attend because their parents are prominent. But, you've earned the right because you're talented. You're as well, or better, qualified than any of them. This is your chance to prove yourself – don't let it slip away."

He continued to fight himself over the decision for a few days, but ultimately his mother's logic had won out and he accepted the scholarship. Most of his friends were happy for him, but some thought he was being a traitor and succeeded in making him feel guilty. Eventually, over the course of six or seven months, they pretty much stopped doing things with him because he no longer fit in.

His first days at the academy were miserable. Most of the other students simply ignored him, which suited him fine. He wanted to be left alone. But some of the more obnoxious ones taunted him when out of earshot of a teacher. One day, while changing after soccer practice, he saw Travis Eaves and a bunch of his friends turn and look at him, then laugh. It infuriated him. Eaves was cocky and self-assured and seemed to represent everything that Magill hated about the upper class. He should have let it alone, but instead he strode over to Eaves and shoved him against a locker.

"If you've got a problem with me, why don't you say it to my face!"

"What makes you think I have a problem with you," Eaves shot back. "What makes you think I even think about you?"

"I saw you looking at me and laughing. You think you're so good, don't you? Well, as I remember it my friends and I kicked your ass in the ninth grade and I'll be glad to do it again here, if you like."

The blood had pounded in his forehead and he knew he was in trouble.

He didn't have any friends here and Eaves was surrounded by them. *Who cares? Maybe they'll beat the crap out of me and I'll get thrown out of the place.*

Instead of pushing him back, though, Eaves said earnestly, "I don't know why you've got such an attitude, Magill. Nobody here is against you. We were laughing because we thought it was great how you shot past the goalie in practice yesterday. Nobody's ever pulled it off like that and he's been pouting all day. We'd tell you that to your face, but you never let anybody talk to you."

It was such an unexpected response that it shook Magill. Eaves continued. "The truth is that you're the only one in this whole place who cares that you went to a public school. Hell, you're the only one who's really earned the right to be here, the rest of us just had to be born."

"What about Wells and Jamison?" Magill said rather lamely. "They're always hassling me."

"Those guys? Try to tell me that your public school didn't have jerks just like that. They've been jackasses since kindergarten."

Magill couldn't think of anything to say.

"Why don't you relax, Sean? Maybe you like school, but I don't. It's bad enough we have to be here. Why do you want to go through it alone? Can't you lighten up, a little?"

With that, Eaves made a friend. And Magill started to let go of some of his prejudice. In time, he started to fit in. So much so that he joined Travis in some truly world class practical jokes in which he more than gained his revenge on Wells and Jamison. His grades and soccer playing were good enough to avoid expulsion. It also helped that Eaves' grandfather was a cabinet secretary. Still, even though he made a lot of friends and nearly everyone treated him as an equal, there was still a lot of prejudice against the lower-classes. Not an overt kind of prejudice that says they're inferior. It was more benign – a simple recognition that everyone has a place in society and those at the Kalenden Arms were at the top of the leadership ladder. The only real change is that people started thinking of Magill as a first-class.

Back in the present Magill found himself thinking, *Someday I'll get a position on the Quadrant Council and then I can help those in leadership understand what it's like to have talent with no way to express it. I will make a difference.*

"Making a speech in your mind again, Sean? What foreign embassy are you lecturing to about the virtues of Kalenden society now?"

Magill cast an irritated glance at Eaves. "You know, there's a lot more to life than just shooting up asteroids or rebel bases. Someone with your talent should be a leader."

"I am a leader. It's just that I want to lead a squadron, while you want to lead a population." He saw the fire in Magill's eyes and added, "But, it's okay, Sean – the universe needs both kinds. I hope you do get to be President of the Council someday. I think you'd be great."

Magill calmed down and replied, "The problem is that I care about it too much, so people think I'm a zealot. You don't give a damn, so people relax and follow your lead. I wish I could figure out how to care a little less and inspire a little more."

"All you need is time, Sean. This action on Keswick is the perfect opportunity for you. You can gain military experience, maybe win a medal or two and if you're really lucky get killed and become a martyr. Then you'd really have some influence." He burst out laughing as Magill shoved him against the wall.

* * *

"Captain, may I have a private word with you?"

"Certainly, Commander, step into my bridge cabin."

Once outside the scrutiny of the other members of the bridge crew, Brighton let down his guard a bit. Jesik offered him a cup of kelp tea, which he accepted gratefully. The warm liquid soothed the back of his throat and helped him relax. Jesik looked at him expectantly.

"Sir, I'd like to request a leave-of-absence when we reach Space Station 12 next week. I need to spend a day on Stirium." Jesik's face flushed, but rather than give him time to interrupt Brighton continued, "I've checked it out and I can join the battle-cruiser Fortissimo prior to its rendezvous with Allegro three weeks later. That should still give me plenty of time to work with the crew prior to battle."

"Stirium's a rather mystical place, Commander, usually reserved for discreet romantic liaisons or shady business dealings."

Brighton could see that Jesik was flustered. Who wouldn't be – a senior officer requesting a personal leave just as the ship is preparing for battle?

"Sir, it's an urgent personal problem that simply can't wait. If there was any other way to solve this problem I'd do it."

"I'm afraid that's not good enough, Commander, the ship needs your full and undivided attention. If this personal problem prevents you from doing that perhaps you need a temporary reassignment to a non-combat role."

Brighton rubbed his temples. *It's already started – this thing is already starting to ruin my career, just when I have a chance to prove myself.*

"Tom?"

Brighton looked up, startled. Jesik almost never called another officer by his first name.

"Tom, normally I wouldn't intrude on your privacy, no matter the circumstance. But, you have to give me some help here. How can I possibly justify authorizing your absence at a critical time like this?"

Brighton sighed. It was now or never. Clearing his throat he resolved to tell the whole story. "There's a young woman named Sondra Vivendel from Tatrius. We met during our last layover there and I spent several days with her. She called earlier today to tell me that she's pregnant."

Jesik sat down hard. "Is it certain that you're the father?"

Brighton nodded.

In an uncharacteristic display of emotion Jesik blurted out, "How could you be so careless, Commander?"

Brighton was surprised to see that the Captain's hands were trembling.

"I thought she'd taken protection. Believe me, I had no idea I was at risk."

With a fierceness Brighton had never seen before Jesik fired back, "Do you know what this can do to your career—to your life? You may never escape its shadow, not as long as you live!"

Jesik's intensity was so over the top for someone so usually reserved that it unnerved Brighton. And made him angry.

"With all due respect, Sir, this is my problem and I just need a few days to meet Ms. Vivendel to work it out. I'd hoped you could accommodate me."

Jesik sighed. "I'm not the problem, Tom. Of course you can have a leave. But, the service is a small club, even though it's spread out over a few light-years. You may well find there's no way to avoid a scandal. Or, if you do, that there's an awful price to pay for silence."

Jesik spoke to the computer, "Formal leave granted to Thomas Brighton, Commander, on my authority. Dates and times to be entered separately." The computer acknowledged the command and started printing the appropriate e-paper. Jesik signed the form and handed it to Brighton. "Do you love this woman?"

"I don't think so. Of course I've had no experience with love, so I'm not really qualified to answer."

"My only advice is that you consider her needs and those of your child first, Commander. Your career's important, but so are they."

Brighton swallowed and raised his eyes. "I was an orphan, Sir. Believe me when I tell you that I understand." He shook Jesik's hand and left the room.

Jesik sat down in his chair again. "Why does it all have to be so complicated?"

"Was that a question?" the computer asked.

"Only if you have a good answer."

The computer was silent.

3 - AN UNEXPECTED ATTACK

The battle was scheduled to take place on two fronts – the Keswick surface and the in atmosphere, but not among the ships in orbit – which is why the first laser blast was unexpected when it temporarily blinded the Allegro's forward sensor array.

"Which ship fired at us?" yelled Jesik.

There was a moment of silence as their Helmsman, Lieutenant Kevin Wight, waited for his console to stabilize. "It appears to be a Zeronion freighter, Sir."

"A freighter, my ass," Gentry retorted. "That beam had the force of a Star Cruiser with a nuclear generator."

Jesik looked as confused as everyone else. "What's the ship doing now?"

"He's taken cover behind one of the Keswick moons, Sir."

Jesik bit his lip, a nervous habit he was completely unaware of. "Your thoughts, Mr. Barrows," he said, turning to the Political Officer.

Before Barrows could answer, Gentry interrupted, "I don't know his motive, Sir, but I do know why he chose that moment to attack. While we were blind, he launched a missile at the planet's surface at their main communication terminal."

"Any damage?"

"No Sir. Lieutenant Eaves managed to launch counter-measures from his fighter just before the moment of impact. Some of the ground crew was hit by the debris, but the reports indicate the equipment was undamaged."

Jesik shook his head in wonderment. It was almost impossible for an airborne fighter to sense an incoming missile, classify it as hostile and launch a counter missile that intercepts the intruder. It's like shooting a basketball from three football lengths away and having it drop in the basket as the buzzer sounds.

Williams saw the Captain's expression and asked, "Luck or skill?"

Jesik couldn't help but laugh. "Mr. Eaves certainly is the luckiest pilot I know. Still, it wasn't luck that he pushed the fire control lever in time. Now, Mr. Barrows, tell us the motive for the attack."

Barrows was glad to have the additional information about the attack. It gave him a vital piece to the puzzle he was trying to solve and now he could follow a new line of inquiry.

"Of course I can't answer definitively, Sir, but available intelligence suggests it's either a pirate wanting to take advantage of the confusion on the planet's surface to raid the mines, or," he paused to study the ship's profile once again, "or it's acting as a surrogate for Alturus."

"A surrogate? What do you mean?"

"Well, Sir, if you compare the profile of the freighter to the star cruisers we've observed from Alturus, you'll see a striking similarity in their underbellies." Everyone on the bridge studied the diagrams on the two monitors at the front of the bridge. "I believe that's where the nuclear weapons array is housed. The shape of the hull at that point certainly isn't consistent with a freighter, even though the rest of the craft is constructed to look like your run-of-the-mill cargo ship."

"So we don't know what it is for sure—freighter or starship. I wish you could tell me which it is, though. If it's a pirate, then it's simple enough to chase and eliminate him. But, if it's from Alturus, we have to consider their three star cruisers in orbit, as well as the safety of our ground forces." Jesik paced impatiently, the sound of systems coming back online and damage control stations checking in providing background noise to mask the silence.

"Well, it does no good to sit here, wondering. The question is whether he's hiding behind the moon to avoid us, or to snare us in a trap. Mr. Wight, move to a 78,000 kilometer orbit."

Wight shook his head ever so slightly. 78,000 kilometers on such a small planetoid meant that the gravity could hardly hold them in orbit, so he'd have to constantly monitor the ship to make certain they weren't drifting. Of course that position also placed them at a distance where it would be easy to observe the various moons. Locking in the new course, Wight listened intently for the soft crescendo of the engines as he engaged the forward thrusters. It was a maneuver that could easily be executed by the automatic sequencing of a computer, but Fleet Command had learned years ago that people prefer the feel of employing a well-balanced lever instead of simply pushing a button on a computer console. It kept their attention focused and their skills sharp. The ship accelerated smoothly into an ever-increasing arc around the planet.

As the ship approached its optimal orbit, the sky was illuminated by a brilliant flash of indigo. Their new trajectory had brought them into the line of fire of the "freighter," which immediately used the occasion to try to dazzle their sensor array again.

"Not this time," said Jesik with satisfaction. He'd made certain that when they rounded the moon their alinite hull would present itself, rather than the exposed instrument array. The laser beams reflected harmlessly off the hull at an angle that intercepted the main inter-quadrant trade route some ten or twenty kiloceks away. Some poor merchantman might find himself dazzled in two or three days if his path inadvertently intercepted the wayward beams, which would arrive there in approximately 70 hours.

"Direct your lasers at his sensors and then fire a Category 6 nuclear missile at their main weapons array, enough to slap them around a little!"

Lieutenant Commander Gentry felt a surge of excitement as he confirmed the targeting lock and depressed the laser fire control. Instantaneously six emerald rays shot out from the Allegro to match the brilliant blue beams from the enemy ship. It looked like an ancient sword fight, fought with shimmering rapiers. Then he launched the missile, which streaked from the Forward Weapons Bay, leaving a trail of vapor to mark its path as it closed on the rapidly retreating freighter. Even close-in drills like this were fought over such great distances that it took nearly four minutes for the missile to overtake the accelerating ship. All the while the laser attack continued, but skillful maneuvering on the part of Wight kept all vital components of the ship out of harm's way.

When the missile exploded near the enemy ship, the shrapnel canisters sparkled like a hundred thousand stars shimmering against the blackness of space. From this distance they seemed harmless enough, but Jesik knew the damage they would inflict on the other ship's exposed instrumentation, like the ragged edges of aluminum cans ripped open by a metal shredder. The enemy came to a dead halt in space.

"A direct hit, Sir," Lieutenant Wight reported. "It looks like we knocked them out."

"What's your assessment, Mr. Gentry?"

"Too easy, Sir. Even if we did knock out some of their weapons array, we certainly didn't damage their propulsion systems. I think they're trying to lure us closer."

"Okay, anyone care to speculate why they used a laser attack, rather than hit us with something that could cause some real damage?"

In the early days of space travel, everyone assumed that energy-beam weapons would be the most natural way to destroy an enemy. After all, in the vastness of space nothing could travel faster than the speed of light, which gave beam weapons the most immediate effect. Plus, targeting was simple because you only had to adjust the beam to follow the target. The most creative scientific talent in the universe was diverted to the task of designing and building huge power generators capable of stimulating the solid state or gas canisters of a laser cannon to levels sufficient for the beam to penetrate the hulls of enemy spacecraft. These efforts led to some spectacular battles with multi-colored beams firing through the darkness of space. Crimson, indigo-blue, violet, alabaster and other iridescent beams could be seen blasting away from up to a parsec away. Each combatant chose a color and beam pattern that became a unique identifier, much like ancient ships hoisting their battle Ensigns as they joined battle. Perhaps the most exciting part of the battle was trying to dodge the ricochets and reflections that made it seem like a thousand ships were firing, rather than merely three or four.

Unfortunately, there were some problems with energy-beam weapons. First, they're notoriously inefficient, losing up to 80% of the power that's used in creating them. It took incredibly powerful nuclear generators to create the electricity needed to stimulate the particles to the degree of excitement that caused them to emit the perfectly phased light that, when focused, could spell death for an enemy cruiser. Unfortunately, as ships increased their armor, it was difficult to build containment cells strong enough to house the amount of gas or rare earth elements required in the ever-larger cannons. It was simply a lot more efficient to launch a missile armed with a nuclear warhead, even though it took longer to reach the target.

The second big problem with energy-beam weapons is that their force was easily deflected once alinite was discovered. By creating a highly polished reflective surface using the high-density alinite, the beams could be reflected away from the ship.

So, even though the lasers made for a terrific Technicolor light show, their usefulness as a weapon of destruction was limited. In time, ultra high-speed missile torpedoes were substituted for energy beam weapons. Their nuclear warheads could either directly damage the enemy craft or contaminate it with enough radiation that its crew's fighting abilities were compromised.

Two things the laser cannons could still do well, however, was to harass ground troops on a planet's surface, since the beams could instantly incinerate wood buildings, and even lightly armored metal troop carriers. They could also blind an enemy ships' instrument panel, which could never be fully protected if it was to gather the necessary intelligence needed to manage a battle.

"So," said Jesik expectantly, "Why energy beams instead of warheads?"

After a pause, "A diversionary tactic to shield an attack on the surface?"

"Obviously, Mr. Williams, since that's what they did, but even the most inexperienced combatant would know it can only work once."

"Something to keep us occupied while an enemy task force slips past long-range sensors on the way to our home star system?"

"Very sinister, Mr. Wight and maybe even true, but it seems to me there'd be an energy signature we could detect after the fact – does anything show up on your sensors?"

Silence confirmed the negative.

"Perhaps, Sir," said Ensign Wight haltingly, "it's a deliberate attempt to provoke us into a counter-attack which would provide a pretext for greater hostilities."

"But why camouflage the ship as a merchant?"

"An even better cause celebre'. The Fleet's most powerful battleship attacking a relatively harmless merchantman."

All this while Jesik had been watching the freighter drift closer and closer to the Allegro. He planned to allow the enemy crew to reveal their intention. With the Allegro on full alert, there should be minimal threat, even if the freighter was not fully crippled. Then he saw something out of the corner of his eye – a brief glint of light near the freighter's main forward thrusters so slight as to be almost imperceptible. Suddenly his face clouded and he shouted, "Red Alert! Ensign Wight, maximum thrust into deepspace . . . Now!"

Wight was so startled he jammed the forward thruster controls to maximum while simultaneously plotting and programming an escape route that would avoid heading directly into the planet's atmosphere. The force of the acceleration knocked people from their feet all over the ship, initiating unusually rich curses in the galley and latrines. The crew was dazed as they scrambled to battle stations.

Any questions about the Captain's motives were erased a few moments later, however, when the aft monitors flooded the bridge with a brilliant white light.

"My lord! The freighter's exploded," Williams announced in astonishment.

Commander Brighton declared, "Now we know why they used laser weapons. There was no one onboard to launch missiles. It was a suicide drone, pre-programmed for the laser attacks, then set to explode when we closed to investigate."

"The only question remaining," interjected Lieutenant Wight, "is if we can put enough distance behind us to avoid being torn apart by the concussion." A nuclear explosion has greater acceleration than a starship. At this very moment a million fragments of shredded alinite were accelerating towards the Allegro. "All hands, brace yourselves," shouted the Captain into the ship's interphone.

* * *

"I don't know what is going on up there, but so far there's been two laser fights and two nuclear explosions. The first was fairly modest, but the second had to be at least a Category 3."

Eaves nodded agreement and settled more comfortably into his seat to watch the show. Debris from the freighter was showering the night sky as fragments burned up in the atmosphere. "I wish we could contact the Allegro to see if everything's okay, but Jesik would bust us if we violated the communications blackout."

His Navigator, Jason Carter, checked their position and confirmed that they were hovering precisely 382 meters above the planet surface, with an orientation 42 degrees above the horizon. With the surrounding mountains acting as shields, this position made them virtually invisible to both ground and atmosphere based radar. Eaves had powered-down the ship so it could float without creating any noise or turbulence. The residual charge in the hull provided enough power for them to hover for several hours before activating the engine (which would immediately reveal their position to the enemy).

Looking around in the darkness, Carter could make out the rebel campfires on the foothills to the east. "It still amazes me that we can slip in here each night and observe without being detected."

Eaves shook his head in the darkness. This was an old theme with Carter. Somehow he was obsessed by the fact that technology allowed them to seemingly defy the laws of nature, so he changed the subject. "The laser battle was really something, wasn't it? It hurt my eyes to even look at it, the beams were so bright. I bet the ricochets alone incinerated one or two of those worthless asteroids they call moons."

"I suppose so," responded Carter lazily.

His companion amazed Eaves, yet again. How was it that Carter could be so impressed by something as simple as a stealth shield, while totally uninterested in the fabulous excitement of a space battle? He sighed. *Oh well, Carter is a great Navigator who never gets rattled in battle simulations. So, if we had nothing else in common what does it matter?*

In some ways Carter and Eaves were exact opposites. Carter was descended from a prominent Earth family on the British Caribbean island of Tortolla and spoke with the clipped accent of his New Boston home-town. At five feet, eight inches, he was slender, trim and good looking. Meticulous in his dress and personal grooming, his ebony skin, brown eyes and tightly curled hair added to the sense of precision that characterized how he interacted with people. For example, he was an obsessive note taker, recording everything on his personal digital assistant in step-by-step bullet points. More than one conversation had been slowed to a snail's pace by Carter's insistent, "Just a minute, can you repeat that?" to which Eaves inevitably replied, "Why don't you just record it and listen to it?" to which Carter replied in an endless loop, "because I don't trust the transcription." It was ridiculous to Eaves. Worst of all, from Eaves' point of view, Carter was also a lacrosse player.

Eaves, on the other hand was taller at six feet, with blond hair, medium blue eyes and fair skin that tanned evenly. He often had a sly grin on his face, like he was privy to an inside joke. Carter took that for smugness and it irritated him to no end. Remarkably agile, Eaves loved personal sports, like water-skiing and snowboarding. As for keeping track of what he was told, he rarely took notes. One of his favorite phrases was "If it's important, I'll remember it!" Perhaps that's why he came late or was absent from so many meetings. A scion of a wealthy family, he got by as a mediocre student and passable athlete and was so seldom serious that it took people by sur-prise when he acted responsibly. Now, he was chained to this automaton.

"It's so boring up here," Eaves muttered. "I thought we'd be in aerial combat, not running a stake-out on a bunch of overage boy scouts camping in the wilderness!"

This time it was Carter's turn to sigh. *Why can't Eaves understand the importance of intelligence in a land battle?* They'd already provided enough information to the Kalenden and Alturian observers to help the Keswick Special Forces knock out two Rebellion brigades. Of course if it had been up to Eaves and the other fighter pilots, they would have shot off a bunch of atmosphere-to-surface missiles when they spotted the enemy and have won the battle directly. But, that would have given away their intelligence advantage completely. *And Eaves calls the rebels 'overage boy scouts'.* Still, it was curious that there had been virtually no rebel fighters to challenge them, even during daylight when the ships would make themselves visible. Their Alturian "allies" had led them to believe that the rebels had a fairly substantial number of both atmosphere and low-space fighters available, but none had been used in the battle at this point.

"What was that," asked Eaves urgently.

"What was what?"

"I thought I saw some kind of movement at three o'clock, elevation forty-five degrees."

Carter checked the instruments. They registered nothing. Then he did a visual scan of the star field in question.

"Everything looks fine to me. What exactly did it look like to you?" Even though Eaves was arrogant, he had an uncanny knack for sensing trouble. Therefore, Carter didn't take his warning lightly.

"It was like some of the stars became blurry for a moment, but in a pattern that indicated movement."

"Hmm, don't know what it is. Campfire smoke can have that effect, particularly with this much humidity in the atmosphere."

Eaves didn't reply. He continued scanning the horizon, first with his eyes, then with night-vision binoculars. Then he repeated his actions.

"You're making me feel creepy," said Carter. "Even if the Keswick rebels managed to steal an invisibility-display ship, the location you identified would make them detectable to instruments and our sensors show nothing there."

Eaves remained quiet for a few moments, then blurted out, "Give me a plot to the shelter of that rock! And make it fast."

"What! We can't leave formation—we'll lose sight of two of the five rebel outposts! You can't disobey orders just because you saw some stars go blurry for an instant. You probably had just rubbed your eyes and they were re-focusing."

"Give me the reading! Something's definitely wrong and we've got to get out of here."

Even though Carter was Eaves' superior, a full lieutenant while Travis was a lieutenant junior grade, he was the pilot which gave him authority to act independently in extreme emergencies. So there was nothing Carter could do but give him the reading. *But, when we get back to base I'll report your irrational action and request a transfer from you…you very lucky, very famous, adolescent.*

With almost no perceptible movement, Eaves edged in the direction of a large rock outcrop in the hills northeast of their assigned position. He was so gentle in maneuvering the ship in concert with the light breeze, that the ship's movement created virtually no air disturbance. Carter held his breath to maintain absolute silence, even though the craft was fully insulated against sound. Slowly, slowly, they drifted until they came under the lee of the outcrop, just a few feet above ground. Glancing down Carter could see a small rodent bolt from his burrow, aware of the huge aircraft floating overhead, even though the hull made the ship invisible.

The way it accomplished that was rather ingenious. Cameras on one side of the hull projected the image of their view to a molded video display screen that surrounded the hull on the opposite side of the ship, which made the ship invisible to an observer. Carter smiled as he thought about it. *Now that was a great invention. Who'd have thought of turning the entire hull of a ship into a video screen?* It was the perfect camouflage, also extremely expensive, since the "screen" had to be able to stand the heat of acceleration in and out of the atmosphere, as well as take a direct hit from enemy beams. Out of the twenty-three fighters on the Allegro, only two were equipped with the invisibility-display hull and it was a compliment to Eaves and Carter to trust them with the most expensive fighter in the ship's arsenal. On the other, it condemned them to reconnaissance, which frustrated Eaves, but thrilled Carter.

Carter and Eaves peered anxiously into space, straining to identify the danger. Their bodies mobilized for action by diverting blood to vital organs and away from their outer skin. The environmental controls responded to the tense mood of the occupants by warming the cabin two degrees. The night was cold anyway and Carter had felt a tingling in his hands and feet, so the additional heat was welcome.

After about an hour, though, he started to relax. It was nearly three A.M. and in an hour, the other invisibility-hull fighter would relieve them. *Or, they'll report to the assigned position and find we're nowhere to be found!* Just thinking about it perturbed him even more.

At 3:23 a.m. Carter reached for an enviro-towel to wash his face and hands. He looked up just in time to see flashes of three, high-intensity, scarlet lasers flare into view, lighting up the night sky from the rebel camps. Two lasers illuminated the two Alturian invisibility-hull fighters, undoubtedly blinding their instrument array. The third beam shot directly through the area of space where Eaves and Carter had been. After a few moments, the laser beam began roving the sky, looking for them. The angle was such that no matter how wide an arc it followed, it could never hit them under their rock hiding place. *Eaves has done it again.*

"How'd you know?" Carter asked in exasperation.

"Don't know, doesn't really matter. Be ready to fast-start the battle-active targeting computer."

"Are you going to knock out the lasers?" In the distance they could see the Alturian fighters gyrating about drunkenly in an attempt to escape the blinding rays. Clearly the cannons weren't strong enough to disable them, but without instrumentation, they were flying blind. Perhaps, the crew were now actually blind, since usual procedure was for the pilot to deactivate the anti-laser window coating to make better visual observations, making it likely that they had permanently lost their eyesight when the first beams hit. Even a reflected beam could cause temporary blindness, but the number of direct hits they'd taken almost assured it. Carter got a sick feeling in his stomach. After all, he and Eaves always had their coating down during nighttime reconnaissance. He could only imagine the result if Eaves hadn't moved out of harm's way.

"I asked if you were going to help those poor guys and knock out the lasers?"

Eaves turned to him. "The rebel ground troops wouldn't use lasers unless something else was under way. Obviously they've known about us for a long time, even though they played dumb. We've got to wait a little longer to learn what's going on. I want them to think we were taken off station early—because if they think we're still up here they won't launch the next phase of their attack!"

Carter swallowed hard, "You're right. But, I sure hate to think of what those Alturians are going through right now."

"Why don't you program three mini-torpedoes to hit their laser cannons. If nothing happens in the next sixty seconds, we'll blast our way out of here."

Carter made the calculations and programmed them into the computer. In their first real battle with live opponents, Eaves was showing himself to be a capable battlefield commander.

At forty-five seconds Eaves was ready to initiate the flight pattern to launch three missiles within a seven second firing window to completely disable the ground-based cannons. At fifty seconds, however, the night sky burst into flame as a dozen rebel fighters screamed in from the west and launched a ferocious attack on the two Alturian fighters. With a precision rarely seen in even the finest academies back on Kalenden, their missiles found their way to their targets, setting the sky ablaze with the explosion of the two doomed fighters. Holding their position a few more moments, Eaves and Carter watched as another dozen or so missiles were launched into the darkness of the forest canopy, precisely where the Alliance ground troops had been mobilizing for a dawn raid. Acrid smoke filled the air.

Even though the odds were twelve to one against them, Eaves programmed the targeting computer to launch all eight of their mini-missiles. It was far more important now to knock out the enemy fighters than to worry about the lasers. Without air cover, the Alliance troops were sitting ducks waiting to be slaughtered. "Jason, it's impossible for us to get even eight of the fighters, since the heat flumes alone will confuse some of our missiles. If we're to stand any chance at all of getting out of here, you'll need to be prepared to fire our laser cannons directly into the canopy of any remaining fighters. If we surprise them we ought to be able to break the battle up, particularly since we're firing from their blind side. You ready?"

Carter swallowed hard. He thought he'd been in battle in the previous few weeks, but now realized it was a phony battle where they encountered only token resistance. Now it meant life or death. Once the enemy detected their presence, they'd become the most important target of the evening. And after launching every weapon they had in the first attack, they'd be defenseless. "I'm ready," he said with as much confidence as he could muster.

The force of the acceleration here in the thick Keswick atmosphere literally took his breath away. Eaves flew out in a loop-to-loop pattern that allowed them to gain altitude at the steepest possible angle. For hovering they used anti-gravity membranes. But, in battle they used forward thrusters to provide the overwhelming speed that would provide lift to the slender fins they used as wings. Theirs was the most maneuverable aircraft in the history of atmosphere-based fighters.

Even though the invisibility shield made the aircraft itself invisible, their exhaust could be seen for at least twenty kilometers. It took the rebel fighter group just a few moments to discern the threat and as a unit they turned to engage them. Flying directly at the rebels, Eaves held his fire long past the standard launch protocol. As they approached the group at a combined airspeed of over 1200 kilometers per hour, Eaves waited until the outer aircraft in the group started to peel away so the lead aircraft would have an escape path if it needed to get out of Eaves's way. Something like an ultra-high speed game of chicken. Just as they were about to crash head-on, the rebel fighter broke to starboard and Eaves shouted "launch all weapons." The recoil of the missiles firing dropped their airspeed immediately, throwing Carter forward against his restraining belts. Of course all the missiles couldn't be launched simultaneously, since they had only four tubes, but the automatic launch sequencer immediately reloaded the tube as soon as a missile had cleared the front of the ship. In all, it took just twelve seconds to launch all the weapons.

The radar alarm had been sounding continuously since they initiated their solitary attack, but now it really became shrill. Eaves glanced down to see that there were twelve orange bogeys headed their way, indicating enemy missiles. Then blue lights started appearing on the screen, which meant Alliance fighters were joining the battle.

"Hang on Jason, there's a dozen hostile missiles headed directly for us."

Restraints or no, Eaves's next move straight towards the ground created such force that it threw Carter against the overhead canopy. They jerked crazily to the starboard, then hard to port. Next thing he knew, Carter felt tree branches crashing against the ship's hull as they tore through the forest canopy. In his aft monitor, he could see that at least four of the hostile missiles had collided with each other because of Eaves' canopy maneuver, but eight were still hot on their trail.

"What are you doing in the trees?" he screamed, "They're gonna tear the ship apart!" Carter could sense the missiles getting closer.

"Do you think they use impact missiles or magnetic?" queried Eaves into his microphone.

"What?"

"Impact or magnetic warheads – you've got about five seconds to decide?"

"Both, damn it!"

"Ah, that's what I think too."

Carter saw one of the lights on his panel flash as two large grape canisters fired out of the rear torpedo tube. Four of the hostile missiles exploded as they neared the highly charged electro-magnets in the canisters.

"Only four left!" Suddenly Eaves dove even farther into the trees. Where before they'd been tearing off light foliage at tree-top level, now they were slicing through branches four to six centimeters thick. The ship shuddered violently with each impact. At 600 kilometers per hour, they were like a razor blade cutting through wood paneling.

"What are you doing?!"

The night sky flared into a brilliant flash as first one, then another and finally all of the hostile missiles exploded, literally a few meters behind their aircraft. The impact warheads couldn't tell the difference between an enemy ship and a heavy tree branch. Still, the concussions were close enough that the ship was thrown head-over-heels, bouncing from treetop to treetop. Eaves fought savagely to regain control. With just seconds to spare he caught sight of a relatively open meadow to starboard and managed to bank the ship in that direction. In what had to be the highest speed drive-by ever recorded, he brought the ship down, skipped it across the surface of the standing water until the water helped stabilize their forward motion to the point where he regained enough control to bring the nose back up into the air. Giving it full acceleration they shot up into the sky to rejoin the battle.

"What a sight to make eyes sore," cried Eaves exuberantly. "Just look at that." At least six rebel fighters had been hit by their missiles and crashed into the forest below. The smoke from their fires gave the remaining enemy lasers an opaque appearance as they tried to sort out friendly from unfriendly aircraft. The Alliance fighters were clearly not as experienced as the rebel forces, but they now had a numerical advantage and were chasing the rebels in a furious aerial combat.

"This should take about five more minutes," Eaves exulted. Then the control console confirmed what he and Carter saw with their night vision goggles. "Ten, no make that eleven new bogeys coming in at 09:00," Carter sighed.

The ship banked into a steep dive to port as Eaves evaded a ground-based laser. They were out of offensive weapons except for their energy beams, but all the other fighters had shielding now, so the lasers weren't much help. The best Eaves could hope to accomplish was to pass so close to enemy fighters that they'd lose their concentration while chasing down the Alliance craft.

It worked pretty well. The sky was churning with fighters going in all directions, other ships launching missiles against ground troops to keep that part of the battle stirred up and occasional explosions when fighters blew up in mid-air or crash-landed.

It started to look like the Alliance was going to come out ahead, when disaster struck. A Kalenden fighter launched a missile at a rebel fighter so that it would pass undetected under an Alturian aircraft until it was too late for the rebel to take evasive action. Unfortunately, the missile's intelligence system failed and the missile smashed into the Alturian. The explosion lit up the entire sky. Misunderstanding what had happened, two Alturian fighters turned on the hapless Kalendener and blew him from the air. Chaos ensued and in seconds the sky was ablaze with Alliance missiles firing at each other, as well as the rebels. It was the kind of madness that comes from inexperience and the frenzy of battle. In short order, some eight Rebellion Fighters were destroyed, as well as seven Kalendens and ten Alturians. It was impossible to tell who had killed whom.

It was also becoming apparent that it wasn't going to end until every single aircraft had been destroyed.

"We've got to do something," Eaves shouted. "Hold on!"

He headed directly for the heart of the melee. Immediately a rebel ship started chasing, followed by an Alturian and Kalenden ship. As he approached the center he started a gentle arc up and out. Soon other ships followed and before long he'd achieved his objective of creating a spiral pattern that involved all the ships in the battle. Lasers were firing, but the upward curve of the arc was such that it was difficult for them to gain a lock on each other. For a few moments, every fighter was preoccupied with maintaining their position, rather than firing missiles; the precise moment Eaves had hoped for. Just as he reached the apex of the spiral, he flipped the controls and dove straight down so that he brought himself into the center of the fighter group. That's when he fired the only weapon he had left – a double-charged dazzle blast. Dazzles were hardly ever used in battle, since they did no real damage, but in this case it had the desired effect. In the most brilliant explosion of the night everything for at least twenty kilometers was illuminated. The dazzle blast had virtually no concussion, but it created an electromagnetic wave that was powerful enough to temporarily stun all electronics in the area. Ships fell from the sky like electrocuted flies. Including, of course, Eaves and Carter's.

"Brilliant," shouted Carter, "It's been good knowing you."

"Shut up and fire the parachute!"

At least four fighters fell to their death because the crew was too stunned to remember their parachutes. The rest drifted lazily towards the ground while other crews ejected to safety. Eaves had the presence of mind to manually fire some small rockets that brought their ship down at least ten kilometers from their nearest enemy. There they hit the trees hard and were jerked into a nose position as they crashed into the forest floor.

Carter imagined that his head had smashed into his instrument console. Of course that was impossible, since it would require all of his safety restrains to be torn from their mounting brackets. *But it does feel wet on my face*, he thought dreamily as his eyes closed and his body slumped out of his chair.

4 — MAGILL, LOYALISTS, AND REBELS

Before falling asleep, Lieutenant Junior Grade Sean Magill re-read his report of the land operations to date. While he didn't know all the details of the various deployments, he had been given clearance by Captain Jesik to take notes at various planning meetings, and then to send them directly to the Allegro. Writing notes, as opposed to dictating them where they might be overheard, provided a potential increase in security. The land battle proved more complicated than the Alliance had been led to believe. The Royal Keswicks promised to field 40,000 soldiers against a rebel force estimated at 25,000-30,000. Plus, the government assured their allies that they could instantly activate a military draft, if required. That appeared more than adequate to meet the threat. Because of a lingering mistrust of outsiders, however, the Royal family was directed by the military to give instructions to the Alliance that the only assistance required was to protect the Keswick orbit from marauders and pirates and to provide military advisers on the ground. History demonstrated that on too many occasions, powerful allies turned conqueror.

"So, our unit joined three hundred advisers from Kalenden to help protect the capitol city of Keston," he wrote, " while another three hundred from other planets in the Kalenden system were assigned to the orchidite mines. Alturus also placed twelve hundred of their specialists in nearby camps. Although these feeble numbers will not be decisive in battle, it put the rebels on notice that both neighboring star systems are on the side of the Loyalists. Both the Kalendens and Alturians do their best to avoid each other, resorting to strict military etiquette when our paths crossed."

He struggled with the next few lines, finally settling on, "At first, everything appeared to be going well for the Alliance. The rebels made several attacks on the Loyalist positions at the 178-kilometer corridor that

enclosed the city and the mines, but were easily repulsed and pushed further back into the jungles. Desiring to end the threat once and for all, but
against the advice of their Alliance advisers, the Keswick military command
sent an ever-increasing number of squadrons to pursue the rebels. Before
long, dangerous gaps opened in the Loyalist lines. When an Alliance general called attention to this, the Keswicks assured him that the rebels were
nothing more than ill-mannered thugs who had no clue how to run a military campaign. So, 'thanks for the advice, but we have everything under
control.'"

What Magill didn't know is that on the same day that the Allegro came
under attack in orbit the night battle erupted in the skies over Keswick.
With more than seventy percent of their army deployed in the jungles,
the military found it had just 6,000 troops to defend Keston. But, 6,000
seemed adequate since most of the rebel units were also in the jungle, starting their ground attack on the Loyalist units. But the military leadership
had not counted on infiltrators and guerillas, who began harassing the Alliance troops from behind.

As they learned later, the first step in the rebel campaign was to destroy
the Keswick Air Force. That was accomplished in short order when 300
Keswick fighter aircraft exploded in flight shortly after take-off. Rebel sympathizers among the maintenance crews had managed to place small beads
of altitude sensitive plastic explosives around the fuel caps of each fighter.
As an aircraft reached an altitude of 3,000 meters the explosives detonated,
igniting the ship's fuel tanks. It was such a subtle tactic that at first no one
figured out what was happening. So, wave after wave took to the air, looking for the external threat that was destroying the aircraft, only to be incinerated themselves. Finally, Air Command grounded all remaining fighters
to figure out what was going on. That saved some aircraft, but took them
out of the battle while bomb squads searched for and disabled the explosives.

That left the Alliance fighters, which had been under constant guard,
as the only ones left to engage the enemy. The rebels kept inserting enough
fighters to the battle to keep the Alturians and Kalendens fully occupied,
leaving the remaining rebel fighters to attack ground positions.

It was unfortunate that Lieutenant Magill was unaware of these facts as
he drifted off to sleep as it would have made a great deal of difference in the
outcome of his life because of events that were about to unfold.

* * *

Magill, was sleeping soundly when the battle began. He thought it was a dream when he heard Corporal Wakely shouted "Wake up, Lieutenant! We're under attack!"

"What?"

"Wake up!"

Just then an air-to-surface laser beam sliced through Magill's tent with a brilliant crimson flash, which helped him to wake up very, very quickly.

"What the hell's going on?" he shouted to no one in particular.

An impact missile blowing up a fuel dump 50 kilometers away answered his question. The heat from the nuclear shock wave vaporized the fabric of his tent, but his sleeping bag was made of Baccharite fibers, which provided protection up to 1200 degrees Celsius. Like a tortoise, he pulled his head in at the sight of the flash, just in time to avoid being incinerated. Corporal Wakely was not so lucky. Magill stuck his head out and saw that all that was left of his friend were ashes and smoldering flames. He retched at the sight, then stood and, in a crouch, started running with the sleeping bag draped over his shoulders. He was bare footed and in his underwear. His clothes were atomized and his shoes had melted. What was left of the jungle was on fire all around him and huge trees and branches crashed down around him.

He remembered a small lake about 100 meters to the northeast of his tent, so he ran in that direction in his bare feet, trying not to inhale the acrid smoke. His feet were being scorched by the burning grass and falling debris, the hair on his legs quickly singed off and the hot air tore at the linings of his lungs and the skin on his face. The fires were so intense that it was difficult to inhale any oxygen, making each breath desperately labored. In his panic, he was barely aware of other figures stumbling through the night in the same direction. Just as he thought he couldn't take anymore, he reached the lake and jumped in. There wasn't a lot of room, since everyone else who survived had come to the lake as well.

Life is full of contrasts. While the air was scorching hot, the lake itself was fed by a cold spring from deep within the planet. The blast had instantly vaporized several centimeters of water from the surface, but the spring had already restored the lake to its natural temperature of one or two degrees above freezing. The shock to Magill's nervous system took his breath away and he found himself foundering, wrapped in his now-soggy sleeping bag and in real danger of drowning. He gasped for breath, but got a mouthful of water. Panicking, he swallowed even more and began to slip under the surface. He tried desperately to expel the water in his lungs, but couldn't reach the surface. *This is it*, he thought, as his arms stopped flailing. Suddenly he was grabbed by his hair and pulled to the surface. A hand was now slapping him on the back as he coughed violently and water flooded out of his mouth. A giant breath filled his lungs as another round of coughing finally cleared the remaining water.

"You're okay. Take a second to get your breath." Magill struggled for a moment, but the hand yanked his hair a little harder.

"Ow, that hurts," he cried. But the act of shouting calmed him down enough to start treading water. Now he was glad he didn't have any clothing on to weigh him down. His sleeping bag floated nearby.

"What's going on?" he asked the nameless face in the dark.

"It looks like the rebels are more sophisticated than the Loyalists gave them credit for. From what I can see from the flashes in the sky, they've launched a massive attack all along the line."

Magill recognized the voice of Marine Major Ernest Wilkerson. As his eyes adjusted to the darkness he could see Wilkerson peering anxiously into the night sky.

"If the rebels are as organized as I think they are, we can expect a ground assault within the next hour or two. As close as we are to the city, they'll have to move through our position to reach the main gate."

Magill's body was going numb. He couldn't think of enemy troops right now. He was anxious to leave the water and said, urgently, "Major, we've got to get out of this lake or they'll find me frozen at the bottom."

"Of course. We should get moving." Wilkerson pointed Magill in the right direction, retrieved their sleeping bags, and together they swam to the shore opposite the explosion. Wilkerson stayed close, in case Magill had any trouble. As they waded out onto the beach, which was surrounded by a shallow marsh, the heat from the trees burning in the distance actually felt good against Magill's skin. The sand on his feet, however, told a different story. The flesh was raw from burns and he cried out in pain as he tried to put weight on his legs. He tried to make progress, but fell forward in a heap, sobbing in agony.

Wilkerson rolled him over onto his back and looked at his feet. He paused so his voice would be steady, "I'm sorry, soldier, but your 'uniform' doesn't give me any indication of your rank or name, even though I'm sure we've met before."

Magill looked down at his bare legs and torso, his body matted in ash and slime, and found strength for a modest laugh. "I see your problem, Sir. I'm Lieutenant Junior Grade Sean Magill of the Allegro. I recognize you from our morning briefings."

"The Allegro? Pietr Jesik's ship? He's a good man – a strong leader."

"Yes, Sir, the best."

Wilkerson could see the desperate look in the young man's eyes and wanted to keep him talking. "Magill?" Wilkerson pondered the name. "Weren't you one of those academy students involved in the Cambriol incident?"

Magill never knew what to expect when someone asked this question. In the civilian population he and Eaves were generally seen as heroes. In the military, however, they were often looked upon as careless renegades who got lucky.

"Yes, Sir, that's where I first met Captain Jesik."

"You guys were nuts, but thank goodness you were there. When I watched the replay of the video recordings, I couldn't believe the reflexes of your pilot. I doubt one-in-a-hundred could have pulled off that maneuver."

"He's my best friend," Magill paused to steady his breathing. "Probably engaged in the air battle right now."

"Ironic, isn't it—the soldiers on duty were all killed, while those of us who were snug in our sleeping bags are alive." Then he looked Magill straight in the eyes. "I'm afraid you've got a real problem, Lieutenant. Your feet are burned terribly, but we've got to get moving or the rebels will kill us right here on the beach." Wilkerson pulled off his shirt and tore it into bandages that he wrapped around Magill's feet. They sat for a few moments to gain their bearings, while other half-naked soldiers and marines crept up on the beach.

Magill liked Wilkerson, because he always appeared calm and in control. And, right now, that was exactly what Magill needed, for as one who worked to be perfectly prepared for any contingency, uniform pressed and starched, hair trimmed and combed, he was unnerved by the present circumstances. Looking down at himself, he thought, *I'm on an alien beach in nothing but my boxers, surrounded by a burning jungle, feet throbbing and enemy troops about to overtake our position. How can this be happening?* And all of it just a few minutes away from a calm and relaxed sleep.

He'd never felt so disoriented or vulnerable in his life. More than that, it was his fault that his feet were burned. The military gave men the option of sleeping in their clothes, (including heat resistant socks when in battle), or undressing. Those who chose to undress were required to keep their clothing under their sleeping bag just in case something like this happened. Magill had followed orders, but when Wakely called him, he'd rolled over, leaving his clothing exposed. It was at that precise moment that the nuclear blast ended Wakely's life and destroyed his own protective gear.

Why didn't I keep my uniform on? he agonized. The answer was that he'd never been able to sleep very well and did sleep better when undressed. Plus, he liked to give his uniform and shoes a chance to air out. It had never been a problem, since he could fully dress himself in well under the thirty seconds required of all personnel in battle conditions. *Now I'm crippled!* He almost hyperventilated at the thought of holding everyone else up if they had to carry him.

Wilkerson immediately saw Magill's distress and pulled himself to a standing position. After what they'd been through, these men needed action. "Attention everyone on the beach!" The men had been talking among themselves, but immediately quieted down at the obvious authority in the major's voice.

"First, you should know that I'm Major Ernest Wilkerson of Kalenden. Is there anyone on the beach who outranks me?"

When no one spoke, he continued, "Then I'll assume command, regardless of your regular service unit. The rebels fired a small nuclear warhead, which means we've all been exposed to a potentially lethal dose of radiation. We have to get into the city as quickly as possible to find medication."

"Excuse me, Sir," a somewhat timid voice said out of the darkness.

"Identify yourself!"

"Corporal Wallace Bingham, Medical Corps. My kit was covered by my sleeping bag and I was able to retrieve it after the blast. I have enough medication for at least fifty people."

Wilkerson drew a deep breath. Here was a small sign of hope in the midst of the nightmare. "Very good, Corporal. We all need to move across the marsh to the campsite over there. It looks like the small knoll provided some protection from the flash – at least I see signs that some of their equipment is still intact. Once we get there, Corporal Wallace will administer a radiation antidote to all personnel." He paused to collect his thoughts. *The sooner the better, since the antidote preserves the DNA signature it finds at the time of administration and the goal is to have as little mutation from the radiation as possible.* "Now, everyone take two minutes to pair up and then form over here so we can get a count. And render assistance to anyone who was partially incapacitated by the explosion. Any questions?"

No questions were forthcoming and the survivors started forming up. When everyone had hobbled into formation, Wilkerson counted a mere twenty men of the more than two hundred who had been in camp. "I suppose even twenty is a miracle," he muttered under his breath.

It was exasperating to not have complete uniforms. He didn't know who were officers, non-coms, or enlisted men. But, time was short and he had to know who he was dealing with. "Men, quickly, I want each of you to tell me your name, rank and unit. Also tell me if you're wounded or otherwise incapacitated. And having the crap scared out of you doesn't count."

Some men laughed and started the report. When finished he found that he had two Lieutenants, one Sergeant, one Corporal and an Ensign. Six officers out of twenty were too many, but at least he had men who could provide leadership. He quickly made the uninjured Lieutenant his second-in-command and then ordered the Sergeant and Corporals to pair up with the most seriously injured. Some had had a hand burned off because it was outside their sleeping bag when the blast hit, while others had hair singed, causing weeping wounds to their scalp. A few besides Magill had foot burns, as well. Wilkerson put his arm down to help the young Lieutenant to his feet, but the pain was so great that Magill passed out. Wilkerson pulled his arm up and over his own shoulder, distributed the weight of Magill's body on his back and attempted to bend down and pick up his and Magill's sleeping bags. A soldier came up and picked up the sleeping bags without a word and the ragtag group started silently into the swamp.

The heat of the explosion had incinerated the grass above the waterline, which thickened the mud they waded through. Wilkerson fell a couple of times, but others always helped him get Magill back on his shoulder. Eventually they reached solid ground.

What a sight greeted them. Before the blast, this had been an Alturian camp on the edge of a forest. They'd built the camp on the north side of a small hill, which had sheltered their equipment from the blast. The pattern of the explosion drew air from this area, leaving the men who somehow survived the crushing impact and heat of the blast to suffocate from lack of oxygen. Many were still in their tents, looking like they were asleep.

Most of his men sat down where they could, exhausted from the effort of traversing the swamp. When the mind is overwhelmed, it saps strength from the body once the initial crisis is over.

"Corporal Bingham, please administer the anti-toxin. Choose anyone to help you."

Bingham and a friend rose and moved from soldier to soldier, administering an old-fashioned syringe shot. When Wilkerson looked surprised, the Corporal explained, "My auto-canister lost all programming from the magnetic pulse of the blast, so I have to give the shots manually."

"No problem," Never in his life had Wilkerson worried about an auto-canister; it was merely something doctors had when they needed it. They were so simple to use that even he could have administered the anti-toxin if there hadn't been a medic to do it. Yet, now his life was in the hands of a twenty-year old boy who had paid enough attention in his training class so that he knew how to use a needle. It was at times like this that he appreciated the thoroughness of the military.

As he was about to give an order to rifle through the dead Alturians' belongings to find uniforms and supplies, he heard a rustling in the forest.

"Everyone, hit the ground!" he ordered.

"Identify yourselves," came a voice from the trees. Wilkerson recognized the accent as Alturian.

"I'm Major Ernest Wilkerson from Kalenden. I hold a First Rate clearance from the Alliance Council."

"Password?"

"Sirian Sunrise!"

"What are you doing in an Alturian Camp?" the voice called back.

It was perfectly appropriate for the Alturians to be suspicious. After all, the rebels knew the common language as well as anyone else and since it had been hundreds of years since Alturus and Kalenden had any contact, who could tell for sure which accent was authentic? Given the obvious depth of the rebel's intelligence operation, it wasn't at all unreasonable to question if they'd stolen the password.

Wilkerson decided he needed to show some trust, so he called back, "May I please stand so you can see and talk with me? We're all unarmed – in fact many of us are undressed and injured."

There was hurried consultation in the bushes and then permission was granted for him to stand up.

Wilkerson stood and told the hidden figures in the trees what had happened. When instructed, he had all his troops stand to show that they were unarmed. At that point the Alturians moved out of their hiding places into the camp.

The Alturians were darker skinned than Kalendens, perhaps because their system-star burned hotter than Kalenden. But they had the same ethnic diversity and, if not for their accent and uniforms, could easily pass as Kalendens. When fifteen Alturians entered the center of the camp, their leader approached Wilkerson and gave him a formal salute. "My name is Captain Arnaud Desani of the Alturian Royal Grenadiers. May I ask what your intentions are, Major?"

"I'm afraid I have something rather unpleasant to ask of you. The only troops in our camp to survive were those asleep in their sleeping bags. Most are without uniforms or weapons and unprotected from the elements. I was hoping to acquire the shoes and uniforms of your fallen comrades. I hope this request in no way dishonors you or them."

Wilkerson braced for a hostile response and was surprised by the mildness of the reply. "These men are dead and have no use for uniforms. Of course your people can take whatever they need. We intend to do so, as well." Desani continued, "Do you have any seriously wounded? My assistant, Captain Carling, has medical training."

Wilkerson thanked the Captain and asked if his assistant could assist Lieutenant Magill with his feet. Magill was lying on the ground near the lake, now awake and conscious, as a soldier periodically poured cold water on his soggy bandages. The pain was unbearable and he writhed back and forth, almost delirious. The Alturian Captain moved to Magill, knelt by his side and lifted his head to her lap. Magill looked up into the most beautiful eyes he'd ever seen in his life. They were like dark brown pools of warmth, set in an exquisite face, framed by short, dark brown hair. He seriously thought he must have fainted and was dreaming.

"What is your name, Lieutenant?" the girl asked soothingly.

"I'm Sean Magill," he replied weakly. "I mean Lieutenant Magill."

For a moment he was embarrassed by his condition, but as he looked down at his filthy body, she rubbed his hair gently and said, "It's fine, Lieutenant, you're just fine. I can help with the pain." Her voice calmed him for a moment. He certainly needed help, for the pain from his feet was unlike anything he'd ever felt before. He wanted to reach down and tear at his feet, but knew that would be disastrous.

Tears streamed down his face as he tried to stifle a sob, "I can't stand the pain! My feet hurt so badly!" He buried his face in her lap. It was humiliating, but the pain was simply unbearable.

Reaching into her kit, she kept talking, "My name is Tara. I'm going to give you something to drink that will calm you down and ease the pain." She held a cup to his lips and he drank the bitter liquid. To his amazement the pain eased within seconds and he felt his body go limp as his eyelids grew heavy.

"I can't go to sleep," he pleaded, "we've got to escape or the rebels will get us. I need to stay awake…"

"Don't worry, Lieutenant, we'll escape. Now, you just relax, let go." He looked up into her face and was astonished once again that anyone so attractive could actually be touching and caressing him.

"You're so beautiful," he muttered, his voice trailing off. He saw her smile. *Even her teeth are beautiful.* Magill slipped into a dreamless sleep. The pain was gone and his body was at rest.

* * *

"Damage report?"

The debris of the exploding freighter had struck the Allegro multiple times, sending a shudder through the ship. It wasn't like an explosion in the atmosphere, where the damage occurs when the effect of the expanding gas or nuclear reaction creates a shock wave from the air displaced. For example, some petroleum-based products have an expansion ratio of 5500-to-one, meaning that one unit in liquid form occupies 5500 times as much space when converted to a gas by heat. This massive expansion instantly displaces the same amount of air, compressing it into a shock wave that creates such dramatic results as buildings being blown apart from the force of the blast. But in space there's no air to compress and the chemicals quickly dissipate into the vastness of space. So the explosion itself creates little danger. But the threat comes from fragments blown out by the explosion that have no air to slow their acceleration. Traveling at unbelievable speed, they can tear through even the strongest reinforced hull of a nearby ship, rupturing the environmental seals that keep its occupants safe. From the number of impacts heard against their hull, Jesik felt it was inevitable that the Allegro had been damaged.

"All decks reporting Sir. We've had a hull breach in the engine room barracks on level twelve and another in the shuttle maintenance ready room on level three. Both areas have been sealed and hull integrity is not threatened."

"Thank you, Mr. Brighton. How many casualties?"

"Forty-five already confirmed dead, the total as of yet unknown. Fortunately your Red Alert had pretty much cleared the barracks, but the ready room was fully occupied."

It was usual on a battleship for essential functions, like tactical and engineering, to be isolated well within the center of the ship where they were least likely to be damaged, while less critical functions, like maintenance and sleeping quarters, were located on the outer edge, next to the hull, where they could sustain damage without disabling the ship. Ironically, most of the men liked it this way, because it helped fend off the occasional claustrophobia one feels in the center of the ship. After more than six centuries in space, people still liked a window, even though it placed them directly in harm's way.

"Any systems damaged by debris that did not penetrate the hull?"

"Communications reports that some short-distance transmitters have been temporarily disabled and there are scratches and blemishes on the hull that make those areas sensitive to laser attack, but nothing that directly interferes with battle readiness."

Jesik sighed in relief. It could have been so much worse.

After re-positioning the ship into an orbit out of visual range of all Alturian ships, he ordered the Captains of his assigned support ships, the Fermata and Stanza, to stand-by for a video link. All three ships moved to Yellow alert since there were no signs of any imminent threat of hostilities.

Then, turning to the officers on the bridge he said quietly, "The next step is to find out who the hell was responsible for this. Senior officers, please assemble in my ready room in thirty minutes. I'll need a report from each operational area."

Jesik used the intervening minutes to sketch out what he knew about the attack. He always found that an old-fashioned paper and pencil helped him collect and organize his thoughts. When the staff began to assemble, Jesik was ready with some pointed questions.

As they entered the room, he scrutinized each officer for any sign of distress or panic. For many, this was the first hostile activity they'd ever experienced and it would be foolish to think they'd be unaffected by the death of more than forty of their crewmates in a particularly gruesome and painful fashion. When the hull is breached, automated systems immediately protect the ship by sealing off all exits from the area, which sucks the air inside the quarantined area out of the ship. The oxygen in the crews' bodies has to escape as well, which collapses their lungs and ruptures tissue throughout their body until the pressure is equalized. The bloody mass remaining is hard to recognize as human.

Hopefully their suffering ended quickly.

He welcomed the Commanders of his support ships and asked them to be seated. Of course they physically took a chair on-board their own ship, but the holographic projector made it appear as if they were seated comfortably in two chairs at the Allegro's own boardroom table.

In response to Captain Rowley's inquiry, Jesik explained the damage sustained by Allegro and the loss of life. Both Commanders expressed their condolences and offered assistance, along with assurances that their ships were ready and eager to join in Allegro's defense.

Turning to his own staff, Jesik asked, "Mr. Gentry, are all weapons fully operational?"

"Yes, Sir. No damage to report."

"Mr. Williams, did the shrapnel impair our communications ability in anyway?"

"Communication with the planet was temporarily interrupted, but we've established an alternate link to communicate with ground forces. Our deep-space Esper links are fine, although encountering some kind of disturbance in communications with Kalenden, probably a space storm. Still, we have almost contemporaneous communications with the home planet."

"Please relay all logs of this incidence. I also want you to communicate video images of the alien ship before and during the explosion. Perhaps Fleet can give us a better idea who initiated the attack."

"Mr. O'Casey, status of the engines and necessary repairs?"

The Chief Engineer was listening hard to his ear-piece, but looked up immediately to respond to the question. "Robot polishers are working on the hull as we speak. We'll need at least three hours to remove all blemishes. The hull breaches have been sealed with molten alinite, which should cool in one or two days, after which we can reopen the damaged sections. Then we can recover the dead crewmember's bodies. Engines are at full capacity."

"Very good. Well, gentlemen, at this point all we know is that an unmarked freighter took hostile laser action against the Allegro. We disabled it and, as it drifted towards us, a nuclear detonation destroyed it and inflicted damage on our ship. The weapon's profile and signature pattern of the blast are Alturian, although the ship itself was an unmanned drone. Anyone have anything to add?"

"The missiles and nuclear reactors appear Alturian, but the lasers didn't use any of the standard Alturian colors or lancing patterns. The closest match is to Keswick Boundary Patrol."

"That makes it even more interesting, doesn't it, Mr. Gentry? I think it's time we contact our Alturian allies and see what light they can shed. Mr. Rowley, please maneuver Fermata to a protected position behind the third moon and Mr. Talbot, bring your ship six kilometers aft of our starboard and we'll move in range of the Alturians. Everyone else, return to your battle stations."

Even though the Alturians had superior numbers, a battleship, frigate and destroyer still provided considerable firepower to give the Alturians pause. So, when everyone was in position, Jesik ordered Lieutenant Wight to move the Allegro into full view of the Alturian Flagship. He was pleased that Wight maneuvered the ship with an unusually brisk acceleration that showed she was at full strength, yet on a flight path that also made it clear the move was not hostile.

"Mr. Williams, please signal the Alturian Commander."

The communications console issued the distinctive hail on three different frequencies. So far, communications between the two battle-groups had been limited to an initial acknowledgement, followed by a joint agreement on zones of responsibility and flight plans. Members of Jesik's crew had executed coordination of the ground and atmosphere fighters, all of which means that Jesik had not yet had occasion to speak to his Alturian counterpart.

Just as he was getting impatient for a response, the main view screen displayed the image of a young Alturian.

"This is His Majesties ship Princeton, of the Alturian Empire Royal Navy. Identify yourself."

"Captain Pietr Jesik, commander of the Allegro – first ship in the Kalenden System Star Fleet. I wish to speak with your Senior Officer regarding a recent attack on our vessel."

The image on the screen changed from that of the rather uncertain young communications officer to that of an obviously self-assured leader.

"Admiral Lucien Rameira, Captain Jesik. I'm pleased we have a chance to speak to one another. I confess that we witnessed the laser exchange between you and the alien freighter, but thought it best not to involve ourselves in your affairs. Are you injured in some way? How can we be of assistance at this point?"

Very smooth, thought Jesik.

"Actually, Admiral, we were hoping you could shed some light on our attacker. It seems the nuclear signature of their main weapons array matched that of an Alturian destroyer, rather than an orchidite transport. We feared we had somehow provoked your animosity."

Jesik smiled slightly as he said this, as a show of good humor, while fingering the trigger of his alert activator that would initiate a massive missile volley if the Alturians took any hostile action.

Rameira forced a smile in return. "Why Captain Jesik, our first conversation and you think it wise to accuse me of an unprovoked attack?"

"No accusation intended, Sir. We're simply confused and in need of military intelligence. We're concerned for our ground troops and need to know what threats face us. I have absolutely no reason to doubt that you and your government are completely ethical in standing by the Keswick Mutual Assistance Protocol. Is it possible you have any information that can help us?"

Political Officer Barrows listened to this exchange in astonishment. Jesik had never received any diplomatic training, yet in just a few sentences he managed to alert the Alturians to the fact that they appeared to be a threat, while rather humbly preserving their options to negotiate.

Admiral Rameira pursed his lips, turned to an assistant for a few moments, then returned his gaze to the screen.

"Captain, in different times I'd enjoy stretching this out a bit, just to see how you Kalendens respond. But, it's clear that you reacted out of self-defense. I believe I have some information that may be helpful to you; actually helpful to both of us. As it turns out, I believe we face a common threat. Can you arrange a secure video conference so I can speak with you privately?"

"Certainly. My communications officer, Mr. Williams, will be glad to work with yours to establish the link. I'd like to meet as soon as possible. You set the time."

A meeting was arranged for one hour later. In the meantime, as a sign of good faith, both ships powered down their laser generators and took their missiles offline. Jesik ordered the crew to Condition Green, which kept them ready to move quickly to action stations, but took all potentially nervous fingers off the buttons that could launch weapons and start an accidental war.

"Strange," he said to Commander Brighton as they retreated to the most secure conference chamber, "but I somehow feel safer now than before … as though the Alturians feel as threatened as we do."

"I sensed the same thing, Captain. At least for the moment all the capital ships in both fleets in orbit are in communicating status with one another, so we'll know if anyone turns into a threat."

Jesik shook his head. "How long before we can break communications silence with the ground and atmosphere teams? I need to know if anything odd is taking place on the planet."

"Another two hours, Sir. Of course you can override the blackout if you like."

"No, I think we're okay for now. But keep a close eye on the planet while I'm meeting with Rameira." With that said, Jesik entered the conference chamber, which was like retreating to a cave 1,000 kilometers in the middle of a planet. His isolation was complete.

At the appointed time, Lieutenant Williams broke the silence to report that a secure communications link was now established between the two ships. To accomplish that, a high intensity laser beam connected the two communications arrays. This beam was surrounded by a virtual sheath of two dozen other beams that were loaded down with meaningless data and high frequency magnetic fields that would prevent any listening in by an unauthorized source.

"Activate the link, Lieutenant. Then see that no one interrupts me, except in the most extreme emergency. Commander Brighton is in operational control of the ship during this conference."

"As you wish, Sir, link is now active."

Admiral Rameira appeared in the seat opposite Jesik. He too, was alone. As the Senior Officer, Rameira broke the silence. "Captain, it's been a hundred and fifty earth years since our cultures have interacted and now it seems we're off to a rocky start. I'm sincerely sorry for that."

"Thank you, Admiral. I had hoped that past animosities would have faded by now so that our systems might extend a few tentative links with one another. We share so much from our common heritage."

Jesik had decided early on to avoid accusations until after he had a chance to take Rameira's measure. So far he was handling the situation with remarkable calm and poise.

"Captain, we've done an analysis of the nuclear reaction you encountered and concur with your conclusion that the ship is of Alturian design. On behalf of the empire, please accept our apologies."

"Perhaps you can help me understand the circumstances of the attack, so that I can reassure our people and Fleet Command that your intentions are benign?"

Rameira was obviously distressed and looked away while he composed his thoughts. Glancing up at Jesik he studied his face for the longest time. For his part, Jesik was content to sit quietly and wait.

"Captain, we're strangers and yet I must share with you secrets that are largely unknown to most of our own population. We had no idea that our enemies would use the Keswick campaign as an excuse to further their terrorist cause at your expense." Rameira looked away again. Jesik could feel the tension in his body, even though he saw only a holographic image. Clearing his throat, the Admiral continued. "There is a fringe element in our society that is distressed by our Royal Family. In the early years of colonization after the Earth migration, a number of prominent families vied for power. The Carlisles, Pomeroys and Sterlings rose to power, while the

LeMons lost ground.

"You were kind to omit the name Jesik from those that lost influence. I've lived in the shadow of the prominent families of Kalenden all my life, which includes many of the names you mentioned."

"Ah, yes, Captain, as have I. While I know I may be repeating information you already have, I'd like to make certain we have a mutual understanding."

Jesik indicated he should continue.

"After consolidating power, there was a rift in the Royal Family itself which prompted the split that drove the initial migration from Alturus to Kalenden, with a few stragglers settling on the border at Keswick. It's my understanding that the people of Kalenden and its related settlements rejected enthroning a Royal Family there."

"True, but the same prominent families, along with the Kensingtons and Wights, still rule in an indirect fashion. We have no king, but our House of Lords can stop any legislation passed by the popularly elected Assembly."

"Then the historical animosity of our greater and lesser families is the cause of our present distress. Once the blood feud with Kalenden was resolved, our society moved on. But the hard feelings between at least some of the families continue. Now, the rebels wish to destabilize the government and perhaps gain control of the government. In that effort they have allied themselves with the rebels on Keswick. We also believe they've been in communication with some of the second and third-class families on Kalenden."

That threw Jesik, and his face must have shown his discomfiture. "Then what you're telling me, Admiral, is that the attack on Allegro was somehow accomplished by Alturian rebels who are most likely working in concert with rebels on Keswick?"

"I'm sorry to report that my own First Officer detonated the drone ship, which means that I had no idea of the real strength of the rebels. Fortunately, the Captain of the Princeton had operational control of our vessel or the rebels would have turned that on you as well. When we detected the conspiracy, I moved immediately to crush it and have already arrested twenty conspirators onboard this vessel. We'll proceed to Summary Judgment as soon as I end this conference. We've been in contact with the Royal Family and they've given authority to execute those found guilty. Please be assured that those who attacked your ship will be dead within a few hours."

Jesik was shocked. On Kalenden, even a military tribunal would be months in scheduling and preparing. That the Alturians could move so quickly to destroy their own people was completely outside his thinking.

"Do you believe all who pose a threat have been identified?"

"I'm not certain of anything, Captain. It may be that our rebels have even been in communication with members of your own crew."

"I've seen no evidence of that, but of course I'll take your warning seriously. With the Loyalist forces rather firmly in control on Keswick, what possible advantage can the rebels gain by taking on the combined governments of Alturus and Kalenden. Certainly they can see that our combined military forces enjoy an overwhelming superiority that will tighten and crush them immediately if they interfere with our interests!"

"Of course I don't have any firm answers, but I suspect the rebels are hoping to stir up movements to de-stabilize the governments on both Alturus and Kalenden. Even better, from the rebels' point-of-view, would be to draw Alturus and Kalenden into another war with each other, leaving our militaries depleted and susceptible to infiltration and sabotage."

Jesik needed time to ponder all this. In posting the Allegro to the Keswick operation, Fleet Command had provided no indication that Kalenden itself might be the focus of the conflict.

"What do you propose we do next, Admiral Rameira?"

"From our point of view, the best thing would be for you or ourselves to withdraw from this field of battle so that we pose no further risk to you. But, politically, it would be suicide for either of us to withdraw and leave the Keswick orchidite mines under the domination of the other system, so I doubt we can disengage. Please trust me that we have taken extraordinary precautions to assure this ship cannot be turned against itself or you."

Jesik stood and walked off screen, picked up a carafe of water and poured it slowly into a glass. He needed time to think without Rameira seeing his face. *Can I believe this man? Is this some kind of trap? If so, why give us a warning and a plea to increase our own security?*

"I'll need to communicate with my superiors before reaching any decision."

"I give you authority to convey the essence of this message on a Need-to-Know basis only. Should word of this conspiracy reach our population before our civil authorities are prepared to respond, we could see system-wide chaos. I suspect your own government is in jeopardy as well, if there is an active rebel movement there. Normal communications and reporting would be too vulnerable to rebel espionage."

"I have no intentions of reporting the details of our conversation to

Fleet until I have more solid intelligence. Until then I'll even use caution in sharing it with my crew."

"Understood. Frankly my politicians had better deal with this quickly or the rebels will make a public move on Alturus. Keswick is clearly a rehearsal for whatever is yet to come. Perhaps this incident will speed our preparations."

Jesik liked Rameira. *I do trust him. He's taken a huge risk in sharing this with me, while I've given nothing in return.*

He was about to ask Rameira about additional protection for their ground troops when Commander Brighton's voice broke into the conversation.

"Captain, we have an emergency that requires your immediate attention." Brighton sounded anxious.

It better be a real emergency to interrupt this conference.

"Admiral, apparently something's happened that has prompted an interruption."

"Yes, there's been a nuclear explosion on the planet surface and it appears there's an active laser and missile attack taking place in the atmosphere. Perhaps we can meet again later. Rameira out."

It was phrased as a question, but stated as a fact. They would meet again.

By the time Jesik got to the bridge, data was streaming in to all monitors. He could see flashes illuminating the area around Keston and the orchidite mines.

"What can you tell me, Mr. Brighton?"

"There's been a nuclear attack by rebel fighters on ground units assigned to protect Keston. While not a direct hit on our base camp near the city, I can't imagine that there are many survivors, given the force of the blast and the likely area of destruction. We haven't been able to establish communications with any of our troops at this time. There's also intense fighter action some sixty kilometers to the south, along the corridor perimeter. We've ordered the fighters to open their communications links so we can hear what's going on, but so far none have responded."

Jesik settled into his seat, brought up his individual monitor and quickly replayed the events up to that point. The thing that struck him most was the perfect execution of the rebel attack that opened all along the line simultaneously. And it was clear from the bombing patterns, that the rebels had full knowledge of Alliance strongholds.

"We were suckered, gentlemen, plain and simple!"

The Bridge Officers turned to look at the Captain, who stepped lightly out of his seat. "The rebels played the Loyalist forces perfectly. They feigned being beaten back so they would draw ever-larger contingents away from the city and mines. Like fools, the ground troops fell for it and we failed to insist they not enter the trap. Now they can cut our ground forces up piecemeal."

The Captain was fully engrossed in his analysis, which gave everyone more confidence.

Brighton stepped closer to Jesik and lowered his voice. "Is there anything we should know about a threat from the Alturians, Sir?"

"What, Mr. Brighton?" Jesik looked up from his screen as the question registered. "Ah, my conversation with Rameira. All I can tell you is that the flagship poses no immediate threat. The freighter was Alturian, but not under control of Royal Forces. I suspect there may be collusion between Alturian and Keswick rebels, so we'll need to maintain full alert. For now, please keep it confidential." He paused. "Now, Mr. Gentry, how can we help our troops on the ground?"

Gentry wanted, more than anything, to blast some rebel fighters out of the sky, but at this moment the melee was so thick that it was impossible to tell which ship was whose. Just as he was about to reply, a voice crackled through the intercom.

"Allegro, Allegro, this is Lieutenant Eaves. We're under heavy assault from land and aerial assault troops. We're holding our own, destroyed at least a dozen of their fighters. Do you read us Allegro?"

"We hear you, Mr. Eaves. I see you're in trouble again."

"Why, yes, Captain, we are." You could almost hear the grin in his voice. "But I think we can handle it."

"What you may not know, Lieutenant, is that the rebels launched a nuclear weapon against our base camp sixty kilometers from your position. We haven't been able to establish contact to see if there were survivors. This is a well-coordinated attack along the line."

This news was greeted by a long silence. "We knew there'd been a nuclear explosion, because we saw the blast. But, we didn't know where. Lieutenant Magill was at that camp, wasn't he, Sir?"

"Yes, he was." Jesik knew Magill was Eaves' best friend, but there was no time for that now. "What can we do to help?"

Eaves voice steadied. "We observed what appeared to be an explosion in the upper atmosphere. Does that have any bearing on us?"

Jesik switched from open microphone to a headset, where he spoke quietly so only Eaves could hear.

"The Allegro was attacked by an Alturian, disguised as a freighter. We sustained minor damage. There's evidence of an Alturian rebel element working in concert with those on Keswick. This is confidential at this point, but you have to be extra alert to danger."

There was the sound of a laser cannon firing and Eaves shouted orders to his other fighters. Jesik returned the conversation to full monitor so everyone on the bridge could hear.

"Oh, I can't believe it – he hit an Alturian!"

Jesik and Brighton moved toward the monitor screen. No matter how urgent their need for intelligence, they could not break the Lieutenant's concentration while in battle.

Finally, Eaves' voice came over the intercom. "Captain, we've got a real problem. One of our fighters attempted to use an Alturian as a decoy to shoot down a rebel fighter, but the missile misread the target and took out the Alturian. Apparently his buddies thought it was an intentional attack, because two of them just killed our guy. It's a free-for-all down here."

"Lieutenant, get your men out! Return to the ship immediately!"

"We can't disengage Sir—the Alturians and rebels are pursuing us, we've got to figure out something to untangle this mess. Eaves out!"

Brighton walked over to study the tactical board. The red, green and yellow lights that distinguished one fighter from another were so close to each other that the screen appeared brown. It was impossible to launch any kind of attack from space until they scattered a bit. Or, until they were all killed.

"What was that?" asked Lieutenant Wight. Everyone turned to look at him.

"What was what, Lieutenant?" Brighton asked with irritation.

"Sorry for the outburst, Sir. There was an unidentified blast in the middle of the fighter group and all fighters in the area are powering down."

There was silence on the bridge as every officer did his best to figure out what the new data on their display screen was trying to tell them. Wight said quietly, "If I'm not mistaken Sir, Lieutenant Eaves launched a dazzle blast. I think he's single-handedly ended the air battle in that sector."

"Amazing," said Jesik, dropping his voice. "Of course he would have disabled himself as well. And naturally his communications are gone, so we won't be able to find out what actually occurred. Well, he's on his own for a while. Commander Gentry, where else is the attack a little more orderly so we can intervene? It feels pretty foolish for the most powerful ship in the fleet to stand idly by while all this is going on!"

5 - THE EYE OF THE STORM

The feel of silk sheets against his skin betrayed the dream Magill was having. In his dream there was an incredible rushing sound like a wall of water engulfing him and carrying him forward in a great torrent. But, it wasn't exactly water, since a searing blast of heat and light preceded the deafening sound. He rolled clumsily to his back and opened his eyes. What he saw was enough to disorient anyone. He was in an ornate bed, gilded in gold and platinum, with a peach covered-canopy overhead. He rubbed his eyes and looked out into the room, which was even gaudier. He recognized the furnishings as "French Provincial," the style the architectural books he'd studied in school said was so popular among the leading families of Kalenden. Certainly no one decorated like this in the neighborhood where he grew up; all he'd ever seen of the style were in pictures.

I must still be dreaming. He rubbed his eyes again. Then a voice came from the other side of the room. "Ah, so you've decided to rejoin us, Lieutenant?" It was a feminine voice and somehow Magill thought he recognized it. He was almost afraid to turn and look.

But, he didn't have to, for the owner of the voice came around the bed into his field of vision. Seeing her face brought back the memories he'd been trying to run away from in his dream. Instinctively he tried to move his feet to see if they were still there. Then he remembered the dream. "I can't feel my feet! Have they been amputated?" Panic flooded his eyes and the girl sat down on the side of the bed.

"No, they're still there, Lieutenant Magill. You can't feel them because they've been anesthetized so you'd stop trying to kick them in your sleep. Go ahead, reach down and feel."

He was a little embarrassed not to trust her, but he did have to know for himself, so he reached down under the covers. His calves were wrapped in some kind of bandage. Touching his feet, however, he was shocked at what seemed to be a pair of boots.

"My feet are in combat boots?"

She laughed. A most remarkable laugh that drove away his feeling of panic. "It is a bit odd, given the room you're lounging in. Perhaps I should catch you up on what brought us here and then the boots will make sense. When I first saw your feet back at the Alturian base camp, I knew shock would overtake you in just a few moments, so I gave you a shot that quickly knocked you out. Your Major Wilkerson told us we had to hurry to avoid a rebel ambush, so we quickly dressed you in the uniform of one of our dead Alturian soldiers and made a litter for you. Our combined forces then retreated through the jungle toward the entrance to the city. About halfway there, we were able to join a Loyalist contingent that was returning to help strengthen the Royal Guard and when we told them about your condition, they agreed to let you recuperate in the palace. So, here you are." She smiled again, which caused an instinctive smile from Magill.

"But, what about the boots?"

"Oh, yes, the boots. Ours is a rather vain society on Alturus and an enormous amount of research has gone into skin care and beauty enhancement. One of the practical discoveries from that research is a medicating gel that can protect serious burns while the individual recovers. Our medical corps figured out a way to incorporate the gel inside a membrane in our soldier's footwear. If the foot ever becomes damaged, the soldier activates an electronic monitor that quickly dissolves the membrane so that the gel can soothe and protect the skin. Monitors can sense your level of pain and numb the affected nerves until you can bear it."

"How long will I need to wear the boots?"

"Once activated, the gel needs to stay in constant contact with your skin until you're ready to come under the care of a physician. We could have taken the gel packet out and wrapped you in bandages, but not knowing when we'd need your help in getting you mobile, we decided to leave the boots on to support you if the need comes for you to walk before your feet have healed."

"Thank you – for everything. I'm sorry I was a burden to anyone."

She smiled again. "That's what you said to me while falling unconscious. You have no reason to feel guilty for being wounded in action. You'd have helped any of us, I'm sure."

He dropped his eyes and said, "I do feel guilty because it was my own fault that my footwear was destroyed." He explained about putting them under his sleeping bag, but rolling off his clothing to talk to Corporal Wakely.

"That sleeping bag of yours is unbelievable. We don't have anything like it. What an amazing material that cools you when it's hot outside, warms when it's cold and also manages to resist a nuclear blast. We Alturians survived the explosion because we had our night camp in the entrance to a cave on the side of a hill away from the blast. It still about cooked us, but we made it through. But, if we'd have had your sleeping bags, there would have been a lot less suffering."

She looked at him and saw he was still distressed.

"Oh, for heaven's sake, Lieutenant, any human being alive would have leaned forward to talk to someone shouting at him from the door of his tent. You did nothing wrong. Even if you had, you've more than suffered for it. So, get over it."

His face flushed, but he appreciated what she said.

"Alright, I'm over it. How bad are my feet and what's happening with the battle?"

"Your feet are badly burned, in some spots into the bone. I'm sure there's nerve damage that, even on Alturus, would be difficult to repair. But I don't know what your doctors' are capable of. The medicating gel pack should have stopped any gangrene or infection, so I think you should hope for the best?"

"But can I walk?"

"I'm a military officer with only basic medical training. But, aside from being clumsy from having diminished feeling in your feet, they can certainly bear weight. The gel pack will absorb any shock and protect the skin."

"At least that's something. I feel so helpless here in bed." He clenched his hands in frustration, but out of her sight.

"As to the military situation, it's about as bad as your feet. The rebels have successfully jammed all communications with our ships in orbit and our fighters have been put out of action. The rebels managed to destroy enough Loyalist and Alliance troops during their attack that they now hold a numerical advantage which they are using to advance on Keston. No one knows if they have more than one nuclear weapon, so many people are afraid to resist them in fear of another nuclear attack. Meanwhile, the Loyalists temporarily lost the means to deliver a counter-attack using nuclear weapons. Unless they get some fighters into the air soon, it's merely a matter of time before the rebels get here."

"What about the orchidite mines?"

"Still under Alliance control, mostly because the miners have taken up defensive positions around the equipment. The rebels know that if the miners destroy the equipment, they lose their negotiating power and will likely face a complete planetary takeover by outside governments. So, for now they're content to sit tight, outside the perimeter and let the situation develop. But, they could also attack at any time and overwhelm the defenders."

Magill was thoughtful. "That means civilians must protect the Royal Family in the event of an all-out assault on the city. That will see hand-to-hand fighting in the streets, particularly if air evacuation for the royals is impossible. The greatest danger will come from rebel cells in the civilian population. It's almost impossible for the guerillas to have grown this strong without discontent in the general citizenry." Tara watched Magill with growing respect. "Amazing that all this could happen because of a small crystal formation the shape and color of orchid petals." He smiled wanly, shook his head.

"You seem quite aware of the political situation."

"Politics is my hobby and most of my military friends think I'm foolish to get so interested in it. They say our job is to simply implement whatever policy comes our way, but I believe we have to understand the dynamics of what's going on in a society, both our enemy's and our own, if we hope to be effective. My ship's captain asked me to be a political observer as well as part of the ground team."

"Your captain? Do you mind if I ask his name?"

Magill raised an eyebrow. "Captain Jesik – Pietr Jesik. Why do you ask?"

"Because you've been using his name in your dreams. While the things you said were a bit muddled, it seems you have a great deal of respect for him."

Magill nodded, aggravated that he had talked in his sleep, and even more so that he felt so emotional. "He's a great man. Since transferring onto his ship he's gone out of his way to help Lieutenant Eaves and me learn the ropes, so to speak, of military life. He's really probably the best in the whole service."

"That's good to know. Things are pretty tense right now, so I'm glad you have someone with self-control on your flagship." Tara paused before posing her next question. A bit nervously she started, paused, then re-started. "I understand, Lieutenant that you are from a lower-class family on Kalenden." She was embarrassed when he looked up sharply. "Please don't be offended, it's just that I'd not heard your name before and asked. One man from your unit explained about your acceptance into Kalenden Arms. But, you don't need to answer."

"No, it's okay. I'm not ashamed of my background. I'm a third-class guy who's learned to get along with some first-class friends. I sometimes tell myself that it really makes no difference, but then a conversation like this comes up and I have to explain myself."

She dropped her eyes, obviously embarrassed.

He felt sorry that he embarrassed her, even though he was angry that his social class would come up as a topic of conversation.

"Here's the deal," he said. "If I had a first-class name, you would simply judge me as a stupid, young Kalenden Lieutenant who didn't take care to protect his feet and, *oh, well, everybody makes mistakes.* But, because I'm from a lower-class, everyone will wonder if my feet are toast because of inferior breeding or poor training. After all, isn't it just like *those people* to forget something as simple as that?" In spite of his best effort, he failed to conceal the anger in his voice.

Tara looked up and said evenly, "You have misunderstood me completely, Lieutenant. Most of your first-class officers are dead because they were lying on top of their sleeping bags to enjoy the night air. That, of course, was against regulations. So when it comes to being stupid, the evidence goes against your first-class families. And the reason I asked about your class is that I'm interested in how classes interact in Kalenden society and I thought you might be the person who could explain it to me, confidentially." She tried to conceal the hurt in her voice, but failed, and Magill felt miserable.

"I'm sorry, but I guess I still carry a chip on my shoulder. It seems like I've spent a lifetime explaining myself. First to my third-class friends who think I'm a traitor for going to Kalenden Arms and then to my first-class friends who can't imagine how we lower-class people get upset and think they're bigoted when they treat us so kindly. They just don't get what it means to feel patronized."

"Now, that's what I mean," she said earnestly. "I'm from a leading family on Alturus and I'm sure I don't know how our lower-class families feel. I want to, very much. But, none of them will talk to me, at least not honestly. They only say what they think I want to hear. Maybe you can help me understand."

"Alright," Magill answered. "I'll try. But I'm not sure I can be that helpful, since Kalenden is probably quite different from Alturus. You have royalty, we don't. On Alturus, both government leadership and social status are hereditary. On Kalenden, it's possible for lower-classes to make it into government service."

"That's basically correct," Tara confirmed, "but in practice, many of our bureaucrats also come from the lower-classes and hold responsible positions."

"On Kalenden we have a constitutional democracy with no Royal Family. That's why there was a split between our two planets. Our House of Commons is responsible for government operations, with the Prime Minister selected from within the ruling party. Of course, even though elections are open, most PM's are from prominent families since they have the most money to run an election. We also have a House of Hereditary Peers that can exercise a veto by a two-thirds vote, but only in matters of property rights and social conventions. As a group, the Peer's have preserved their unity through the years to make sure there are no estate or inheritance taxes to break up their fortunes and that private schools can segregate against members of the lower-classes. With private funding, the best professors and teachers strive to work in private schools, so education for the lower-classes is quite limited. In theory, anyone from any class can attain leadership, but in practice, political parties favor members of the ruling families. Consequently, it's been more than a hundred years since a member of the lower-class rose to a significant position of leadership, either within the cabinet or as Prime Minister. In my mind that's de facto aristocracy."

"Does your government function efficiently?"

"Yes, surprisingly, it does."

"Is it generally fair to the lower-classes."

"It is."

"Then why do you resent it?'

Magill looked around the room. "Take a look at this place. This room is large enough to house four apartments in the neighborhood where I grew up. What an incredible waste of resources to heat, furnish and pamper a Royal Family that will never know what it's like to make a house payment or acquire adequate food and clothing. This bed I'm in probably costs more than an average family spends to furnish their entire house."

"Is it envy, then, that makes the lower-classes resent the upper class?"

"Maybe, for some. Not for me. I'm not jealous of this at all. How much space does one person need, anyway? What I hate is the presumption that heredity qualifies one for leadership. Genetic diversity in the general population is far more likely to produce outstanding character traits than selective breeding among the upper crust. While it's true that some positive traits are strengthened over time, the weaknesses are, too. I think it's deplorable that the most able and intelligent person on the planet may never get a chance to serve because his last name isn't properly hyphenated."

Magill was taking shallow breaths again, which frustrated him. He could feel the old anger rising. Tara continued though, in spite of his frustration.

"But, we believe it's efficient to assign people roles early in life so their training can be customized. By giving each class specialized functions, society works at maximum efficiency. And since there are strict laws against discrimination, no one can speak down to a person of a lower-class. On Alturus a custodian receives the same regard as a cabinet minister."

"Ah, yes, 'noblesse oblige,' the ancient Earth custom of royalty showing gratitude to their subjects. Don't you see how patronizing that is? 'Your work is just as important as ours. Of course our financial reward is a hundred thousand times greater than yours, but you are just as important to society.' Sorry, but that's a bunch of bunk."

Her cheeks colored, but she continued, "And how would you organize society, Lieutenant?"

"Meritocracy. Create an open society where talent, ability and ambition determines who gets ahead. On Kalenden, only the kids from the upper class have a choice. The second and third-class families seldom get the opportunity, even if qualified. It's a huge waste of talent."

"What about you, it seems you progressed to the finest school?" She should have left it at that, but he'd irritated her. "Aren't you a little ungrateful to the society that opened itself up for you?"

"Oh, yes, the token third-class student. It shows the universe that our society is really open by admitting one out of a class of four hundred. But, watch what happens if I ever fall in love with a girl of the first-class. Her family would put her on an extended tour of the Tatrian system so fast, her head would spin. 'Nothing personal,' of course. I may move far enough ahead to one day make it into the Quadrant Council – perhaps even a minister. The publicity would be great for the government. After all, I'd be a third-class success story. But, it'll be a minor ministry, where I can't do much damage. "

Tara paused to catch her breath. There was a fire in Magill's eye and his rhetoric was both appealing and frightening. His dark black hair framed his slender face with its sharply tapered chin, all of which added effect to his earnest authority and sense of lurking danger. She'd never been spoken to this way before and she found it intriguing. So she decided to push just a little more.

"You've got to remember, Lieutenant, that the early colonists were from democracies on earth and willingly chose to return to monarchy. The democracies had become decadent, with no social order. When every person was supreme in his or her own eyes, it became impossible to judge right and wrong. Their philosophy was 'How can you condemn someone else when their morality is different than yours?' In the end, the democracies became more lawless and the people were constantly anxious, even though they shared freely in the material abundance of their society."

Magill started to interrupt, but hesitated as she continued. "Not only that, but their supposed equality was a sham. The money of the corporations and media combined to create a false sense of independence, while controlling the common people by taking advantage of their moral weaknesses. Gambling, material goods, and sexuality – all was available for a flat monthly fee. The rich grew incredibly rich, while the middle class was content thinking they were in control. All that changed when space travel became possible and hereditary leadership took over out here in the quadrants, making good and evil became fashionable again so people could begin living meaningful lives. I can't see why that's so bad. What's wrong with creating an intellectual-elite with the inclination and intelligence to sort those things out and properly order society?"

Now it she was speaking with passion and Magill found himself wanting to slap or kiss her, for he'd never known anyone like her before.

"But, what if a first-class kid is an idiot? Does he still deserve a prime posting? No matter what you say, an aristocracy elevates the undeserving and still holds other people down. Think of China in ancient earth of the 21st century. They pretended to be Communists, with all people sharing in the common good, but the children of the political elite could get away with anything. At least that's what the history books say. So, regardless of how benevolent the class system wants to be, it's just not fair!"

Tara flashed, "It sounds like you're pretty sympathetic to the rebels, while at the same time taking advantage of the hospitality of the Royal Family!"

Magill was about to lose it when he heard the confident voice of Major Wilkerson. "Did I just hear we rescued and harbor a rebel?"

Tara backed down immediately. "I'm afraid I provoked Lieutenant Magill. I asked him for some insight into Kalenden society, then argued with him when I didn't like his answers."

Magill's irritation evaporated. "The last two people I want to fight with are you two. You saved my life, even though it slowed your own escape, so I owe you everything." He swallowed hard. "I just get so anxious to do something to help the lower-classes attain their potential." He looked from Tara to Wilkerson to see if they understood. "I'm not a rebel. And I'm certainly in no position to judge the monarchies of either Keswick or Alturus. All I know is that it's hard for people in the upper class to understand what it's like to grow up with limitations. I've had an opportunity to see things from both sides and when I talk like this, it's not that I'm on the rebel's side, but I do think it makes sense to try and understand your enemy. If you don't understand what motivates them, how can you defeat them, or better, find a way to make peace?"

"That's a rare insight," said Tara. She took his hand. "Thank you for being honest. It's what I asked for."

"Lieutenant," Wilkerson said, "when you are feeling up to it perhaps you wouldn't mind if I joined you two for dinner. I don't understand the rebels at all and whatever insight you can give me would be appreciated. They're shrewd and likely to win if we don't figure out how to stop them in the next few days. So, any information you or your friends can give me will help."

"Speaking of friends," said Tara, "there's a brash, young, fighter pilot who claims he's your best friend and demands to see you."

"Travis Eaves is here?"

"That's it, 'Eaves!' He's notorious for having fired a dazzle blast that ended the atmosphere battle some twenty kilometers from here. It was the only thing that could end the mayhem."

"Yeah, that would be Travis. May I see him?"

"I'll go find him. But, remember, you've been in shock and shouldn't let him get you too excited." She laughed at herself and added, "And then I'll try to stop sounding like your mother. I look forward to dinner with the two of you, Major." She and Major Wilkerson left the room.

Magill grinned but didn't notice he'd started whistling. The door opened and he looked up expectantly.

"Damn ground troops – a real nuisance when there's heavy fighting to be done."

"Inept fighters that leave us open to something as minor as a nuclear attack!"

Eaves approached and grabbed Magill's cheeks. "You don't look nearly as bad as they said you would. You should try to look sicker when they take your hero-photo. How do you feel?"

"Lucky. Wakely was incinerated and more than 90% of my unit was wiped out. Yet somehow I'm still alive."

"Alive, but not kicking, I understand."

"Yeah, I'm afraid I'm an invalid, at least for a while. But boy do I have the most beautiful nurse in the quadrant!"

"I saw her. She is beautiful. I hope you think of her as a sister, because I intend to ask her out."

"You should hope. You know a woman can't help but love a man in pain. Go find your own date."

They laughed.

"I was really scared when Jesik said your camp had been hit by a nuclear blast. Then there was no communication with the base camp and I had to break our link to Allegro before I received a full report. I thought you'd bought it for sure. Of course death would have been great for your reputation."

"The Allegro? I thought all communications with the ship were broken."

"Mine was the last one to get through. The rebels learned our communications patterns and blocked them. If we had some decent equipment down here, we could overcome their jamming, but nearly all our fighters are out of commission and behind enemy lines. Mine's hidden in the jungle and I'm working on an escape plan to get the Alliance personnel back into orbit."

Magill felt better. Eaves was a great innovator and together they might come up with workable ideas. Their situation didn't seem nearly as hopeless as just ten minutes earlier.

"Do, you plan to stay in that bed forever?"

"Uh, hadn't really thought about it. It does feel pretty good."

Eaves spoke into his communicator, "Captain Carling, please come in here for a moment?"

As Tara re-entered the room, Magill's eyes grew wide and he whispered, "Captain?" Eaves smiled rather wickedly.

"What is it, Lieutenant?"

"Sorry to bother you ma'am, but in my opinion we have a slacker on our hands. This man has slept through nearly the whole battle. Isn't it time he made himself useful?"

"Oh, you're a doctor as well as a fighter pilot?"

Magill smiled and said, "It would feel great to take a shower, if that's possible. I feel pretty grimy."

"That's too bad," she said, "I hoped to give you another sponge bath, but, if you insist, I don't see why not."

Magill's face flushed and Eaves burst out laughing.

"Perhaps you can call your partner, Lieutenant Eaves, and the two of you can help this man get used to walking on what used to be his feet."

"Glad to, ma'am." Eaves clicked a button on his communicator and said, "Mr. Carter, would you please join me in the Ambassador Suite. We've been asked to render aid to a stricken comrade." He turned to Magill, "He does outrank me, so I have to make him think things are his idea."

Tara sat down on the edge of Magill's bed. "Let me tell you about walking. Right now the electronic monitors in your boots sense you're not using your feet, so they've numbed them completely to erase the pain. When you attempt to stand, however, the boots will sense the pressure and reduce the masking effect so that you have enough feeling to move forward. But, it's likely to be quite painful at first and you may flinch or think you're injuring your feet. Don't worry, though, you can't do additional harm to them. In fact, it's probably good for you to walk regularly before the nerves die. Eaves and Carter can support you to the shower."

"At which time we'll leave you on your own, no matter how painful it is," added Eaves, "because there's good naked and bad naked and you're definitely not good."

Captain Carling shook her head as if dealing with adolescents and said, "The boots are waterproof, so you don't need to wrap them. Good luck." She stood to leave the room.

"Well, no time like the present." Magill sat up rather clumsily and swung his legs out to the floor.

"What about the bandages around my calves?"

"Oh, yes," she said, turning, "The bandages aren't attached to a monitor, so they'll keep your legs numb below your knees. That will increase the challenge of walking, but you'll have to do your best until you figure it out."

Magill pulled the covers off his legs and Eaves helped him swing them off the bed. Another Lieutenant, about their same age joined them.

"Sean, this is Jason Carter. A decent Navigator, but even more serious than you, if that's possible. I've decided my biggest combat risk is being bored to death by my friends."

Magill looked up at the nasty scar on Carter's face.

"A remnant of Lieutenant Eaves' outstanding piloting," said Carter. "He did his best to kill us both, but wasn't quite up to it."

"Of course Carter wouldn't know all the details since I had to drag his scrawny body out of a dangling fighter. That's another thing you two have in common – you both tend to fall asleep in the heat of battle."

"I'm ready," Magill interjected, "if you don't mind."

Eaves and Carter placed their hands under Magill's arms and lifted him to his feet. As weight was applied to his feet his legs buckled at the knees. Then, after another second or two, Magill let out a howl that almost caused them to drop him.

"Judas priest," he said breathlessly, "How can anything hurt this much?" Tears filled his eyes and he tried to sit back down on the bed.

"Hardest part's over," said Eaves. "Let's just stand here until your boots figure out how to deal with this. Amazing, when you think about it – intelligent boots."

After another ninety seconds of trembling, Magill regained his composure and declared, uncertainly, "Okay, let's try to go forward." He stumbled on his first two steps, began to walk properly on the third and then shuffled toward the bathroom. Eaves and Carter supported most of his weight, but with each step he gained some confidence.

"What does it feel like?" asked Carter.

"It's strange. As I put my foot down, I sense there's going to be a shooting pain, but then the feeling instantly subsides and I get a slight hint that I have a foot. It's just enough to help me figure out where I am. But, the hardest part is not feeling my lower legs."

Together the three of them made it across the room. Magill was relieved to see there was a shower chair for him to sit on and after settling onto it, Eaves and Carter left him alone. It was a lot more painful than he'd let on and tears now streamed down his face. He was grateful for the warm water to wash them away.

After one of the longest showers of his life, he dried himself off and pulled on the freshly-cleaned, Alturian uniform that had been left for him. It felt strange to be in foreign clothes for the fabric was coarse, stiff, and didn't feel good against the unwrapped part of his burned legs. But even that couldn't offset the joy he felt in being clean and dressed again. He called out to Eaves and Carter and they helped him back into the bedroom. They tried to steer him to the bed, but he had them help him to a chair next to the small conference table. A footrest allowed him to elevate his feet.

"I need to know what's going on. You've got to bring me up to speed."

For the next two hours, they poured over maps of the surrounding territory, trying to come up with a plan to escape the planet surface. They didn't want to become hostages. Eaves relayed that their parachute landing brought them down on trees next to a small river and, after regaining consciousness, he dragged Carter down and then used portable lasers to cut branches to lower the ship. There was enough remaining fuel for thrusters to move the ship into the river, where they floated downstream for nine or ten kilometers closer to the city. They found a secluded spot to beach the fighter and camouflaged it with branches and debris. Using their locator, they beat a path through the jungle to the main city entrance. At about five kilometers out, they connected with Major Wilkerson and his party and collected stragglers along the way. Finally the group reached the city and were taken in by Loyalist troops.

"You'll like Wilkerson," Eaves said. "He's a leader in Jesik's mold, cool under fire and fearless in battle. We were attacked on two separate occasions and he deployed the limited men under his command to make the rebels think there were hundreds of us. Even the Alturians obeyed his orders."

"I know Major Wilkerson," Magill replied. "He saved my life by carrying me through the swamp." Magill shuddered at the memory. "I never felt so helpless."

Carter interjected, "He was particularly worried about you and never strayed far from your litter. He took a personal interest in your welfare."

Magill could see Carter was stressed out and that Wilkerson's attention to an unconscious man meant a lot to him.

"Are you two still here?" Captain Carling's voice showed irritation. "Lieutenant Magill needs rest and you two need to spell the advisers to the Palace Guard. So get a move on!"

"Yes, Sir!" said Eaves, giving her a formal salute and a wink to Magill. Carter sighed as they left the room.

"How're you feeling?"

"Surprisingly good. These boots are really amazing, giving me enough feeling to know I have feet, but the intense pain is gone."

"I've asked the carpenter to make crutches, so he should be in shortly to do the measurements. In the meantime do you think you can make it to the bed."

Magill blushed at the thought of what he would look like stumbling to his bed and hated himself for it. Either she didn't notice his blush or pretended not to. He stood up uncertainly, wanting to walk on his own, but his first step forward landed him in a heap. He couldn't get used to not feeling his knees.

"Stupid legs." He felt Captain Carling put her arms under his armpits.

She had surprising strength and helped him to stand. Walking like a zombie in an old earth movie, he stumbled to the bed.

"Thank you, Captain," he said as he slumped onto the bed. "Back on Kalenden, I was on the All-Continent Soccer team, although you wouldn't know it to look at me now."

"Oh, I can see that you're athletic and I'm convinced the shock of the burns would have killed you if you hadn't been in such great physical condition."

He was relieved to think she could see past his injuries. Plus, he liked the phrase, "Great physical condition." Still, it was so strange to talk to this woman, who was all business, yet tender. Not many women served in the Kalenden armed forces and none of those he'd dealt with were this beautiful. He knew he shouldn't be attracted to her since she was from Alturus, but she was the most interesting person he'd ever met.

Laying his head on the pillow, he picked up on their earlier conversation, but resolved to stay level-headed this time, "Carling is a fairly prominent name on Kalenden; one of the leading families. How about on Alturus?"

"We're considered part of the snobbish class there as well."

"Magill is pretty common where I come from. I'm adopted, so I don't really know my heritage – probably mongrel – but I couldn't have had better parents if I'd tried. Fortunately, I did well on my military and scholastic exams, which is why I received the scholarship to Kalenden Arms, even though we're not a prominent family." She didn't say anything, probably nervous that she'd set him off again.

"You asked me to tell you about Kalenden and now maybe you can tell me about Alturus. Different cultures and customs fascinate me. Would you mind?"

For the next thirty minutes the two of them talked back and forth, occasionally laughing, but mostly speaking earnestly of the differences between their two peoples, finally agreeing there were more similarities than differences.

"What exactly do you hope to do with your life, Lieutenant?" she asked.

"Eventually I want to go into diplomatic service, but not until I've gained distinction in the military. You go a lot farther in our system if you have military contacts." Then he looked down at his legs and added, "That probably won't happen now. One needs to be in top form to stay in the service – particularly the fleet."

Tara wanted to lift his face and try to get a smile back, but his mind had taken him deep into his own thoughts.

"Well, Lieutenant, I've stayed far longer than I should have. I didn't even follow my own orders to let you rest."

"Don't go," he pleaded. "It's been years since I've been able to talk so freely." A yawn betrayed him and he laid his head back on the pillow.

"Take a nap and then it'll be time to join Major Wilkerson for dinner."

"I still stick with what I said as I was conking out from the sedative you gave me at the base camp. You're the most beautiful woman I've ever met." He was pleased with her surprised look. "You thought I forgot, didn't you?"

"I thought you were delirious. Perhaps you're having a relapse." He smiled and closed his eyes.

As he breathed deeply, she gently stroked his face. "I wonder what it would be like to come from a planet where people join together in love, not duty?" She stood and quietly left the room, being careful to wipe her eyes before entering the corridor. But, she couldn't stop thinking about his comment that his military career was over. It certainly would be on Alturus. When dinnertime arrived, Lieutenant Magill was still sound asleep, so Wilkerson and Carling dined alone.

* * *

The next morning Eaves burst into Magill's room. "Wake up Sean! You've gotta get out of bed!"

Magill had slept in his borrowed uniform, so instinctively he tried to swing his legs out. But they were still fairly numb.

"I can't move fast, Travis. Help me. What's going on?"

"I don't know for sure, but there's a commotion in the hallway. We've got to move to protect the Royal Family, but I don't want to leave you here in case of prowling rebels."

Magill stepped down. His feet again screamed in agony for a short time. He put his arm around Eaves' shoulders and they hobbled into the corridor and turned towards a magnificent door. When they reached it, an Alliance guard swung the heavy door open and they stepped inside a large, elegantly-decorated room.

About forty feet away, a well-dressed family huddled close to each other, surrounded by a fierce-looking contingent of Palace Guards, weapons pointed at the gathering crowd. Eaves spied Carter to one side of the room, standing next to a member of the household staff. They were leaning against a wall painting, which struck Magill as odd. Carter beckoned them to join him.

"Try to move quietly, Sean, so we don't attract attention." They joined Carter. Eaves whispered to ask what was happening. There were fifteen or twenty Alturian advisers in the room, along with a number of Loyalist troops, all of whom held weapons. Captain Carling moved silently in the direction of Magill and the others.

"I think there was a disturbance at the main palace gates," Carter whispered. "Some of the household staff turned on the guards and shot them. No one knows what's happening for sure, but it looks like there's an attempted palace coup."

Gunfire erupted in the outside hall. Eaves, Carter and Magill raised their weapons and pointed expectantly in that direction. Magill turned to look at the Royal Family just as, without warning, the guards swung around and opened fire. Before anyone could react, the Royal Family was heaped in an expanding pool of blood.

Acting on impulse Magill fired at the lead guard, who had already aimed at the Prime Minister. The Prime Minister stood motionless, stunned by what just happened to the Royal Family. The blast from Magill cut the guard in half. He then turned to a second guard rushing towards the Prime Minister and shot him as well. As he was about to fire again, a bullet tore the laser from his hands and a second bullet grazed his head. The combined impact of the two bullets knocked him to the floor. As he sat up, he saw a guard racing toward him, his weapon pointed at his face. Instinctively, he rolled to one side to protect his face. He saw the guard squeeze the trigger and braced for the impact, but instead, a searing blast flared next to Magill as Eaves blasted the guard into his next life. Still, the soldier's bullet also grazed Magill's head, tearing a gash through his hair, but leaving just a surface wound.

"Get out of the way, Sean, fast!"

Magill tried to rise to his feet, but the pain was too great, so he rose on all fours and crawled toward the wall where Carter stood.

Chaos ruled in the room, with members of the royal guard firing at both Loyalist troops and Alturians. A few managed to return fire with lasers, setting furnishings on fire, while others used impact weapons that shredded bodies and furniture alike. Many more fell, while others ducked behind protective pillars, or found other protection. With bullets and laser beams flying in all directions, there was no place safe.

Carter shouted "Everybody, push against the painting." Eaves looked at him like he was crazy, but the wall behind Carter gave way and he and the Keswick staff member disappeared into the blackness.

"I'll be damned," Eaves muttered. He pushed Magill and Carling through the opening while maintaining withering fire to cover their escape. When everyone else had gone through the opening, he fired off a final blast, then turned and dove toward the hole. But just as he was about to enter the opening, a bullet struck his left arm, spinning him around and away from the portal with blood spattering the wall behind him. He groaned and fell to the floor. Immediately, Tara dashed out, dragged Eaves through the opening and Carter and the Keswick shoved the heavy wall back into place. Numerous bullets slammed into the wall, but it was thick enough to absorb their impact. Carter dropped an old-fashioned bar across the doorway, effectively locking out the others.

"Come on," he shouted, "we've got to get out of here. Follow me!"

By this time Eaves had regained his balance and in spite of his wounded arm, leaned down to help Magill to his feet.

"Not this time, Travis," said Carter quickly. He gently moved him aside so he could help Magill stand. Sean's right foot hurt more than his left, but he grimaced and walked as fast as he could, holding onto Carter for support. Blood trickled down his face from the head wound, but there was no time to deal with that now. Meanwhile, Tara had ripped the sleeve off her uniform and wrapped it around Eaves wounded arm to staunch the bleeding.

"Which way do we go?" she asked.

The Keswick replied, "Down this corridor and into the left passageway. It'll take us down into a subterranean hallway that leads to a boat landing on the Palace Lake."

"He's telling us the truth," said Carter.

"How do you know that?" asked Eaves.

"While you were talking with the other Alliance fighters, I made friends with some of the palace staff. I guess they liked me, because two of the housekeepers brought me into the crown room and showed me the secret passage. They said if we ever needed to get out, this was the way to go."

"It sounds like they had a pretty good idea that something was going to happen," said Carling, anger evident in her voice. "They were probably involved with the murder of the Royal Family." She was trembling with rage.

"I'm afraid it's an old story," said Magill. "It goes clear back to the ancient days of Earth, when palace coups dethroned hereditary monarchies."

"Yes," Tara said, "but in those days the monarchs were tyrannical. This family has provided stability to Keswick for more than 200 years, letting everyone share in the profits from the mines. They didn't hurt anyone and look how they ended up!"

She was so angry she was crying, which made her even more furious. She strode ahead down the corridor so fast that Magill couldn't keep up, though he tried. Finally, she heard him gasping from the pain and stopped, turned to look at him. His face was flushed from the exertion. Eaves was ashen colored, obviously losing blood.

"I'm sorry," she said. "We need to slow down. Everyone stop and let me listen." Since she was the senior officer, she assumed command. The corridor fell silent and they strained to hear if anyone was following. There was no sound except for dripping water. "Okay, let's take a five minute break."

Magill and Eaves slumped to the floor, trying to catch their breath. They were both too tired to talk.

"How much farther?" Tara asked the Keswick. "And, what is your name and how is it that you were with Lieutenant Carter?"

"They call me Paval, madam and the Royal family asked me to assure your safety, as well as the Kalenden Lieutenants." Tara eyed him suspiciously, but didn't choose to follow-up. "How much farther?"

"Not far. There's an underground grotto the Royal Family used when they wished to sneak onto the lake to seek a reprieve from official duties. The lake ties into the main river and may offer a means of escape. We will meet friends there."

"Perhaps we can work our way upstream to our fighter," said Carter, "although it doesn't have room for four."

He looked dejected. Tactical thinking wasn't his strong point and they now had few options.

"We'll take it one step at a time," said Tara. "Right now we need to get Lieutenant Eaves into the daylight so I can look at his arm. The bandage is soaked through and I may have to apply a tourniquet to stop the bleeding."

Carter lifted Magill and Tara helped Eaves back to his feet. Slowly they started working their way down the corridor. Magill turned to Carter and asked hesitantly, "How do you know the household staff wasn't setting you up? Maybe we're walking into a trap."

"I don't know, but I trust them. Besides, if we were still in that room we'd already be dead. I don't see how anyone could make it out alive.. You can be sure that the rebels didn't want any witnesses."

The tunnel walls had taken on a different color. "I think there's daylight ahead," Tara called out. Then, as they rounded the next bend, she suddenly stopped. There were voices ahead.

Carter listened intently and said, quietly, "It's my friends. What should I do?" He and Tara whispered furtively for a few moments. It looked to Magill that she was arguing against Carter revealing himself and them, but he eventually won the discussion. Carter helped Magill sit on the floor and Tara eased Eaves down. There was just enough light for her to remove the dressing and look at his arm. Meanwhile, Carter and Paval slipped quietly around the corner and approached the Keswicks.

War's certainly a lot different than I dreamed of, Magill thought. Eaves let out a low groan as Tara poured a white powder into his wound. Magill saw Eaves blood foam around the edge of the wound. Then she scrubbed furiously, which must have been agony for Eaves. *She's a tough one. Even when she knows she's hurting you, she keeps going to see the job's done right.* He thought back on all his daydreams about being in combat and how he'd valiantly lead the charge that turned the tide of battle. In reality, war was seeing friends turned into nuclear powder or a horribly disfigured corpse and parents with their children turned into a bloody mess by people sworn to protect them. *And I certainly haven't heroically led anyone anywhere.* Instead, he'd been a burden to everybody. *So much for daydreams!*

Tara spoke some soothing words to Eaves and, watching, Magill thought, *At least I got a chance to meet her. I could have lived a lifetime without ever meeting anyone like her. I'm grateful this war gave me that.*

Voices approached them. Instinctively Magill pressed against the wall, hoping to become invisible. Then he recognized Jason Carter's voice and was relieved to hear he was still alive.

"They're ahead," said Carter as he came into view, followed by an elderly man and woman, plus two Palace Guards pointing their weapons. Carter stepped past Magill to introduce them to Tara.

"Captain Carling, please meet John and Linda LeMons. They were personal attendants to the king and queen. They're the ones who showed me how to save our lives, but now they have some urgent questions." Tara rose and deeply bowed.

"Thank you for your kindness," she said formally, "we owe you much. How can we possibly repay you."

Mr. LeMons spoke quietly, "You must speak candidly and tell us the full truth, or our hospitality and your lives may end in this corridor."

Tara responded darkly, "By all means. Pose your questions."

"We have, in our native language, interrogated our assistant about what happened in the throne room. Now we would like to hear your version."

Tara explained that they had slipped into the room, recounted the various troops there and reported that the Palace Guard turned their weapons on the family and all others in the room.

"But, why would the family's own guard turn on them and then the foreigners?"

Magill spoke up, "Because they intend to turn Kalenden against Alturus!"

Tara turned to him with a flash in her eyes. "What do you mean by that?"

Magill glanced at LeMons, who indicated for him to continue.

"If I'm right, everyone in that room is dead now, including the Palace Guards. They must have been rebel sympathizers who were sacrificed after completing their assignment. By killing the Royal Family, they effectively ended the monarchy. But their leaders know that Loyalist elements would continue the fight, perhaps for years, seeking to return an heir to the throne. But if the rebels make it appear an outside force was involved in the murders, they can unite the populace against the external threat. My guess is that after we disappeared, rebel forces entered the Crown Room, killed any Alturians that remained alive, then murdered the Palace Guards so there are no witnesses. They've probably already announced that the Alturians killed their monarch and loyal Palace Guards. They will have expressed sympathy and remorse that the family was killed, proclaiming their own innocence."

"That's ridiculous," said Tara, "everyone knows the rebels were planning to attack the palace."

"Yes, but the people would like to believe it was only to place the royals in protective custody until a new power-sharing arrangement was worked out—one that was more fair to everyone. That way they can avoid more battles."

"But, why would they claim Alturians were responsible – why not the Loyalists themselves, or Kalenden?"

LeMons motioned Magill to continue.

"If I'm right, the answer is that the Alturian Royal Family has hereditary ties to the Keswick Royal family and there are some grudges that go back centuries. If the rebels can make it look like this was an Alturian plot to finish an old blood feud, they can stir up more anti-royal feelings on Alturus, making it appear that Alturus is making a grab for the orchidite mines. That way, they can draw Kalenden into a war with Alturus. The chaos that would inevitably follow, along with an increased demand for orchidite to fuel the warships, will only strengthen the rebel's hands."

Tara was having none of it. "It makes no sense. While it's true that the royal families of Keswick and Alturus haven't been close for many years, there's no hidden animosity. And there are no rebel elements on Alturus to appeal to!"

Eaves cleared his throat and said, "I'm afraid you may be mistaken, Captain. In my last communication with the Allegro, Captain Jesik warned me that an Alturian freighter had been used to attack the Allegro. Apparently it was under the control of an Alturian rebel group."

Tara slumped against the wall and put her hands to her temples.

After a few moments of an embarrassed silence, LeMons spoke up. "Captain Carling, it appears to me that Lieutenant Magill has analyzed the problem correctly. The official news networks are reporting that a group of Alturians attacked the Royal Family and killed their guard, just as Mr. Magill predicted. The rebels claimed they entered the palace too late to prevent the devastation, because they were detained by Alliance fighters at the city's perimeter. The rebel Coalition also claims it knew all along that an outside government was plotting against Keswick, which is why they started the rebellion. And now, for the protection of the people, they've proclaimed martial law."

"What about the Alturian warships in orbit? Aren't the rebels worried about them?" Tara expressed defiantly.

Eaves answered. "They've been stalemated by the attack on the Allegro. For the Alturian forces to make any hostile move whatsoever, Fleet Command would immediately attack. So, the rebel's plan has already had an effect."

Tara sighed. "So, my planet is to be drawn into a war with both Keswick and Kalenden. It's a great story these rebels tell. Yet, those of us in this tunnel are eyewitnesses that it's all a lie."

"Eyewitnesses who, if discovered, could ruin everything for the rebels. Captain, if the rebels know we're alive, we're in mortal danger. They have to kill us to maintain their story."

"Then what do you suggest, Lieutenant Magill?"

Magill felt the sting in her voice. Obviously his comments had irritated her, but he knew he was right and ignoring the truth would increase their risk.

"First of all, I think we've got some time. Since all those who saw us in the room died, no one saw our escape. But, they may know we're missing and will have spies out looking for Alturians and Kalendens. And with my feet and Lieutenant Eaves' arm, we'll be easy to spot. What we need is to get back to our ships. But without control of the atmosphere, I don't see how we can get past planetary defenses. Perhaps we can contact the Allegro or your ship and hope for a rescue."

"Captain," Eaves broke in, "If Sean is right, there's no time for a rescue mission. We must escape and I have an idea – maybe not a good one – but with luck it might work."

Tara's voice softened, "From my conversations with Lieutenant Magill, it sounds as though your ideas, improbable as they often are, often seem to work out. Tell us."

"First, we'll need help. Mr. LeMons, are there any remaining Loyalists that you can trust?"

"There are many of us, although no one will be able to admit it publicly, now."

"Good. Here's what we'd need to pull this off."

6 — A PAINFULLY SLOW ESCAPE ATTEMPT

"Captain, We're receiving an interesting broadcast from the Keswick Palace."

"Put it up on the monitor, please, Mr. Williams."

"... therefore, in view of the unprovoked attack by Alturian forces which resulted in the death of the Royal Family and their Palace Guard, the rebel Coalition has taken control of all government bureaus and their administrative functions..."

Jesik settled into his seat and wondered what else could happen in this strange war.

"Mr. Williams, you must try to establish communications with our ground forces now! If we need to destroy a jamming tower, feed the coordinates to Mr. Gentry, who is authorized to take immediate action."

Williams had never been given that kind of assignment before, so he quickly set to plotting the point of contact for the jamming equipment and fed the data to Gentry.

"We have the coordinates, Captain."

"Then fire, Mr. Gentry. Your choice – warheads or lasers."

A brilliant beam stabbed the planet's atmosphere, broke off, then reappeared at a slightly different angle as the beam focused on a second target.

"The jamming towers have been destroyed, Sir."

Jesik listened as Williams hailed Kalenden troops on all frequencies. Before any could reply, an urgent message came from the planet surface.

"A Mr. Lansing from the Rebel Coalition, Sir. Should I patch him through to your station?"

"No, put him on the main monitor."

A face appeared on the viewer, ruggedly handsome and clearly upset.

"Kalenden ship Allegro, we demand to know why you have taken hostile action against this planet!"

"Because, Mr. Lansing, you've been blocking our communications with the surface since this battle began. We will not tolerate your interference any longer." He didn't need to add, "and what do you want to do about it?" even though that's what everyone on the bridge was thinking.

"Captain, we apologize for the disruption. As you may have heard, the Alturians have destroyed our Royal Family and we felt we needed to secure our position without interference. Of course you are free to communicate with your troops, since we believe we now share a common interest in preventing an Alturian take-over of the orchidite mines."

"I am aware of your claims of Alturian interference. But, at this point, I consider those unsubstantiated charges, in need of further investigation."

"Investigation, Captain? Was it not an Alturian vessel that attacked you? How much investigation do you require before you protect innocent lives?"

"We'll be in touch, Mr. Lansing, but for now I need a report from my ground troops. Any information you have on prisoners will be greatly appreciated. Please transmit it to my First Officer, Brighton. Jesik out."

Jesik was furious. No one on the bridge dared approach him.

"Mr. Williams, where are our ground troops?"

"I have contact with Major Wilkerson, who wishes to speak to you privately, Sir."

"I'll take it in my day cabin."

"Sir, Admiral Rameira is also hailing us."

"Give the Admiral my regards and my regrets that I can't talk to him for a few moments. Please indicate I'll return his hail momentarily. Commander Brighton, please join me." Jesik left the bridge without returning any salutes.

"What's your status, Wilkerson? What's happened to our troops?"

Wilkerson looked exhausted and grimy from battle. "I haven't been able to connect with our troops at the mines, but it's pretty grim here in the city. The blast on our base camp wiped out more than 90% of our troops. The rest of us managed to move to the city, where we've been directing both alliance and Loyalist troops. This morning the rebels launched an attack on our position, a rather feeble one, but enough to keep us tied down. Then we received word of the assault on the Royal Family and the rebels have since taken the city from inside. They were well prepared with a fifth column infiltrated among the population."

"Are you telling me we had no one in the palace?"

"We had two units inside, one group of fifteen that was wiped out by rebel forces making their way to the throne room. The other group, if you'd call it that, was your three Lieutenants and an Alturian Captain. Their bodies have not been found, so I can't report on their status."

"What is your current situation?"

"We're still in our position, but surrounded by rebel forces. When word was received that the Royal Family was dead, the Loyalists laid down their arms. Effectively we're prisoners-of-war."

"I'll be making contact with the rebel Coalition shortly and negotiate your return to the ship. In the meantime, insist on your rights. For the moment it appears that the rebels wish to make us their allies against the Alturians. While I'm not sure how that will play out, it should work to your advantage in the short term."

Wilkerson could be seen reaching to turn off his communicator when Jesik added, "By the way, Major, you have my deepest regrets for the loss of your men. I appreciate your courage and theirs against these odds."

Wilkerson nodded at the recognition.

"Mr. Williams, please hail Admiral Rameira." The request was immediately acknowledged.

"Admiral, reports from the planet indicate Alturian complicity in the deaths of the Royal Family. Please explain what happened."

"Yes, Captain and reports from our fighters indicate that Kalenden fighters openly attacked our airships. It's been a confusing day, at best."

For the next forty minutes Jesik, Brighton, and Rameira attempted to sort out what happened. The rebels had prevented any surviving Alturians from communicating with their ship, holding them as hostages, so, Rameira had no hard information to provide. Although he doubted that Alturians had taken part in the murder, he admitted that it was a possibility. It was clear there was provocation for either side to act against the other, but in the end they agreed to give the situation a bit more time. Jesik made it clear, though, that any attack by the Alturians would be met by an immediate response from the Kalenden ships. Rameira ended the conversation with a request for Jesik to assist in protecting the remaining Alturians on the surface and showed particular interest in a female captain named Carling.

Finally, Jesik hailed Lansing of the Rebel Coalition.

"Captain Jesik here, Mr. Lansing. Have you had a chance to gather the information we requested?"

"We have, Captain Jesik. You have 200 survivors at the orchidite mines. Fortunately, the miners have abandoned their plans to sabotage the mines, particularly since the Coalition governing board has followed through on its promise to increase their salaries by more than forty percent."

"A very shrewd accommodation, Mr. Lansing. I assume you'll be arranging for the return transport of our troops as soon as possible?"

"There's something of a problem, Captain. There's an Alturian officer who was in the palace at the time of the assault who remains unaccounted for. She was accompanied by a Lieutenant from Alturus with disabled legs and two Kalendens. We're concerned that your people may be hostages, so we're scouring the palace and grounds, as we speak, in an attempt to locate them. Until then, we think it better to not let any ships leave the surface."

"Are you holding my men as prisoners, then?"

"As guests, Captain. We're a small planet and have no desire to engage you Kalendens in hostilities. You're our best orchidite customer, so I hope you'll be a bit patient with us while we establish order here."

"Patient yes, tolerant no. You have twelve hours. Then transport must begin. In the meantime, I have determined it is not in our best interest to take any hostile action against the Alturians. I advise you to show restraint as well."

Lansing was obviously irritated to be spoken to this way. After all, he'd just won the battle of a lifetime. But he agreed to Jesik's terms and ended the conversation as gracefully as possible.

"So, Tom, what do you think?"

"Well, Sir, it's obvious we're being lied to, either by the Alturians or the rebels. It can't be both ways. We also know we have more than 200 people on the planet's surface. So, I think you've adopted the right course for the moment. My fear is for Magill, Eaves and Carter. It sounds like two of them are with the Alturian Captain and the other is missing. I don't know why, but somehow I sense they're in danger."

"Either that or they are dead. Assuming the positive, they must have some role in this, the rebels wouldn't be concerned about them."

Inasmuch as there wasn't anything they could do at the moment, Jesik stood and moved to his food console. He poured himself a soft drink and took a handful of crackers. Brighton accepted a cup of herbal tea and settled into his seat.

"By the way, we haven't had a chance to talk about your trip to Stirium. I don't mean to pry, but were you able to make the progress you hoped for."

"It went far better than I hoped for, Captain. Once this is settled, I'd like to talk to you about it more." Jesik was about to pursue the topic further when the overhead speaker crackled to life.

"Captain Jesik, Colonel Kensington has made an Esper contact and demands to speak with you."

Jesik sighed, "Put him through." At this distance it would be an audio conversation only.

"Jesik, I've been monitoring status reports and it sounds to me like you have a royal mess up there. For pity's sake man, an Alturian ship attacked you, the Alturians have murdered the Royal Family and there's nothing to show you've taken any action. Just how much provocation does it take to move you to action?"

"Colonel, I've been in almost constant contact with Admiral Rameira on the Princeton, have attacked and destroyed the rebel jamming towers and spoken to the rebel Coalition about our ground troops. The situation is well in control."

"In control? It's obvious to everyone but you that the Alturians intend to take Keswick and leave us out in the cold. You should launch a counter-attack immediately to neutralize the threat!"

Although he couldn't see Kensington's face, he could picture it easily enough, flushed and sweaty.

"With all due respect, Sir, I can initiate an interplanetary war with Alturus immediately, or I can wait twelve hours to do it. By waiting, there's a chance that we'll have enough intelligence to make an informed choice, rather than a reactionary one. As you know, I accepted this assignment on condition I have plenipotentiary powers, so as not to be obligated to refer to Kalenden as I make my decisions."

Brighton shook his head in amazement. He knew that Jesik was perfectly aware that Kensington had fought the delegation of authority with everything he had and was furious that Jesik had won. Now, to throw it back at him was adding insult to injury. *I hope the Captain knows what he's doing?*

"I'm well aware of the extent and limits of your authority, Captain. I only caution you that there are many opportunities in this conflict and I hope you're not being too timid to capitalize on them. Kensington out!"

"It's easy to be brave when you're three months away from the scene of battle," muttered Jesik under his breath.

"He gave in rather easily."

"Don't underestimate him, Commander. That was just a warning shot across the bow. He was letting me know he's busy telling everyone I'm a coward who's afraid to engage the enemy. Believe me, he's doing his best to have my authority to act independently withdrawn."

"The Colonel isn't a very pleasant man, is he, Sir?"

"You don't know the half of it, Tom, and I hope things work out so you never have to feel the full force of his wrath."

Brighton wanted to pursue this, but Jesik quickly added, "That will be all for the moment. Please see to the repairs and make certain we have staff assigned to monitor all planetary broadcasts for information we can obtain about our missing people."

"Of course, Captain. I've got double teams assigned to all monitoring stations. I'll keep you informed as new intelligence is gathered.

* * *

Mr. LeMons commented, "Captain Carling, the rebel Coalition is aware of your existence and is anxious to search you out. Inter-palace communications are abuzz with orders to find you and the young Lieutenants. From what I gather, the rebels have grounded all ships to make certain you don't escape. And the tone of the orders has angered the Kalendens, who wish their remaining troops returned to their ships."

"I'm sure it's angered Admiral Rameira on my ship, as well. Thank you, Mr. LeMons. Obviously they want to hunt us down and kill us, so there'll be no witnesses to the massacre. It also means we can't hope for help in attempting our escape."

Turning to Eaves she said simply, "We'll go with your plan. We have to make it happen quickly or we'll certainly be discovered. Tell us how to proceed."

"Mr. LeMons and his accomplices have given me the piece needed to complete the puzzle. There's a small garbage ship launched each evening at twenty hundred hours to take refuse from the palace into an orbit and released. The release position assures that the garbage will be completely burned up as it reenters the atmosphere, providing complete privacy to the Royal Family's dealings. Because the launch is automatic, I'm hoping we can make it aboard without arousing suspicion. Lieutenant Carter will take manual control if something goes wrong. He'll be joined by Captain Carling, the LeMons, and four other members of the household staff."

The LeMons protested. They didn't want to leave Keswick. Eaves carefully pointed out that since they aided both he and the others, they would be considered traitors to the new government. They had to go or they would be tried for treason.

"Magill will be the navigator on our fighter. We'll activate our invisibility shield and launch slightly lower than the garbage scow so we can merge our contrails with its. That way we'll be hidden and available to defend against any enemy fighters that attempt to destroy the scow. We scrounged some missiles from other disabled Kalenden fighters and, once we're in low space orbit, I'll activate the "friendly forces" beacon so the Allegro knows who we are. At that point they can use their lasers to beat off any attacks.

"Two wounded men piloting a fighter? Somehow that isn't reassuring," said Carling.

"I've got great feet, Magill has two good arms. Between us we'll get the job done."

Tara studied the flight plan of the scow and remarked, "This really doesn't bring us very close to either the Allegro or the Princeton. We'll be exposed for at least a third of the distance. How can we protect ourselves against ground lasers?"

"We managed to find some reflective grape canisters in an abandoned palace armory. If we're attacked, we'll scatter enough reflective debris between us and the planet so that they can't get a clear beam on us. We'll easily create thousands of reflections, which will confuse their targeting."

"Okay," she said. "Sounds pretty convincing. Where's the risk?"

"I think Lieutenant Carter can best address risk," said Eaves in a flat voice.

Carter flashed him an irritated glance, but delivered, "The risk is that the rebels may shoot the scow down before we clear the lower atmosphere. While we doubt their sensors are accurate enough to detect life onboard, they may decide that even a drone shouldn't violate their grounding order. So, if we're engaged at too low an altitude, Lieutenant Eaves won't have time to eliminate the opposition."

"Well, my guess is that we'll be toast before we reach 30,000 meters," Tara said, "but frankly I'd rather die in space than be held as a hostage. I guess it's time to retrieve your fighter."

It was agreed that Carter and Carling would dress in civilian clothes and proceed upriver in a fishing boat, pretending to be husband and wife. Once they reached the fighter, they'd activate the invisibility shield and float downstream to the Palace Lake, where their accomplices would disable the alarms and open the gate to the garbage bay. Given the time required to get upstream, drift back and get everyone secured inside, it was going to be very, very tight timing.

The LeMons shoved them off and Lieutenant Carter immediately activated the anti-gravity-membrane cell to silently propelled the boat forward at a surprisingly brisk speed. Located below the water line with a horizontal orientation, the cell acted against the water in much the same way as two magnets that repel one another. As they drifted out of sight, they looked like a peasant couple out trying to land a fish or two.

"I know you're jealous," said Eaves to Magill. "Carter's out there with your girl."

"You know, Travis, sometimes you're a real jerk." Magill turned and hobbled towards the ancient dungeon which had been chosen as their hiding place until evening. Glancing up at John LeMons, he said, "Thanks for the crutches. It's nice not to have to depend on my friends for assistance."

* * *

"Captain, there's something odd happening in the lower atmosphere."

"What is it Lieutenant Wight?"

"It appears that a small ship has started a slow ascent into the atmosphere. It was launched from the palace grounds."

Jesik's stomach did a flip-flop. Just thirty minutes earlier he'd spoken with Lansing, who indicated they still hadn't found the missing Alturians and so wanted an extension of time to maintain a no-fly zone. Jesik said he'd review it when twelve hours were up, which was just forty minutes away. Now this.

"Lieutenant Gentry, can you provide a better idea what kind of ship it is?"

Gentry bent over his view screen, running a search against all known ships of that physical configuration and displacement. He also scanned the ship for signs of life.

"It appears to be a garbage scow, Sir. Probably an automatic launch set for this time each day."

"Any life onboard?"

"None that I can detect. Of course, rotting organic matter often gives off false readings, so it's impossible to get a good fix."

"The flight path is obviously under automatic control, if that helps, Sir."

"Thank you Ensign Wight. Gentlemen, I can't say why, but I want to see that this ship makes it into orbit. Inform me immediately if any action is taken against it."

As his words left his mouth, their sensors indicated that at least two rebel fighters were now heading toward the small ship.

"Mr. Gentry, track those two ships and if it appears they're going to fire on the drone, blind them with a laser blast."

Gentry acknowledged the order and made the appropriate plot. Fortunately, the ships simply did a cursory search of the area around the drone, then broke off and left it on its flight path.

"Apparently they've decided to let it do its duty, Sir."

Jesik took his seat and pondered his next conversation with Lansing and Rameira. He'd played tough with Lansing, but with nearly 200 potential hostages on the planet, his flexibility was very limited. His only hope for demanding their release was to threaten the use of his ship's weapons to cause so much destruction that it wasn't worth it for the rebels to keep his men. But, if he did that, it was certain that many would be killed. In addition, he didn't know what the rebels would do to the Alturians. He'd hate to see Rameira forced into battle. That would obligate Jesik to intervene to protect the mines. A full-scale war was still a possibility and things would come to a head in approximately thirty-five minutes.

"Sir!" said Lieutenant Wight urgently.

"What is it, Navigator," snapped Jesik.

"For just a moment I detected a second exhaust from the drone ship."

"Are you certain?"

The moment he spoke, Jesik realized how foolish the question was. Wight was always certain about such things.

"Yes Sir, but now it's consolidated back into a single trail."

"What do you think caused it, Lieutenant?"

Wight carefully considered his answer. Jesik wished he would hurry, but that would simply reduce the reliability of his response. After punching a number of commands into his console, Wight looked up and said, "I believe there's a second ship, Sir – probably a fighter."

"How can that be possible?" asked Gentry, "It's virtually impossible to fly two ships into the upper atmosphere that close together."

"Yes, it is, Lieutenant," said Jesik. "That's what tells me that Lieutenant Eaves is piloting the fighter. Gentlemen, go to silent alert and prepare to defend the drone ship from both ground and atmosphere attacks."

Red lights flashed silently on the bridge and all consoles went to double illumination and maximum tactile responsiveness. During regular operations, the console keyboards were quite stiff, so that a bored or inattentive crewman didn't accidentally relax and push the wrong button. In battle however, the keypads were sensitively tuned to each operator. That way, commands could be executed instantly.

"Fighters have been launched from the planet's surface under maximum acceleration."

"Mr. Gentry, when they clear the lower atmosphere, give each fighter a laser blast strong enough to disorient their pilot and automatic systems."

"Yes Sir. In approximately thirty seconds."

Those thirty seconds presented the greatest risk to the escapees. The rebels could take a number of offensive actions too complicated for a space-based ship to counter.

"Williams, contact Rameira and Lansing and tell them the garbage ship is under my protection and they should take no offensive action against it. Do it now!"

Jesik tuned into William's calls and heard Lansing's voice go shrill as he shouted an obscenity at Williams. He also heard Rameira reply that the Princeton would assist in the defense of the ship however Allegro requested.

Lieutenant Wight reported, "Ground-based lasers have been fired." Just as the screen lit up to register the lasers, a thousand targets burst into view.

"What on earth?" asked Brighton.

"Mr. Eaves has apparently launched grape canisters to confuse the laser targeting systems," Gentry reported. It worked. The laser beams were scattered in a hundred directions, while the two little ships, now clearly separated from one another, continued their labored ascent into the atmosphere. Meanwhile, the ground-based fighters were rapidly gaining on them.

"Can you fire on them, yet?" asked Jesik.

Three brilliant beams emanating from the weapons array answered his question. Two of the fighters spun out of control and burned up in the atmosphere. That left five. Unfortunately, the grape was reflecting the Allegro's beams, as well, which provided the enemy fighters a measure of protection.

"Captain, the Princeton has modified its orbit and is closing range with the drone. Should we alter course to meet them."

"No, leave them to it. They're going to attempt a rescue. How long before the drone has cleared the upper atmosphere?" Wight reported that there were two minutes to go.

"Blast it, the fighters will overtake them in forty seconds."

Jesik bit his lower lip. Then he saw the exhaust trail of Eaves' fighter as it broke away from the drone, heading straight for the enemy fighters. The enemy launched a number of missiles at Eaves, but he was able to avoid them. At point blank range, he fired five missiles. In a series of explosions, the five rebel ships each took a direct hit. But, Eaves' ship was so close that it too lost power and began drifting.

"Mr. Wight, see how close you can bring our ship to the planet's atmosphere without gravity overtaking us."

Wight immediately took manual control of the Allegro and maneuvered it toward Eaves' stricken fighter. At least two of the enemy fighters showed signs of life and were powering up to launch another missile. With sixty seconds to go until they could magnetically grapple their fighter, one launched a missile at Eaves. Immediately, even before Jesik could issue an order, a missile streaked out from Allegro. It intercepted the hostile missile a mere ten kilometers from Eaves' ship, sending Eaves and Magill end-over-end towards the Allegro. Ten seconds later the magnetic grapple captured the fighter and drew it into their docking bay.

"Good work, Mr. Gentry," said Brighton. "That's about as tight a shot as possible."

"I owe it all to you, Mr. Brighton. That's the corner pocket shot you taught me in pool!"

The crew laughed, which relieved the tension on the bridge.

Jesik looked to learn the status of the drone and saw it had been ingested by the Princeton.

"Admiral Rameira, it appears you've taken possession of some very valuable garbage."

"We're inspecting it right now, Captain. It appears we've recovered our missing Captain and one of your Lieutenants. They're unharmed."

"Admiral, I've recovered one of our fighters, but I don't yet know the condition of its occupants. I'll get back to you in a few moments."

Jesik turned the bridge over to Brighton and rushed to the nearest transport tube. He arrived at the docking bay just as Lieutenant Eaves and an Alturian were being lifted onto the deck, either unconscious or dead. As he came closer, he saw that the Alturian was really Lieutenant Magill.

"Are they alive?"

The medical officer looked up. "Yes, Sir, they're alive, just knocked out. But both have been wounded and I have no idea what happened to Lieutenant Magill's legs and feet. I've never seen that kind of damage." Holding smelling salts under their nose quickly revived them.

"Mr. Eaves, do you ever intend to make a normal entrance on this ship?"

Shaking his head to clear his thoughts, Eaves said, "I hope so, Captain, I really do." Then, he added, "Did the garbage scow make it okay? Carter's onboard."

"They're safe on the Princeton."

Magill sat up slowly and voiced, "Thank God they're alright!"

"Sorry I can't give you time to recover, gentlemen, but I've got 200 men on the planet now under rebel control. And the rebel Coalition is mad as hell because of your escape. Talk to me on our way to the bridge." Eaves pushed Magill, in a wheelchair, through the ship. Eaves did his best to explain to Jesik intelligence on the military situation on the planet as Magill filled in details of the political situation.

By the time they reached the bridge, Jesik opened a line to Rameira and asked him to join his conversation with Lansing. Carling and Carter had already briefed Rameira.

"Mr. Lansing, you chose to disobey my instructions and fired on our ships in spite of my warning. Please explain yourself."

"Explain myself?" Lansing replied indignantly. You violated a planetary grounding order and killed seven of my best fighter pilots. I'm afraid that was an act of war. Your men here are now our prisoners."

"Before you do that, Mr. Lansing, you should hear from my three subordinates and the Alturian Captain. They were in the room when the Palace Guard murdered the Royal Family and the Alturian advisers."

"That's preposterous, Captain. Your people are saying that to cover their own duplicity in the murders. We demand your officers surrender themselves to a planetary military tribunal."

"You are in no position to make demands, Mr. Lansing. We do not negotiate for hostages and, as you know, we have enough firepower to completely destroy your planetoid. So, you will listen and negotiate with us."

Other members of the rebel Coalition clamored around Lansing with angry faces

"Captain, we've tried to be civil with you and the Alturians. But you will not blackmail us. We have powerful friends outside your two systems and if you attack, we will destroy the orchidite mines. You have no right to interfere with our internal affairs; particularly with no proof of your accusations."

Jesik paused. He had no proof. While he believed Magill and Eaves, their testimony would not stand up in court. He was trying to decide how much farther he could push his bluff when he heard Lieutenant Carter's voice come over the speaker.

"Captain Jesik, perhaps I can help."

The various monitors showed Jesik, Rameira and Lansing turn to this unexpected interruption.

"What is it, Lieutenant?"

"Well, Sir, perhaps you're aware that I'm enrolled in a Social Studies class through the electronic Academy."

"A Social Studies class?" asked Jesik in astonished voice.

"Yes, Sir and I have an assignment to write a paper about an alien social system. So, while I was assigned to the palace, I took it upon myself to interview members of the household staff. To make certain I could recreate the conversations later, I recorded them on a portable video recorder." He pulled a small device out of his pocket. "As it turns out, this was operating during the attack on the Royal Family. Perhaps it will show everyone what really happened."

A man next to Lansing shouted that they would not view any contraband videos, but Jesik hit a control that made it impossible for them to break the connection. For the next three minutes, everyone aboard the Allegro, the Princeton and at the rebel Coalition watched as the horror unfolded before their eyes. Carter then skipped ahead to the corridor where Magill gave his explanation of the motives of the rebels in executing the family and the Alturians.

Jesik turned to the monitor and said in an icy voice, "Mr. Lansing, yours has been a cruel and vicious coup d´ e´ tat, laced with nuclear assault and assassination. Perhaps they're all that way, but this is the first time it's cost the lives of any of my crew."

Lansing looked completely abashed, struggling with his emotions. He tried to interrupt, "Captain, I had no idea…" but Jesik was in no mood to listen.

"Save it, Mr. Lansing! You'll have a chance to explain yourself, later. But for now you have no reason to restrain my troops. If you agree to the immediate return of all Kalenden and Alturian troops, we'll refrain from destroying the buildings in which you now stand. Once our troops are safely onboard, we'll meet with you aboard the Allegro to talk about the interim government that will take control on Keswick. Do you agree to these terms?"

The men around Lansing looked like trapped animals who wanted to lash out and kill every Kalenden and Alturian they could get their hands on. Nevertheless, Lansing said firmly, "We agree to your terms, Captain. We will guarantee the safety of your troops. Will you provide assurances of our planet's safety from an Alturian counter-attack?"

Jesik looked to Rameira's monitor. He'd been joined by a beautiful young woman in a military uniform. The two of them consulted briefly and Rameira said, "We will refrain from any attacks, provided the transfer of our troops begin within the next four hours. After that, we will meet aboard the Allegro."

"Mr. Lansing, work out the launch arrangements with my First Officer. If all goes as agreed, we'll see you tomorrow at 09:00 aboard the Allegro. Jesik out."

"Captain," Lansing managed to say before the line went dead, "I ask you to keep an open mind at the conference." Jesik gave him a scowl and terminated the connection.

Turning to Rameira he said, "Thank you, Admiral, for showing restraint. You've been seriously injured by these people, but your willingness to refrain from revenge may well prevent an interplanetary war."

"You're the man of the hour, Captain. You were the first to spot and protect the ships that brought us the evidence we need. I look forward to your leadership at tomorrow's conference. Now if you'll excuse me, I have some urgent issues to attend to."

Jesik turned to the members of his bridge crew and congratulated them on a great job. Relief was evident in his face as he smiled while exiting the bridge.

7 — THE PEACE CONFERENCE OF KESWICK

Jesik watched apprehensively as Lieutenant Magill made his way painfully into the conference room, struggling on a pair of crutches. The Chief Medical Officer had reported they could save his feet, thanks to the effectiveness of the Alturian gel pack, but the radiation had destroyed enough nerve endings that he would never have full feeling. Jesik assured Magill that he'd have time to recuperate with assignments suited to his recovery. "I also think I should be honest with you," said Jesik, "and tell you that you are not likely to advance any farther in the military. Even if your physical limitations don't interfere, there is prejudice in the command structure." The distressed look on the young man's face confirmed his understanding of this reality.

He undoubtedly uses crutches instead of a wheelchair to show his determination to overcome his disability, thought Jesik, *but unfortunately, it actually draws attention to it.*

Looking around the room, Jesik quickly assessed the members of the various delegations. He was surprised to see Rameira was taller in person than he had appeared on the holographic projector. Usually it was the other way around. His dark complexion and jet black hair framed his face and eyes in such a way that they conveyed a sense of solid confidence and intelligence. Yet, he conducted his affairs with remarkable modesty. For example, even though he was the senior military officer present, he asked Jesik to preside. Rameira and Jesik had met privately for more than ninety minutes prior to this session and had mapped out the agenda and a rough outline of their plan for disciplining the Keswick rebels.

While Rameira was cordial during introductions, his aides were decidedly unpleasant, making little effort to conceal their contempt at being aboard a Kalenden ship. Jesik's experiences with the Alturians so far made him think they weren't a very happy group of people.

The person who intrigued Jesik the most, however, was the young woman Captain who accompanied the Alturian delegation. She moved with a grace and dignity uncommon for one so young and she enjoyed a prominence that wasn't normally warranted by someone of her rank. *Probably the novelty of a woman serving in a combat role.*

Glancing at the clock on the wall, Jesik saw it was time to begin. Everyone was assembled, except the rebels, including Loyalist Party ministers. The various delegations sat apart from each other, quietly chatting with members of their own group.

"Captain, the delegation from the rebel Coalition has arrived and is now onboard."

"Have a double guard accompany them to the conference room, Chief, showing appropriate courtesy."

A few minutes later the doors slid open and four rebel leaders entered the room. All were relatively young, but had a hardened look to their features that spoke of the hardship they'd endured as outcasts of their society. They formed a single line and stood at attention.

"Mr. Lansing, I presume? I'm Pietr Jesik of Kalenden and this is Admiral Lucien Rameira of Alturus."

"John Lansing, gentlemen." He extended a rough hand.

Lansing was ruggedly handsome, about six feet, two, with a high forehead, dark brown eyes and wavy hair that apparently refused to stay combed. He wore camouflage fatigues, the de facto uniform of the rebel Alliance. Not the usual dress for a peace conference, but on Lansing the crisply-pressed creases of his trousers and open shirt seemed appropriate and gave him the appearance of one who leaves nothing to chance. While the others in his party looked at the Alturians and Kalendens suspiciously, Lansing was remarkably controlled, fixing a steady gaze on Jesik. The intensity behind his eyes was almost unnerving and it was apparent why he'd risen to the top of the command ladder.

After accepting Lansing's hand, Jesik said, "Please be seated and we'll make introductions around the room."

Jesik introduced each member of the Kalenden delegation, which included Commander Brighton, Lieutenant Commander Gentry, and Political Officer Barrows, who was seconded by Lieutenant Magill. Rameira, the Loyalists, and Lansing followed suit.

When everyone was seated, Jesik rang an ornate mariner bell, salvaged from a sailing vessel on ancient Earth, to officially begin the conference. He'd chosen to use the bell to remind everyone of their common ancestry.

Clearing his throat, Jesik said, "The battles of Keswick have brought a number of unfortunate surprises that have created an atmosphere of distrust and animosity. Things certainly turned out differently than my superiors anticipated or desired. Each party at this table has numerous grievances, some legitimate, some imagined. In the absence of open and uncensored information, misunderstandings are inevitable. Having spoken with Admiral Rameira, I know that when we arrived at Keswick we all had our own ideas of how to resolve these problems. Yet, now that the Loyalist government has collapsed, we're faced with the new reality of bringing order to Keswick with new players and demands. While it may appear that this is an internal Keswick problem, humanitarian concerns, as well as an interest in the orchidite mines, forces both Kalenden and Alturus to take an active part in that re-organization."

Both the Loyalist and rebel delegations glowered at this, but were wise enough to hold their tongues.

"Normally, the first order of business would be to have my political officer review the history of the conflict so we can speak from a common understanding. However, I cut Mr. Lansing short yesterday when he attempted to explain the circumstances surrounding the execution of the Royal Family. Since that's the most serious charge hanging over the heads of the rebel Coalition, perhaps we should start there."

Lansing rose from his chair, quietly looked around the table until he'd made brief eye contact with each person in the room. "Thank you, Captain. Admiral Rameira and Captain Jesik, first accept my sincere apologies for the deaths of your advisers in the attack on the palace. It was not intended that way. I'm aware that your ships monitored our planet-wide broadcast condemning Alturian mercenaries for the murder of the Royal Family. In that broadcast we indicated that the rebel Coalition had simply sought to take the family into protective custody, while the government and our relationship to the monarchy was revised. We also expressed surprise by the murder. Our attribution of the assassinations to Alturus were, as events proved, entirely false."

Captain Carling brooded in her chair, arms folded, eyes narrowed, as Lansing spoke. He saw her out of the corner of his eye and it unnerved even as cool a character as him. It was obvious she was using all her self-control to suppress her rage.

"What you need to know is that when we made that broadcast, I believed it was true. Later, when you aided your soldiers in their escape from the planet, I also believed you were helping them avoid justice. At that moment my comrades and I felt a continuing outrage that our group was not taken seriously, even though we spoke for the vast majority of our people."

Lansing paused and looked around the room. By now everyone was brooding, waiting for their chance to respond. "Which is why, when Lieutenant Carter played his recording of the actual execution, I was sickened beyond words to find that it was rebel forces. Perhaps none of you have ever been betrayed and used in a most horrible fashion. Everything I believed to be true was proven false and I was left with the realization that people I considered my friends actually used me for their own dark purposes." He took a sip of water.

"What I'm trying to explain is that several members of the Coalition Council orchestrated the execution as well as the scheme to blame the Alturians, without the knowledge or consent of the rest of us. They were the ones you saw standing next to me yesterday, trying to cut the connection. Fortunately, you had the means to make that impossible."

"An old trick we learned in deep-space communications experiments," said Jesik.

"At any rate, I knew instantly that we had lost much of the moral ground for our cause. That's why we fully complied with your demands. All Kalenden and Alturian personnel have been returned to their respective ships and are safe. Are there any we are unaware of?"

"All our surviving troops have been accounted for," said Admiral Rameira quietly. "Once the Allegro knocked out your jamming towers, we were able to tune into our electronic self-identification devices, which tell us if a person is alive or dead, as well as their location. We've retrieved all our personnel and destroyed the remains of those who were killed." Commander Brighton indicated that all Kalenden troops had been retrieved as well.

As Lansing started to speak Rameira interrupted. "Before you go on, Mr. Lansing, tell me why we should believe you? Yesterday you told your people that it was my forces that destroyed the monarchy. Now that we've presented proof of that lie, you make a fine speech blaming other members of your council. Is this just another way to avoid punishment for your outrageous conduct?"

"There are two reasons why you may believe us. The first is that we have the four men responsible for the treachery in a prison ship, docked securely to the Allegro. They have each confessed to their part in the conspiracy and you can use your own interrogation techniques to determine the truthfulness of their confessions. For our part, their statements have been fully documented under Keswickian laws and our military tribunal has sentenced them to death. We chose not to execute them without first submitting the case to you. As a sign of good faith, you can choose whether to take them as prisoners yourself and try them under your separate laws, or you can allow us to exercise our jurisdiction. In addition to their signed confessions, a search of their personal belongings amassed documents and recordings that provide irrefutable evidence that the plot was planned in advance and without knowledge of the other members of the Coalition Council. All this will be made available for your inspection."

"I accept that," said Rameira. "What's the second reason we should believe you."

"As a council, we've prepared an announcement accepting full responsibility for the attack on the Royal Family. For those of our citizens who wish to see the grisly details, we will provide a link through the interstellar net to Lieutenant Carter's footage of the execution. We'll explain that while those who actually committed the assassination did so without our authority, they were part of our leadership team. We will also resign in favor of another group not implicated in the murder scheme, if the people decide they don't want us. After a lifetime of living with censored news and propaganda, we want the citizens of Keswick to have complete, honest information to decide their own future, no matter what the cost is to any of us as individuals."

Captain Carling signaled a desire to speak and was acknowledged by Jesik.

"So, Mr. Lansing, assuming this is all true, can you tell me what this war was about? Why are more than 500 Kalenden and 1000 Alturian troops dead, as well as untold casualties among the Keswicks? What did you possibly hope to gain to justify this suffering?"

Lansing felt her suppressed fury, but answered as calmly as he could.

"In the first place, Captain, it was never our wish that Kalendens or Alturians involve themselves in what we viewed as an internal affair. From the outset, we provided assurances that the rebel Coalition would protect the mines and secure the safety of the general population. But, the Royal Family was unwilling to consider any of our concerns, choosing instead to drive us into the jungles in an attempt to silence us. After centuries of living as second-class citizens in our own society, we simply could not tolerate that any longer. So we consolidated our strength among the citizenry. When it became apparent to the Loyalist government that they could not maintain control, they brought you in. By making you their allies, you became our enemies. Thus, your men and equipment became fair game for our attacks. That's how it's always been in war and we were fully justified in the attacks we launched against your military. The truth is, while Captain Jesik speaks of humanitarian concerns, the real motivation for your systems to become involved was to maintain control of the orchidite mines. While the cost of everything in the adjoining three quadrants has tripled over the past fifty years, the price of orchidite has remained essentially unchanged. Why? The answer is simple. The Royal Family continually increased production to maintain their lifestyle, while sacrificing the welfare of the general population so as to keep the peace with you. With all due respect, we do not consider our actions illegal or unnatural. We simply assert our right to play a role in the society in which we live."

Carling opened her mouth as if to reply, but thought better of it. The duplicity of the monarchy was apparent and it would be futile to dispute it.

Admiral Rameira interceded. "I'll accept, for the moment, that you were the victim of the same treachery that sought to implicate Alturus. What you haven't addressed, yet, is what purpose this treachery would serve." He paused and furrowed his brow before continuing. "Of course that's obvious when one thinks of it. By making it appear that we are culpable, your comrades in the rebel Coalition could incite the second-class families of Alturus and perhaps even Kalenden, into joining a general revolt. I'm afraid that your words do little to reduce that threat. We are more vulnerable than ever."

Lansing attempted to suggest that the Coalition sought no allies, but he had to acknowledge under a withering cross-examination that there were many in the rebel movement who hoped for that very objective.

"In fact," Rameira fired back at one point, "members of your group were in contact with members of my crew and together you plotted the attack on the Allegro. It would well suit your purposes to have us fight each other, while ignoring your threat to the government of Keswick." That brought on a whole new round of accusations and when the discussion heated to the boiling point, Jesik signaled a recess.

As the groups parted into individual delegations, Jesik was thankful for his political officer's advice that a separate room be provided for each delegation, so they could get away from each other and cool down. *There's certainly a shortage of cool, right now*, he thought.

Rameira stepped close to him and whispered, "A private word, Captain?" He and Jesik moved down the hall to Rameira's stateroom, where they huddled for the next twenty minutes. "The stakes are escalating," said Rameira. "The royalist government on Alturus is clamoring for me to blockade Keswick until an Alturian assault force can be assembled with enough power to subdue the rebels."

"In other words, they want to invade and conquer?"

"Exactly, Captain."

"And what do they think we will do while you take over the orchidite mines."

"I'm sure they hope that you will allow us to become your supplier. But if Kalenden intervenes we will be obliged to fight you, as well.

Jesik felt his face flush. To be challenged on his own ship was an outrage, but before he could respond Rameira added, "I personally think it would be a disaster, both for Keswick and Alturus," continued Ramiera. "I'm not sure our Royals can count on unqualified support from the second and third-class families in an assault on their ancestral relatives who finally have a chance for equality."

"For my part," said Jesik, "Kalenden is secure enough in its pseudo-democracy that my government isn't frightened by internal rebellion. But we're a proud people and my leaders think I've been too passive in not launching a counter-attack to avenge the attack on Allegro. They're concerned, too, I'm being too accommodating of your needs, even though events prove you were in no way responsible for the freighter attack."

"Then what are we to do?"

"First, as an outsider looking in on your system, it seems to me that it's better to isolate the violent rebel element that initiated the attacks on the Allegro and the Keswick Royals from the more moderate members of the rebel Coalition. If your government runs roughshod over the coalition, sympathy will build at home for the entire rebel movement. But it would be easier to maintain the loyalty of your second tier families if your government is supportive of the rebels governing along with remnants of the Loyalist government. With that support, it would be easy to come down hard on the fringe elements on both Alturus and Keswick."

Rameira agreed. "Your course also has the advantage of avoiding a confrontation with Kalenden, since I assume any move on our part to unilaterally blockade the planet would be met with resistance."

"It would."

"Then I'm agreed that we have to find a way to strengthen the moderate elements of the coalition."

In the brief discussion that followed, they decided the best way to proceed was with a much more limited peace conference. While it would be impossible for either outside system to exercise real control on the planet, given their limited numbers, they could enforce a blockade that would eventually force the rebels into negotiations. So, in spite of all that happened, the new objective of the conference was to forget recriminations and come up with a workable plan for governing Keswick.

Returning to the conference room, Jesik signaled for order.

"After private communications with our planets and taking at face value Mr. Lansing's willingness to assume responsibility for rebel atrocities, we have decided to limit the focus of this meeting to a set of specific objectives. The situation on the ground is extremely unstable at this point, so it's vital we help form a functioning government as quickly as possible. Toward that end, we'll restrict this assembly to just two participants from each interested party. Normally, I would select my First Officer or political officer, but because of his direct experience in the Keswick Campaign, I'll ask Major Wilkerson to assist me in representing Kalenden." It was a little unusual for a Fleet officer to voluntarily share authority with the Army, but Wilkerson had handled the crisis on the ground with such skill that he was the best qualified.

Rameira surprised Jesik by asking Captain Carling, a relatively junior officer, to be his aide. In spite of the fact that he bypassed a number of more senior officers, no one in the Alturian delegation registered concern by this choice.

The leading Loyalist Party member proclaimed that, as the legitimate government of Keswick, they should have as many representatives as they desired.

Rameira responded to this demand with dispatch! "Gentlemen, it's obvious from the speed with which your troops laid down their weapons after the palace coup, that the people of Keswick are ready to accept members of the rebel Coalition as their legitimate representatives. I come from a planet ruled by monarchy, yet even I can see that the time has come for Keswick to adapt. The simple truth is that you have little standing, either here or on your planet. You woefully underestimated the strength of your enemy, went against our advice of how to conduct the military campaign, and your support evaporated once the rebels captured the palace. You're invited to stay only to provide legitimacy to the process. In return, we'll do our best to support you and a select group of other Loyalists, but it can only be in conjunction with the rebel Coalition. In other words, you are in no position to demand anything!"

The leader of the Loyalist group went pale and protested, but the other delegates quieted him. They were more realistic in assessing their diminished status.

John Lansing chose his second, and the surviving group of eight went behind closed doors, where they spent the next two days working out details of an interim government, with open elections scheduled one year hence. A Unified Governing Council (UGC) would replace the rebel Coalition Council, with the Loyalist Party given eight seats in the council and authorized to form their own political party in for the upcoming elections. The rebels would also form a party, the Democrats, and have ten seats on the council. The Prime Minister would be selected by the council, with the power to appoint a cabinet to administer the bureaus and agencies.

During the transition period, the special representative of Kalenden and Alturus would also hold a voting interest in the UGC, which meant they could effectively veto any legislative or executive action imposed by the rebel majority by choosing to vote with the eight members of the Loyalist group. The two special representatives could also block any move that in their opinion threatened the safety or continuing production of the orchidite mines. If they ever made such a decision against the advice of the local members of the UGC, their decision could be appealed to the Home Offices of Kalenden and Alturus. Once open elections were held, the special representatives would lose their seats on the council and the relationship between the two systems and Keswick would be re-negotiated, with terms depending on the stability of the new government.

Probably the biggest stumbling block to the negotiations was the concern on the part of the Loyalists that the ruling families were essentially being stripped of all their authority. This also concerned the Alturians, who feared a precedent that might inspire a rebellion on Alturus. Jesik pointed out that those families continued to own the vast majority of businesses and real estate, which would enable them to readily afford the cost of promoting their party and interests. In the absence of estate transfer restrictions or taxes, the imbalance was likely to continue for many years, giving those historical families the same kind of edge they enjoyed on Kalenden. "It is a situation that will resolve itself over the course of time," he assured them, "but at least the second and third-class families now have a stronger hand in participating in the planet's political future." Eventually the Loyalists conceded the point and surrendered claim to special recognition.

Once the outlines of the plan had been settled, Rameira returned to his ship to communicate with Alturus, and the Keswicks returned to the planet surface to announce to the population what was proposed. A general plebiscite was scheduled for seven days hence so that the adult population could either approve the arrangement or demand additional negotiations. It would be the first open election at the planetary level ever held on Keswick.

Even though he had plenipotentiary (unrestricted) powers in the negotiations, Jesik wanted the official approval of the Kalenden leadership, so he initiated a private Esper link with the Prime Minister.

After lengthy discussion the plan was accepted by the Kalenden Cabinet, with private congratulations to Jesik for the peaceful settlement of the conflict.

Rameira had a more difficult negotiation with his high command. There were many in the government violently opposed to any compromise with the rebels. Admiral Rameira argued the points to the best of his ability, but there was still indecision on the part of Alturus that threatened to destabilize the situation on Keswick even further. Finally, Rameira asked Jesik to join him in a video briefing with his leaders to explain the position of Kalenden, along with the reasoning of the peace conference. As the briefing began, Jesik could see that the Alturians both on the planet and onboard the Princeton were shocked when a senior member of the Royal Family entered unexpectedly, asking to join the discussion. His participation, however, proved to be the turning point in the discussions.

After learning that his leadership team was divided, he asked Rameira for his recommendation.

"With all due regard to the concerns of our leading families, I believe the situation here warrants adoption of the plan as proposed. It will maintain peace with Kalenden, assure the safety of the mines and avoid further bloodshed between first and second families. Captain Jesik has made a persuasive argument that the first families will continue their leadership role by virtue of their property ownership and experience."

"And what do you think, Captain Carling?" asked this unknown royal. Rameira stiffened as he awaited her reply.

"I was opposed to the settlement in the beginning, because it appeared to excuse the destruction of the Royal Family. But, now I'm confident the murders were the result of a fringe element. Of course I strongly advocate monarchy, but setting my personal feelings aside, I believe the conference should be supported."

Jesik braced for additional questions, but there were none. The Royal simply said, "Then we are agreed. You have authority to proceed, Admiral." He turned and strode from the room. Everyone in his presence quickly stood at attention to honor his departure. As one who had never experienced the efficiency of monarchy, Jesik was astonished by this quick acquiescence on the part of the military.

Once the Royal had departed, the holographic image of the leader of the Alturian group turned to Rameira and said, "Admiral, you'll have a signed copy of the protocol within the hour. Please work with our distinguished colleagues from Kalenden to encourage the population of Keswick to accept this agreement. Alturus out."

"I'm beginning to see some of the advantages of a monarchy," said Jesik as everyone settled back in their seats with a sigh. "It's breathtaking to see how quickly things happen when authority is so well defined."

Rameira smiled for the first time since Jesik had met him. "Captain, as an outsider you simply can't know what a courageous decision the Royal Family just made. To formally accept a plan that ignores hereditary leadership on a planet that is vital to our interests, shows a pragmatic flexibility of which our ministers have been incapable. Rather than being isolated from the concerns of our citizens, as appears to have happened to the Keswick monarchy, our leading family is very much in tune with current events. I'm confident that our citizens will feel even greater loyalty than before." Rameira turned and smiled at Carling, thanking her for her participation.

She returned his gesture and, turning to leave the room, addressed Jesik, "Captain, I came to Keswick with many prejudices, but you and your associates have made me rethink my ideas of the universe. You're a remarkable man and we're fortunate you were in command. Perhaps Admiral Rameira will communicate that sentiment through diplomatic channels to your superiors."

Jesik blushed slightly, which was not natural for him, even though it was an indirect sleight of his second class heritage. Still, the blush drew the first smile he'd ever seen on her face and he was glad.

From that point forward, things moved quickly. During the next seven days, Jesik was busy promoting the plan on all fronts. In addition to responding to an endless list of questions from the Kalenden Quadrant Council, overseeing the completion of repairs to the Allegro and whatever fighters that could be salvaged, his senior staff conducted an internal investigation, checking if any of his crew were in league with the Alturian rebels. Fortunately, there were no signs of that.

He also descended to the planet for two days, appearing at a number of press conferences, where he responded to reporters' questions as well as appearing on a number of holographic video interviews. Although he didn't consider himself suited to such activities, his participation added credibility to the plan.

The most surprising part of the interviews, from Jesik's point of view, was the intense interest in the Cambriol incident. His reputation had pre-

ceded him and the local talk shows even requested permission to interview
Eaves and Magill, who became minor celebrities. The scene of Magill trying
to save the life of the Prime Minister during the attack on the palace was
replayed endlessly and created a reputation for Magill as a fearless war-
rior, even if it was in support of the former government. Their response to
Magill showed how mixed people's feelings were and how fragile the UGC's
hold on the government was likely to be.

When the election day finally arrived, and the results tabulated, Jesik
initiated a conversation with John Lansing. "So, today is the first plebiscite
since leaving earth? How does it feel to have both questions pass with so
resounding a margin?" The first question was whether to accept the Unified
Governing Coalition while the second asked if Lansing and the remaining members of the former Rebel Coalition should retain their standing as
members of the new Unified Governing Coalition. "It's obvious that you
will be the new Prime Minister of Keswick."

"It is gratifying, of course. But I have no allusions that it will be easy.
People have been terrorized by all that has occurred, we have nuclear fallout
to manage, and–please don't take this wrong, but we have you and Alturus
looking over our shoulders—so it will be difficult, to say the least.

"Well, you are a man well suited to the task. We'll try to keep our
involvement to a minimum."

The next morning, Jesik invited Ernest Wilkerson into his office.

"Major, I've recommended you as Kalenden's Special Representative to
the Keswick Unified Governing Council and our Prime Minster has authorized me to invite you to accept."

Wilkerson's surprise registered immediately. "Me? A political advisor? I
hardly think I'm the one; I'm a military man, not a diplomat. And frankly,
I'm quite biased against the rebels. Nearly all my men were killed in the
nuclear attack and the rebels were ruthless in the hand-to-hand combat we
encountered trying to defend the city. I'm certain that your political officer
would do a better job."

"Mr. Barrows would do a good job. As it turns out, though, his wife is
about to have a baby back on Kalenden and he's requested assignment to
the home planet to be with her. But, even if he were available, I'd still ask
you to take the job."

"But why, in view of my reservations?"

"Three reasons. First, we need someone here who is skeptical and will
make sure the UGC follows through on its commitments to Kalenden. I
want a military man who understands what's happening and will intervene

when needed. Second, I'm convinced that you're fair-minded and will deal with the issues that arise, based on their merit, regardless of your personal feelings. Finally, and to me this is most important, you're a compassionate man. As I've talked to members of my crew, they've told me how you cared for Lieutenant Magill. The people of Keswick have suffered an overwhelming trauma to their social system and are caught up in the joy of having the struggle end. But, before long the enormity of overthrowing a monarchy will rest heavily on the new government and they will need a steady hand as they learn the art of governance. I believe you can help Lansing temper his passion. It's quite different to govern in peace than it is to foment a rebellion. The truth is, there's no one as well suited as you."

"Then I have just one request. I'll take this position if you'll assign Lieutenant Magill as my aide-de-camp."

"Lieutenant Magill? But his feet will take at least a year to heal to the point where he walks without crutches or a wheelchair."

"You told me why you thought I was qualified. I'm telling you that he has the qualities I lack, particularly a shrewd political insight into the rebels' frame of mind. He has a keen interest, almost a passion, for the role that social institutions play in helping people live more meaningful lives. As to his feet, where better to recuperate than here? If you keep him on active military assignment they'll post him to some no-account job on Kalenden and he'll end up leaving the service as soon as he's healed. What a waste of talent that would be. At least out here, he can gain experience and recognition that can help him later. Plus, he's popular with the Keswick people. 'The hero of Cambriol.' I can use all the goodwill we can gather. So, will you meet my condition?"

"Rather proves what I said about you, doesn't it, Major? Why don't you offer the job to Lieutenant Magill yourself?" Jesik smiled as Wilkerson rose and the two shook hands.

"By the way, Captain, how does Fleet Command feel about your giving this assignment to an Army man?"

Jesik laughed. "Fleet command is convinced that I'm unusually skilled at snatching a political defeat from the jaws of victory. Just as we gain recognition, I give it away. But, you're the right man for the job. So, that's that."

Later that afternoon Colonel Kensington gave Jesik a dressing down over Magill. "Jesik, you astonish me. As a member of Unified Command, I was shocked that you appointed Wilkerson as our Special Representative. As a member of the Army, I was gratified, of course and thought that maybe you've started to mature in your judgment. But then I hear that you're appointing a Lieutenant, Junior Grade to the second most influential role on the planet? For crying out loud, Jesik, the man's an invalid and will be an embarrassment. While the Alturian delegation strides forcefully about, pictures of Kalenden will feature a boyish face hobbling along on crutches. What kind of an image is that to project to this corner of the galaxy?"

"It was Major Wilkerson who requested Magill, Sir."

"A sentimental reaction to their shared misery on the planet. You should have told him 'no' immediately. But you're a sentimentalist, too. That's your greatest weakness—it always has been. Now I have to do it and I'm tired of cleaning up your messes, Jesik. You have to have Magill withdraw his name immediately. That's an order. And do it in a way that doesn't embarrass us."

Kensington was about to break the connection, but hesitated before adding, "I'll be sending my own aide-de-camp to assume that position. Wilkerson will be grateful to have someone truly qualified by seniority and experience. Plus, the man's from a well-established family."

Jesik tried hard to conceal his contempt for Kensington's never-ending self-promotion. Finally, unable to rein in his anger, he said, "Speaking to your earlier point, Colonel, you're certainly right about how withdrawing Mr. Magill's name will embarrass us, particularly in view of the correspondence I received fifteen minutes ago from the Prime Minister. But, naturally I'll follow your orders."

"What correspondence? I'm not aware of any message from the Prime Minister."

"Probably hasn't been delivered to you yet, Sir." Jesik picked up a piece of paper and read, "On behalf of the Quadrant Council, please accept our congratulations of your choice of Major Wilkerson and Lieutenant Magill. You should immediately promote Magill to Lieutenant Commander to give proper status to his position. Having one of the prominent figures in the Cambriol incident chosen for this assignment has strengthened our own political situation immeasurably, particularly since Lieutenant Commander Magill is from a third-class family. In view of the rebel discontent on both Keswick and Alturus it's vital to keeping our citizens content that we demonstrate that advancement opportunities are available to every Kalenden, regardless of family background or status." Jesik looked up, eyes narrowed and taunted, "It's signed by the Prime Minister."

"Of course, the Council is wise in their decision…" Kensington paled as he mentally fumbled for a way to rescind his order. Finally, "It's a sad day when political considerations outweigh seniority and tenure, but we constantly have to stroke the egos of the second and third-class families to keep peace. Let Lieutenant, that is, Lieutenant Commander Magill know of my interest in his promotion. Kensington out."

Jesik nearly collided with Brighton as he exited his cabin.

"Why the smile, Captain?"

"No reason, other than every once in a while fate gives you a particularly good moment to relish. I just had one of those. By the way, have you seen Lieutenant Magill? I need to have a word with him."

"I believe he's in the officer's mess, Captain."

"Thank you, Commander."

Brighton smiled as he heard Jesik whistling softly down the corridor. Another good ending, thought Brighton cheerfully.

8 — SHUTTLECRAFT COMPETITION

Captain Rowley of the Fermata stood up and gathered his papers.

"Remember, Rick," said Jesik, "there's a whole quadrant full of privateers who would love to see us lose our grip on the orchidite mines, so that they could become power brokers. You and Talbot will have your hands full patrolling the solar system and returning to orbit often enough to provide support to Major Wilkerson on the planet's surface. It'll be particularly tough to maintain ship's discipline when so many marines are coming and going between shore duty and onboard assignments. I'd keep the rotation pretty tight so that no one has too much time on the planet – there are still plenty of rebels who would like to subvert the men from our second and third-class families."

"I appreciate the advice, Sir. Fortunately, I'm from good second-class stock, myself, so the men won't have any reason to be angry at me for my genealogy."

Jesik laughed. "We have that in common, as Colonel Kensington likes to remind me whenever he gets the chance." Jesik looked Rowley over. *He's awfully young to be commanding a Frigate, particularly in the hottest spot in the quadrant. But, he was steady under fire and should do fine.*

"A little free advice, Rick?"

"Yes, Sir."

"I'd find occasion to spend some time with Lieutenant Commander Magill. He has a natural feel for the politics of this place and he'll know the problems that Wilkerson's dealing with. It might help you keep the peace with the Alturians, who aren't elated to share the system with us. Plus, he needs to stay connected with the fleet to bolster his own morale."

Rowley acknowledged the advice and added, "I know it probably sounds strange, Sir, since most people would find it frustrating to receive an eighteen-month assignment on customs duty this far from home, but I'm actually looking forward to this cruise. I think the Keswick Rebellion's going to have some long-term implications for Kalenden society that will take years to fully understand and I like being in the action."

With that, Jesik's concern about Rowley's lack of experience evaporated. "Keep the lines of communication open, Rick, and may the wind always be at your back."

"Good luck to you, too, Sir – and to Lieutenant Eaves and Carter in the competition."

"So you've heard their entry into the Shuttlecraft trials has been accepted? I imagine everybody knows it by now."

"Only everyone within three parsecs. Eaves isn't quiet when he's excited."

"He ought to be terrified. This is the first challenge he's likely to lose and who knows what it will do to his self-assurance?"

"I wish I could be there," said Rowley with a grin, "I can see Mr. 'Instant Reflex' fighting the controls of a shuttlecraft. It'll be like having the number one striker on the Kalenden Interstellar Soccer Team trying to shoot goals with a medicine ball."

"Well, when you hear that the Allegro's reputation is tarnished, feel free to send your condolences. Good luck, Captain Rowley."

Rowley left the room to catch a shuttle back to the Fermata. Speaking into his communications device, Jesik said, "Mr. Brighton, is the ship ready for departure?"

"All in order, Sir."

"Good, I'll be in the shuttle bay to bid Major Wilkerson and Lieutenant Commander Magill farewell."

"Acknowledged, Sir. Wish them well for all of us on the bridge."

When Jesik arrived in the shuttle bay he found Eaves shaking his head with contempt. "Lieutenant Commander; a two-step promotion because of your unique 'political skills.'"

Jesik couldn't help but smile when he heard Magill reply, "I told you to pay more attention in our Political Science classes. Politics is where the real power is; and now I have the rank to prove it." Before Magill could react, he added, "And you really should stand at attention in the presence of a superior officer!"

"Going to your head so soon?" asked Jesik, coming up from behind Magill. The sound of his voice nearly startled Magill out of his wits, and he teetered on his crutches.

"Sorry, Sir! And not really—just to Mr. Eaves. A person needs every advantage they can get when talking with him." Magill looked absolutely miserable until Jesik broke into a grin.

"I understand— on more than occasion I've found myself trying to remind Lieutenant Eaves that even a lowly starship captain outranks a Lieutenant Junior Grade."

"Ganging up on me?" Eaves looked stricken. "Sir…Sirs!"

"But on a more serious note, Commander Magill, do you really think it's fair that you get a promotion out of this while Mr. Eaves languishes,?"

Magill shook his head. "I suppose not. Although it's quite nice on a personal level. But in spite of all his bluster he really did have a huge impact on the battle."

"Then we'll promote him to full Lieutenant right now—how about that?"

Sean Magill smiled. "I actually wish you could make him outrank me, Sir. He saved my life, after all."

"Afraid I don't have that much authority. But I can do a one-step field promotion. How does that sound to you, Lieutenant?"

"It sounds great, Sir. It means I'll be of equal rank with Jason Carter, and he needs some humility."

"Well, you're certainly the one to teach people about humility, Lieutenant Eaves." Jesik then spoke his command firmly to the computer, and Lieutenant Junior Grade Eaves became simply Lieutenant Eaves.

"Congratulations!" said Magill sincerely, then stepped forward and dropped his crutches to give Travis a hug. "Good luck in the competition. Stay in touch."

"You get this government good and organized so you can return to real duty!" Eaves actually held the hug a bit longer than Magill expected, which was his way of expressing the emotion that he felt.

"Enough of that, gentlemen. We've got to be on our way."

Ten minutes later Magill was on a shuttle to the surface of Keswick and the Allegro had left orbit for the three-month journey back to Kalenden.

* * *

One of the greatest difficulties of deep-space service is the mind-numbing boredom one encounters during voyages that take months, sometimes even years to complete. Part of the problem is that even in vortex drive, space itself is so vast that there's no way to experience a sense of progress because at any given moment there's very little change in the position of the ship relative to the stars. It always feels like you're absolutely motionless, even though the ship is traveling at an incredible rate of speed. The only time things get exciting is when a ship draws close to a planet or another ship, where speed becomes obvious in relationship to the other object.

At first, Fleet Command tried to deal with this by providing a well-stocked library of books and movies. But that wasn't enough to effectively occupy the crew's off-duty time in a meaningful way. In time, the boredom of travel made it ever more difficult to recruit top talent into deep-space service, a real problem in maintaining defense and control of the trade routes.

The solution came by accident during an after-dinner drink between several ship Captains attending a training conference. One bragged that he had the best Helmsman in the service, one who could dock a space cruiser to a soap bubble without breaking it. Another disagreed and soon a bet was made. Since both ships would be rendezvousing at Tatrius in four months, the challenge was that they'd have a formal competition of docking to the orbiting space station, with points awarded for accuracy, speed and style. At this point, nearly everyone in the room joined the conversation and there was agreement that a competition was a great idea. Thus was born the first service competition. The effect on the morale of the two ships was profound, since nearly the entire time during the journey was spent getting ready for the competition. The respective helmsmen spent days in the flight simulators, practicing various maneuvers, while the rest of the ship's company spent their time rehearsing their roles in the docking procedures and thoroughly checking all relevant equipment to make sure nothing would go wrong. By the time the two ships arrived, they found that news of the competition had preceded them and they were met by video crews who had set up interplanetary links so that military personnel from all branches of the services could watch the maneuvers. The victor was then awarded the "Docking Cup," with a promise of a rematch the next time the two ships shared the same orbit.

Fleet Command recognized that was just what they'd been looking for and so over time they sponsored a number of high-profile competitions that ships could choose to enter on a regional basis, with the top twelve in the fleet (based on service-points, rather than actual success in the regional trials) competing at a system-wide festival. The service points idea was a masterstroke, since it required everyone on the ship to do their best on every cruise, instead of occupying the time of just crewmembers who would directly compete. Of course, success in a regional trial helped qualify as one of the top twelve for the system competition given that additional service points were awarded to ships who competed in the various trials.

The sites of the competitions were scattered throughout the system, so that major planets had a chance to host an event. The local citizenry of each planet also became involved, competing vigorously to see who could throw the best party. Huge festivals grew around the competitions and before long, both civilian and military authorities looked upon them as the premier events of the year.

Because the ship was still so new, Allegro had not yet competed in any of the competitions. But with the combat points earned at Keswick, she could pick which trial to enter, without regard to any regional competition.

Which lead to an interesting conversation taking place in the Allegro's shuttle bay shortly after the departure from Keswick.

"Have you actually ever piloted a shuttlecraft, Mr. Eaves?"

"Well, not on an actual shuttlecraft, Sir, but I did successfully land a training shuttle in a simulator at the academy. I'm the only one who didn't crash."

"Heaven help us," cursed Chief Engineer Timothy O'Casey. His red face complimented his red hair.

"And what about you, Mr. Carter?"

He hesitated before answering. "I had to run the calculations for a shuttle landing during a navigational mathematics class."

"Just what the blazes were you guys thinking, signing up for the competition? Do you have any idea the scale of humiliation we're all in for? You're going to disgrace the ship and screw up my shuttle."

Carter looked at Eaves with fire in his eyes. "It was actually Lieutenant Eaves' idea, Sir. I wasn't aware we'd been entered until it was announced during the ship's daily briefing."

Eaves did not look repentant. "With all due respect, how hard can it be? A ship's a ship and once you know the layout of its control panel, the rest just sort of happens."

O'Casey snorted. "You are so full of yourself! Well, this competition should help you get over it. You see, Lieutenant, a shuttlecraft is not a ship like any other ship. Nearly every maneuver you execute to control a fighter is dead wrong in a shuttle. You hit resistance in a fighter, you power through it. Try that in a shuttle and you'll fold the thing like an accordion. You want to bank to starboard in a fighter, you tip the controls to starboard and the ship makes the turn instantly. In a shuttle you have to turn the controls to port for at least thirty seconds before making the starboard bank, or you'll roll the ship into a giant loop. Therefore, if you actually succeed in becoming a shuttlecraft pilot, you'll be so screwed up mentally that you'll never be able to manage a fighter again. I hope you learn to like piloting a large, slow, giant steel feather that dances slowly through the atmosphere, because that's where you'll spend the rest of your career."

Eaves still looked defiant, although he felt not nearly as confident. "But Sir, out of the twelve teams competing, they always have three fighter crews. So, I figured we ought to be one of them."

"Oh? That's why you signed up?" O'Casey stroked his bushy red beard and smiled. "Lieutenant, they always invite three fighter crews to provide comedy. It's hilarious to watch nine crews make nearly perfect hook-ups, while three ships do their level best to avoid crashing into buildings or the spectators' gallery. At best, you're facing better than five hundred to one odds that you'll wreck the shuttle on the first try. MY SHUTTLE, dammit! Then, you'll go off to some glamorous assignment in your fighter while I'm left to repair the damage." O'Casey smoldered. Nothing was said for at least thirty seconds.

"Sir, maybe this is a mistake, but, Carter and I have three months to get ready and I promise you we'll get prepared. While I don't want to screw up my skill as a fighter, I'm willing to take that chance. I think we can win."

"Win, with just three months practice in a simulator? Get real, Lieutenant. You might learn enough to avoid wrecking the shuttle, but you'll be up against men who have made this their life's work and who have piloted their ships through every kind of weather on every type of planet. You won't win."

"Sir," said Eaves with a sideward glance at Carter, "You may find this hard to believe, but this really isn't about my ego. It's about developing skills. I want to be able to fly anything that can move in the atmosphere or space." He searched their faces for understanding, but both men remained stoic.

He continued. "Fighter pilots have ten years at most and then what do they do with their lives? I'm a pilot. Not just a fighter pilot. Before I'm done, I want to design ships and improve things, and to do that I need to know everything there is about every type of craft in the fleet, including shuttles." His face tightened with resolve. "Mr. O'Casey, I want to learn to fly the shuttle, even though it's as big as a hundred fighters. So will you please help me?"

O'Casey pursed his lips and straightened, a bit. "Well Lieutenant Eaves, I had no idea there was any depth to you. And while I'd hate to have to change my opinion, maybe you can learn. Three months in deep-space can be boring and watching you crash a simulator can give me a break from my routine. But I'm warning you, if I ever get the feeling, for even a second, that this is just a game, or that you're in this to make fun of the shuttle service, I'll personally take our shuttle out of service so fast your head will spin, and you will have to forfeit. Do you understand?"

"Yes Sir."

"Are you in this with your friend, Mr. Carter?"

Carter grimaced and let out an irritated sigh. But, he nodded his head in the affirmative.

"All right then, be here tomorrow morning at 05:00 for your first lesson."

"05:00!"

O'Casey smiled.

* * *

The lesson started with a review of the principles involved in shuttlecraft propulsion. When deep-space travel became viable through the invention of the vortex drive, it became necessary to find a low-cost way to get people and materials from a planet's surface into orbit. At first, designers tried to use deep-space ships to take off and land within the atmosphere, but the sheer weight and volume of fuel made that impossible, (with a typical ratio of one-to-five fuel-to-ship weight). Plus, the cost of recovering booster engines made the entire process impractical for routine service. So what was needed was a reliable way to shuttle goods and people to an orbiting ship that never traveled anywhere but in deep space.

"But, even that presented a problem," O'Casey explained. "Using explosive propellants for shuttles was extraordinarily expensive and damaging to the environment. Ironically, the answer to the problem came from Earth's Merchant Marine. To make military submarines ever quieter and avoid detection by hostile forces, scientists developed a membrane that attracts or repels water, depending on how an electrical charge is applied to it. At first, the surface of the membrane had to be so large, relative to the submarine, that it was impractical. Eventually, though, the process was perfected to where large panels at the bow could be charged to attract water, in essence pulling the ship forward, while panels aft carried the opposite charge to push the ship forward. That ingenious solution eliminated most of the mechanical equipment aboard the ship. Thus, interior space formerly allocated to propulsion was available for cargo and supplies."

"Are you with me?" O'Casey asked. The two nodded affirmatively, so he continued. "As scientists pondered ways to make surface-to-orbit shuttles practical, someone thought of the idea of adapting the membrane to attract and repel other materials, including air. Dubbed the "Anti-Gravity-Membrane," a substance was developed that could be manipulated electronically to resist or attract nearby objects. Practically anything could be used, but different materials provided varying attraction rates. If electrical power was lost, the membrane lost the orientation needed to hold the molecules in the opposing position and the membrane simply reverted to its inert state.

"While the water-only membrane had become efficient enough to propel large ocean-going tankers at speeds in excess of fifty knots, it was difficult to apply the same process to a shuttlecraft because of the lower density of air compared to water. The size of the membrane was simply too large for traditional shuttles that carried forty or fifty troops. Ultimately, the solution was to build extremely large, but lightweight, shuttles that had enormous panels on the bottom and top. A typical shuttle is roughly the size of a soccer field and its boxy shape makes it look more like a large warehouse than a spaceship. Sophisticated computers constantly monitor the environment for the best material to oppose or attract, then modify the structure of the membrane to match that material. So, for example, the panels on the top of the shuttle might be programmed to attract themselves to gases in the atmosphere, while the bottom panels are set to repel the ground itself. All this can be accomplished with relatively-small, cold fusion generators and batteries, eliminating propellants.

Eaves and Carter were impressed by O'Casey's knowledge. "Of course every solution creates new problems. First, was speed. The acceleration rate of a shuttlecraft is just a little faster than a hot-air balloon. Actually, the rate is variable, with quite a bit of lift when close to the ground, where the atmosphere is of a higher density and the minerals in the ground are closer. But, as the shuttle climbs ever higher in the atmosphere, its speed slackens until it ultimately comes to a standstill. Then the space ship makes an approach to give the shuttle something to pull against. While a high-speed, rocket-borne shuttle can reach orbit in less than thirty minutes, it takes a membrane shuttle some twelve to fifteen hours, depending on the weather. It's inexpensive, but slow.

"Which is why," said Eaves, the light going on in his brain, "most planets maintain a variety of shuttles – propellant shuttles for emergencies and rapid transport for VIP's and strictly membrane shuttles for routine re-supply missions and crew transfers. And the combo shuttles that use both membrane and propellants!

"That's right. The combination craft are much smaller than a membrane ship, about the size of a large, ocean-going yacht and their shape is more along traditional aircraft lines. The combo shuttles can make the trip in approximately four or five hours, with the propellants starting the journey, then going idle while they drift up, and finally kicking in again as they reach the upper atmosphere."

"Another problem early shuttle designers had to work through was how to store a shuttle to use on distant planets that didn't have their own fleet. Making them collapsible, like a giant accordion, solved this problem. The Allegro's shuttle reduces by ninety percent when fully collapsed. After the shuttle docks with the ship and unloads its cargo and/or passengers, winches collapse the panels into a compact cube that is drawn into a specially designed storage bay by large hydraulic arms."

"I guess I just always took all that for granted," said Carter. "But it's really pretty great engineering."

O'Casey was pleased with that, and continued the briefing, pointing out that "piloting a shuttle is very much like trying to control a soap bubble – a silent breeze can send it flying in an unexpected direction."

When Eaves furrowed his brow, Casey tried a more direct approach. "The shuttle's tremendous surface area acts like a sail that makes it vulnerable to changes in air currents or turbulence created by other aircraft. Generally, these disruptions offset each other, so you can continue on your original course, with just a few occasional adjustments. But every so often, an unexpected wind shear will catch a corner of the ship, causing it to roll. If you encounter such a condition in a fighter, how do you respond?"

"You immediately oppose the shear, powering through the disturbance."

"Right. In a shuttle, however, that maneuver would almost certainly cause you to lose control. Here's why." O'Casey moved to a three-dimensional whiteboard where he drew the boxy image of a shuttlecraft. "Suppose the wind catches the forward starboard corner, let's call it northeast. The aircraft lifts and begins to roll to port. Your natural inclination is to oppose the roll, so you execute a turn to starboard."

Carter and Eaves nodded in agreement.

O'Casey then animated the diagram. As expected, the northeast quarter settled nicely. But then the aft port, or southwest corner, rose at an alarming rate.

"If you were in a fighter, what would you do now?"

Eaves responded, "Execute a turn to port, but ..."

"Hold your comments for a moment and let's see what happens." O'Casey touched the diagram in such a way that the shuttle began a port turn. This lifted the northeast corner, as expected, which should have compensated for the rise on the southwest corner aft. But, the ship continued to rise at both corners, while sagging mid-ship. Carter and Eaves watched in amazement as the ship succumbed to the stress of lifting in opposing corners. In less than two minutes it buckled in the center, breaching the lower deck. The contents spilled out and the sickening sound of tearing metal confirmed its ultimate fate.

"As you can see, gentlemen, as the two corners continued to rise, the ship tore itself in half. The resulting loss of electrical power to the anti-gravity-membranes caused the entire structure to crash. Even if the occupants managed to bail out, the ship would likely crush them on its fall to the ground."

"How did it happen?" Carter asked.

Before O'Casey could respond, Eaves said, "The wind shear is like a wave. When it hit the northeast corner it started the lift, but then continued to pass under the structure lifting each section in turn. By the time we had turned to starboard, depressing that quarter, the wave was lifting the southwest corner, which aggravated, rather than relieved, the original condition. By trying to counteract that turn, we created a fatal stress in the center."

"Very good, Mr. Eaves. Why is that a problem unique to shuttles?"

"Actually, Sir, it's similar to what was experienced on large aircraft carriers on ancient earth. They were so long that when the ship encountered a long wave on the bow it would lift the ship in sections as it passed from bow to stern. That made it a real challenge for an aircraft attempting a landing in heavy seas to anticipate the rise and fall of each section."

O'Casey nodded appreciatively.

"So, how do we compensate for it?" Carter asked. "We have to do something."

"Actually, most of the time doing nothing is the best answer," O'Casey replied. "Think of a leaf falling from a tree. As it falls to earth, it flutters back and forth in the wind, ultimately self-correcting for all the currents that hit it."

"I can see that, but we're not drifting down. Instead we're powering our way up through the atmosphere, trying to reach a pre-determined spot."

"While you do use power, that's not the best way to think about it. The anti-gravity-membrane is really causing you to float up – like a leaf going in reverse."

Eaves interrupted. "But what if it's a sustained wind, rather than a shear? At some point you have to react or it will tip the ship over." O'Casey was annoyed by the interruption.

"You're correct, Mr. Eaves. The solution is counter-intuitive to most people. What you need to do is create your own roll, so you can then cut through the wave. "

He walked to the diagram again and tapped on the northeast corner. "The wave hits you here, on your right side. Instruments tell you it's a sustained wind, not a shear. The way you respond will determine whether or not the ship survives the next maneuver. First, you have to turn to Port, generally for thirty seconds. This will overemphasize the roll and cause the southwest corner to fall, relative to the rest of the ship. Then, you'll apply full power to a starboard turn, dropping the front as fast as possible. What do you expect will happen next, Mr. Carter?"

Carter tried to picture it in his mind, then spoke carefully. "First, we'll be rolling with the wind, northeast quarter rising. Then we resist, so the northeast quarter will settle. When the wind catches it from the top, it will dip sharply and come to equilibrium."

"Good so far, what are the risks?"

"If you let the northeast corner rise too far before the starboard turn, the correction will warp the ship in the center. As the northeast corner settles, the wind will hit it from the top while the southwest corner is still supported from underneath by the wind. It seems to me that it will snap the ship in two, again."

"Not if you simultaneously apply full bottom thrust to the aft-port quarter," Eaves said instinctively. "That way the wind will support it in the maneuver, so the stress isn't too great. In essence we slice right through the wind as we bring the ship head-on into the wave. From that point we'll be going perpendicular to our original course, but can match the speed of the wind and continue rising until we get above it." He looked up and added, "I'm sorry, Sir, I keep interrupting without permission."

"It's okay, Lieutenant, you analyzed the situation perfectly." This time O'Casey gave a slight smile.

Carter looked like his head hurt. "I'm sorry, but I still don't get it."

"Care to diagram it, Lieutenant Eaves?"

Eaves stepped forward and took the pointer. For the next two hours the three of them practiced various maneuvers on the board until the mathematics of the task came into focus.

Concluding the session, O'Casey said, "You've had a good start. A remarkably good start. Tomorrow's lesson will take place in the simulator, where you can feel the effect of all this first hand.

Rising early, Carter and Eaves made their way to the simulator with high expectations. But, their first attempt was a dismal failure. "It's like dancing in a slow motion ballet," Carter said at one point, frustrated.

"It's so darn big," Eaves responded. "Most of the time there's nothing to do but let it rise or settle. But then a problem hits and it takes all your concentration to avoid wrecking it."

One of the problems that proved hardest to deal with was the variable rate of speed depending on the material being attracted or repelled, as well as a particular planet's gravitational field. Trying to match all the competing forces in such a way that they didn't tear the flimsy shuttle apart was remarkably challenging. By the third day O'Casey had simplified the simulations to match only those that the team would encounter at Kalenden. Even these proved just as frustrating as O'Casey had predicted. Still, the Lieutenants showed up on time, every day and practiced every drill until it began to become second nature. The shuttle support crew actually cheered when they completed their first successful bad-weather landing.

As the final withdrawal date approached, Jesik dropped in unexpectedly "How are they doing, Mr. O'Casey?"

"Better than expected, Captain. Which means that if the weather is half-way decent, they probably won't humiliate us?"

"And if the weather's bad?"

"I hope our insurance premiums are current."

Jesik laughed. "Should they withdraw from the competition?"

"That's up to you and the Lieutenants, Sir. But, if they stay at it, I think they'll do alright. I'd certainly bet they'll do better than the other two fighter crews."

Eaves and Carter walked up as O'Casey said that and grinned.

"Hey, you two, beating the other fighter pilots doesn't begin to put you in league with some of the experienced crews. So that was a modest compliment, at best."

"Thanks for the clarification, Mr. O'Casey."

Jesik returned the Lieutenants' salute.

"I was just asking if you two ought to exercise your option to withdraw."

Jesik expected a flippant answer, but was surprised when Eaves responded seriously.

"I don't think so, Sir. But, I admit this is much more difficult than I imagined. I've probably sat on a shuttle a hundred times as a passenger and, if I ever thought of the crew at all, it was to wonder why anyone would enter such a boring service. Shows how ignorant I was." O'Casey raised an appreciative eyebrow at that.

"I'm sure you'll do fine in the competition," said Jesik, "but I'm worried about what it's doing to your skills as a fighter pilot. I don't want this to interfere with your combat skills."

"We've kept that in mind during our trials and so far, I think I'm doing okay. "

"Well, then, if Mr. O'Casey clears you, you have my permission to confirm your entry. But, I'd like a private word with you, Mr. Eaves, before I leave." Jesik walked around the shuttle bay for a few moments chatting with the maintenance crew, then drew Eaves to the side. Eaves nodded, apparently in agreement with whatever the Captain said and saluted him.

"By the way, Mr. O'Casey," Jesik called out. "We've been making better time than expected through the asteroid field. I think we'll give the men a three-day shore leave on Stirium on our way home. I want to check the political situation there, to see how the Keswick action affects other out-planets. Perhaps Lieutenant Eaves and Carter can help you with shuttle service there?"

"I believe they can, Captain. The Stirium gravitational field and planet composition is very similar to Kalenden. But, I'm sure you already thought of that, Sir." Cheerful demeanor aside, under his breath O'Casey muttered, "I hope our shuttle survives the ordeal of a first time pilot. It's only the most expensive shuttle in the fleet."

09—KESWICK GROWING PAINS

"Well, that didn't go so well, did it Commander?"

Magill shook his head. "I have the strongest desire to tell these people to just stuff it. Both sides are so stubborn!"

"But of course we can't. We need the orchidite. And if we try to just take it we have the Alturians to deal with."

Magill was thoughtful. "From my reading of history energy has been one of the major causes of wars since the beginning of human society 8,000 years before the common era on Earth. When people were the main source of energy nations raided their neighbors and took slaves. If one country found coal deposits, everyone else wanted them. In the days of sailing ships, when whale oil sold at a premium, nations threatened war in competition for killing whales. And when fossil fuels became the main source of energy the whole planet was in constant turmoil for more than 200 years. That was the darkest time of all. When the great oil fields in the Middle East started to run out the nuclear wars broke out, threatening the very survival of the species. Then orchidite was discovered on Saturn and interplanetary travel became possible. And now here we are, almost a millennium removed and still quibbling over fuel. It seems like the answer is to find a reliable source of energy that is everywhere—like water, or air, or sunlight! But none of those "renewable" have the energy needed for space travel, so we have to make nice with those who have orchidite."

Wilkerson smiled. "That's why I need you, Commander. It's all a lot simpler for me—we need it, we should take it. If we're stronger, we ought to have it."

Sean laughed. "Sometimes I'd like to come to your point-of-view, I really would." He paused and reflected on his life on Keswick. It was a mixed bag, so far. Since no one here had ever known him as anything but crippled his legs were no longer a liability. In fact in some ways it actually helped his cause since his pain was so obvious to everyone he dealt with, which caused them to recognize the sacrifice he was making to take part in their discussions. But on the downside his inexperience had caused some very embarrassing gaffes that gave an advantage to the far more experienced ministers from Alturus. They were constantly scheming to gain an advantage with the governing coalition and he knew they would strive to renegotiate their orchidite contracts at rates more favorable than those awarded to Kalendan. More than anything he wished he and Wilkerson had the help of some experienced commodities traders. As naïve and inexperienced as Magill was, Wilkerson was absolutely out his depth. But he was a fast learner and on the positive side, Prime Minister Lansing seemed to identify very strongly with Major Wilkerson, distrusting the royal ministers from Alturus, so they remained well-connected at the top. *As I said, a mixed bag!* It was all very puzzling

"Well, we better go back in. Prime Minister Lansing has his hands full and it seems like we're always the ones to back him up," said Wilkerson.

Magill nodded his agreement. "From my point-of-view it's critical that we keep him in power. If the Loyalists gain any ground it strengthens the hands of the Alturians."

"I'm telling you – a couple of starships to blast them out of orbit…"

Magill laughed. As he made his way back into the conference room he had a momentary image of Tara Carling and his heart suddenly hurt. *I can't believe you miss her—you meant nothing to her. She's a nurse, you were a patient. She helped you. Then she helped Travis when his arm was injured. Then she…"* He forced himself to stop thinking, at least for the moment. Yet no matter how hard he tried to convince himself otherwise, he somehow wanted to believe that Tara felt something more than just professional pity for him. *Probably all her patients think that way. STOP THINKING ABOUT IT!*

10 — PREPARING FOR "THE MANHATTAN TRIALS"

O'Casey wanted to grab the shuttle controls away from Lieutenant Eaves on a minimum of a hundred occasions. Not that Eaves' first attempt to land the shuttle was worse than any of the other trainees. In fact, it was better than most. But his other newcomers had first flown a training shuttlecraft into a secure environment, where Eaves' landing was with the Allegro's brand-new shuttle in the heart of the business district. Given the planet's obsessive concern for secrecy, they'd been harassed by ground control each time they drifted, fearing they were spying on the planet's guests, there to enjoy the spas and private estates.

Finally, Eaves floated the thing down to an acceptable landing, even if the last 2,000 meters had been at twice the preferred rate of descent. His launch from the planet had also gone well, but his first attempt at docking with Allegro nearly crushed the hydraulic docking arm. O'Casey had to take control before any real damage was done. Eaves was humiliated and upset, insisting he could have regained control of the shuttle in time, but the look on the Captain's face confirmed the wisdom of O'Casey's intervention.

Captain Jesik was patient and held the Allegro in low space orbit for an extra twelve hours while Eaves and Carter mastered the docking maneuver. Being in low orbit consumed an inordinate amount of fuel and risked creating a film on the alinite hull that made it less resistant to laser attack. Fortunately, Stirium had an unusually thin atmosphere, so the ship came through without any problems.

The only problem with the live practice was that the Stirium weather system did not produce a single storm, so O'Casey had to create artificial turbulence. The two Lieutenants handled that okay, but O'Casey still felt vulnerable, particularly since the Manhattan Trials were held in the dead of winter, when Kalenden weather was the most unstable.

"Why are they called the Manhattan Trials?" Lieutenant Carter asked at a briefing one morning.

"The island on which the trials are conducted on Kalenden is about twenty by eight kilometers. It bears a striking resemblance to the chief borough of New York City on Earth. So, the trials were named in its honor. Manhattan was the chief financial district on Earth, even after China became the leading economy."

This was a good a time to address the physical layout of the games, so O'Casey activated a three-dimensional image of the playing field. "For nine months each year, the entire island is occupied with shuttle training and maintenance. For the remaining three, it's converted into a replica of the ancient city, complete with hardened holographic buildings. The real Manhattan had a large open area in the middle called Central Park and that's where the takeoffs and landings will take place. The shuttle crews must show their ability to bring the shuttles in without disrupting the city's normal activities. Of course, the buildings present an unusual challenge, since they create wind canyons that make it difficult to predict landing conditions. Anyone who crashes into a building is automatically disqualified."

"The buildings on either side of the park look different than the others," Eaves observed.

"That's because they're permanent structures that house the observation platforms. To maintain the illusion of New York City, the platforms resemble prominent apartment buildings and museums that once lined the prestigious streets alongside the park. During the trials they'll be filled with dignitaries from all over the quadrant." He zoomed in on the image to show just Central Park and its surrounding streets. "Do you see the cables and tracks running up Fifth Avenue and Central Park West?" Eaves and Carter bent closer to the image and saw miniature railroad locomotives tethered to the now floating platforms. "During the trials, these observation platforms use anti-gravity-membranes to hover parallel to the playing field so that spectators can get the best view. The operator can adjust altitude to match the incoming shuttles and use the cable system to move north and south as shuttles land at various points in the park."

"Cool," Eaves said, "Who gets to observe?"

"The Quadrant Council, the Joint Chiefs of Staff, Shuttle and Fighter Command and nearly every influential business person in this corner of the galaxy. It's a chance for these luminaries to get together and do some unofficial wagering. Plus, most of the big business contracts for the next year are signed during the trials. They love this competition, because the shuttles move so slowly that there's plenty of time to conduct business. Each of the shuttle crews are also entitled to ten tickets in the VIP observation building, so you can have your parents or girlfriends occupy a premier spot at the trials."

"My mom will love that." Carter said, "It'll be her excuse to buy a whole new wardrobe."

O'Casey continued. "The competition consists of seven trials. Separation and docking from the deep-space host, upper altitude maneuvers, lower altitude approach, interference from proximate aircraft and landing and take-off. Speed is not foremost, although it can be a tie-breaker at the end of the trials. Accuracy, precision and passenger comfort are the three criteria that make up the lion's share of your point total. Additionally, you'll be exposed to two emergency conditions called "randoms," because the timing and nature of the emergency is selected randomly by the course computer, once all twelve teams have logged in. The randoms you encounter may include loss of power, loss of instrumentation, an unruly passenger, or loss of communication with either Ground Control or your ship. In each case, you have to complete the drill you're working on in the best fashion possible."

"But, what if one crew draws two easy randoms, such as an unruly passenger and loss of instrumentation, while another draws really severe problems like loss of power and communications?"

"That's the luck of the draw, I'm afraid. More than once, my assigned team has been in a substantial lead, only to be taken down by two seemingly insurmountable randoms. Plus, you shouldn't underestimate any of the randoms. An unruly passenger may be able to fire a stun blast that knocks you two unconscious."

"Anything else we need to worry about?" O'Casey turned to address Eaves' question.

"Probably the biggest problem is the weather. Some years the sky is clear and stable, other years have seen raging blizzards. No matter what occurs, the trials continue until one team has won all seven trials, or is the only team left."

"Has a fighter team ever won the competition?"

O'Casey smiled. "Not yet."

"At least our odds have gone from 'impossible' to 'not yet,'" Carter voiced.

"I wouldn't be spending the prize money," O'Casey replied mildly.

"Your task today is to memorize the buildings on Manhattan Island, as well as each landing pad in Central Park. Remember, accuracy earns the most points. And so you know what your competition's capable of, last year's second place team lost by being a mere three meters off-center on their landing. The winner has re-entered this year's competition."

"What's the single biggest mistake to cause disqualification?" Eaves had an intense look in his eyes.

"Most people think it's the randoms, so they spend all their time practicing for that. But, I believe it's the canyon winds swooping up Fifth Avenue and the Avenue of the Americas. The danger is greatest at the southern end of the park where the buildings are tall on three sides. That doesn't put the shuttles in danger of crashing, just their being blown off center at the moment of touch down."

"How do you protect against that?"

"That's another homework assignment, Mr. Eaves. I'll program the simulator to give you some unexpected blasts from different quarters as you prepare to land. You figure out what actions to take so that you can land within two meters of center, perfectly squared at every corner. When you can do that consistently, I'll believe you have a real chance in the competition."

O'Casey left and Carter and Eaves poured over the map of Manhattan. Carter detailed a plot of every building and street, programming the coordinates into his personal navigation device. He could have downloaded the program, but that would fail to save the information in his mind, where it would be needed in an emergency. Before he was done, he knew the basic architecture of ancient New York City better than most city planners of the time.

Meanwhile, Eaves fed blue dye into the blowers programmed to simulate the weather conditions that could arise, constantly changing the wind direction to see how the various canyons influenced the flow. It was well past dinner before either of them spoke or even realized they were hungry.

No one saw much of the two Lieutenants after that. Brighton relieved them of all duties except preparing for the competition and the shuttle simulator became their effective quarters. At the end of three weeks, Eaves exited the simulator with a stack of paper and approached O'Casey and Brighton. O'Casey held out his hand as Eaves handed him the papers. Carter quietly joined the group, an expectant look on his face. O'Casey looked down at the stack of paper, read the first page, quickly turned to the second, third, fourth. He started handing them to Commander Brighton, who had done his best to restrain his curiosity.

"Well, then," O'Casey said quietly, "ten landings with the wind coming from every point on the compass, with unexpected turbulence on six of the ten."

Brighton's jaw dropped as he thumbed through the pages.

"This can't be right!" It indicates you landed dead center, with no more than 85 centimeters variance. And square on every corner. That's impossible!" Eaves and Carter said nothing.

"How many attempts did it take to get these ten?" O'Casey asked.

Carter couldn't suppress a grin. "These are the last ten attempts in succession. Look at the time signature and simulator sequence."

"Unbelievable!" said Brighton with a broad grin. "We've probably ruined the best fighter team in the fleet, but gained the most highly-practiced shuttle team ever to enter the competition."

"Don't go giving them false confidence," said O'Casey fiercely. "A simulator isn't the same as the real thing and they'll be up against top-rated crews." Eaves expression remained unchanged. "But, I have to tell you that the two of you are far better prepared than any team I've ever entered. You've done great work and will do us proud."

"Thank you, Sir," Eaves said and started to return to the shuttle.

"Hold up a moment, Lieutenant," Brighton said. "What are your intentions for the next three days before we enter the Kalenden orbit?"

"Practice, Sir," Eaves replied seriously. He and Carter looked exhausted.

"I'm afraid you can't do that, Mr. Eaves. I'm placing the simulator off-limits for the next three days." That shocked all of them, including O'Casey.

Eaves eyes flashed and he replied fiercely, "But, Sir, we have to keep our concentration. We've worked so hard, we can't let down now."

"I understand that, but my orders stand. Dismissed!"

Eaves was furious and Carter looked like he'd been kicked in the stomach. It was obvious that Eaves wanted to smash his fist into Brighton's face or, barring that, the nearest wall.

As Brighton started to walk away, he added, "I'd like both of you in my quarters in one hour." Without turning to look at them he left.

When the door sealed behind Brighton, Eaves turned to O'Casey and pleaded, "Can't you do something about this, Sir? How can he do this to us? Does he have money riding on another team?"

"Don't say that, even if you're angry," O'Casey said sternly. "The Captain and Mr. Brighton have moved mountains to help you two get ready, so there's got to be a reason for the Commander's order. In the meantime, go get some lunch and keep your appointment. You can help us polish the shuttle's logo after that, if you like. Wouldn't want you passing the reviewing stand with any grime on the Allegro's insignia."

Eaves sat down in a chair and put his head in his hands. "I can't believe this, I just can't believe this," he said over and over. Carter walked to the simulator. It knew his footsteps well enough to waive the usual retina scan and had opened its door hundreds of times during the past three months. But, not this time. An order from the First Officer trumps a request from a First Lieutenant. Even the metallic voice of the computer sounded sad when it denied entrance. "Come with me to the lunch room," Carter said, with as much cheer as he could muster.

"Later," Eaves replied sullenly, "I've got to take a walk."

An hour later Eaves and Carter met at Commander Brighton's door, which opened at their approach.

Brighton recognized the anger evident in Eaves' slumped shoulders. He invited them to sit. "I'd like to show you something." He reached for a small object on the end table next to his chair and handed it to Eaves. "Read it aloud, please."

"First Place, Lieutenant Thomas Brighton, in the CCXXVIII Precision Maneuvers Trials of the Kalenden Heavy Battle Fleet. Acting Helmsman."

Eaves looked up and for the first time, met Brighton's gaze.

"The year before we received this, I made a mistake that disqualified my ship from the trials. The Captain was furious with me because our ship had always been one of the top three during the previous ten years, winning first place six times. He was a fanatic about the trials and our disqualification devastated him – he wouldn't talk to me for nearly three months, always issuing orders through a subordinate. I wanted to transfer off the ship, but Fleet Command deployed us on deep-space duty to squelch a drug trafficking ring near Stirium. That was the most miserable time of my life, particularly since there were a couple of other Lieutenants in the wardroom who delighted in my reduced status. The Captain wouldn't let me anywhere near the helm, and assigned me to supervise the guard duty in the brig. What a come down! I was cut from operating a 20,000 ton frigate to watching drunken sailors throw-up on a mattress in lockup. I figured I'd never get another promotion and would be the oldest Lieutenant in the fleet."

"What did you do wrong?" Carter asked.

Brighton ordered a warm drink and continued, "Captain Mackinaw had drilled everyone to the point of exhaustion on precision docking to the space port. He tried to practice every maneuver he could think of, knowing we were likely to get a random. But, as the trials progressed, our random didn't come, which only increased the tension. Not only were we assigned to dock at the Elite Terminal, where all the dignitaries were observing from a glass-walled observation lounge, but the Admiral in charge of the games had been the Skipper of my Captain's first ship, so Captain Mackinaw was anxious to make a good impression. On our final approach, he was speaking very quietly. He always liked to speak just above a whisper when giving his most important orders. I think he believed it made him look calm and in control. But, I was so tired from practicing and practicing and practicing. I'd been sneaking off to the simulator after lights-out so I could work a few more drills. I'd figured out how to hack into the security system and make it appear that I was a member of the cleaning detail whenever I showed up after hours."

Eaves' face colored slightly, but Brighton didn't seem to notice.

"We'd successfully attached three of the four mooring cables when a simulated meteor struck the docking station – our long awaited random. It hit the station's port side, just as we were firing our starboard thrusters to make the final connection. Of course, that meant the station started moving toward us, as we were moving toward it. We were coming in too fast, so I instinctively fired the aft port thrusters to compensate for the terminal's drift. The noise was incredible and the simulation made it sound like the meteor was tearing through two or three levels of the station. That's when the Captain spoke, 'Port thrusters, Mr. Brighton.'"

Brighton paused, his eyes looking up and to the left. "'But Sir,' I protested, 'I've already fired the port thrusters.'"

"Apparently he didn't hear me, because he shouted back, 'Obey my order, Lieutenant!' There was nothing to do but fire the port thrusters a second time. With three tethers attached, our aft port quarter swung away and down, crashing into the docking station's fuel nipple. I felt the sickening crunch as it collapsed and looked on in disbelief as it flooded the docking bay with radioactive coolant. That, of course, forced evacuation of everyone in the observation stand. There was pandemonium on both the station and our ship as we attempted to disentangle ourselves from the rigging."

By now Eaves and Carter were both sitting forward in their seats. "But why did the Captain order you to fire a second time?" Carter inquired.

"That was the question that smothered all other thoughts in my mind, particularly when the Captain bounded up to me and started screaming, 'Why did you disobey my order Lieutenant? Why did you humiliate us?'"

"'But, Sir, you ordered me to fire Port Thrusters. I tried to tell you I'd already fired them.' I was so embarrassed I wanted to scream at him. Then I saw recognition in his eye and he shouted back, 'I ordered you to Abort Thrusters!' I'll never forget the look on his face. It was like his whole world had collapsed and all because of a single confused command. He was furious, ashamed and devastated, all at the same time."

"Why did it matter so, much?" Eaves asked. "Docking errors aren't that rare." This was the first time Eaves had spoken since the shuttle-bay.

"I can't say, for sure. But during my exile, the First Officer took me aside and said the Captain had come from a second-class family and the trials had been the only thing that gave him equal status with the others in his class at the academy. I imagine he saw the crash as the end of his being treated as an equal."

"So how did you win the next year?" Eaves asked earnestly.

"After four months of guard duty, I was walking back to my bunk one night when I bumped into the Captain coming around a corner. I averted my eyes and apologized, then stood there, not knowing what to do. He didn't speak for perhaps twenty or thirty seconds and when I sneaked a glance at his face I saw that he was struggling with his emotions. I braced for the worst but instead he said in his quiet voice, 'Mr. Brighton, join me for a drink in the Officers Lounge.' Wow, that sure took me by surprise."

Looking into the Lieutenant's eyes, Brighton continued, "When we took a booth in a quiet corner, I glanced around and saw that everyone in the room was pretending not to watch us. The Captain must have seen it too, because he leaned forward and said, 'Lieutenant, I owe you an apology. I made two mistakes that day. The obvious one is that I spoke too quietly for you to hear me and then cut you off when you attempted to provide the information I needed to make a correct decision.' I responded that I shouldn't have cut the starboard thrusters and fired the port thrusters until he gave the order and was sorry I ruined everything. The words just came spilling out. He held up his hand for me to stop. 'No, you did exactly what you should have done. I'd given you authority to bring the ship to its final position and shouldn't have interfered.' All I could do was tell him thank you and try not to cry. I was only twenty-three at the time."

"You said the Captain admitted he made two mistakes. What was the second?" Eaves asked.

"That was a real surprise. He told me that he'd been so anxious to win that even when he'd received a report from the Simulator Chief that I was making unauthorized use of the simulator at night, he did nothing to stop me. He apologized for driving us so hard to win."

"I protested that it was my fault, but he brushed that aside. 'It was my mistake. I never should have let you become so tired. In combat, your men need to be as rested as possible. Instead, I let you become fatigued. Who knows if you'd have heard me clearer if you weren't so tired?' That left me too stunned to say anything.

"At any rate, he returned me to full duty and the next year we went through the same drill again. When the time came for the trials we heard the inter-ship jokes about how they were wrapping the fuel nipple with duct tape, just in case we crashed into it again. Captain Mackinaw said nothing. I think that's why our win was so important to all of us. There's nothing quite like being vindicated, particularly when you defeat six of your fellow classmates in the process."

"What made the difference?" Carter asked. "How did you avoid the mistake of the previous year."

"When we came within three days of the trials, the Captain locked the simulator door. He told me I was to relax or work out in the recreation bay. 'Go ski or surf,' he said. 'Don't think about the trials. That's an order.'"

"So did you relax?"

"Yes I did, Lieutenant Eaves. I thought I'd be a nervous wreck thinking about it, but after a couple of hours of brooding, I decided I had nothing to lose since I'd made a fool of myself the year before. So I went water skiing for three days in the rec rooms, worked out in the weight room, and relaxed in the sauna."

Eaves' posture improved. "The point is, Mr. Eaves, that our log for the simulator shows an interesting pattern of use. I had no idea that our Tech Specialist Crane from Accounting was interested in flying shuttles." Eaves bit his lip and averted his eyes.

"Whether you believe it or not, the best thing you can do to perform well in competition is to stop thinking about it. Your brain is like a muscle. You've successfully exhausted it through repetition. Now it needs time to rejuvenate and fortify the neural paths you've created for it over the past three months. When you walk onto that shuttle next Monday, you need to be well rested and clear headed."

He could see they would do what he asked, but still didn't really understand why. "You know, I became really good at piloting capital ships. It's what elevated me through the ranks. But, I was never half as fast as you are. You have the best reflexes of any pilot I've ever seen. But your worst enemy is to think about something. You must simply react to whatever situation comes your way. Your mind and body know what to do. Any more time in that simulator will actually detract from your skill because you'll sec-ond-guess yourself at a crucial moment and then that'll be it. That's why I'm ordering you out of the simulator and into the recreation bay." He stood up. "We'll all be rooting for you and I think you've actually got a chance to win, certainly to place. But, know this, no matter what the result of the competition, the entire crew is proud of your effort. You'll represent the Allegro well."

"Thank you, Sir," they both mumbled.

Eaves looked relieved. "I didn't know you were a pilot, Sir. That's really awesome, winning the System Cup."

Brighton smiled and put his arm on Eaves' shoulder as he escorted them through the door. "Remember, do anything you want between now and Monday, except the shuttle."

For once Eaves obeyed an order perfectly. Three days later he and Car-ter emerged from the recreation bay, suntanned and relaxed.

The navigator saw them and asked, "Where on earth have you two been?"

"I've been skiing the French Alps and Carter's been kayaking in New Zealand."

"Skiing and kayaking, my, my. Meanwhile, I've been spending my time navigating through the Cambriol asteroid belt. Enriched, I might add, by the hundreds of thousand fragments you created."

"It was nothing," said Eaves. "For the right price I'll blow them out of the solar system, if you like."

"No, that's okay, we get nervous whenever you put your finger on a trigger. Those who know you are thrilled you've decided to take up shuttles for a living."

"A friend of yours?" Carter asked, as the navigator disappeared down the corridor.

"What do you expect from a navigator, for crying out loud?"

Carter laughed for a second, then caught the dig and attempted to strangle Eaves.

But Eaves wriggled free and asked, "How's New Zealand this time of year?"

"Great. It's summer down there and the rivers are running high. How about France? "

"Cold. But the snow was unusually fast. I beat my best time ever on the giant slalom."

They walked down the corridor to get lunch where the galley staff noticed, with satisfaction, that they'd eaten more in the last three days than in the previous two weeks.

"Gotta love the Rec Bay," said Carter while standing up to get another sandwich. After a number of crew members went stir crazy on early deep-space flights, human engineers figured out that people need diversions and plenty of sunlight to avoid depression and cabin fever. One of the results of their efforts was creation of the recreation bay. At the extreme forward arc of the ship's bow, the bay spanned all twenty-five stories of the ship's infrastructure. That allowed engineers to do some really remarkable things, including installation of amusement park rides, gyms, saunas, pools, mountain climbing walls and a magnificent atrium. It also provided room for some terrific extreme-sports simulators. Eaves had spent most of his awake time in the snow-skiing simulator, which extended the vertical distance of the bay via a twenty-story treadmill covered with artificial snow. It was a near-perfect substitute for the real thing. The belt went over a series of rollers that could be adjusted to simulate moguls, curves and jumps. Hydraulic lifters simulated runs of varying intensity. Eaves liked to ski the black diamond slopes, the most difficult the simulator could create. As the skier started down the course, the rollers began turning to match his descent. If he came too close to the bottom the belt sped up enough to pull him further up the incline. If he slowed, the belt automatically slowed too. The entire structure was housed in a video tube that recreated a three-dimensional view of the galaxy's best ski resorts. To improve the crew's mental attitude, the lighting could replicate 90% of the Kalenden Star's light spectrum. Natural light was the best antidote for the doldrums. It also accounted for Eaves suntan.

Carter, meanwhile, had been on a horizontal simulator that recreated the great rivers of Kalenden and Earth. The New Zealand program was by far the most popular, since it had the most spectacular natural scenery. The kayak paddled against an artificial current that duplicated traveling down a river, complete with rapids and hazards.

The simulators weren't the only reason the two Lieutenants were relaxed. On their first day of R and R, Eaves slept for fifteen hours and Carter for twelve. During the three days, they caught up for three weeks of sleep deprivation.

As they rounded the corner to the shuttle bay, Captain Jesik joined O'Casey and Brighton for a last minute inspection.

"You look fresh and well-rested," said Jesik.

"Yes, Sir, a gift from Commander Brighton," replied Eaves.

"Wish he could do that for me. Mr. O'Casey, are you going to let Lieutenant Eaves get his hands on your shuttle for our descent to Manhattan Island? We probably should be off if we're going to make the opening receptions."

O'Casey nodded, then added, "The virtual buildings are in place, so watch what you're doing. Every eye in the observation lounge will be on you."

"Yes, Sir," Eaves said crisply and formally. Then he burst into a grin, amused at O'Casey's seriousness.

"Remember what I said, Mr. Eaves. If you think this is a joke, I'll pull you from the controls so fast, your tail will get surface-burned from the friction." Brighton immediately wished he'd ordered O'Casey into the recreation bay, too.

Eaves and Carter entered first and made their way forward to the control cabin. Carter radioed the bridge and planet for clearance and Eaves initiated the unfolding of the shuttle. Because the number of passengers was minimal, the shuttle would only need to be 25% uncompressed, which made it easier to control in flight. When they were ready, the others boarded and settled in to watch the entry into the atmosphere – always a rather spectacular sight as the parent ship faded from view and the shuttle started to flare from the friction. Then there would be time for a movie and dinner, followed by sleep for those not in the control room. They expected to arrive the next morning at around 10:00 hours.

11—AN ILL WIND

Most of the descent to the surface went without incident. As the morning breeze off the ocean found its way up the streets of Manhattan, however, it created some interesting turbulence. Ground control gave the Allegro shuttlecraft its choice of three approaches and naturally Eaves chose the most difficult, directly up Park Avenue from the south. O'Casey hovered over his shoulder as they floated past the Empire State building, two blocks west, then past the Chrysler building, one block east, on Lexington.

At Forty-Ninth street a blast of frigid air hit them from the East River, lifting the starboard side. It was strong enough that it startled Brighton into suggesting a corrective maneuver, but Eaves simply kept his gaze forward and took no action. Everyone there stood nervously, wondering why he didn't do anything as the shuttle drifted west towards Rockefeller Center. Everyone but O'Casey. He actually smiled.

"Well done, Eaves, you were absolutely correct to ignore that."

The breeze rolled under the giant ship like a wave and the shuttle settled back onto its original course. Jesik and Brighton said nothing, but mentally took note to never, ever, pilot a shuttlecraft. As they drifted past Trump tower, Eaves applied a slight banking motion to port, which allowed them to pass lazily over the simulated Plaza Hotel. Carter began calling out coordinates for the landing pad, which was on a soccer field south of the main boathouse.

Eaves activated the forward gels, which reacted against the air, then the trees. The ship came to a dead stop over the assigned pad. The breeze from the east was uneven, but with three or four quick maneuvers with the port membranes, he was able to square the ship properly, then reduce the resistance below, allowing the shuttle to settle gently on the pad. Everyone onboard breathed a huge sigh of relief. Eaves had managed his first landing without incident. And in full view of the maximum number of observers, including the crews of nine of their competitors.

O'Casey peered anxiously over Carter's shoulder as he ran the numbers on the landing.

"One meter off from dead center, to starboard, and off rotation by two-and-a-half meters, aft side trailing."

Everyone onboard burst into applause. Practically a perfect landing.

"I overcorrected for the east wind," muttered Eaves muttered as he powered down the systems. He appeared angry, but Carter knew he was as relieved and happy as everyone else.

"It's just lucky for the two of you that there was no real weather to worry about," O'Casey said laconically. Then, turning to the shuttle ground crew he issued a quick set of orders for post-docking security and maintenance.

"Great job, everyone. Congratulations, Mr. O'Casey. Your training appears to have paid off," Jesik commented

"Thank you Captain."

"Now, I see there's air transport waiting outside. Let's all check into our hotel rooms, to shower and then I'll buy you breakfast at a café I know next to the Helmsley on Fifty-Ninth. After that, we'll go off to our various receptions to start, ah, consultations with senior command." The crew smiled, knowing how the Captain felt about receptions.

Three hours later, Eaves and Carter made their way toward a conference room in one of the permanent structures on Park West. The Dakotas was an ornate apartment building that reminded Eaves of the Palace on Keswick where Magill had been laid up. The room he and Carter shared had twelve foot high ceilings, gold plated faucets in the bathroom and a magnificent view of Central Park out the east windows. Their room overlooked a spot of the park identified as Strawberry Fields.

"Why Strawberry Fields?" Eaves asked, when they first arrived.

Carter barely concealed his irritation at the gaps in Eaves' understanding of history. "It was named in honor of one of the greatest composers of all time, John Lennon. He lived his last days at the original Dakotas and his widow assumed the expense of maintaining this part of the park as a permanent memorial to him."

"Ah. I should have known that."

Forty-five minutes later the two Lieutenants assembled with other crews in a large conference room where the competition's Commanding Officer was about to start the meeting.

"Gentlemen, you should all know the drill by now. To those here for the first time, welcome and good luck. To those of you who are returning, congratulations on qualifying again to represent your ship in the Manhattan Trials. Your exercises over the next three days will be observed by more than three billion people throughout the quadrant. I also understand that this year there will even be an Esper-delayed link to Tatrius, which they'll view next week. So, let's all look sharp and add even more luster to the reputation of Shuttle Command."

Everyone broke into applause.

The Commanding Officer added, "We'd especially like to welcome our three fighter crews who were selected for their skill at high-speed maneuvers. Please do your best, gentlemen, to not wreck any of the permanent structures or deprive your ship of its shuttle."

Everybody laughed except Eaves, who folded his arms and sat back in his chair.

"Five of you have your shuttles docked on the south end of the park, so you can start your take-off and deep-space docking maneuvers tomorrow morning. You'll start your descent Tuesday evening for a Wednesday morning hook-up. The seven shuttles at the north end will start landing drills first thing tomorrow morning, by climbing to 60,000 meters over the ocean off the New Jersey coast, then initiating a normal approach through the city to your assigned landing pad. At noon of the second day, you'll participate in takeoff drills and ascend to your parent ship where you'll permanently dock. If successful, you'll return by high-speed shuttles and join the rest of us at the awards ceremony on Thursday. Any questions?"

There were none. "Your placement at north or south was determined in advance by lottery. In a few moments we'll draw for who goes first in each of the drills. But, before we draw, I'd like our weather officer to brief you on what to expect the next four days."

For the next thirty minutes they endured the most boring, analytical treatise on planetary weather Eaves had ever heard. His mind wandered across most of the known galaxy, with occasional detours back to some of the more interesting adventures of his childhood and he still absorbed the weather report. It wasn't good. That much was clear. High storms were expected, mild on Monday morning, but growing to near-hurricane gale force by Wednesday afternoon. That was great for the takeoff drills but could create havoc for their landing. He mentally went through the modifications he'd designed to give him greater control of the shuttlecraft. At first Carter had been violently opposed to making any changes to the shuttle, threatening to tell O'Casey. But he calmed down after Eaves showed him the research he'd done on the rules of the competition. None of his modifications would get them disqualified. Still, it would cause an uproar in the competition if he actually used any. The hardest part was arranging that O'Casey wouldn't ride with them on the return to the ship. Eaves had already enlisted the maintenance crew to implement the changes, if needed on the trip up. The objects could be placed inconspicuously enough so that O'Casey wouldn't notice until it was too late for him to do anything about it.

Carter nudged him. "They're getting ready to draw names, so pay attention." Eaves looked up expectantly.

"First, the names for take-off and orbiting maneuvers." The Commanding Officer reached into a large crystal vase and drew out a piece of paper. "Ah, very good. First take-off will be the Allegro, piloted by Lieutenant Travis Eaves, with Lieutenant Jason Carter as Navigator. I'm sure we'll all love seeing the hero of Cambriol master the morning breezes with the sunrise in his eyes." Everyone laughed. Eaves smoldered inside, but stood and took a theatrical bow. *What good is it to react to a jerk like that anyway?* The officer glowered at him, annoyed to have someone steal the stage. But, Eaves' cavalier attitude had stolen the officer's thunder in that each of the succeeding crews did something theatrical to acknowledge their place in the lottery. His earnest "Gentlemen, please," went unheeded for Eaves had succeeded in showing that he was just a regular guy. After the meeting, many members of competing crews welcomed Eaves and Carter. The general sentiment was it was unfair to have fighter crews in the competition, since they were at such a disadvantage. The four Lieutenants of the other fighter crews made it clear that they were there for fun and planned to fly obsolete shuttles their Captains had borrowed for the trials. So it didn't matter if they wrecked them, for they were scheduled for the scrap heap anyway.

"But, we want to win," Carter whispered to Eaves.

"It's just as well we let them think we're not serious. Why give guys like the Commanding Officer ammunition to taunt us with? Let's get out of here and look at the city before the banquet and variety show."

The simulation of New York City in the last years of the Twentieth Century offered far too much variety for the two Lieutenants to take in with just four hours. Each year during the tournament, the entire island was turned into a giant art festival that attracted upwards of four million people coming to sample the diverse ethnic cuisine, stroll up holographic avenues that meticulously reconstructed the ancient borough of Manhattan and to interact with local citizens in period costumes. The chaos and disorder of the Old World was in stark contrast to the orderly ways of Kalenden. Most people stayed on the broad boulevards, like Fifth Avenue, where retailers set up temporary quarters in plywood buildings that were given electronic façades to make them look like buildings of the past. Stores with odd names like Macy's, Tiffany, Saks and Bergdorf-Goodman competed furiously with each other and some people waited all year for the festival, to buy their fine clothing, oriental carpets, jewelry and electronics.

Others, who wished to maintain anonymity, slipped off to the West Side of Eighth Avenue, where the buildings resembled old brothels and porn houses, but without actual pictures or prostitutes. There were, however, enough dark corners in which some ancient vices were actually played out. Parents passing through these areas in quaint old wheeled-vehicles called busses lectured their children sternly about the wickedness of the ancient times and about how lucky they were to grow up in a civilized society. They were often embarrassed when their kids asked them what was evil, back when.

Kalenden's theatre community added to the festivities by building numerous temporary playhouses to perform old shows like "Cats," "Phantom" and "Les Miserable."

The bazaar and competition was a grand extravaganza that left everyone exhausted when it was done, but immediately afterward, planning for the next year's event began.

Like most first-time visitors, Eaves and Carter wanted to try everything, but ended up spending most of their time moving between lines without doing much of anything. Finally they contented themselves by walking down Broadway to a busy intersection called Times Square where they enjoyed a delicious, old-world delicacy called pizza.

"What a mess of a place this city must have been," Carter said in awe. "Imagine, having a series of streets set up on a grid, only to be sliced through by another street that runs on a north-south diagonal."

"The historic guide says that Broadway was originally a Native American trail that was left where it was, as the rest of the city grew around it."

"Well, from an engineering point-of-view, this place is crazy," Carter continued, "and the sooner we get out of here, the better. Besides, these people are acting like idiots." He said that as they walked past a somber fellow wearing a wig and playing a stringed instrument called a sitar.

"Jason, if you stay with me long enough, I may be able to help you see that there's more to life than right angles and quadrants. Personally, I love this place – it's so alive with energy and fun. It makes me wish time travel was possible, so I could go back and see what it was really like. But, good old Stephen Hawking took the idea of time travel away from us with his stab at unified theory, how many hundred years ago?"

"I wish you'd show proper respect when talking about the great philosophers," Carter hissed. "The reason we're here is because of men like Hawking. And he didn't take time travel away, he just stated the natural law that makes it impossible. You can be so juvenile, sometimes."

"I'll try to be more serious when talking about important people. Just promise you'll help us win the competition, so we get invited back next year. There's a lot more of this place I want to see. Besides, I'll bet Stephen Hawking and Einstein both liked New York."

Carter shook his head and hailed a yellow device called a taxi. Fifteen minutes later, the two Lieutenants emerged at a drab place called Pennsylvania Station and entered a permanent structure named Madison Square Garden, although it didn't look like there was a garden within thirty blocks of the place.

"Wow and I thought it was exciting to fly space fighters," Eaves said exultantly. "When I get really good, I may try driving a taxi at the Manhattan Festival."

"Well, that's where our partnership ends," said Carter, rubbing his temples. "There's no way you'll ever get me back into one of those things. It's no wonder our ancestors couldn't wait to leave Earth."

The evening variety show in "the Garden" was a lot of fun, with period actors singing and dancing and loud bands playing outlandish music. In any normal circumstance, people would have left the place disgusted, but a festival gives everyone the chance to loosen up a bit. Even four hundred years of the best genetic engineering wasn't enough to breed out every single aspect of mankind's ancient urges and impulses, although the government certainly tried its best.

The next morning dawned bright and clear, with a stiff breeze blowing in from the west.   At 06:40 O'Casey grasped Eaves hands and implored, "Are you sure you don't want me to come along. I'm certain I can get an exception since you're a fighter pilot."

"You'd embarrass us if you did, Chief," Eaves replied simply. "Carter and I either have it, or we don't. With all due respect, Sir, I'll be more relaxed if you're not there."

"I suppose so," O'Casey said with resignation. "But, if you damage my shuttle…"

"You'll kill us where we stand," Carter and Eaves said in unison.

"To hell with you, then," O'Casey retorted. "If you need me, I'll be at a place called an Irish pub somewhere south of here. Find your own way out of a jam!"

"Thank you Sir. Thanks very much for all your time." Eaves sounded unusually sincere. "And thanks, too, for believing in us. It means a lot."

O'Casey blustered about the atmosphere on Kalenden in winter as he wiped some moisture from his eye and hurried out of the shuttle. Jesik wished them luck, then turned to the maintenance crew and shook each of their hands in turn. Then he, too, departed. Left onboard were Carter, Eaves, seven engineers assigned to the technical crew and five stewards to serve the twenty-five guests seated in the passenger cabin. Normally, a passenger shuttle would accommodate fifteen hundred, but there was no need to move so many for the competition.

Eaves gave last minute, unmonitored instructions to the technical crew. There was one engineer assigned to the reactor and electric generator, one crew member for each corner and two rovers who directed the small platoon of robots that fixed any external damage while the shuttle was in flight.

"Everyone clear on what we need to get done on the trip back down? You need to slip the modifications onboard the shuttle while we're docked with Allegro."

"We're clear, Lieutenant. I sure hope you're right about these enhancements. If not, O'Casey will bust us all."

"He's right," Carter chirped in. "Plus, we'll be a laughingstock, forever known as the guys who aren't smart enough to know the difference between a shuttle and a fighter. Are you sure you want to do this?" Everyone looked at Eaves expectantly.

"If we lose, no one will give us trouble. If we win, they'll have to check the rules and we're on solid ground. I don't plan to use any of these things unless the competition is close. You know the weather reports as well as I do – a gale warning for Wednesday. If it becomes as bad as they predict, most crews will forfeit the day's competition, rather than risk damaging their shuttle or a permanent structure. We can, too, but that means a lot of time wasted in training and practice. But, with these adjustments, I believe I can control the ship no matter how bad it gets outside. Then, nobody will laugh."

"I've got a bad feeling about this," said Master Sergeant Price, "but if you promise you'll only use them in an emergency, we'll get to work."

"Promise. Now assume your assigned positions for take-off." Even though barely twenty-three years old, Eaves spoke with the authority of a line officer and the crew responded instantly. Many were at least a decade older than him.

The view out the front of the shuttlecraft presented a stark winter landscape, sculpted by drifted snow. Perched nearly thirty feet above the ground, Eaves looked out on the crowd assembled to watch their take-off. Glancing at the video monitors providing a 360-degree view of their surroundings, he noted the large apartment buildings that floated on either side of the park, hosting some of the system's most influential politicians and military leaders. The advantage of an early start was that most of them were still asleep, thanks to the previous night's partying.

With an acknowledging signal from the Judges' Platform, Eaves turned to Carter and spoke briskly, "Coordinates for a direct ascent to Allegro?"

Carter punched controls on his navigation console. Displaying a large map on their common video monitor, he acknowledged, "Course laid in for a three-quarter orbit ascent." That meant the planet would complete approximately three-quarters of a revolution in the fourteen hours expected for the ship to rise to the Allegro which, at the moment, was in a geo-synchronous orbit directly above them.

"Any traffic concerns?"

"There are routine flights out of JFK and LaGuardia airports so you'll need to watch your drift to avoid their flight paths." It had been hundreds of years since people boarded aircraft to go from city to city. Now, individual membrane pods propelled forward by an excellent grid of high-powered super-magnets provided far greater speed, using far less energy. But, to keep the Twentieth Century feel of the competition, the shuttles had to maneuver between ancient air lanes populated by holographic jet aircraft.

With a final "All Clear" from the control tower, Eaves pushed the electrical control lever that released the cold fusion rod in the main reactor forward, which, in turn, sent a flow of current to the lower membranes. Their anti-gravity-membrane computer instantly analyzed the content of the bedrock just a few feet under the surface of Central Park and the ship began to rise up confidently. Eaves delayed activating the upper membranes until he could get a feel for the various air currents.

"All four landing paws left the ground at precisely the same moment," said Carter with obvious satisfaction. As they reached an altitude of fifty meters, the breeze off the Hudson River caught their port side and the ship started to drift. Eaves activated the starboard membranes, advancing the control stick slowly until it's resistance matched the force of the wind. At five hundred feet the wind intensified and they sensed a rolling motion caused by updrafts from the city canyons.

"I think it's time to get out of here." Eaves cheerfully activated the massive upper membrane, which had lots of moisture to pull against in the heavy cloud cover. The ship's ascent rate increased noticeably and the wind started a rolling motion that was briefly disorienting. Eaves divided the upper and lower membranes into the traditional four quadrants, which allowed him to electronically compensate for some of the rolling motion by opposing the waves as they passed under and above the ship. In a few moments, the passenger cabin amidships was rock steady, although the outer edges of the ship continued to flex with each succeeding blast. Carter glanced at the passenger monitor and saw that everyone was settled comfortably in their seats.

"Clear of the buildings and well out of the airline flight paths," Carter called out in his routine voice. Their intra-ship communications were now being monitored in the judges' booth and the observation buildings. Once above 60,000 kilometers, they would have privacy, except for surface-to-shuttle or ship-to-shuttle communications, which would also be available for those wishing to listen in via the inter-stellar net.

Their assigned flight path called for a pass over New Jersey as the planet rotated beneath them. As the Hudson River drifted 40,000 meters below them, this was a perfectly routine flight. Suddenly alarm bells sounded and red warning lights started flashing on the instrument panel.

"Collision Warning! Collision Warning!" the computer repeated in an urgent tone.

Eaves reached down and hit the mute button.

"A high speed private jet is off course for a landing at Newark International," Carter said evenly. He pushed a button on his console and called out, "Unidentified aircraft, acknowledge hail and change course to 180 degrees east, vector 12 south." He'd activated an all-frequencies hail that would override all other communications in the area. It was standard operating procedure. The jet aircraft, however, continued its approach.

"Control tower, please identify alien jet and advise action." Protocol required that military aircraft submit to the direction of civilian command in such situations. But, at this point it was impossible to determine if the jet was a routine flight that was off-course or had a more sinister intent.

"Control tower, please respond!"

There was no response from the unidentified aircraft or the control tower. In fact there was absolute silence from all communications ports.

"I believe we've had two randoms thrown at us," said Carter, "An unidentified bogey and a communications failure."

"A great way to start the morning. How long before collision?"

"238 seconds on present course."

Eaves had a number of choices. If the unidentified aircraft continued on its present course, the standard response was to initiate an emergency descent, using maximum power to both upper and lower membranes. He took just five seconds to determine that because of the strength of the wind current, which was lifting the ship from the west, there was not enough time for the standard procedure. His only real choice was to re-direct all power to the forward membranes and depress their attitude more sharply, thus barely avoiding a collision. However, that would also throw the passengers out of their seats and perhaps start an uncontrolled spin towards the planet.

Instead of instituting the emergency dive, however, Eaves zoomed the starboard cameras to bring the unidentified ship into close focus.

"Quit wasting time!" said Carter as the computer screamed, "Collision Imminent! Collision Imminent! Take Evasive Action!"

"Travis, do something!"

Eaves punched a spot on his computer screen, which responded with an acknowledging beep. He shouted, "Hostile Alien! Fire anti-ship lasers and an air-to-air missile."

Carter froze for a moment, as did the passengers and crewmembers who were following the action on their video screen. But, his military discipline took over and Carter's fingers moved faster than the eye could follow. A blinding light seared out from the starboard side of the shuttlecraft as a missile deployed from its underbelly. The laser caught the enemy craft head on, obviously destroying its sensors. It started a high-speed spin towards the ground. Then the missile struck, incinerating it a fiery ball.

"What have you done?" cried Carter. "That was a real target, not a holograph. We've just killed people!"

Their instruments picked up an approaching missile launched by the destroyed alien ship. Eaves thrust the two forward quadrant controls to provide maximum lift, while executing a sharp turn to port. He mashed a button that Carter had never seen used before that controlled an old-fashioned grape canister cannon, which shot out debris three points below their starboard side. The lumbering shuttle inched up precipitously in the forward two quadrants while the aft quarters settled back. The missile was expected to strike in twelve seconds but, at ten seconds, it veered off course and exploded as it impacted one of the grape clusters. A tearing noise ground throughout the shuttle. The lights went out, throwing the passenger cabin into complete darkness.

Now there was absolute silence, except for the sound of Eaves working to bring the ship back level with the horizon. Then, all hell broke lose! The lights came back on, the communications panel lit up with more than a dozen incoming hails and the sound of all seven maintenance stations trying to report simultaneously overwhelmed the intercom system.

"Everyone quiet!" ordered Eaves. "Carter, don't answer any hails until I get a damage report. Mr. Price, follow standard reporting procedures and let me know the condition of the ship!"

"Yes, Sir. We've taken a number of shrapnel hits on the northeast quadrant, but fortunately there's enough outside air pressure to maintain environmental integrity. One power line was cut, which is why we went dark, but we've managed to restore power. All systems are functional."

"Casualties?"

"None among the crew and the chief steward reports just minor bruises and perhaps an arm sprain among the passengers."

"Very good."

Before he could turn to Carter, Price interrupted, "What happened, Sir? Why would a real ship attack us? There's never been a random like that."

Eaves looked at the anxious faces in the monitors, as well as Carter's, and replied, "I don't know for sure, but I do have a theory which I need to confirm with ground control. Mr. Price, how long will repairs take?"

"I've got all robots deployed and they should be able to patch the holes in about three hours. You can continue an ascent if you wish, but at some point I'll need to complete a pressure check for any small holes."

"Let me know when you're ready and we'll bring the ship to neutral. Will you be able to isolate the passenger cabin during the test? A pressure test is extremely painful to people's ears."

"Yes, Sir, I can."

"Thank you… and thank your crew for the excellent work. Okay, Jason, get me ground control."

"You have an Admiral on another hail."

"Like I said, ground control."

Upon contact, Eaves quickly brought ground control up to speed on the action they'd taken, as well as the damage suffered.

"Maintain your position and clear communications for an urgent connect to Fleet Command."

Colonel Kensington's face appeared on their monitor. "What the blazes have you two done up there? You shot down a live fighter in full view of half the quadrant. Explain yourself."

Four other monitors activated as others in the command structure came on line, including the image of the Chairman of the Joint Chief of Staff, the highest ranking Admiral in the Fleet, the Defense Minister and Captain Jesik. It was intimidating to say the least and Eaves hesitated briefly.

"Just tell us what happened, Travis," said Jesik.

"Yes, Sir. At first I thought it was a random and was about to take standard evasive action. But something in the shape of the ship caught my attention. I knew I'd seen it before and something was wrong. So I hesitated just long enough to confirm with the computer. I checked to see if it was a live ship or holographic image. Then I had three independent systems confirm its identity before I fired our laser blast and missile. Finally, I took evasive action to avoid their missile."

Kensington began to shout again, saying it was natural for the ship to launch a counter-missile after Eaves' attack, but the Chairman of the Joint Chiefs interrupted. "Tell us what you saw that made you launch your missile."

"Sir, the configuration was identical to the rebel fighters we encountered on Keswick. It is not part of our active fleet. Its approach was clearly hostile and if I didn't take action when I did it would be impossible to avoid contact."

"But how could you know it was hostile and not just an unexpected variation to the trials?"

"I wish I could tell you I had absolute knowledge, Sir, but I didn't. There wasn't time. But I could see from its exhaust plume that the ship was accelerating, not decelerating and it was aimed amidships, not forward or aft as one would expect if it was a fly-by. Finally, the computer positively identified it as Keswick rebel and so I felt I had no choice but to fire."

Eaves looked at the monitors, expectantly, saw that his explanation had done little to quell their uncertainty. Kensington glanced up several times, fury in his eyes.

"One more thing, Sir."

"Yes, Lieutenant?"

"I believe you'll find, Sir, that they actually fired their missile before we fired our weapons. It's just that the laser was instantaneous and it masked their launch."

Carter's fingers moved frantically over the keys. "He's right," said Carter in astonishment. "They did launch their missile first."

There was some whispered conversations on the monitors and then an unidentified officer came into the Admiral's monitor and handed him a printed readout. The Admiral looked up and said, "Our records verify what you've reported, Lieutenant. They did fire first. It appears your actions were definitely defensive in nature, although for the life of me I can't see how you figured that all out in fifteen seconds. Hold your current position while we assess what's happened. We'll need a political decision as to whether the trials can proceed."

"Yes Sir."

" And don't share this intelligence with anyone."

Kensington glowered from his monitor, but kept silent. A few moments later all four monitors went blank.

Carter saw Eaves relax, loosen his grip on the ship's controls. Even the color returned to his knuckles.

"So, how do you think the Keswick rebels got past Boundary Patrol?"

"You saw the ship, it was almost perfectly disguised as a private commercial aircraft. Boundary Patrol probably thought it was coming to join one of the parades."

"But, why disrupt the shuttle trials. What's to be gained? They had to know it would infuriate the entire system."

"You'll have to talk to Magill for a good answer for that." Eaves sounded dejected. "Politics is his specialty. My guess is that they hoped to provoke an overreaction by the government, which would piss off all the second and third-class families here. That would create the needed dissent to bring their revolution to Kalenden. I'd bet everything in my wallet that a similar incident has, or will happen on Alturus. It's an act of terrorism that'll shake up a few star systems and that turned you and me into killers."

Glancing down, Eaves saw that Carter's hands were trembling. "You did great, Jason. I know you thought I was crazy to order the attack, but you followed my orders anyway. It took a lot of courage. Thanks."

Carter looked away momentarily and acted like he wanted to say something, but couldn't. It had probably been a lot tougher to follow that order than he wanted to admit.

"Let's check on our passengers. After all, their comfort is the second most important factor in our overall score."

Carter smiled and said, "I think that's the ship's Commanders job. I'll watch the console while you go back and talk with them."

Eaves was more than his usual charming self. He apologized for the bumpy ride, explained that a non-holographic ship had launched a missile and that he'd taken the necessary precautions to protect the ship. The minor damage they'd suffered would soon be repaired and their shuttle was now in the safest place in the universe, since a full-scale military alert was providing them with complete fighter protection. Perhaps it was the confident demeanor that he exuded but the passengers all relaxed.

Turning to a steward he said, "I understand you have new clothing for each of our passengers." Then, looking at the floor, which still showed spilled coffee and snacks, he continued, "Perhaps this would be a good time for them to take a break and clean up."

"Yes, Sir," said the steward, happy to be noticed. "Before takeoff, we contacted their home planet to learn each of our guest's measurements, fabric preference, etc. We'll be glad to provide them each a private cubicle to collect their thoughts and change. Then we'll serve an early luncheon, if that's alright with you, Sir."

Eaves looked around at the astonished passengers, amazed that life was to go on as normal in spite of what they'd been through. He was pleased and embarrassed when they applauded.

"Show them the way, Steward. It seems they like your style!"

Nearly three hours later they received word from Fleet Headquarters. Fortunately, the guests weren't impatient, since they'd all budgeted plenty of time for a leisurely ascent to the Allegro. But it had been nerve-wracking for Eaves and Carter. Every communications hail was answered immediately, but all proved to be routine updates and course corrections. While their shuttle sat motionless in the atmosphere, the planet continued to rotate, which meant they'd passed into a new air control sector.

Finally, exhausted by the waiting, Captain Jesik initiated the awaited hail. Eaves was visibly relieved when Jesik informed him that it was decided that the Trials would continue. A planetary search confirmed the destroyed fighter as the only one of its kind on the planet and so the Prime Minister announced that he was not going to let the terrorists stop the games. The entire planetary defense establishment went on full alert and the increased security would make it safe for the games to carry on. Eaves wished Jesik had used a secure channel, so he could pass on a concern he'd been thinking about, but it was an open link and anyone might be listening, so he kept his thoughts to himself. Jesik wished them good luck and signed off.

The robots finished their initial repair to the hull, so Carter cleared a new flight plan and Eaves resumed their ascent.

"I guess it was dumb luck that at the precise moment the fighter attacked us, the computer threw us our first random, the communications blackout."

Eaves smiled at Carter and agreed. Then he initiated a quick communications blackout, so that no one could overhear his next comment. "It was either bad luck, or someone in the command structure is in league with the terrorists."

A cold chill shot up Carter's spine. "There might be more?"

"I don't know. Probably not. But we have to be on full alert for the next four days, which is why I want you to take a nap right now so that you'll be fresh when I get tired. But make it a short one."

Carter knew better than to argue with Eaves, so he stepped back to the small cot nestled in an alcove behind his position. He assumed it'd be impossible to fall asleep, but was startled when the alarm woke him a couple of hours later.

The rest of the ascent went without incident. They reached static orbit, where the anti-gravity-membranes lost their effectiveness, at precisely three hours behind their initial estimated time of arrival. Commander Brighton positioned the Allegro ten kilometers above them and the shuttle pulled forward. The docking maneuver was flawless and the shuttle's passengers stepped easily through the pressure seal into the comfort of the Allegro where they were escorted to visitor's quarters for a shower and some much needed-sleep.

The only dangerous part of the whole operation was when O'Casey got a look at the shuttle's hull. He'd flown up earlier on a high-speed propellant shuttle and now widely cursed the terrorists, Eaves, Carter, even his own parents for having children. He deployed his entire maintenance crew to inspect the shuttle, with special attention to the robot welds.

Then, after making an appropriate show of indignation, he pulled Carter and Eaves aside quietly and said, "Naturally the entire shuttle service is up-in-arms about what happened. Everyone on the planet is speculating whether you were the specific target of the terrorist attack because of the Allegro's role in suppressing the Keswick Rebellion, or if the fighter simply meant to destroy the first shuttlecraft to launch. One thing for sure, if it had been any other team, their shuttle would lie in pieces on the planet surface. At any rate, I'm not sure it's over, so you two have to be extra cautious."

It was Carter who replied. "Thank you, Mr. O'Casey, but I think that if we were specifically targeted, the reason may be that we're both from first-class families. It wouldn't do the rebels any good to blow up just anybody."

Eaves was surprised by Carter's words. They showed good insight to the political aspect of the situation, something Carter usually ignored.

"Could be." O'Casey nodded. "With your permission, I'll pass that comment along to Shuttle Command. They need all the information they can get right now, for the whole planet is in an uproar and the authorities are scrambling to make it look like they're in full control of the situation."

He studied the two Lieutenants, who looked dead tired. "I know you have some post-flight details to follow-up on, but leave them to me if you will. I want you to both to head to your quarters for some food and high-quality sleep. You're already three hours behind schedule and will have to leave early tomorrow afternoon for your next round of trials. So good night!"

Carter and Eaves gratefully accepted his offer and stumbled off to their cabins where they skipped the food and went straight to bed.

* * *

At 07:00 the next morning, Eaves made his way to the Recreation Deck, where he spent an hour water-skiing on the simulator. He loved skiing when the surface of the water was smooth as a highly-polished mirror, a phenomenon that occurred twice each day as the sun rose above the horizon and again when it set. The calming red-rock scenery of Colorado provided a needed diversion to the winter storms that occur on Kalenden. After that, he played racquetball for another hour, then took a leisurely shower and steam bath. By noon, he was famished, but chose to eat only a simulated seafood salad and fruit juice since he made it his policy to never eat anything heavy before flying.

Carter dealt with his nervous energy in a different way. He spent the morning reading a novel he'd put off for three months. It was an old Earth science-fiction novel that was a real scream to read some four hundred years after it was written. The ancient English grammar was sometimes difficult to interpret, but was the kind of challenge he enjoyed.

At 16:00, he met Eaves at the shuttle to review their flight plan and at 17:00 the small crew re-boarded. As it unfolded from its docking bay, Eaves strained to see signs of the damage from the previous day but found none, for O'Casey had his crew work all through the night to reinforce the robot welds and buff the exterior to a dazzling silver sheen. A maintenance man whispered that O'Casey had even unfolded it in the middle of the night and ran a second pressure check on the structure, including the passenger compartment. So, barring any new threats, they were in great shape mechanically.

I wish the same could be said about the weather, thought Eaves. The forecast for Wednesday showed gale warnings. Two shuttles had already washed out of the competition by either forfeiture or getting so far off course, they couldn't complete their drills.

"Jason, I think we're going to need our modifications. Can you configure the computer to make the necessary adjustments to the membranes?"

"I've already stored the program, so I can initiate it immediately. And, I've noticed you don't give a person a lot of warning when you need something."

"I always intend to do better, but then life throws me the equivalent of a random. Sorry about that."

Only two-thirds of their scheduled passengers boarded, all a bit nervous. There were no further incidents since their encounter the previous day, but the risk of another attack was enough to frighten some of them into taking the high-speed shuttle back with O'Casey. Still, the stewards did their best to reassure those who did board and made them as comfortable as possible.

Separation from the Allegro was always an impressive sight. As large as the shuttle was, it was dwarfed by the massive hulk of the battle-cruiser and at the moment of separation, the morning star splashed the alinite hull with a brilliant crimson reflection that increased the ship's grandeur. The planet's atmosphere radiated an iridescent golden glow that also illuminated the natural skylights of the shuttle. It produced a good omen for the trip ahead.

As they drifted into the lower atmosphere, they hadn't yet encountered their second random and Carter had convinced himself that Flight Control was going to count the terrorist attack in lieu of another random. That's when all onboard power failed, causing a sickening lurch as the shuttle began dropping uncontrolled to the planet below. At 300,000 meters, the only thing to do was to let the ship drift, leaf-like, back and forth in the atmosphere. There was no danger at this point, but it did make some of the crew and passengers a bit nauseous. Eaves instructed the crew to manually unfurl several large sails that slowed their descent even further. Then he made his way back to engineering.

"Is this a real emergency or a random?" he asked Sergeant Price.

"I'm not supposed to tell you until you figure it out, but after yesterday, you deserve to know it's a random."

"Good, I'm not up for anything too serious. Let's figure why the system failed, so we can program in a correction and regain power."

It took about fifteen minutes to isolate the computer-generated problem. The cold fusion rod was supposed to have slipped from its mount inside the reactor because of some earlier turbulence. Using a robotic arm, Sergeant Price was able to re-establish the connection and full lighting and power replaced the puny emergency lighting of the previous half-hour. Through the intercom system they could hear the passengers applaud.

Returning to the bridge, he turned to Carter as he settled into his seat, "See, I'm not always a jinx!"

They prepared for the storms now just 100,000 meters below. The sails were furled, all unoccupied compartments were folded in to increase structural integrity and non-essential systems idled so that maximum power could be directed to the anti-gravity-membranes. Then there was nothing to do but wait.

Their flight plan called for an approach up the East River until they were even with Sixty-Seventh Street, then drift over the Upper East Side until they reached their assigned landing pad in Central Park. The problem with this approach were the high winds blowing from the southeast and they would have to pass over the observation buildings, meaning they'd have to come in higher than usual, with greater exposure to the wind. One wrong move could prove very embarrassing. At 09:30, they were being buffeted mercilessly, although Eaves was able to keep most of the movement to the outer edges. The passengers had acceded to his request that they buckle their lap and shoulder belts, although that was a seldom used precaution on shuttle trips. Of course, most shuttles would simply not fly on a day like this, or choose an alternate landing point several hundred kilometers to the west.

At 09:50 they successfully fought their way up the river and started their drift eastward. With no forward motion to steady them, the ship began to warp violently, creating the real risk that a sudden downdraft might pull them into the buildings below.

"Time for Phase I modification," said Eaves. This time he received absolutely no static from anyone. They were all scared witless and ready to do anything to stabilize the ship. Carter punched in a series of commands to his computer and the systems' monitor immediately reorganized itself from the standard four control zones on upper and lower membrane into twelve. That meant Eaves could now use twenty-four anti-gravity-membrane zones to respond to changes in the air pressure above and below the ship. Such a thing had never been tried before and the communications panel immediately lit up with hails from ground control asking what was going on.

"Carter, you tell them what they need to know" Eaves voice betrayed the strain he was under. "I need full concentration to manage all this." His face was buried in his main video monitor, which was programmed to display the air currents passing around the ship. He used a second monitor to control twenty-four virtual joysticks that controlled each one of the membrane panels. At first the ship bucked even more violently than before the reorientation and there was the sound of dinner plates crashing to the floor in the galley behind them. Then slowly, but surely, Eaves found the rhythm of the wind and acted in harmony with it. Instead of huge, lurching motions that threatened to tip the ship on its side, it undulated evenly in the breeze, with the air currents moving across it like a wave through water. Even though the winds were nearly hurricane force on the ground, the passenger cabin stabilized to where it was almost motionless. More confident than before, he moved the shuttle to the proper position above their landing pad and began his final descent. Now nearly full power was being channeled to the port membranes to resist the wind coming at them from starboard. Ever so slowly the giant ship settled towards the ground as Eaves' hands flashed madly, controlling drift and descent. At 10:06, just fifteen minutes after their scheduled arrival, the ship was about to land.

"Steady, steady, There!" Eaves yelled exultantly, as he released the final energy.

"What's that," Carter replied.

"What?"

"Look, Travis, the main observation building has torn free from its mooring cables and is headed straight for us!"

They felt the giant landing paws touch, but immediately Eaves shoved the lift controls forward to rise as quickly as possible. That close to the ground, the greater than 100% humidity in the air gave them incredible lift and the vehicle shot up like a rocket.

Eaves quickly illuminated his side view panel to see what was happening to the observation building (which was shaped like the whimsical Guggenheim Museum). It was still tethered by a single mooring cable, but clearly could not hold for long. The anti-gravity-membrane on the observation platform was programmed for only repulsion from the ground, since gravity was used to lower it onto its foundation. There was no way the pilot of the platform could resist the force of the wind and re-land it. Just as Eaves feared, the final cable snapped and the giant platform began a tumble to the west, directly through the Park.

"Time for modification two," as Eaves activated a second virtual panel. Judging the drift of the building, which was also rising, he told Carter and

Price "We've got to get under the building and use our anti-gravity-membrane to attract it to us. We'll act like a magnet and gain control of both structures.

"But its weight will crush us," Price replied.

"Not if we tell their commander to keep his anti-gravity repulsion on. That should keep the building significantly lighter than normal, right until we cinch up. Then we'll have to use a pattern of attraction and repulsion to balance the weight while it's tethered to us. Carter, establish contact with their control room. Price, I need you and your men to mobilize the robots to tie the building down as we near the ground. Let's go!"

Their plan appeared futile, since the building was about to roll over. There was simply no way the shuttle could respond fast enough to maneuver into position. At least no traditional way.

"Firing starboard thrusters," called Eaves into the microphone. Until now, there had never been starboard thrusters on a full membrane shuttle. The flames from four thrusters quickly illuminated the outside video monitors as the ship shot eastward. Eaves half-listened on Carter's conversation with Ground Control and the observation platform and understood the disbelief in their voices. But what else was there to do?

Using a visual approach, the shuttle came up rather sharply under the building. Then Eaves executed a series of commands to the upper anti-gravity-membrane. In what had to be a frightening scene, a ten-story airship, made to resemble a building, began to move directly towards them. Their membranes had made a successful lock on the building. Eaves now fired the rockets at the bow of the shuttle to hold it in place as the building drew nearer, threatening to crash into the shuttle and destroying all forward compartments.

"Execute pulsing maneuvers on the membrane, Mr. Price!" Price initiated the pattern on his own control panel and the pulsing sound was different than anything ever heard on a shuttle, but its effectiveness was immediate as the building slowed its advance and stabilized.

"Now we'll use the upper twelve-panel array to pull it above us so its weight is distributed evenly over us. Since we're three times larger than the building platform, I want to center it on our front third, so that no matter what happens we don't injure our passengers."

Price acknowledged and helped Eaves with the controls. As the weight of the huge platform connected with the shuttle, both started settling dangerously and Eaves directed maximum power to the lower membranes. "I need more power, Mr. Price."

Price pushed the cold-fusion reactor past its' redline and held his breath.

They were able to stop the descent and rise farther above the buildings on Park West, including the Dakotas, which was now directly under the shuttle/observation building combo. Looking at his underbelly monitor, Eaves could see hundreds of people streaming from the Dakotas, including most of the competing crews.

A warning siren sounded on the port side. "The rockets are running low on fuel and without them, we're dead. Can you divert fuel from the starboard rockets?"

"I'll get on it, Sir." Price ran from the control room, shouting into his communications device as he went.

"All we need is a three-minute burn," said Carter anxiously.

At ninety seconds one of the rockets flamed out. Then another. The ship started drifting west again.

"Mr. Price, now would be a really great time for that fuel transfer."

"Try now, Mr. Eaves."

Eaves punched the rocket firing control and both rockets flared back to life. It took a ninety second burn to compensate for the drift and to center them over the observation buildings' mooring locomotives.

"Deploy the robots."

Outside the aircraft, a small army of robots swarmed up the side of the shuttle and onto the corners of the observation shuttle, snaking cables along the way. Small arc welders flamed as they attached cables to the observation shuttle and then dropped them to the ground where a waiting maintenance crew reattached them. After what seemed an eternity, the surface-to-ship communications port reported, "Cables secure!"

Everyone cheered, including Eaves.

"Jason, instruct the building to float up and away from us. I'll release our attraction on your word."

Carter spoke into his headset, then gave Eaves a thumbs-up. The pulsing sound ceased and the building lifted away from the shuttlecraft with a large groan. Eaves fired the starboard rockets and the shuttlecraft slipped out from under the building, into the safety of Central Park. He quickly maneuvered the shuttle in the direction of their landing pod, then cut all the rockets.

"Why are you shutting down the thrusters?" Carter asked.

"We're going to land this the right way—I don't want any smart-ass saying we couldn't." Now using only the membranes, Eaves brought the shuttle in for a near perfect landing, just twenty-two centimeters off center and less than one meter off square at the corners. As the ship settled onto its paws, Eaves powered down the overheated reactor and, after catching his breath, stood to leave the control room, his uniform dripping in sweat. He'd been so caught up in the crisis, he hadn't thought about what was coming next, which is why he was startled to be greeted the thunderous applause of the passengers and assembled crew. Then they all charged him, slapping him on the back and congratulating him and Carter. It was one of those rare occasions when Travis Eaves was speechless.

12 — THE SECOND KESWICK REBELLION

"The problem with rebellions is that they attract rebellious people," said Magill a bit desperately. For the second time in his brief diplomatic career he was holed up in the former Royal Palace, now called the Palace of the People. Outside there was gunfire—the old fashioned kind where bullets are propelled by exploding cartridges. While not as dramatic as laser blasts, their victim is every bit as dead if hit in the proper place. Or wounded and maimed if hit elsewhere.

"We've got to get Lansing. As shrewd as he is, he underestimated the antipathy of the former Loyalists, and now he's the one holed up in the palace with an angry mob swarming outside." Major Wilkerson was, indeed, the right man for the job—because now the job had become military; defending the new governing council. In just a matter of months, well before any long-term changes to the political system could settle in, the general populous had become restive, in part because of the genuine suffering caused by the destruction of their crops from the effects of the nuclear blasts that had left the current harvest ruined by radiation. Hunger was growing, traders from distant quadrants had stopped calling because of the uncertainty of the political situation, and the promised prosperity of the great rebellion had not yet materialized. That it would be improbable-to-impossible for all the promises to be fulfilled in such a short time made little difference, particularly when a group of fanatical Loyalists produced a new heir to throne—the supposed grand-nephew of the King.

Magill shook his head. "The one rule that has to be obeyed in a revolution is that if you're going to take out a royal family you have to be sure kill all potential heirs. That's the only way to end the monarchy once and for all. It was a lesson that well served Lenin in the 20th Century Wars back on Earth."

"Now you're the one who sounds bloodthirsty," said Wilkerson, quickly checking around a corner.

"Not bloodthirsty; dismayed. I thought all of that was ancient history and that humans had overcome such things. It's depressing to think that we act just like the ancient Romans, the Nazis, the Communists, the City Gangs of the 21st Century, and the Separatists of the 22nd. For all our morality we haven't learned anything!"

"You go ahead and be depressed about history, I'm worried about right now. Are you okay to move out?"

Magill nodded, and followed Wilkerson into the hallway. It sounded as if there was fighting going on some place in the palace, but it wasn't here. The Unified Governing Coalition had taken up residence in what had formerly been the king's cabinet room. That's where they expected to find Lansing. "We've got to get him out to a safe location where he can still tie into the planetary broadcast system," said Wilkerson. "The thing I do know about revolutions is that they most often go to the side that controls the flow of information."

Magill had grown so accustomed to his crutches by now that he was easily able to keep up with Wilkerson. "There it is. Stop, Look, Listen. That's the most basic of commands." So they stopped, looked at both what was visible and used their personal assistants to scan for traces of heartbeats or other indications of life in the hallway and surrounding corridors, and then they listened. They could hear voices in the Cabinet Room, but nothing to indicate hostility, so they made their way to the door, flashed their security keys, and then stepped in when the door opened automatically.

Not a good move. They stepped through just in time to see someone wearing Loyalist colors slug Lansing in the gut, sending him to the ground. Lansing's body guard's lay dead on the floor, blood staining the rich carpet under their bodies. As dismaying as this was to Wilkerson and Magill, it was remarkably energizing to the four assailants, who now turned and attempted to fire on Magill and Wilkerson. But, as skilled as they were, they weren't fast enough for the Major, who, with the advantage of being the one to open the door, had time to bring his weapon to bear on three of the four, firing his laser in an arc that tore open their bellies, thus sending them gurgling to the floor in agony. The fourth, who was standing close to the door where Magill had entered, was not in the line of fire and he quickly brought his weapon to bear on Wilkerson. Seeing the danger, Magill cried out in a furious shout, "Noooooo…." and lunged for the assailant. The sight of a crippled man with crutches flying through the air was so unnerving that the fellow turned his weapon on Magill. "Not good enough," shouted Magill as he expertly extended the crutch in his right hand to bat away the weapon. The shock of that maneuver was enough to make the fellow fall back, which meant that Magill's only recourse at this point, given that his feet had given out from under him, was to fall on top of the would be assassin. Magill started pounding, the Loyalist pounded back, in what was a fairly even match until the fellow managed to get his hands around Magill's throat. Struggling to free his airway with his right hand, Magill placed his left hand on the throat of his opponent and now it was a fight to see who could hold out for air the longest. Magill struggled desperately, knowing the outcome was life for one and death for the other. He wasn't at all certain he would be the survivor.

Then Wilkerson shot a piercing green ray, 1/64 of an inch in diameter, directly through the Loyalist's skull. The light blinded Sean and the heat of the beam instantly cauterized all the blood vessels that were ruptured by the beam so that there was no blood. The hand that had been gripping Magill's throat loosened immediately, but the hand at the end of Magill's arm continued to strangle the now dead assailant. "It's alright Sean," said Wilkerson quietly. "You can let go now." The sound of his first name shocked him out of the almost trancelike state he was in, and he recoiled in horror. "What happened!"

"You saved my life. That's what happened."

"But, you killed him. You saved me."

Wilkerson reached down and extended a hand to Sean. "You were willing to die for me. That's the greatest sacrifice a soldier can make." He pulled Magill up; the young man was trembling. "It's alright to feel bad that a man has died. I hope I always feel remorse, even when I know it's the right thing." By now Lansing had joined them. He too was shaken.

"I don't know how they got in. We were alone in here, monitoring the situation outside the palace, when all of a sudden these four just materialized. They must have rehearsed it all because they knew exactly who my guards were, and they killed them before we even realized what was happening!"

"It's hidden panels and tunnels," said Magill. "They're all over this palace. It's how we made our escape after the royal family was murdered." By now Wilkerson had handed him his crutch and Sean made his way to a chair where he sat down to take pressure off his feet.

"I suppose more will be coming in a few moments," said Wilkerson, checking to make sure that his energy pack was fully recharged.

Lansing shook his head. "Not right now. I just got a message that our guard held at the palace gates. We had to turn water cannons on the protesters, but we've managed to drive them back. The whole episode was likely a ruse to make it possible for these guys to get in. Once their life monitors winked out the organizers, whoever they are, undoubtedly concluded that it was time to fall back. But this is far from over."

Just as Wilkerson was about to say something the door burst open and a half dozen men came tumbling in the room. Lansing held up his hands to let them know that he was alive and then stepped between the newcomers and Wilkerson and Magill to protect them from being blasted into eternity. "It's alright—they're Kalenden's who just saved my life!" The leader of the group looked skeptical, but told his men to stand down. "So what happened in here?" asked the man.

"I'll explain it to you later, if that's alright. Right now I need to assemble the Council to figure out what to do next. Would you mind seeing to these bodies?"

The man nodded and Lansing motioned for Wilkerson and Magill to follow him to an adjoining room. Sean stood up painfully, but refused help. He quickly followed them out of the room.

Once they had a private place Lansing opened a number of communications links to summon the council. When he was finished he turned to them and said, "We have about twenty minutes. I'd appreciate your thoughts on what's happening and how we can stabilize things—that is assuming that you want them stabilized."

Wilkerson turned to Sean. "That's more a question for Commander Magill. All I know is that we were attacked and we survived. What are your thoughts, Commander?"

Sean bit his lip. "At this point I haven't heard anything from the Alturians to suggest that they are ready to throw in with the Loyalists, even though they may have natural sympathies that way. They are a hard lot to figure out. The fact that their Royal family told them to support the UCG is likely enough to keep them loyal. But we need to seek them out and find out where they stand for sure. A move back to Royalty could play to their benefit."

"As all this heated up their ambassador assured me they were firmly on the side of the UCG," said Lansing. "But who knows what will happen?"

"It also surprises me that the situation could turn so quickly. If I were you I'd do an instant planet-wide poll to see what people are thinking. They can respond to a limited set of questions through the social network and you'll know pretty quickly how deep this division runs. Your people will have to be careful how they pose the questions since whoever is leading this new rebellion will try to flood the response system with their own supporters to make it look like they have more strength than they really do."

"Makes good sense," said Lansing.

"But no matter what it shows," said Lansing, "as long as there is an aspiring successor to the throne we'll have trouble."

"Commander Magill tells me that in the old days you'd just have him killed." They couldn't tell if Wilkerson was attempting humor or if he was actually serious.

"Yes, well, that's not an option. But it is a problem."

The three of them fell silent. The odds against a peaceful resolution seemed very remote, now.

Magill broke the silence. "What do you know about this grand-nephew?"

"Not much. We have a name and a face. The name is consistent with the royal family and he looks like he could be related."

"Would it matter if he were illegitimate?"

Lansing raised an eyebrow. "It would make all the difference in the world. We have never recognized a bastard child as a legitimate successor."

"So, how do you know if he is legitimate or not?"

"We don't. I suppose all that will have to be worked out if this fringe element gains more popular support."

"But why don't you just check out his DNA signature?" asked Wilkerson.

Lansing sighed. "Because one of the ways we chose to distinguish ourselves from Alturus and Kalenden is that we never joined the international DNA registry. You've got to remember that many of our founding families were considered outcast by the Alturus elite, so they didn't want to give them any more information they had to. Unlike the two of you, privacy laws keep our records private."

Magill shook his head. "I wish Captain Jesik were here. He'd have an idea."

Wilkerson smiled at the thought that Magill didn't realize what a potential insult that was to Wilkerson's leadership. "I wish so, too. He's kind of the perfect blend between us; me the military man, you the political philosopher."

Magill looked up quickly and stumbled on his words, "I didn't mean any offense, Major. You're the best there is…"

Wilkerson waved his hand. "No offense taken. The captain is a remarkably agile thinker."

"It's just that he liked to pose dilemmas and have us struggle to find unorthodox solutions. Dilemmas are problems that appear to have no favorable solution since one answer comes at the expense of another."

Lansing nodded. "Well, I have to get ready for my cabinet meeting…"

"Wait! I have an idea." Magill's countenance had fallen as a result of this revelation, not brightened as one would expect.

"What is it, Commander? Somehow I don't think I'll like it," said Wilkerson.

"How would I get close to this aspirant to the throne—really close; close enough to touch him?"

"I think that's virtually impossible unless we discover where he's hiding and storm the place. That would not go down well on the social network."

Magill shook his head slowly. "That's what I thought. So we'll have to do it another way."

Lansing sat back down. "Tell me what you're thinking. I need to know quickly."

Magill looked up, resolve forming on his features. "I can't tell you my plan, Prime Minister. If I'm wrong it would discredit you. I need to go in there on my own, taking my chances that my hunch is right."

"And if it's wrong?" asked Wilkerson.

"Then you two will have to figure this out on your own, because I will very likely not come out of it alive."

"What is it? You've got to tell us." Lansing was impatient now.

"No. If you let me do this it may save the situation. I honestly don't see any other way."

"But how will you get close to this man—particularly without our help?"

Magill bit his lower lip. "Because I will publicly disavow you and say that I am sympathetic to the Loyalist revolt."

"What?" said the two in unison. Then, Lansing, "No way, that would shake our coalition completely." In trying to get that out he competed with Wilkerson's, "There's no way; it would completely discredit Kalenden in future negotiations."

Magill held up his hand to quiet them. "You'll both have to disavow me publicly. I'll disappear into the underground and I promise that they'll find me. The chance to have a Kalenden delegate on their side will prove irresistible, and once I'm in I can execute my plan. Remember, I'm adopted into a second class family – maybe natural born to the third class."

"How will we know if you're successful?" Wilkerson was truly shaken at this point.

Magill smiled. "If I'm successful the whole planet will know it – at least if PM Lansing will let me switch protocols on my personal assistant with one of your clear channel ones."

Lansing glanced down at his assistant. "You mean you'd send a signal out to the entire network at once?"

Magill nodded. "If I'm right, I can discredit this movement completely. But to do so I've got to infiltrate them first."

"But we'll send in someone anonymous. You're not the only one who can do this. And with your feet…"

"I'm the only one who will gain instant acceptance because of my notoriety. It could take months for a non-descript operative to gain their confidence."

Lansing sat back in his chair, tipped his head back, and rubbed his forehead with his fingers.

"But if you're wrong…"

"If I'm wrong, I will disappear into obscurity. You'll find another way to maintain control and I'll be a footnote in history."

"But why would you do this, Sean? You're putting everything on the line—your life and your reputation."

"Because there is much more than the success or failure of the United Governing Coalition at stake here. If the Loyalists succeed in upsetting the revolution the second and third class families on Alturus, and maybe even Kalenden will be outraged. I'm absolutely certain that there will be elements on both planets that believe the Alturian royalty was behind the coup, and that will completely destabilize things there. What happens on Keswick will not stay on Keswick. So the stakes are too high to take a risk."

"And you'd risk your own life?" asked Lansing.

"You both have—why should I do any less?"

"And how do I know you are not truly defecting?" Lansing's eyes narrowed.

Magill raised his hand to silence Wilkerson's indignant response. "You will have to decide for yourself if I've done anything to suggest betrayal. All I have is what you see."

Lansing took a deep breath, turned to Wilkerson who nodded. "I never really questioned your loyalty, but I had to ask." He took a deep breath. "Alright then, we'll have to trust you to implement your idea. But we're going to record the fact that this is an espionage mission and if you don't make it out we will not let your name be tarnished. We will not do that."

"You'll have to for a while," replied Sean. "Otherwise the population will think that it was your idea and they will be furious with you." When they started to protest he cut them short, "It's alright. I'll die someday, anyway. And, when the records are released, however many years from now, people will either think me heroic or traitorous depending on who ultimately wins control here." He smiled. "Which means that if I'm one day to be exonerated you two have to maintain control!"

No one laughed. Wilkerson felt sick to his stomach, and said so. But he knew they must proceed. "Alright then, how do we make it happen?"

"Well, the most important thing is this. If you get the signal that I hope to send, then that's when you send in the Cavalry with guns blazing, if necessary. The moment the message goes out I will be in trouble."

"Where do you come up with these homilies?" asked Wilkerson. "Cavalry and guns blazing?"

"Doesn't anyone around here like ancient history?" He paused, but neither replied. "Just be prepared to move in fast. I'll need you."

13— MANHATTAN TRIALS

The celebration on the shuttlecraft was nothing compared to what awaited them at the observation platform that evening. The first two hours after their landing was spent in intense debriefing at Sector Control, followed by an impromptu parade down Broadway, where the crowds were jubilant. Fortunately, the bad weather had eased and everyone was festive again.

The shuttle crew made the trip north, up Park Avenue, to the Guggenheim. A line of dignitaries, wanting to have their picture taken with members of the crew, made them instant celebrities. Even the Allegro's passengers were sought after for their first-hand account of events, since it wasn't not every day that members of the Quadrant Council and CEO's of more than four dozen of the Quadrant's largest corporations nearly lost their lives.

Both Eaves and Carter had grown up in influential families, so the idea of a reception wasn't as intimidating to them as to other members of the crew, but it was hard for them to concentrate when so many people were trying to get their attention. Twice Eaves saw Captain Jesik in the distance, but was never able to make his way over to talk with him. Finally, after nearly two hours of mingling, the crowd eased a bit and he was able to move to the side of the room where Jesik motioned for him to bring Carter to him. As they came closer, Eaves saw Colonel Kensington standing next to Jesik and he didn't look happy. *What now?*

Jesik ushered them into a small conference room and closed the door. Brighton and O'Casey were already there, looking sullen. Kensington told them to sit down and puffed himself up to deliver what was obviously a well-rehearsed speech.

"You two are to be commended for saving the observation platform. I can't deny you acted with great presence of mind. Some call it brilliant, which is clearly an exaggeration, since all you did was your duty. Still, I believe in giving credit where it's due."

Carter shifted uneasily in his chair, wondering what the next "but" was going to bring.

"However, having acknowledged your contribution, I have to express the shame I feel for the callous attempt on your part to win the competition through subterfuge and deceit."

"What subterfuge?" Carter nudged Eaves' knee under the table. There was no sense stirring Kensington up even more.

"The modifications you made to your ship placed all the other competitors at a disadvantage, enabling you to win at their expense.

"But, Sir, we did nothing that was outside the rules!"

"Of course not. But as gentlemen you should know that the spirit of the games are far more important than the actual outcome. We are a planet of time-honored traditions and as members of the best families you should know that. Instead you've brought shame on your service and your own good names."

Eaves was ready to jump up and hit Kensington, but Carter grabbed his leg so hard Eaves let out a small yelp.

"Sir, the Lieutenants were simply attempting to give the very best performance they were capable of."

"So, Jesik, you were part of this shameless conspiracy? Why am I not surprised?"

"Captain Jesik and Mister O'Casey had no idea of these modifications, Sir, so they bear no responsibility."

"Even worse, Mr. Eaves. It's inconceivable that you would deceive your leaders or that they would be so…"

Eaves attempted to interrupt again, but Kensington cut him off sharply.

"So, Lieutenant, the honorable course is to disqualify yourself from the competition and issue an apology for what you've done. I'm sure your popularity will overshadow the deceit and perhaps even allow you to one day advance in the service. Of course Allegro will not be allowed to engage in the games for a very long time."

Just then a young Lieutenant stuck his head in the door. Kensington turned on him with a fury, "Can't you see we're in an important conference. Close the door immediately!"

"Begging your pardon, Sir, but Admiral Showalter wishes to speak to the crew of the Allegro shuttlecraft, as well as their commanding officers."

The Lieutenant pushed the door open all the way, as Kensington moved back against the whiteboard behind him. Admiral Showalter, acting chairman of the Joint Chiefs of Staff and the highest ranking officer in Space Fleet Command, entered the room, accompanied by Commodore Park, head of Shuttle of Service and General Josephs, chief of Homeland Security. Everyone rose and saluted. Kensington attempted to say something, but Admiral Showalter went straight to Jesik and shook his hand.

"Jesik, congratulations to you and your crew on a magnificent performance at the trials today. What a splendid example of courage and ingenuity." Then turning to the two Lieutenants he said, "It turns out that I owe my life to you two and your crew. I was aboard the observation platform. On behalf of everyone there, please accept our thanks."

Carter's face flushed and Eaves averted his eyes as he took the Admiral's hand. Continuing, the Admiral said, "I knew your father at the Academy, Lieutenant Eaves. A very solid person, but I didn't get the sense that he was as unorthodox as you are."

"No, Sir, he isn't. I'm afraid I've caused him some sleepless nights throughout the years."

"Well, he should be proud today. Your handling of the shuttlecraft was superb, the best I've ever seen."

Kensington was quiet, but the smoldering look in his eyes indicated the battle wasn't over.

Admiral Showalter continued. "The reason I interrupted your meeting is that my two associates have some urgent business to conduct with you. Commodore…"

"Thank you, Admiral. Please accept my congratulations as well. As far as I can tell that's the first time in history a shuttle has used its anti-gravity-membranes to control another ship. It was simply brilliant."

That did it! Kensington couldn't stand it any longer. He wanted to be acknowledged as the first to recognize their affront to the rules of the games, so he interrupted.

"Their rescue was indeed remarkable, Commodore, but I was in the process of explaining to the Lieutenants how their modifications to the shuttlecraft were entirely out of harmony with the spirit of the games and I was urging them to withdraw from the competition. Of course the ultimate responsibility for their behavior falls on Captain Jesik." He attempted to show the gravity of the situation, while suppressing his obvious pleasure at jabbing Jesik.

"Withdraw from the competition?" asked Park in an incredulous voice. "Why would they withdraw from the competition? Their performance today was in the best tradition of the games."

The statement completely discomfited Kensington, whose satisfaction turned slowly to horror. "But, Sir, they violated time honored traditions of keeping the competition equal."

"Ah," said Park, "there's the old 'let's keep it civil' approach. Also, the safe way to mediocrity." Turning from Kensington to Eaves and Carter he said, "I don't know if you're aware of this or not, but the original purpose of the Shuttle Trials was to foster a spirit of innovation in the service. The earliest contests were absolute nightmares for everyone involved; passengers, crew and the ships they docked with. The trials were envisioned as a way to encourage teams to think outside the usual and to come up with ways to use the shuttles more effectively. Some of our greatest advances came as a result of secret modifications made for the trials. For example, moving the passenger compartment to the center of the ship where there's less turbulence was one. One year, a ship added stewards and the four-panel membrane came about as a result of a ship crashing when hit by a wind-shear."

Turning back to Kensington he continued, "Colonel, I'm sure your motives are well-intentioned, but in this instance these lieutenants did exactly what was expected of them. In fact, I'm here to request the services of Lieutenant Eaves and Carter to help us redesign the entire shuttle fleet and take advantage of their twelve-panel membrane. And the thrusters are such an obvious and inexpensive modification, it's embarrassing we didn't think of it before. How'd you come up with this, Lieutenant?"

Eaves looked bewildered, since the conversation had taken such a considered turn from Kensington's assault. It was hard to know where to start. But fast thinking was an Eaves specialty, and quickly collecting his thoughts, he replied, "Actually, Sir, dividing the panel was an idea I thought of in one of Chief O'Casey's training sessions. He compared the shuttle to a giant leaf floating through the sky, flexing with the wind. One day on the simulator I was having a hard time keeping the passenger compartment stable while dealing with high wind. As a fighter pilot I wanted to continually correct for it, but Mr. O'Casey's leaf analogy came to mind and I kept my hands off the control. His advice worked. By letting the ship flutter a bit, we avoided being flipped, but it was still uncomfortable. Then I thought about actual leaves falling. When they're old and brittle, they drop much faster and in a less controlled fashion than when they're fresh and supple. I realized that if I could somehow add additional flexibility to the ship, it would be much easier to control in high winds. That's when I did what I always do when confronted by a complex problem." He flashed one of his trademark smiles.

"Which is?" asked Park.

"I turned it over to Lieutenant Carter to do the calculations. He's a genius when it comes to the computer and after only three days he came up with the basic programming to subdivide the panels. After that, we worked on developing the full code at night, in our cabins."

"You were doing all that under my nose?" O'Casey growled. "Why didn't you tell me what you were up to?"

"No offense, Mr. O'Casey, but if this failed I didn't want to put you at risk. Plus, you can sometimes be intimidating and …." It was clear O'Casey didn't want to hear where this conversation was going.

"I think we get the picture, Lieutenant," said Parks. "So the entire division was handled by computer?"

Eaves looked at Carter, who asserted, "Yes, Sir. Although it would be much easier for a pilot to control if there were hardwire separations, rather than virtual." Park nodded to indicate his understanding.

"What about the thrusters?"

"That was easy. I'm basically a fighter pilot and it drove me nuts not having the ability to execute quick changes when needed. Since we didn't need a whole bunch of additional maneuverability, I figured small thrusters would give me insurance against unusual events."

"I seriously doubt you ever contemplated events as unusual these. Without the thrusters, you never could have controlled both ships. That saved the day. That and the pulsing maneuver you used to control the building as it drew near. Our engineering team was astounded that you pulled that off."

Admiral Showalter broke into the conversation. "Speaking of being a fighter pilot, Lieutenant, I've been concerned that your attention to the shuttle competition may have interfered with your skills in a fighter. Has this competition changed your career path?"

"Actually, Sir, I believe I'll be a better fighter pilot than before for a couple of reasons. First, all the homework I've had to do has given me a much better understanding of aerodynamics, which should make it easier to control my fighter in the atmosphere. Plus, Captain Jesik intervened and required me to spend at least two hours each day in a fighter simulator, to make certain I kept those skills current."

"You mean that after six to ten hours a day, I made you fly in the shuttle simulator, you flew a fighter simulator for another two?" said O'Casey, a guilty tinge to his voice.

"Yes, Sir. In fact, when Commander Brighton chastised us for using other names to get into the simulators, it was actually to obey Captain

Jesik's orders." At that, Brighton's face colored slightly.

Turning to Brighton, he said "You were right to throw us out those last three days. Carter and I were exhausted and the break gave us the edge we needed."

"Obviously, from what I've heard, the entire Allegro command was interested in your success." Looking around at the group, the Commodore added. "Well done, all of you. And thanks on behalf of the shuttle service. "

Everyone relaxed, except Kensington, who stood back.

General Josephs interrupted, "Gentlemen, we have some urgent business to get started on."

"Yes, sorry," Park continued. "Captain Jesik, can you release Lieutenants Eaves and Carter to work with us while you're refitting. I believe you're scheduled for three months."

"Of course, Sir. We'll be glad to provide whatever support possible."

"Excellent. Also, in view of the Lieutenants' praise for Mr. O'Casey's training, perhaps you will help me renew an old appeal that he assume leadership of the In-Flight Training Wing of the Shuttle Academy."

Turning to O'Casey he said, "I know you love being in space, Tim, but with this terrorist threat hanging over our heads it's more critical than ever that our new pilots have the best training possible. Shuttles make a particularly vulnerable target and you're the best person I know to help our crews get ready. What do you say?"

O'Casey was clearly flustered, but said, "I'll give it very serious consideration, Sir. I promise."

"Good. Well, gentlemen, I've gotten everything I hoped for. Now, General Josephs has some business to transact."

Josephs was a very intense man, with a dark, almost ominous look. Small and compact, he obviously had great physical power, yet moved with a catlike grace. He spoke earnestly. "With the Admiral's permission, I'd like to excuse everyone but Captain Jesik and the two Lieutenants." Brighton, O'Casey and Park rose immediately and started out the door.

Addressing Kensington, "I'm afraid this discussion is classified, Colonel, which precludes your attendance, as well."

"Yes, of course," said Kensington, bumping a chair as he moved toward the door. His irritation showed clearly on his face, but there was nothing he could do but leave. Events had certainly taken a different turn than he had anticipated.

Once the room was empty, the Admiral and four remaining men sat down at the conference table. Josephs pulled out a small electronic device, about the size of a personal digital assistant and set in on the table. A red light began blinking in a random pattern.

"A simple precaution," he explained, "in case there's anyone else interested in what we have to say. Gentlemen, you were the subject of two attacks in the past three days. The ship that attacked you during your ascent has been positively identified as a Keswick rebel, brought in more than six months ago, apparently for this very purpose. One of the crewmembers was a Keswick, but the other was a young Kalenden from a third-class family. He belonged to an insurgent group we've been watching for the past three years. We've known they were extremists, but until now didn't realize the extent of their preparation or commitment to their cause. It's obvious from documents found at the flat in which they were staying, that they expected to be shot down after destroying a shuttlecraft, meaning they were willing to commit suicide to start a broader rebellion."

"Why did they choose our shuttlecraft?" asked Jesik.

"We don't know for sure, but preliminary clues indicate it was simply the luck of the draw. They wanted to get the first shuttle of the day, so they could be on all the news services as people were going to work."

"You said there was a second attack, Sir," Carter recounted.

"Yes. That's why this meeting is classified. Everyone, including the news services, believes the observation platform broke from its tethers because of the gale force winds. But the steel mooring cables are strong enough to withstand winds at least a dozen times stronger than those encountered today. Surveillance tapes show one of the maintenance engineers used an acetylene torch to weaken the cables. Further investigation revealed he's a member of the same resistance group as the pilots who attacked your shuttle. So, now we're faced with the prospect of future terrorism and while we don't think the rebel cause has broad appeal, our society hasn't had to deal with terrorism in over three hundred years. The effect of additional attacks could be devastating to public morale."

Jesik frowned thoughtfully before saying, "How can we help?"

"We need to know everything you learned about the rebels during the Keswick campaign, Captain. We need to profile the rebels to understand what they hope to accomplish here."

Jesik picked his words with even more than his usual caution.

"I hope you're right about the rebels being a small group. But we underestimated their strength on Keswick. They were far better prepared than any intelligence reports had indicated, even though we had the participation of both Keswick and Alturian intelligence agencies."

"I don't see how the situation on Keswick is similar to ours," the Admiral intoned. "The rebels were fighting against an entrenched bureaucracy legitimized by the monarchy. Our government is far more open."

"That's true, Sir. Still, how long has it been since a second or third-class family sent a representative to the Quadrant Council, or furnished the system with a Prime Minister? It's amazing how easy it is for a skilled orator to make a minority group feel aggrieved. And the rebel leader, John Lansing, is a man of incredible skill and persuasion. If he's involved, there's no telling how much influence our rebels have."

The Admiral shifted uncomfortably in his seat.

"Then it's obvious we have a lot to learn," said Josephs. "I didn't want to alarm Commodore Park, so it's important you Lieutenants work closely with him. Unfortunately, the Allegro will be leaving orbit in one month, not three and we'll need part of your time to brief us on the terrorist tactics you learned while in combat on Keswick." Eaves and Carter acknowledged his order and withdrew from the meeting.

Admiral Showalter turned to Jesik. "Now, Captain, I'll tell you what's next. I suspect you'll be unhappy with part of what we have to tell you."

"Sir?"

"We need you to return to Keswick to engage in a dialogue with Mr. Lansing. It seems there's trouble brewing with unhappy Loyalists and some kind fringe element. Our Esper communications from Major Wilkerson indicates that Lansing and his cabinet often refer to you in their dialogue. You've earned his confidence and we need your help. We have to persuade Lansing that it's in his best interest to contain any further unrest on Keswick before it spreads here to Kalenden. We're going to pull you into some high-level briefings with the Prime Minister and cabinet ministers in the next few weeks, so you'll be prepared."

"I've never thought of myself as a diplomat, Sir, but I'll certainly do what I can."

The Admiral nodded, looked around a bit nervously. "Your negotiations must be conducted in secret, so that rebel spies here and on Alturus are unaware of your influence. If we're to maintain you as an informal communications channel, we have to provide a cover for you. Which is why the Quadrant Council has named Colonel Kensington as their official representative to Alturus, a position approved because of the Keswick insurrection. He'll be traveling with you."

Admiral Showalter winced as he said this and braced for Jesik's reaction.

After a moment of stunned silence, Jesik responded, "You want Kensington as leader of the delegation?"

"Yes. I know you have issues with Kensington and we've anticipated that by transferring him to the Diplomatic Corps. He'll have no operational command of your vessel during the journey and, once on Keswick, he'll assume ceremonial functions only, while Wilkerson carries on the day-to-day management of our affairs."

Jesik's mind was reeling and he felt that, no matter what he said, it would come out wrong. Still, a man like Kensington could ruin everything, so he had to give it a try.

"With all due respect, Sir, Colonel Kensington's demeanor may prove annoying to the Keswick rebels. For one thing, he's from a most prominent family on Kalenden, which is what the rebel's opposed." That was dangerous to say, since Showalter was also from a leading family.

"Captain, we understand far more than you might imagine. We intend for the Colonel to stay on Keswick for a month or two, at most – just enough to throw some lavish receptions and show the Kalenden flag. Then he will continue on to Alturus as our charge-d´ affairs."

Jesik rubbed his temples for a moment. The thought of spending the next nine or ten months with Kensington was almost too much for his mind to absorb. But, the plan had merit. "Appointing Colonel Kensington may actually work out alright, since the Alturians still have a very strong monarchy. Colonel Kensington should fit right in."

"Actually, the Kensington family still has royal ties, which is why he was chosen."

Jesik sat quietly, trying to absorb the full impact of sharing a dinner table with Kensington. It's like his worst nightmare had just exploded into daylight, but there was no way to awaken and make it go away.

"Captain," the Admiral asked quietly, "Can you tell me what the dispute between you and the Colonel is about?"

Jesik sighed. "It's not really a dispute. In fact, I'd be content to get on with our lives. I'd like to forget I ever knew him. But, his attitude toward me is stuck in a fight we had while cadets at the academy. The ironic part is that he actually bested me, costing me something I valued more than anything else in the world. You'd think he'd be happy about that, but things didn't turn out as he wished and so he continues to try to discredit me." Jesik's knuckles were white and he had to make a conscious effort to unclench his fist. Looking up, he smiled. "But at least up 'til now, I've been able to survive."

"I hope you can deal with this for I can't change his appointment."

Leaning forward, Jesik said, "It isn't about me, Sir. I've learned to live with him. It's that he tries to get at me through people who serve with me like trying to oust Lieutenant Eaves and Carter from the competition today. I can't contradict him publicly so they're made to suffer because of his dislike for me."

"Captain, the sensible solution would be to reassign you and let someone else take Kensington to Alturus. But, you're the one to deal with Lansing and Wilkerson and so I'm asking you to accept this command. In view of what you've told me, though, I'll recommend that Major Wilkerson be promoted to full Colonel, with continuing authority to work with the Keswick government. That will give him military precedence over Kensington, who, of course, will be furious when he learns about it. So perhaps we won't announce it until you're a week or so away from Keswick. In the meantime, I'll issue a formal protocol stating that you are in command of all naval military forces in the sector. Kensington cannot override your decisions and I emphasize that he is going merely as a figurehead. If he stays with his modus operandi, he'll irritate half the quadrant, which will give you perfect cover to get real work done. I can't force you to go, but I hope you will."

Jesik looked up. "I'll go."

Showalter and Josephs both sighed with relief and shook Jesik's hand.

"By the way, your Lieutenant Commander Magill may need a transfer to Alturus for additional surgery on his feet. It seems they are much better at that than we are. Major Wilkerson reports he's invaluable diplomatically but his wounds are failing to heal. The only course left to our doctors is amputation, but communications with Alturian medical authorities indicate they think they can halt the effects of the radiation burns and provide some use of his limbs. For some reason, they've taken a real interest in his case."

"He's one of the best young men I've ever worked with, so I'll do whatever I can to facilitate his full recovery. It seems we're enjoying an unusual amount of contact with Alturus, given nearly two centuries of silence."

"I think the Keswick rebellion has scared the hell out of them. For better or worse, our three planets share a common heritage and the problems of one can't help but impact the others. Perhaps the rebellion will be the means for us to finally close old wounds, eh?"

"I hope so, Sir. And please don't overreact to my comments about Colonel Kensington. It's not my place to be critical of a superior officer."

"For crying out loud, Jesik, you've only had to talk to him by Esper link on a few occasions," said Josephs, speaking up for the first time, "but we work with him every day. If his family didn't have so much influence…"

Admiral Showalter interrupted, "What General Josephs is saying is that you need not worry about our conversation. We asked you to speak frankly and you've been perfectly candid. Now, you've got a lot to do over the next thirty days, so I suggest you get a good night's sleep, enjoy the awards banquet tomorrow, and then get on with your duties."

"Thank you, Sir."

Josephs stood and left the room. Showalter came close to Jesik and said quietly, "Is there anything I can do to settle the problem with Kensington?"

Jesik was so startled by this that all he could come up with was, "What?" But he quickly added, "I'm afraid it's such an old story that nothing can ever be done. But thank you for offering, Sir." Showalter lingered for a moment and Jesik added, "I'll be alright, you don't need to worry."

They saluted and Showalter departed. Looking back through the door he thought Jesik's expression was the most forlorn he'd ever seen.

* * *

The awards banquet for the Manhattan Trials was always a cheerful event, but this night it took extreme center stage. Nearly fifty extra tables had been added at the last moment to accommodate all the additional luminaries who decided to show up. It was clearly the place to be for anyone who wished to keep their name current on the social register.

The Allegro crew sat at a table near the front, joined by the parents of Lieutenants Carter and Eaves, who were overwhelmed by the attention their sons were receiving. The Carters were quiet and unassuming, even though they were from a prominent family. The Eaves were much more at ease circulating among the crowd, although not in a pretentious way. They thanked Jesik and the others for inspiring their son to finally take something seriously.

After a marvelous dinner of simulated steak and lobster, followed by a stunning presentation of cherries flambé, the host for the evening, Commodore Park, called the room to order. He was a genial man who held the affection of everyone in the Shuttle Service and whose goodwill radiated through the microphone. The first order of business was for the previous year's winners to return the coveted alinite chalice to the judges. Of course, each crewmember was allowed to retain a miniature replica of the cup as a permanent award.

"The competition this year was unusually difficult," Park began, "particularly in view of the weather and the unfortunate incident on the first day. Additionally, seven of twelve teams were either disqualified or withdrew from the competition due to the harsh weather conditions."

That wasn't too unusual. There were many years when the weather interfered with the games. It was seen as just another factor to be conquered.

The Allegro's helmsman, Kevin Wight, leaned over to Jason Carter and whispered, "In view of your practically perfect landing, I don't see how anyone else could possibly win." One way the judges added an element of suspense to the trials was to not post their scores until the awards banquet. Thus, there was no way to know in advance who the actual winner was.

"Normally, we only announce the first and second runner-ups before awarding the cup to the top point winner. But, this year we feel the need to give an explanation about the fifth place team."

This prompted a slight murmur from the crowd.

"Let me get right to the point. When we first ran the calculations, the Allegro shuttlecraft was number one in points. But before the results were made final, Colonel Kensington asked if he could review the tapes, to provide a verification of the results."

"What's he done this time?" Wight whispered, a bit too loudly.

"The tapes indicate a problem with the Allegro's first landing attempt. Although the placement was almost dead center, the problem with the observation platform apparently caused them to lift off before all four paws had firmly settled on the pad. Assuming that's correct, the first attempt was incomplete and so we need to count their second attempt, which, by the way, was also excellent. But of course, the time spent in the rescue effort deducted points, all of which places them last among the competitors."

At this point the crowd did more than murmur. There were shouts of "Shame! Shame!" and "Give them the cup!" Among those shouting most loudly were members of the four teams that had remained in the competition.

Park used the gavel to bring the group back to order. "The Allegro crew now has the chance to formally protest and the judges can exercise their judgment in determining their qualification. After all, these truly were unique circumstances. It falls to the shuttle's commander, Lieutenant Travis Eaves, to request a review."

Carter was sick to his stomach, not at losing, but at what Eaves might do next. No one had ever worked harder to win a competition and the thought that Kensington had found a way to disqualify them was infuriating.

The spotlights swung to the Allegro table and a steward brought Eaves a microphone. Everyone waited to hear his challenge, which was likely to include a heavy layer of his trademark sarcasm. Eaves stood with a placid expression on his face, cleared his throat and spoke easily into the microphone. "Until this moment I hadn't taken time to review the first landing. But as I think about it, Colonel Kensington is absolutely correct. We settled stern first and I remember I hadn't fully released the bow membrane when Lieutenant Carter reported the danger to the observation building. So, he's right. We didn't complete the landing."

The crowd was at first stunned, then it went wild, with people yelling for him to contest the decision anyway.

"Am I to understand, Lieutenant, that you do not exercise your right to request a judges' decision?"

"Of course not," said Eaves, "we didn't win. It's as simple as that." Then he sat down.

After a moment of stunned silence, a growling noise grew among the crowd and quickly turned into a cheer for the Allegro crew. Jesik touched his hand to his brow in a silent salute for Eaves' decision and Commodore Park looked down at his notes for the longest time, to give everyone time to collect their thoughts. Finally he asked the audience to again come to order and proceeded to announce the runner-ups and winners. The response to these announcements was subdued, but no one applauded louder for each winner than the people from Allegro. Carter still had an ache in the pit of his stomach and noticed that Commander Brighton took more than his one customary drink. In fact, the only two who were unaffected by the decision were those with the greatest stake in the competition, Eaves and O'Casey. It just didn't make sense.

As the ceremony drew to a close, Colonel Kensington at the head table stood as if to leave, but was forced back into his seat when Commodore Park continued, rather than bringing the meeting to an end as expected.

"If you please, ladies and gentlemen, Prime Minister Larimore has asked for a moment of your time."

The Prime Minister both looked and acted his part. His gray hair gave him the distinguished look of age and maturity while his optimistic attitude and outgoing personality produced a youthful appearance that allowed him to relate to citizens of all ages. With more than eleven years of service, he had the opportunity to become the longest-serving Prime Minister in the history of Kalenden. Stepping to the microphone, he spoke in a reassuring voice.

"The events of the past few days have reminded us that in spite of our best efforts to minimize the risks of life while maximizing the potential for individual achievement, life is fragile. I was one of those who faced the prospect of losing my life when the anchoring cables of the observation platform were severed. Like most of the men and women who shared that event, I was prepared to face the end, grateful that I'd been given the chance of a meaningful life that has included service on your behalf." Everyone in the hall and the video audience hung on every word. "Still," he said with a twinkle, "I'm glad that I'm here, taking an active role at this ceremony, instead of being a passive participant at my own funeral." There was an appreciative laugh.

"It's interesting that we don't often think about the men and women who risk their lives in military service. It's been easy to overlook their contribution, having lived in relative peace for two hundred years. But, the troubles on Keswick and the events here on Kalenden have brought back remembrance of the risks they assume. I'd like every member of the military to please stand so we can express our appreciation." The house lights went up as the crowd cheered for the people who were now standing.

As order returned, the Prime Minister continued. "I now have the honor of representing the Quadrant Council in bestowing special recognition on the crew of the Allegro shuttlecraft, whose unusual creativity and courageous action intervened to save the lives of innocents at great peril to themselves. Accordingly, prior to this banquet and their surprised standing in the competition, the Council passed legislation to recognize the members of the crew, including Chief Engineer Timothy O'Casey, with the Council Medallion of Merit. And for their contribution of designing modifications that made the rescue possible and successful execution of those modifications in extremity, Lieutenants Travis Eaves and Jason Carter will receive the Council Medal of Honor, the highest recognition bestowed by the Congress on active military personnel for risking their lives to save another. Gentlemen, would you please come forward with your Captain and accept these tokens of our appreciation."

The crowd erupted and gave a standing ovation even as the crews of the winning three ships carried the men of the Allegro on their shoulders to the platform. Jesik asked the Carter and Eaves families to join him as his men received their commendation.

For the Prime Minister and members of the Council it was a perfect event giving them the chance to acknowledge their constituents as their own political standing flourished. For Jesik, it was exciting recognition for his crewmembers who, he was convinced, were the best in the fleet. For Travis Eaves' parents, it was the chance to see their son's recklessness mature into willing self-sacrifice that was being commended, rather than punished, a wonderful contrast to his teenage years. And for the citizens of the Kalenden System, it was one of those rare moments when people came together in recognition of their good fortune.

Allegro's loss at the Manhattan Trials was heralded as the most successful defeat in history.

14 — THE DANGEROUS GAME OF ESPIONAGE

Sean Magill never liked drinking. The few times he tried it made him sick and stupid. But to pull this off he had to at least appear to be a bit drunk, so he slipped the bartender 20 CC (Common Currency) to keep his mouth shut about the fact that the apple juice he was drinking wasn't really hard liquor. The bartender just shrugged and poured the glass below the level of the counter. After a couple of shots Sean said to the fellow next to him, "These Loyalist sympathizers have got it right, you know?" The guy shoved Sean back into an upright position and told him to shut up. But Sean just took another sip and added, "It always works out that the original conspirators end up being worse than the royal family they depose."

The fellow next to him was irritated enough that he got up and moved away. Sean bit his lip, trying to decide what to do next. But he didn't have to. He'd picked his tavern wisely—the one where most of the log writers hung out to sympathize with each other how they could never get paid properly for all the work they did—and sure enough, one of the best known slipped into the chair next to him. "I couldn't help but overhear what you had to say, Commander. Okay if I buy you a drink?" Sean's eyes widened. He hadn't counted on his source being both beautiful and willing to buy him a drink—it could all fall apart right here. But his bartender held up both hands, indicating another 10CC was in order, acknowledged Sean's slight tip of his head authorizing the deal, and took his glass below the counter to fill it again.

"Thanks! But why would that be of interest to someone like you?" He regretted saying it that way just as soon as the words were out of his mouth because of the implication that beautiful women weren't interested in politics.

But she overlooked it and smiled. "I'm just curious how a Kalenden representative could say something like that. Everyone thinks Prime Minister Lansing has you guys in his pocket!"

Nice, he thought, *she challenges me right off the bat. Touché!* But he was too smart, even if he had been drunk, to fall quite so easily. "I didn't say anything about PM Lansing. He's a good guy and trying to do the right thing."

"Then why do you say that the Loyalists have it right?"

Sean sipped on his glass as if considering how much he could say. Of course he knew exactly what he was going to say, but it had to look impromptu. "I'm just saying that anybody who's ever studied history knows that rebellions like this sound great in the beginning and almost always start out with good intentions. But once the cool guys get in power they become just like the ones they threw out – except that they don't feel the same level of responsibility."

The lady smiled. "My name's Janet. And you're Lieutenant Commander Magill, if I'm not mistaken."

Magill looked down at his feet and the crutches leaning against the bar. "That's pretty brilliant on your part since I'm about the only person on the planet who uses crutches!" He really didn't like being obnoxious, but he had a role to play in this discussion.

"I recognized you by your face. I always thought you were kind of cute. But let's get to the point, if that's what you want. Tell me more about this history thing and how it ends up being worse after a revolution than before."

Magill's face darkened. "Listen, you're not going to print any of this are you, because they'd have my butt in a sling in no time and I don't need that."

"We're just talking—that's all."

"Well, aside from Mr. Lansing, who really is a good guy, what always happens in situations like this is that the rebels kick out a king or queen who's lost touch with their subjects. The new crowd comes in all bent on reshaping the government to their particular favorite ideal governing system and pretty soon they're out their killing all the people who disagree with them and blaming others for the failures of the new system. They get into office by promising the moon and the stars and then when they can't deliver they just get more and more violent. In the end its worse than it was before."

"Can you give me examples?"

Magill struggled to straighten up. "That's the problem isn't it – that I have to give the examples. Everybody should know the examples if they'd just study a little history."

"I was good in math—so maybe you'll humor me." Her voice had a seductive quality to it.

"Think about it—the Czar of Russia sits fat and lazy with his big family in the Winter Palace while his subjects are starving in 1917. So Lenin comes into town promising that the Bolsheviks will fix it all. Sure enough, they kill the Czar and impose Communism and everything is supposed to get better – except for the fact that Lenin and Stalin proceed to murder more than twenty million of their own citizens, starving millions of others in the process. Then it happens in China under Mao Zedong. Then it happens in Cambodia under Pol Pot. Then in the 22nd Century it happens in Africa. And then our ancestors proclaim that their sick of all that and get the hell out of Dodge when space travel becomes viable and we're supposed to have put all that in the past, except that now your royal family gets murdered and people are hungry. So where does that put us now?"

"I've never understood where that comes from, 'Get out of Dodge?'"

Magill shook his head in disgust. "No, you probably wouldn't because you'd actually have to study history to understand the reference." He was tempted to add "moron" but thought that would put her off.

"I've kind of heard of all those things, but that's like in the ancient world. It doesn't happen now!"

"That's what they all thought before it happened to them." He pretended to nurse his drink, then looked up at her and said earnestly, "Listen, I've just had a few too many. I don't want you to repeat any of this. I'm just shooting off my mouth because it gets so frustrating."

"But you think that the UCG could turn out worse than the Keswick monarchy…"

"I didn't say that—I just said that there's a reason these Loyalists want things to go back to the way they used to be—that's all I'm saying." With that he looked down at his glass and pretended to brood. She got the hint and got up and left.

* * *

The next morning proved the validity of his theory that using reporters pretending to promise confidentiality was the easiest way to get a message out, inasmuch as the whole planetoid went crazy over the headline, "Kalenden Envoy Predicts Mass Murder By UCG."

"Well, he certainly made it easy for us to disavow him, didn't he?" said Lansing to Wilkerson, as he read the report.

"If you read the whole interview you'd see that he never said anything like what the headline suggests. The lady printed the interview exactly as he said it and he went out of his way to compliment you…"

Lansing held up his hand. "I know—but it's the headline that's going to give me headaches for who knows how long."

"At least I have a couple of hours before the Esper Links can get word back to Kalenden. Then I'm going to have my ass chewed right off."

"Well, it's been reported that he's gone into hiding, so it looks like his plan is working."

"I hope his plan doesn't take a long time. This may prove harder to manage than we thought."

Wilkerson nodded. He felt so out of his element in all this intrigue and hoped that Magill knew what he was doing. *You better know what you're doing—because I couldn't stand the thought of…*" He forced himself to stop thinking about it and to start working on what he'd say to Colonel Kensington when the call from Kalenden came in. *It will come in!* At least he could count on that.

* * *

Magill was sitting in an easy chair in the small motel room he'd taken the night before when the door came crashing down. He successfully resisted the urge to say, "What kept you," and instead did his best to act alarmed. Given the roughness with which they put the bag over his head and ripped him into a standing position it wasn't as hard to act alarmed as he thought it would be.

"You're coming with us…" said a rough voice and Magill found himself stumbling forward.

"I need my crutches!" he shouted, but the men just laughed, put their arms under his armpits, and dragged him out the door and into some kind of vehicle. The fact that it made no noise when it accelerated suggested that it was an anti-gravity land cruiser that floated above the surface. *Makes sense if they don't want to be tracked.* Sean did his best not to throw up. He was genuinely frightened, now. Even if his plan were solid, he might never make it out alive.

* * *

"Sir, we have a very strange message that just came through."

Jesik looked up at Williams with a quizzical look. "So, read it."

Williams hesitated. "I'm not sure – maybe you'd like to read it privately, first."

Jesik stood up and moved over to the communications console. After reading the message he said quietly, "Mr. Williams, please treat this as confidential for the moment. Would you ask Lieutenant Eaves to meet me in my quarters?"

"Certainly, Sir." Even Williams was disturbed enough by the message that he wouldn't have told anyone else on the crew even if Jesik hadn't coded it confidential. *Not until we hear his side of the story!* Fortunately they were in deep space so only cleared communications and news could be shared with the ship's company. For now Magill's reputation was safe.

* * *

"But you said that these things always turn out badly—that the rebels turn out worse than the kings they depose."

"I gave some examples. But that doesn't mean this has to be the same way."

"But it could turn out that way."

Magill looked around the room. He was, as he hoped, right square in the middle of the Loyalist uprising command structure. He was being interrogated by some former general in the Keswick Military who had obviously defected, but not yet made that known to the Unified Governing Coalition. And right there next to him was the young man who was supposed to be the rightful heir to the throne of Keswick. But not close enough for him to brush up against him. The way the guards in the room were positioned—rather the way their weapons were positioned—made it impossible for him to make any kind of a move towards the prince without getting blasted.

"So, what do you want me to do? I shot off my mouth in a bar."

"Were you sincere in what you said? That's the whole point!"

Magill pondered. He actually was sincere. Every single incident he cited was true. Things often worked out unfortunately when an historic ruling family was deposed. It had caused problems in the Middle East on Earth, in Africa, and—well almost everywhere. So he nodded.

"Then own up to the statement—that's all we ask. We've written a communication that we are going to send out." The general, whoever he was, added, "We've already taken pictures of you here that we intend to attach to the broadcast and we'll make it sound like you wrote it, whether or not you give us permission, so you might as well read it first."

"But how will people know it's really me and not some doctored picture. You could take a picture of me and a picture of the royal nephew here and put them together electronically."

The general creased his brow. "You're right. We could and everyone would thing that we'd doctored the picture. That's why you're going to go stand right next to him with your arm around his shoulder. That's a pose that's almost impossible to fake. And then we'll send our message and before you know it we'll have people joining us in droves."

"No—I didn't mean that," stammered Magill, even though that's exactly what he'd hoped for. As the guards moved close to force him next to the prince he fingered the personal assistant that they had foolishly neglected to check for. *A piece of skin is all I need. An exposed piece of skin and two seconds."*

* * *

"We've got to do something!" Wilkerson couldn't remember the name of the minister who was shouting. He just knew that the Keswick UCG was going crazy over Magill's indiscretion and they were shouting at Lansing to find him and haul him up on charges of sedition.

"We can't do that, and you know it – he's a Kalenden!"

"Then send him back to Kalenden!" someone else shouted.

Lansing nodded. "Gentlemen, things aren't always as they seem. My experience tells me that Commander Magill is a reasonable fellow. I'm sure he's got a good explanation for this."

"You'd defend him!" Now the room did erupt in a firestorm and Wilkerson put his hand next to his holster. Dealing with a group of rebels turned government ministers wasn't exactly the safest thing in the world.

Just when he thought they'd have to give into the demand to going after Magill he heard the distinctive "ping" that indicated he'd received a high level communication on his assistant. Glancing down to read the message his eyes widened. "Why you little devil—you've done it!" He looked up and caught Lansing's eye. "He's done it! It just went out over the social network!" Lansing pulled out his own assistant and then pounded the gavel to bring order to the room.

Wilkerson sat back down astonished. Then he heard the words, "Send in the Cavalry…" inside his head. He didn't actually hear them, of course, but he might as well have because the thought alarmed him so quickly that he jumped up shouting, "We've got to get over there. What's the fastest way to deploy a SWOT team!" Lansing looked down at the message quickly, realized what Wilkerson was talking about, and jammed a red button on the table. The room lit up like a starship in the night and alarms sounded. The cavalry had been summoned.

* * *

In some ways Magill hated what he had done. The young man was undoubtedly innocent and actually believed that he was related to the royal family. It was probably the general who had flattered him into thinking he was special, most likely because of the way he looked. But when Sean had put his arm up around the young man's shoulder he allowed the assistant to come into contact with the boy's neck, which set off the automatic protocol that he'd previously programmed. In less than two seconds of contact the assistant scanned a DNA sequence, connected to the web and compared it to all known samples of the deceased royal family, confirmed that there was no relationship, and then transmitted that information with a pre-written message to everyone connected to the social network—in other words everyone on Keswick and all the foreign nationals stationed on the planet. The fact that it also activated the reflective camera in the device, which allowed an electronic image of him standing next to the boy to be constructed from reflected surfaces all around the room, proved to the world that the scan was legitimate, because there was Magill holding it next to the false prince's neck. The message he'd written was headlined, "Supposed Royal Nephew a Fraud – Proved by DNA Sequence."

Of course the message also instantly alerted everyone to the fact that he was an infiltrator who really was on the side of the Unified Governing Coalition. That would please some people and aggravate others. The people it aggravated the most happened to be standing in the room with him just at the very moment. When the general spied the probe he lunged from across the room, knocking both Magill and the pretender down as he screamed at Magill. But it was too late and the general knew it.

"So, in reality you are a spy—one of Lansing's puppets as everyone supposed!" shouted the general, as he stood up, furious. Then, seeing Sean lying at his feet he stomped on his right foot, which caused the most intense pain Sean had ever felt. The wounds were already bad enough without this. "I'll kill you for this you bloody little fool!" shouted the general, pointing an impact weapon at Magill. And that was the last thing Sean heard before passing out.

The general would have been right about Sean dying, had it not been for one of the Loyalist guards in the room who had actually believed that the boy was a royal relative. The moment he saw the headline, recognized that the general had deceived them, and was now about to shoot Magill, the guard simply shot the general before he could kill Sean. The uprising ended even more quickly than it began.

Reflecting on the sequence of events later Magill concluded, "There's nothing more dangerous in the universe than a disillusioned idealist." In this case it was a disillusioned, but well principled guard, who saved his life.

* * *

"So you used me?" The woman's voice was just as silky smooth as when he'd met her in the bar.

"I didn't use you. Everything I said was true. And I asked you not to print it."

"But you knew I would."

"I thought you might."

She bit her lip. "But if it's true, why didn't you stand by your convictions and assist the insurgency? If all those horrible things happened after revolutions on ancient Earth, are we not in danger of the same thing now?"

Magill inhaled. "Is this on the record?"

She seemed surprised. "Not if you don't want it to be."

"No—I do want it to be. I want everyone to hear what I say now because it's essential that they have confidence in Prime Minister Lansing."

She nodded. "Alright—it's on the record."

"I mentioned the failures—but not the successes. The United States is an example of a revolution that changed the history of mankind. The new government formed after the Revolutionary War became a light on the hill for democratic movements for hundreds of years. The revolution in France was bloody, but ultimately led to a successful and enduring democracy. And while England kept their monarch, it was only as a symbol of the state as they became a successful constitutional monarchy. Even Germany after Hitler—kind of the worst example, went on to develop democracy. And everyone knows how the Middle East, at one time a source of great contention, eventually prospered. So the examples of success far outweigh the negative examples I gave."

"So you said what you did just so you could get inside the uprising to prove that the claim of royalty was false."

Sean nodded. "That's exactly why I did it."

"But what if you'd been wrong? What if he really was royal."

Magill smiled. "Then I'd have had to think of something else. But it just didn't ring true—someone like that would have known long before now that he had royal connections. For him to show up at such a convenient time made no sense, so I placed my bet on the fact that he was a phony."

He looked down. "At any rate, I'm sorry if you felt deceived, and I'm sorry that sincere Loyalists were troubled by what I said. But I really do believe the Unified Governing Coalition is the best hope for Keswick. If I were a betting man, I'd wager that PM Lansing will lead this country on to a very bright future."

The young woman turned to her recorder so that her face was highlighted in the camera. "And there you have it—from the Hero of Cambriol himself—Lieutenant Commander Sean Magill, explaining why he helped end the uprising."

Sean took a deep breath to steady his hands. It had been a very trying week. And his feet really hurt.

15—A PROBLEM AT THE HELM

"Too bad about the disqualification of your ship in the trials." Kensington taunted Jesik as they walked down the hall. "But I'm sure you recognize the wisdom of my intervention. We have to maintain integrity in everything we do or the service becomes soft and sloppy."

"Of course, Sir."

"Still," said Kensington amiably, "events turned out well for the fleet that night. I was pleased that so many people acknowledged my original decision to let your team compete."

Jesik swallowed hard, continued walking. Fortunately, one didn't have to say much in a conversation with Kensington. In fact, it was difficult to find an opening to say anything. Still, Kensington had seemed in unusually good spirits the previous six weeks that he'd been onboard and hadn't intervened in any way, other than to occasionally reprimand a crewmember for a sloppy uniform or salute. Luckily, the incident with Sean Magill was over before Kensington even became aware of it, and when he did he simply deplored the use of espionage, but didn't really take issue with the outcome. If he continued like this the voyage might be bearable after all.

One thing Jesik did that pleased Kensington was to ask if he would preside over Sabbath services. Even though Kalenden's orbit precluded a day titled Sunday, the tradition of observing religious ceremonies continued to bear that name – a carryover from ancient Earth that had been preserved by early Kalenden colonists. In spite of his pomp and bluster, Kensington could deliver a spellbinding sermon and had actually increased attendance at the services. Though his philosophies were a bit extreme from Jesik's point-of-view, Kensington made a powerful case for adhering to fidelity, sacrifice, and self-denial. Perhaps he had missed his calling and should have stood behind a regular pulpit.

As Kensington turned to enter his quarters, Jesik heard him mutter the now ubiquitous line that popped up in so many conversations, "The first Ambassador to Alturus in more than two hundred years. A great honor, yes, but an even greater responsibility." Modesty was still not a virtue Colonel Kensington had explored.

Jesik believed in an open, cordial atmosphere on the bridge, except during military exercises or a hostile engagement when reporting protocol was strictly observed to prevent distractions or confusion. But during routine patrols it was acceptable for crewmembers to talk quietly with one another. So, it wasn't surprising when he appeared on the bridge to hear light-hearted banter between the Helmsman and other bridge personnel and to see Brighton in heavy conversation with the Communications Officer. He overheard the phrase "Auburn Hills," which immediately told him the discussion was about Williams' favorite professional soccer team and their recent loss at the Quadrant Invitational. No wonder Williams looked so somber.

"Captain on the Bridge!"

All officers acknowledged Jesik's entry by a nod in his direction.

"As you were." Taking his seat, Jesik noticed that, in spite of his tolerant attitude, the conversations now focused on a scheduled shutdown of the main communications array for routine maintenance and testing.

Lieutenant Wight and the current navigator were reviewing the Fleet's various escape maneuvers on their monitors, quietly debating the merits of each, trying to come up with their own variations to recommend to the Captain during the next drills. Since the Allegro's military engagements on Keswick, the crew had come to view these drills as significant, rather than theoretical exercises. The effect on motivation was pronounced. Working through complex evasion patterns wasn't usually humorous, yet Lieutenant Wight and the navigator suddenly burst out laughing. Jesik bit his lower lip and looked stern as they apologized for their outburst. They returned to their conversation in more subdued voices, but continued to enjoy the chance to relive the Allegro's recent battles.

For a moment Jesik felt a yearning for simpler days, when he served at the helm. Back then every waking thought and motion had been directed toward becoming noticed and moving up the ladder of command. *Why was I in such a hurry to leave a post that gave operational control of a powerful star ship without having to worry about strategy and whether a decision will take advantage of our opponents' weakness or cause our own destruction?*

"Mr. Brighton, do you have a moment to review one of our strategies?"

Wight's voice had an innocence about it that immediately involved every-one within hearing. His earnest tone made even the most trivial request sound important. His questions were always delivered with such an abso-lute lack of self-importance that a person couldn't attribute any self-serv-ing motives to what he said. Jesik liked the young man. In fact everyone liked Wight. At six feet even, with a slender, athletic build, he moved with unusual grace—more like a professional gymnast than the aggressive jaunt of a typical junior officer. He was unusually handsome, with deep blue-eyes and dark-brown hair that undoubtedly held special appeal to the young women in his life.

Of course I'm biased. Kevin's mother was a most uncommonly beautiful woman with eyes as deep as a brooding sapphire…

"You've got to be kidding, Lieutenant!" Brighton laughed. "How on earth do you think the starboard stabilizers could stay attached to the ship if you executed a banking maneuver at that angle?"

Wight laughed back, his smile animating his face as he launched into his counter-attack as to why the ship would actually welcome such a move over the Academy's preferred maneuver. The intelligence of his response was confirmed by Brighton's furrowed brow and positive nod.

Jesik was grateful for the distraction. *After two decades I can't afford to start thinking about Helen, again.* He sighed, because that meant he was already thinking about her. *It probably would have been better if Wight had never been assigned to the crew.* But, even as he thought that, he knew that wasn't true. He loved having the young man on the ship, even though he knew nothing about Jesik and his mother. Kevin brought her closer to him.

The port transport tube opened with a swishing sound, its light flood-ing into the more subdued illumination of the bridge. Lieutenant Eaves strode onto the bridge and proceeded confidently to the weapons array.

Jesik glanced around the room and noticed that everyone had turned to follow Eaves, hardly the usual reaction to a Lieutenant's comings and goings. But his obvious panache in the shuttlecraft competition added more luster to his reputation and no one's stock rode higher with the crew.

Eaves was a puzzle. On one hand he was supremely self-confident, so it was easy to assume he was arrogant. Yet, he never pressed for preferen-tial treatment and the reports of his design work were outstanding, which meant that in addition to his natural skill as a pilot there was a good chance he'd go back to school to train as an engineer once his active duty was complete.

Looking up, Jesik became aware that Brighton's conversation with

Wight was coming to a rather subdued end. Whereas moments before they'd been laughing and arguing cheerfully, Wight's entire demeanor had changed dramatically, and his face looked flushed.

"Thank you Commander," said Wight, rather stiffly, "Perhaps the Academy was right after all." Brighton stared at him, puzzled, but wasn't the kind to worry about a Lieutenant's tone of voice, so he moved back to Communications to resume his former conversation.

Jesik shook his head. *What in the world causes such a mood swing?* It was no longer personal – the helm required someone who could stay focused in spite of outside distractions or irritations. Despite his usually bright temperament, Jesik had observed mood changes by Wight on a few other occasions. He'd be smiling one moment, then suddenly turn cold. It was like a thundercloud moving in to ruin an afternoon picnic.

Piloting any kind of vehicle in space presented an unusual set of challenges – far different than those encountered with land or atmosphere based craft. In air or water pilots use the natural resistance of the medium to control turns, acceleration, and braking. Outer space presents a whole new challenge. There is no resistance – nothing to bank against or use to execute your turn. Early deep-space astronauts found there were only three ways to maneuver in the vacuum of space – use a complex array of internal thrusters, skip off a planet's atmosphere, or use the gravity of a nearby star or planet. Modern space travel requires a ship to use a combination of the three. Even the vortex drive was but a method of combining gravitational effects of at least three celestial objects to create a whirlpool in space – a shortcut, as it were, from one place to the other. Finding the center of the vortex was critical to avoid having the ship torn apart by competing gravitational waves. That's why the Helmsman has to be both agile and focused.

"Do you remember the first time I was assigned to bring a cruiser into planetary orbit?" Jesik asked his yeoman, Sergeant Darcy.

"Remember it! I thought it would be the last thing I remembered. Your angle of descent damn near burned the ceramic heat tiles right off the hull!"

"Glad to know I'm still famous. But the depressive thrusters burned hot that day. The follow-up investigation showed it."

"All I know, Sir, is that I remember thinking at the time that if we lived through the experience, I hoped you'd be posted to a fine ship, a long ways away from me." That was twenty-three years ago and Darcy had served with Jesik on every assignment since.

Jesik smiled, but remained silent. Darcy glanced over at Wight. "Turned a bit quiet, didn't he Sir?"

"What? Oh, yes, I suppose he did. What do you make of it?"

"He's hard to know. On the outside, everything about him is open for discussion. He's popular in the wardroom, not as loud as most of the others. Still, he carries on his fair share of the conversation. But then he goes quiet, with no warning, and it's like he's a million kilometers away. I think there's a part of him he's never spoken about – like a pocket of uncharted space."

When Jesik didn't respond Darcy added, "I think it must have something to do with women. They're usually the trouble with the young men."

"Women? That's probably as good an explanation as any." Jesik had heard everything he needed to. "Well, just as long as he doesn't freeze in battle, he can worry about whatever he likes. And, there's nothing better to think about than a girl."

Wight looked up at Jesik just in time to catch his eye. Jesik nodded slightly.

Oh, no, thought Wight, *he's been looking at me. He must have seen my face flush. Everybody must have seen it. They must suspect!*

Just then Lieutenant Eaves saluted the Officer of the Day and exited the bridge. Wight held his gaze steady, not looking at Eaves as departed.

Why do I have these thoughts? His stomach churned and he wondered if he was going to throw up. Oh, dear God, please help me to not feel this way. He looked up at the main viewer desperately. *No one else in a thousand parsecs of outer space thinks like this – why do I?*

The original Kalenden colonizers had been utopians who felt that with a firm grip on ancient values, they could create a society free of the liberal vices that tormented Earth in 2238 A.D.. They felt the basic family structure was threatened. People used so many pharmaceuticals that real personalities had long since disappeared and virtually nothing was considered right and wrong by the majority. Each person determined his or her own morality and no one else had the right to question it. This was anathema to the fundamentalists, who yearned for more certitude and structure.

With the invention of the vortex drive, it became practical for colonies of like-minded individuals to strike out to a distant space quadrant and create their own society, regulated as they wished. God-fearing people who shunned socially liberalized human interactions first colonized Alturus, before the great rift between the major families caused a second exodus to Keswick and Kalenden. All three societies remained socially conservative, however, in contrast to Stirium and Tatrius. That's why Brighton was at such risk with this out-of-wedlock pregnancy. For more than two hundred years, there had been careful monitoring of genetic stock to be sure that unwanted human weaknesses had been bred out of the society, including attraction to a member of one's own gender. Even though accepted as normal by most societies on earth, those 'deviancies' had been effectively eliminated in the fundamentalist societies.

Wight deftly executed a course correction of less than one degree to starboard. For a starship 800 meters long and with a 500 meter beam, that wasn't much. But, in the vastness of space, that tiny correction meant they'd miss the Routienne Star System by more than 276,000 kilometers, rather than crashing directly into the star.

Once he'd finished verifying the correction with the navigator, he returned to his thoughts, desperately trying to erase the image of Eaves' walk onto the bridge from his mind. But the tight cut of Eaves' uniform and open collar of his shirt was hard to dismiss. A few days earlier, he'd stumbled into Eaves exiting the shower. It meant nothing to Eaves, but the experience simply refused to stay out of Wight's thoughts. It had been the most erotic experience of his life as well as the most horrifying. *Why can't I feel that way about women?* he pleaded with himself.

He had tried to--even gone on dates as he was expected to. And he'd kissed his dates, the way he'd seen it done in movies. But it meant nothing to him. *I like women. I like their sensitivity and softness. I enjoy their conversation and companionship, but I'm just not aroused by them.* He licked his lips to moisten them, the internal turmoil having left his mouth dry. *But, if I meet an athletic guy with an assertive personality and the right build my stomach turns to butterflies. That's how it must feel to other males when they see an attractive female.* He shook his head, felt sick to his stomach.

"Kevin, you okay?"

"What?" Wight turned to the navigator.

"The Captain just asked you a question and you didn't answer. Are you alright?"

"He did! Oh, yeah, I'm fine."

Turning to Jesik he said, "I'm sorry, Sir, but I was concentrating on the calculations for our next scheduled correction and didn't hear you." He had a desperate look in his eyes.

Jesik felt a slight panic himself, but answered calmly, "No problem, Lieutenant. I just asked if you'd completed your Third Course Mathematics Trials for the Academy. I know you've been studying for them."

Wight relaxed noticeably and replied, "Yes, Sir, I passed."

"Care to share your score with us?" It was probably the most difficult test in the entire academy experience and most students failed it two or three times before finally passing with the minimum of sixty-three percent on the 300 question exam.

Wight hesitated, then said quietly, "A score of 297, Sir."

At that, nearly everyone on the bridge gasped, then offered congratulations. Wight blushed, tried to turn back to his station, but Jesik wasn't ready to let it go. "How many cadets have achieved a two ninety-seven, do you suppose?"

Brighton observed, "Well less than one hundred in the history of the Academy, Sir."

Wight tried to fade into the fabric of his seat. Jesik wondered how many men would answer the question without revealing the score, yet be embarrassed because it was so high. *Wight is one of those rare people who are truly modest.*

"An outstanding job, Kevin, you've brought great distinction to the ship. Congratulations."

"Thank you Sir." Wight turned back to his monitor.

"Mr. Brighton, I believe such an accomplishment warrants more than a verbal commendation. What do you think would be an appropriate way to recognize Mr. Wight's triumph?"

Brighton smiled, sensing where the Captain was going. "Personally, I think a field promotion is in order."

"A field promotion?" Jesik paused for dramatic effect. "I agree, Mr. Brighton." Then, with an authoritative voice, "Computer, on my authority as Captain of Allegro, note that Lieutenant Kevin Wight is hereby promoted to Lieutenant Commander, with all the rights, privileges and responsibilities attendant to that grade."

The computer confirmed the order, and the entire bridge crew joined in a salute and applause.

Wight's face flushed again, but this time accompanied by a modest smile. After enjoying the scene for a few more moments Jesik said, "As you were." The bridge crew returned to their normal activities.

Sitting at his post, Wight put his hands on the console, to look busy.

He called me Kevin. He never calls anyone by their first name. Thoughts of his problem were immediately replaced by his astonishment at the Captain's recognition. He decided he would march boldly into a pool of boiling tar on the volcanic planet Cirsius, if asked by his Captain. *Kevin.* He smiled.

Jesik settled back in his seat as he observed the Lieutenant Commander's smile. *Well, at least that settled the immediate storm*, he thought. *I sincerely hope Darcy's right and that it's a girl, or something else that simple.*

16—AN OFFICER AND AN IDIOT

The passage to Keswick was routine. The best accomplishment of the journey was that their earlier experience in navigating through the asteroid belt had inspired Lieutenant Commander Wight to develop a new strategy that shortened the transit time by nearly a month. The change was rather revolutionary, in that it called for a slight bend at the inverted end of the Vortex field, to allow them to penetrate nearly one third of the way into the asteroid belt before decelerating. Such a curve had happened occasionally in the past, but never by design. The mathematics involved in warping the vortex were sophisticated enough that Wight invited Eaves and Carter, now on rotating shifts piloting the Allegro, to add their input. The danger of a ship encountering an asteroid while in vortex drive was so significant and possibly lethal that there was absolutely no room for doubt or error. At first, Jesik refused to entertain the idea of coming any closer than 10,000 kilometers to any asteroid. But as the team refined their calculations, they convinced him that the force of a starship's vortex could sweep aside any small fragments or meteors that might not be indicated on their maps, thus making the technique viable. When scientists on Kalenden confirmed the veracity of the idea, Jesik decided to chance it.

Lieutenant Commander Wight attempted to persuade Eaves to pilot the ship during the critical last moments in vortex drive, but Eaves deferred, indicating Wight had more experience with the Allegro and understood the concept better than anyone else. That was a big boost to Wight's self-confidence. He was finally relaxed around Eaves and Carter. Everyone held their breath when the ship entered the asteroid belt under full acceleration, but everything worked exactly as predicted and the ship decelerated smoothly to sub-light drive, significantly ahead of their original schedule.

One of the benefits of Wight's discovery was that freighters couldn't maintain tight enough control of their vortex field to make the necessary curve, which meant that the military finally had a speed advantage over orchidite smugglers. Jesik believed that in time the "Wight Curve," as it was named, would prove a significant weapon in the fight against crime, as well as reducing the cost of deep-space travel.

Kensington blustered a bit about junior officers wasting time on scatter-brained ideas, but the technique was well received at fleet headquarters. Jesik was pleased when his bridge officers showed initiative, particularly since it always improved morale.

During the journey, Colonel Kensington had remained remarkably quiet and unobtrusive, aside from his weekly sermons. For the first two-thirds of the way, he'd maintained the optimistic attitude that characterized his first boarding of the ship. But, for the past few weeks, he'd confined himself to his quarters, working furiously on his computer console. While he didn't talk about what he was doing, there was ominous urgency to his work.

Another item that concerned Jesik was Brighton's patrimony problem. Whenever he attempted to raise the issue, the Commander avoided the topic. He was unusually interested in the arrival of the Legato, a ship that was scheduled to rendezvous with the Allegro approximately half-way between Keswick and Alturus. There was no indication of what he was going to do about the child. It certainly must have been born by now, so Brighton didn't have much time to deal with it. Jesik decided to wait a while longer for him to talk about it, but would eventually have to force the issue.

"Captain on the bridge!"

"At ease, gentlemen."

"We've established geo-synchronous orbit, Sir and received a number of communications from the surface, as well as from Commander Rowley, who arrived in orbit several days ago."

"Very good, Commander. Mr. Williams, please send my regards to Fermata and invite Captain Rowley and his First Officer to join us for dinner this evening?"

"Yes, Sir."

"Mr. Brighton, I hope you'll join us. It looks like our situation is stable enough for you to implement your R&R schedule for crew transfers to the surface. I'm to meet Colonel Wilkerson tomorrow, so I'll need the high-speed shuttle."

"Will Colonel Kensington be joining you, Sir?"

"I don't know. He's been invited, but I think it's his intention to wait for a formal welcoming ceremony consistent with his status as our representative to Alturus. Mr. Darcy, you'll need to stay onboard to help him get ready."

Darcy growled more than replied, but Jesik let it pass.

Kensington did not join Jesik the next day. He hardly glanced up from his computer screen when Jesik stopped by to extend a personal invitation and indicated that he was occupied with important matters that he'd bring to Jesik's attention shortly. Also, it was Lansing and Wilkerson's place to invite him to the planet, not Jesik's. The Captain acknowledged and went to the shuttle bay, relieved to be traveling alone.

On the surface, the shuttle docked at the People's Palace, which appeared quite different than the first time he'd seen it as a result of multiple attacks by the various rebel and insurgency groups. Inside was changed as well, with most of the private living quarters converted into office space and the place was abuzz with activity. From the fresh, young faces walking up and down the hall, it was obvious that Lansing's administration had opened government service to a whole new cadre of civil servants who were there because of talent, not heredity. Colonel Wilkerson chatted amiably as they worked their way toward the Kalenden Special Representative suite of offices. He appeared relaxed, acknowledging greetings from those they passed.

Once inside the privacy of his office, his tone became much more serious. "I'm glad you're here, Captain. After the insurgency Lansing has accomplished a great deal in terms of reorganizing the government, and the economy is finally starting to improve. But his hands are more than full. The Loyalist bureaucrats have instituted a number of "by the book" slowdowns to protest his demands for greater accountability and efficiency. The former rebel coalition is also feeling the strain of having to deal with day-to-day management, which isn't nearly as exciting as coming together in a common cause of bringing a government down. And there's still unease at the thought of another Loyalist uprising. He's under a constant threat of the coalition breaking up and we continue to experience armed fighting in the provinces. Probably the greatest threat to the peace, however, comes from the orchidite traders. They've timed our one-year occupation down to the second and the price of orchidite futures has gone through the roof. It's tempting to an immature government to let the market drive prices up, promising untold wealth for the people of Keswick, with no increase in production. But neither Kalenden nor Alturus would stand for the prices that are in play right now."

"What role do you play in this, Colonel?"

"I try to be the voice of reason. Our stock with the UCG is pretty high after Lieutenant Commander Magill's little trick in ending the uprising. And I think Lansing understands that neither Alturus nor Keswick will allow fully deregulated prices, but the people he associates with don't get it. They admire Magill, but most look at me as an extension of the old Royal Family and can't wait for the day we clear out. Moreover, I'm not sure there won't be additional bloodshed before we finish the first year."

Jesik pondered quietly for a few moments then asked, "Where does Alturus stand on these issues? Have you been able to maintain meaningful contact with them?"

"Yes, but they're much more belligerent than Kalenden, with threats that the price had better not increase more than thirty percent. Considering that the futures are trading at one several hundred percent of current prices you can see why things are so tense. I guess that's why I'm pleased to have Allegro's firepower nearby. It may discourage the traders."

"Unfortunately, we won't be here very long. As soon as Colonel Kensington meets with you and Lansing, we're moving on to Alturus, where he'll take up permanent residence."

"Can't a smaller ship transport Kensington?"

"I'm afraid not. It wouldn't be consistent with the image he hopes to project to Alturus. More than that, however, is the fact that the Quadrant Council is very interested in getting my report of the political situation on Alturus. Fortunately, Legato is scheduled to arrive in a few weeks to relieve Captain Rowley, so at least you'll have a full battle-cruiser at your disposal. While not as heavily armed as Allegro, it's more than a match for anything the traders or smugglers can put up. Plus, at dinner last night, Rowley indicated he would keep the frigate here if needed, at least for awhile,. That would give you nearly twice the firepower you've had the last nine months."

"Then that'll have to do."

Wilkerson was thoughtful. "May I speak off the record, Captain?"

"Of course."

"Why Colonel Kensington? He'll aggravate Lansing and the United Governing Coalition without contributing much to the discussion. And I say that as an Army man."

Jesik laughed. "His reputation precedes him, then?"

"Reputation hell! We're in the same service branch and I've had to put up with some of his lectures personally. The man has no sensitivity whatsoever."

Jesik could see from his expression that Wilkerson wasn't in the mood to joke about this. "My impression is that the Council wants to rile Lansing a bit. If I understand their strategy, and no one has said this to me, they want to strengthen your hand by making you the good cop compared to Kensington. By drawing a contrast between the two of you the Council can make clear that if the Keswicks don't support you, they could wind up with a lot worse. I'm part of the package too, forming a back door line of communication that you and Lansing can use to communicate outside formal diplomatic channels. Plus," said Jesik, "You will shortly be notified of your promotion to full Colonel. They planned to do it earlier, but it got bogged down in the Esper network."

"Really," said Wilkerson, pleased. "But why?"

"Because you deserve it. Plus it puts you at an even rank with Kensington, so he can't try to give you orders."

Wilkerson shook his head appreciatively. At least there was some logic behind what was going on, even if he didn't yet know if he agreed with it.

" As for Alturus, it's the feeling of Admiral Park and Prime Minister Larimore that Colonel Kensington will actually fit in quite nicely with their Royal Family. He certainly flaunts the superiority of his own family line." Jesik smiled ruefully, which made Wilkerson laugh.

"Maybe, but I've got an idea the Royal Family on Alturus is pretty shrewd. They'll recognize an amateur when they see him and if Kensington doesn't watch himself, he'll cede the whole Kalenden Quadrant to Alturus."

Jesik laughed and with their former chemistry reestablished, they talked on for another hour, reviewing specific players and issues in the orchidite drama until Jesik was comfortably ready to meet Lansing again. A call was placed and they scheduled a meeting first thing the following morning. They then adjourned to their rooms to change for dinner.

As Jesik entered the restaurant an hour later, he was surprised to see the place was packed. Perhaps the speed of the revolution minimized the psychological damage, but it looked like once the uprising had been put down the citizenry had adapted quickly to their new government. As he approached the maitre-d, he heard a familiar voice from behind and turned with a smile to greet Lieutenant Commander Magill. He was shocked by what he saw, for though the young man had always been thin, he was athletic. The young officer who stood before him now appeared downright gaunt. Jesik smiled brightly and returned Magill's crisp salute. Still, the surprise must have shown on his face.

"Don't worry, Sir, I don't feel nearly as bad as I look."

"You've lost some weight."

"Yes, Sir. The constant pain in my feet has affected my appetite. Plus, I can't exercise as I'd like to, although I continue to work on upper body strength. I also force myself to eat some high-nutrient supplements in addition to whatever meals I do eat, so the doctors say I'm not in any danger of malnutrition." He looked down at his feet. Jesik followed his gaze and couldn't help but notice that he now used two full length crutches.

"Some people say I should just get it over with and have them amputated. Artificial limb technology makes it possible to have virtually full function again, but I don't want to lose the feeling down there. One of my doctors thinks I should use a wheelchair, but at least for now I prefer to keep my legs as strong as possible so I don't have to go through therapy once the feet heal." He looked up and smiled. "I'd really like to play soccer again and need my real limbs to make it on a sanctioned team."

While Jesik thought it unlikely that Sean would ever play soccer again, he didn't say so. They moved to the table reserved for them. He was surprised that people seemed not to notice Magill's infirmity, even though it would have caused a notable stir on Kalenden, but realized that his prominence here undoubtedly had put people at ease with the condition.

It was Magill's misfortune to have suffered radiation burns prior to taking the antidote and even the most sophisticated medications had failed to cure him. Then there was the injury to his right foot during his espionage. "I'd probably have given up hope for my feet if it weren't for the gel boots the Alturians gave me. As long as the gel remained active I could get by pretty well. But about a month ago, the gel began to harden, so I had to give them up. The pain is getting worse."

"I understand the Alturians have offered to perform surgery for you."

"Yes, Sir. I hope you can find room for me as you transport Colonel Kensington to Alturus. It's the only hope for keeping my feet."

"Of course you'll come with us. Lieutenant Eaves has been pestering me to see you, anyway. Plus, I think your diplomatic experience here will prove useful to our discussions with the Alturians. Colonel Wilkerson tells me you've done a great job helping him sort out the politics of Keswick."

"I've enjoyed working with him, very much. He's a skilled adviser to PM Lansing, but the fact that he comes from a first-class family makes it difficult for many rebels to relate to him. My lower-class credentials open doors into private conversations which we wouldn't otherwise hear."

"And what is your assessment of the long-term prospects of this government?"

"I don't think they'll have any real trouble hanging on. The people love that the government is open to public input."

"And the things you said in support of Mr. Lansing had to help…"

Magill looked surprised.

"I've been thoroughly briefed. It was a very courageous thing for you to do. I'm glad that your life was spared."

"Me, too. Although it was a matter of seconds. I thought the Loyalists would keep me alive as a bargaining chip, but when their leader went berserk I was pretty scared."

"Which adds to the valor—it wouldn't be bravery if a person weren't frightened."

Magill blushed and then continued, as if the previous two paragraphs hadn't been discussed, " I think the biggest danger to Keswick comes from Alturus. I understand there's a much more powerful underground movement there than anyone anticipated. The second and third-class families see what's happening here, in spite of an official government news blackout and there's quite a bit of agitation. The social networks get past the blocking, as they always do. The main problem is that if the Alturian monarchy clamps down at home, they'll likely accompany it with an invasion here, to stop the rebel movement once and for all. I believe that's Mr. Lansing's biggest concern. If he moves too slowly on promised reforms, he comes under criticism from his own party, but if he becomes aggressive in breaking up the old class structure, the Alturians go crazy. He has a high-wire act to perform and I think it's wearing on him. I get the feeling there's a lot of illegal correspondence going on between some of the rebel cells here and their counterparts on Alturus."

Colonel Wilkerson entered. "Sorry I'm late. There's trouble at the mines. The workers want a pay raise immediately and have taken the position that it's the government's fault for caving in to the Alturian and Kalenden demands. So, we're in a diplomatic battle again."

"Perhaps this is one for Colonel Kensington to cut his diplomatic teeth on," said Jesik. They had a good laugh at that.

From then on the dinner discussion picked up from where Jesik and Magill left it. It was obvious that Wilkerson enjoyed his association with Magill and was going to miss him when he left for Alturus.

Jesik was grateful for the briefing when he met with John Lansing the following morning. Lansing looked tired, but had the same, powerful drive that allowed him to dominate a conversation without being overbearing. He was wise enough to first make plans for the official reception of Colonel

Kensington the upcoming weekend, personally extending the invitation. Kensington was pleased to have the Prime Minister himself make the call and humbly accepted. Lansing dispatched his aides to quickly issue invitations to all foreign delegations, as well as to the cabinet and chief government ministers. In a remarkable display of organizational skill, he planned the outline of a formal reception, dinner and entertainment in fewer than thirty minutes, then put it aside. He and Jesik discussed the terrorist attacks at the Manhattan Trials.

"While the news reports are sketchy, I understand it was the skill of your crew that halted the terrorist attacks on your home planet. Congratulations on your leadership."

"I wish I could take credit, Prime Minister, but it was Lieutenant Eaves' quick reactions that saved the day." Lansing nodded in understanding. After all, Eaves had escaped Keswick from under the rebels' noses.

"I wish to get directly to the point, Captain. We were not aware of the Kalenden terrorist attacks until after they occurred. From what our intelligence has gathered the splinter group here on Keswick, which sent the fighter had broken off from our party long before our rebellion had taken place. Apparently we weren't nearly radical enough for them since we were content to focus our ambitions on Keswick, while they wanted to foment rebellion everywhere. I hope Kalenden will not hold our government responsible."

"Nothing of that kind has been said to me," replied Jesik. "But please tell me, what do you believe is the group's ultimate objective?"

"As far as I can tell, it's to destroy all hereditary rights of property ownership, government service and social class distinction throughout all populated star systems. They and the half dozen or so groups like them, are utopian in their ambitions and ruthless in their execution. They say they want to make the galaxy better for all people, no matter how many they hurt or murder in getting there."

"And where do you personally stand regarding their exporting revolution? After all, you were quite ruthless in your decision to use nuclear weapons to achieve your objectives."

Lansing gave Jesik a piercing look, trying to judge how far he could trust him. After an extended pause, he continued. "Our party would eventually like to see greater unity among the leading planets of this system. We believe to accomplish that, all people must be allowed to participate in the processes of their government. Having said that, we also respect the sovereignty of Alturus and Keswick and have no interest in stirring up trouble there. It's taking much of our energy just to manage the transition here, so why would we take on the added burden of interfering on your planet?"

"Perhaps because idealists are never content as long as injustice exists anywhere."

"I think, Captain, that both Colonel Wilkerson and Lieutenant Commander Magill will tell you that I'm more pragmatic than idealistic. I'm perfectly content to take things one step at a time and right now that means focusing on Keswick."

Jesik sat back in his chair, an indicator that he was content with Lansing's answer, even though he didn't address the implications of the nuclear attack.

"To what degree can you provide assurances to our government, as well as to the leaders on Alturus?"

"Well, that's where the serious discussion has to take place. I think Lieutenant Commander Magill is best suited to tell you the depth of antipathy that many of my second and third-class advisers feel about our aiding a monarchy or class-divided culture anywhere. It is an anachronism to exclude the talent and skill of second and third-class families and to my advisers it seems almost criminal that we help either Kalenden or Alturus. Their attitude, too, is that if a revolution is brewing on either planet, let it go forward with our blessing, but not with our help."

"But you will oppose those elements?"

Lansing nodded. "Right now we need a stable relationship with both planets, not a blockade or invasion. I don't sense that Kalenden is nearly as volatile as Alturus, so I've focused most of my energies there. There is limited intelligence I can share with the Alturians, although not through formal diplomatic channels. They're far too leaky to trust. As to Kalenden, you know everything we do about the Keswick participation in the terrorist attacks. To my knowledge, it was an isolated incident by a relatively small group so if your people use common sense security measures and don't overreact, I believe you can keep your planet safe. It's easy for terrorists to destroy complex infrastructure, but that doesn't necessarily win people's hearts to their cause."

Jesik thanked Lansing for his candor and indicated he wished to be open and frank as well. He explained that he was there on special assignment from Prime Minister Larimore to offer his services as an unofficial means of communication with both Keswick and Alturus. The Allegro had been chosen to transport Colonel Kensington in order to provide an innocuous way for Jesik to travel between the three systems.

"Then I'm relieved you're here, because I trust you personally and it indicates maturity by Kalenden's leadership. If I have enough time to complete the transition to a republic, I'm sure we can become stable partners. And now, I have a number of messages I'd like you to deliver to the PM on Alturus." From that point on, their dinner conversation was far more relaxed.

Discussions over the next few days focused on providing stability to the orchidite trade, for Jesik was of the opinion that wildly fluctuating prices would benefit the traders and speculators, not the miners or citizens of Keswick. He supported Wilkerson's recommendation that the Keswicks consider long-term contracts with price escalation clauses that would ease the economic impact on the Kalenden and Alturian economies while providing Keswick with a stable cash flow. He emphasized that although Keswick had some of the highest quality orchidite, they weren't the only available source. Lansing agreed in principle, but explained that even a Prime Minister has to consult with his bureaucracy, so Jesik's recommendations were tabled for review. As a member of a second-class family, Jesik's thoughts were taken more seriously than he might have been otherwise.

Kensington's reception was a grand affair. Old Loyalists showed up in droves, their formal evening wear providing a stark contrast to the business attire of the new cadre of the Governing Council. Kensington made a witty speech that was innocuous enough to offend no one and short enough to please everyone. Lansing handed him the key to the Capitol and everyone applauded. Kensington positively glowed in the attention. Jesik credited him with getting off to a positive start.

After three weeks in port, the Allegro was fully provisioned and staffed and prepared to leave orbit. Eaves flew down to the surface to collect the Allegro delegation and, on the way back up to the ship, he teased Magill by saying that he was probably faking his injuries to have an excuse to go to Alturus and see Tara Carling. His taunting had the desired effect. When Eaves wasn't looking, Magill swung a crutch across the back of his head, which evened the score a bit.

Once onboard, Colonel Kensington remained socially engaged for three or four days, then withdrew into his quarters once again. It appeared he spent most of his seclusion preparing a memorial service over which he was to preside marking the first time a Kalenden ship crossed into Alturian space in more than 200 years. "Inasmuch as the ceremony commemorating those who died in the ancient conflict will be broadcast live to both Alturus and Kalenden, I must be thoroughly prepared," said Kensington in his condescending way.

Prior to reaching the boundary the Allegro decelerated out of vortex drive so that normal communications could be established. It always took the Espers a while to locate each other's thought patterns across the vastness of space and to synchronize their abilities so they could properly relay information. About that time, the Legato appeared out of vortex drive to serve as the Allegro's second when they crossed the boundary. Once on the other side, an Alturian starship would escort the Allegro to the planet and the Legato would proceed to Keswick. Everything was proceeding according to plan and Jesik was actually pleased to have Kensington in charge of the diplomacy because it took the onus off Jesik. Plus, the Colonel was showing promise in his new role.

* * *

"You there, come with me. Now!"

Magill didn't like the look on Colonel Kensington's face and wondered what he was up to. He hobbled along as fast as he could, trying to keep up with Kensington's furious pace. When they reached Captain Jesik's private cabin, Kensington demanded entrance. Magill caught up just as the doors were about to close.

"How can I help you, Colonel?"

"You can summon Commander Brighton and Lieutenant Commander Wight to your cabin immediately."

"They're both on duty. Can we schedule another, more convenient time to meet with them?"

"No! You'll get them here, right now!"

Jesik's face clouded up and he looked to Magill to see if he could indicate what was going on, but Magill just shrugged his shoulders.

"With due respect, Colonel, you are not in command here and I will summon my officers when I think it best."

"You'll get them here right now, Jesik! I have proof of serious misconduct and I must clear it up before this mission can continue. If I have to contact Fleet I will, but I believe it's in your best interest to deal with it first."

Jesik thought about challenging him further, but decided it wasn't worth it. He contacted Brighton and Wight and requested them to come to his quarters immediately. A few moments later they entered, looking apprehensive. Jesik invited everyone to sit, but Kensington remained standing.

"Gentlemen, Colonel Kensington indicates he has concern that requires your attention. I don't know what it is, or why he's also asked Lieutenant Commander Magill to be here, so I'll leave it to the Colonel to explain."

"I asked this man to join us to witness this." He looked sternly at both Brighton and Wight. The young man shrank back in his seat, but Brighton maintained an unconcerned look.

"For the past three months, I have been reviewing the operational efficiency of this vessel. Since my life is in your hands I like to know where things stand."

No one said anything, so Kensington cleared his throat. Apparently whatever he had to say made him a bit nervous.

"While there's always room for improvement, by and large your performance is within fleet standards. However, in reviewing your log of outgoing communications I came across some very disturbing information. I've now had a chance to use my diplomatic clearance to conduct an in-depth review and must now confront the ugly truth."

"What ugly truth?" asked Jesik.

"Just this, Captain. These two officers have engaged in conduct unbecoming an officer. In both instances they've violated Kalenden's morality laws and now place the reputation of the entire fleet at risk."

Brighton shifted in his chair, but maintained eye contact with Kensington, which slightly unnerved the Colonel. Wight, on the other hand, blanched as the color drained from his face.

"Colonel, I don't know what you have to reveal, but perhaps we should meet with each officer individually."

"Curse it Jesik! There's no time for that! In three days the Alturian Starship will be here to escort me to my new posting and I want this cleared up before then."

Jesik glowered, but allowed Kensington to proceed.

"First, let's talk about Commander Brighton. I encountered some interesting messages that prompted me to run a scan of the ship's genetic records. My search turned up evidence that the Commander is the father of a one-month old baby boy born to a Tatrius woman. I was puzzled by that, of course, since I was unaware that Commander Brighton was married. It turns out he isn't married, so has fathered a child out of wedlock. A child seventy-five percent Kalenden, I might add. This is a flagrant violation of our non-fraternization policy and makes the Commander subject to a Courts Martial."

Jesik looked at Brighton, furious with himself for not forcing the issue earlier. Brighton, for his part, continued to look rather peaceful, although clearly annoyed by Kensington's intrusion.

"Well, what do you say to this charge!" Kensington demanded.

"I'm not prepared to discuss it with you at this moment. If you're making this a formal accusation, I'll need time to prepare; at least two days."

"So, you don't deny it!" Kensington shouted.

"I neither deny nor confirm it. If you wish to pursue this matter, I insist it be in a formal hearing." His defiant attitude cowed Kensington a bit, who clearly expected the Commander to fall apart at the accusation.

"Fine, Commander. We'll convene an official inquiry in two days and you will be prepared to explain your breach of military code. If your explanation is acceptable, no formal charges will be filed. If it isn't, as I suspect, you'll be placed under immediate house arrest."

Brighton settled back in his seat, angry, but still fully in control. Turning to Wight, Kensington puffed up for the next round.

Jesik attempted to intervene. "Colonel, I'd like to talk with you privately before you confront Mr. Wight with whatever charges you plan to level. I'll not have you confronting a member of my crew without my prior knowledge."

"Captain, you have no authority in this case. Lieutenant Commander Wight is guilty of violations of both the civil and military code, so I can confront him in my role as an ex-officio member of the Quadrant Council." Jesik could see that Wight was actually trembling and wished desperately that he could somehow help him. But with no idea what was to come, there was no way to provide a shield.

"It seems, Captain, that your Mr. Wight has a problem. A search of his outgoing communications via the interstellar net show that he has visited a number of "unsavory" sites – sites forbidden under the Basic Rules of Morality statutes. Do you care to explain Mr. Wight?"

"But, Sir," Wight stammered, "I only went to those sites to conduct research on a social science paper I'm writing for the academy."

"Rubbish. The sites you've visited have no bearing whatsoever on the academy and you know it."

Jesik attempted to interrupt, but Kensington turned on him with a fury.

"Captain, before you rush to this man's defense, you better watch yourself. The sites he visited carry such labels as 'Men with Men' and 'Same Sex Attractions.' In other words this person is a homosexual, using military equipment to indulge his twisted fantasies!"

The look of astonishment on Jesik's, Brighton's and Magill's face was what Kensington had hoped for. A long pause ensued in which no one said anything. What could prepare them? This type of behavior was so long listed as formally extinct in Kalenden society that it was never even considered.

"Kevin," asked Jesik, "is this true?"

Wight turned to him with a wild look in his eyes.

"It's true I visited those sites, but it isn't the way Colonel Kensington makes it sound. There are no graphics, only text that talks about the ancient practice. It's still practiced on Earth and has general acceptance there and elsewhere."

Kensington moved to retake control from Jesik. "Whether there are graphics or not is immaterial. The sites are forbidden, which means charges must be filed. Plus, there's no reason for anyone to visit such a site unless they have a personal interest in such things. I'm afraid, Lieutenant Commander, that it is my duty to formally charge you with violating the Morality Law. You can ride back to Kalenden on the Legato to face a Courts Martial."

"But, Sir, such a proceeding would be devastating to my mother and to her family," Wight pleaded. "Can't I just resign from the service quietly and avoid a public trial? My mother's done nothing wrong, but she would pay the biggest price."

The mention of Kevin's mother brought Jesik to his feet and he exploded. "Kensington, I will not allow you to destroy this young man or Commander Brighton! Whatever has happened can be dealt with through private discipline and you know it. Your only motive in forcing these incidents into the public spotlight is to embarrass me, even though it ruins the careers of these men. Understand me clearly. I will not stand for it. Not this time!"

Even Brighton shrank back in his seat at this. He'd never seen Jesik in such a fury and the tone in his voice suggested that he was angry enough to actually move against Kensington physically.

Even though he shrunk back in his seat, Kensington did not yield. "Captain, I will not be intimidated by you. You are in no position to make demands at all. It falls to the ship's Captain to keep track of his officers and their breach of the Morality Laws makes you subject to censure as well. That you promoted this man to a line position at such a young age, particularly in view of his egregious conduct, shows the total lack of sound judgment on your part!"

"So, that's it! One last chance to take me down." Jesik clasped his hands together to mask their trembling. "I actually thought you'd changed, that this assignment to Alturus had given you whatever you needed to get on with your life and let old demons die. But, no, you son-of-a-bitch, you have to stay with it no matter who gets hurt. You will not do it to these men! With heaven as my witness, you will not destroy them to get at me!"

"Lieutenant Commander, what's your name?" Kensington looked at Magill, whose name he should have known, but Magill quickly averted his eyes. Still, he quietly repeated his name. "Lieutenant Commander Magill, you will note that Captain Jesik is threatening me."

"I'm not threatening, I'm promising."

For a moment the two of them stared at each other with a fury in their eyes that spoke of ancient grievances. Then Kensington relaxed and smiled.

"Perhaps you're right, Captain. The best way to cure a cancer is to cut out its core. The only thing these two men have in common is your leadership. That they could both commit such flagrant violations of our most sacred laws right under your ineffective nose indicates an appalling lack of supervision on your part. Maybe they're symptoms of the illness, while you are the cause."

"You'll not blame my behavior on Captain Jesik," said Brighton, but Kensington waved him down with a gesture.

"Here's my offer, Jesik. If you will submit your resignation from the service, effective immediately, I will see that Lieutenant Commander Wight is allowed to resign quietly, with no entry of this in his record. He can then slink back to Kalenden or Tatrius to pursue his degenerate practices in private, while you simply disappear from the public scene. I'll even drop the charges against Commander Brighton if he agrees to leave Kalenden permanently."

Jesik slumped in his seat. Wight tried to protest that he would go through the ordeal of a trial rather than have the Captain surrender to this blackmail, but Jesik put his hand on Kevin's arm and told him to say nothing more, since the real attack was against Jesik, not him.

Finally, after what seemed an eternity of silence, Jesik told Kensington that he was likely to accept the offer, but that he needed some time to consider its ramifications. Kensington smiled and moralized that he was a reasonable man and Jesik could have the two days Commander Brighton requested – just as long as he resigned before the Legato left station. Kensington then turned and thanked Magill for his service, indicating that as an officer, he was bound to report all that had happened accurately and without prejudice if ever questioned. Magill nodded glumly in the affirmative and Kensington left the room.

After he was gone Jesik turned to Kevin, whose eyes were now watering as he tried to hold back tears. His humiliation was complete and the force of Kensington's vitriol and Jesik's anger had cowed him completely.

"Kevin, I know this sounds like the worst thing in the world, but I promise that things will work out." Wight didn't look up. He stared at the table in front of him, trance-like.

"Kevin, look at me." The young man caught his breath and looked up with a paralyzed expression.

"Kevin, whatever is going on in your life has little to do with what took place here today. Colonel Kensington has been seeking to destroy me for many years and the charges against you and Commander Brighton are simply his current line of attack. I promise you that he will not use this to hurt you or your mother."

"But, Sir, it's true that I went to those sites. I didn't think they were in violation of the morality laws. But if they're forbidden, I'm guilty."

Jesik caught his own breath, afraid to ask the next question, but knowing he had to.

"Kevin, do you have questions about your own sexuality? Moreover, have you ever acted out your doubts?"

At this Wight couldn't control his emotions any longer and started sobbing, his shoulders heaving up and down as the physical manifestation of the emotional agony he was enduring. Jesik stood up and put his arms on his shoulders, while Magill and Brighton moved closer to provide support. Finally, he quieted down and looked at them with something of a pathetic look.

"I have never acted, Sir. But it's true I don't understand my feelings. I've lived with thoughts that I hate for so many years it's hard not to hate myself. Yet, this is how I've always felt and a part of me says it isn't wrong. I'm sure that this is me, because I've tried so hard to think other ways." He took a deep breath. "It's just me." Wisely, Jesik and the others said nothing. "My greatest fear has been that someone would one day find out about it. Now that's come true and may cost you your career, or make my mother face the public humiliation of a trial." The look of terror returned.

Jesik calmed himself as best he could, taking a number of breaths to steady his own voice.

"Kevin, I have no frame of reference to understand what you're feeling, because I've never personally had such thoughts. I don't pretend to comprehend the complexities of human nature, but I know, first hand, of your character and you're one of the finest men I've ever known. You have a great deal to offer our system, no matter your personal feelings. The only tragedy that can happen today is if you lose faith in yourself. I want you to look at me."

Wight kept his eyes averted until Jesik lifted his chin.

"Kevin, no matter what happens in the next two days, I personally think highly of you. If I end up making a career change, it will be because of events in my life, not yours, so don't give up hope. Trust me to make things work out." Wight tried to avert his eyes again, but Jesik held them with his. "Will you trust me?" Finally, Kevin nodded in the affirmative.

"Good. I want you to go to your room now and collect your thoughts. I also want you to report to duty for your regular shift. You are every bit as capable of piloting this starship now as you were half-an-hour ago before Colonel Kensington summoned you here. Understand?"

"Yes, Sir. Thank you."

"Mr. Magill, will you be kind enough to escort the Mr. Wight to his quarters?"

"Yes, Sir." Magill gave Wight his arm and escorted him from the room. Concerned that Wight might do something drastic if left alone Sean spent the next two hours in his room talking. Magill told him of his own struggles of having been an outsider in school and how lonely it was to feel different from everyone around you. He also talked about what he'd learned from having his feet burned, having to trust other people to help him when he'd prided himself of being independent. For the first time in his life, Magill was offering comfort to another human being by opening up to his own fears, anger and disappointments. Eventually, Wight was able to share his feelings with Magill, telling him everything he'd suppressed through the lonely years he'd nurtured his thoughts. It started with halting words, but eventually flooded out. "I'm embarrassed to say such things openly, but sharing this with another person is helpful."

Magill nodded. He was not as naïve as many of the others and knew perfectly well that there were others on Kalenden who felt as Kevin did – there had always been. He'd had friends whom he suspected of it, but no one in his rank had made an issue of it. When Kevin finally started to nod off to sleep, out of sheer exhaustion, Magill covered him with a blanket and turned out the lights.

Back in his own quarters Magill reflected on what he had learned the past year, painfully aware that before being wounded on Keswick, he would have had a much harder time expressing empathy to Wight. But, now, because of his own suffering, he felt an understanding for Kevin and wished, more than anything, that he could comfort him and give him hope that his life still had meaning, no matter what lay ahead. "Who'd have guessed I'd have to lose my feet to find my heart?" He lay back on his own bed and fell into troubled slumber.

* * *

As soon as Wight and Magill had cleared the room, Jesik turned to Brighton.

"Blast you Commander, why didn't you talk to me about this earlier? I tried, but you always brushed me off. Now Kensington's involved."

"Captain, you don't need to worry on my account. I can take care of myself."

"Not worry? Not worry?" Jesik shook his head, at a loss for words. *How could Brighton be so naïve to his own danger?* "I tried to make you see this could end your career, Tom, but no matter what I did, I couldn't get your attention. You're a great officer, but your cavalier attitude may now ruin everything."

Brighton started to respond, but Jesik interrupted. "Tom, you're the best officer I've ever served with." He hesitated, "And you are my friend. Why didn't you protect yourself?"

"Captain, you have to believe me. I'm okay and my career will not come to an end. There's a reason I asked for a formal inquiry. Please trust me on this. I can handle Colonel Kensington."

Jesik hesitated. "Well, I don't see how, but if you wish to proceed on your own, I guess I have no choice but to trust you."

"I won't be on my own. At the right moment you'll stand up for me. But in the meantime there are some things I need to take care of."

"Then that's how it will be."

"My concern is for Wight," Brighton continued. "I felt like I'd been kicked in the stomach when Kensington accused him. Nothing like this has happened in more than a hundred years, at least as far as I know. But, it sounds like the charges are true."

"I've got to protect him, Tom. It's rotten for Kensington to destroy his life, no matter what you or I may think about Kevin's inclination. He doesn't deserve to be humiliated for what's a part of who he is." Jesik slowly shook his head, as if trying to force his mind to come to terms with this new challenge. "But I don't know how I can help. To do so, I'd have to take on the Morality Laws themselves and it would be hard to find anyone who would support that. I don't know if I support it. So it may be that the only way out of this is to meet Kensington's demand for my own resignation."

"Sir, with all due respect, I need to intrude on your personal life. I don't know how I can help Kevin, but I intend to find a way. But, to do that, I need to know the source of the bad blood between you and Kensington, so I'll know what I'm fighting."

"That's my business, Tom, not anyone else's, not even yours. I put it to rest a long time ago and I don't want to resurrect it." Jesik had a faraway look to his eye that said he was re-living some incident from the past.

"Captain, whether you put it to rest or not, Colonel Kensington hasn't. Please tell me. I need to find some way to stop him." After a moment he added, "You said you think of me as a friend."

Jesik looked up and started to reject his inquiry a second time, then paused. Lowering his face, he sighed. "Why not? There's nothing more that Kensington can do to me, now. He's left no way for me to win this time, just like the first time, except that now I'll go away and never bother him again."

Jesik slumped into his seat and proceeded to tell the story. "When I was a nineteen-year-old Cadet at the Academy, I fell in love with a beautiful young woman named Helen Wentworth. She had the most striking eyes in the world and her personality was the perfect match to mine. While my natural inclination is to take things as they come, she was much more ambitious, but not in an arrogant way. She thought that people who did their very best could make the worlds brighter and more meaningful. She was a true idealist. But, since her ambition was softened by a terrific sense of humor, it was easy to talk with her – and fall in love."

In spite of the circumstances, he smiled at the memory. "She had the kind of laugh that could fill an empty room. At first I had a lot of rivals, but in time it came down to just one – Kensington. I'd gotten into the Academy on one of the three scholarships offered to second-class families, just like Lieutenant Commander Magill. Helen, though, was from a distinguished family. In fact, her father was a minister on the Council. Naturally Kensington thought it was shameful that she showed interest in a second-class person, so he made it his personal mission to win her away from me."

He stopped to sip some water. Brighton sensed whatever was next was obviously painful. "He didn't succeed, though. Helen couldn't stand his posturing and saw through his shallow attempts to flatter her. He thought she should marry him because of his family name, but she cared nothing about that."

Jesik paused, again. Brighton could see that there was another "but" statement coming.

"Unfortunately, her father cared, aghast at the thought of her diminishing the family name by marrying someone from a lower-class. He tried to break us up, even forced her to stop seeing me. But, it didn't work. In fact..." Jesik paused abruptly as if it was hard for him to breathe.

"... In fact, she became pregnant and scared to death. But I was thrilled, because I thought it would force her father to let us marry and I wanted that more than anything. Our confrontation with him was ugly, but when she threatened to run away from home he finally relented. He insisted on a small, private ceremony quickly, so the timing would make the pregnancy appear legitimate."

Jesik stopped again, much of his energy spent. Brighton nudged him to go on.

"Everything seemed to be going right for us and then one day Kensington overheard us talking. He was smart enough to put two-and-two together and bribed a nurse at the clinic to give him a copy of the pregnancy test. Rather than coming to us, he went straight to her father and threatened to reveal the incident, including her father's attempt to cover it up. Of course, that would have ruined her father's career and so he called Helen and me to face Kensington, telling us that we had to give the baby up for adoption and I had to agree never to see Helen again. If we'd do that, Kensington would sign a document promising never to reveal the details in exchange for a recommendation that he be promoted directly to Captain upon graduation. His grades didn't justify that, but cabinet ministers had a way of making their influence felt. So, the devil's deal was struck. Kensington was able to blackmail Helen's family and they could still blackmail him by proving that he didn't deserve his posting to Captain. Thus, a successful balance of terror was established."

"What did you do?"

"What did I do? I pleaded with Helen to go with me to Tatrius or even Earth, where we could get away from all of these narrow-minded, bigoted people and raise our child. I begged her to run away with me. I've never seen anyone struggle so hard emotionally and I hated Kensington for making her suffer such anguish. At one point, it looked like she was going to go with me, but then her father pleaded with her not to ruin his career. She had never seen him show any emotions except anger or impatience previous to this, and it unnerved her. So, she chose her father over me and that night was the last time I ever saw her, at least alone. Her father arranged that I never had the chance to see our baby, or to even know whether it was a boy or girl. I would have been washed out of the Academy, too, if it had been up to Kensington. But Helen's father thought that would look too suspicious and so she went to visit relatives on a distant planet and I was transferred to boundary patrol, while Kensington moved up the military command. He thought that when I was out of the scene he could win Helen's heart. But of course, she hated him more than ever. For someone like Kensington, that meant his victory over me was only partial, so he's spent the past twenty-five years trying to get me kicked out of the service to make his triumph complete."

Jesik looked totally spent from telling the story.

"Forgive me, Sir, but can I ask you a question?"

"Yes."

"Whatever happened to Helen Wentworth?"

Jesik looked up with a wan smile. "That's what makes the story so very interesting. She remained single for a time and then her father arranged for her to marry another cabinet minister, a much older bachelor in his late-forties who was very wealthy, but in need of a wife to help him fill his social calendar. His name was Jonathan Wight and Kevin is their only child. Jonathan died several years ago"

Brighton sat back in his chair and exhaled slowly. "Now Kensington has the chance to hurt both of you again."

"Which is why I've got to stop him, Tom, no matter what it costs me personally." Jesik leaned forward with fire in his eyes. "He hurt Helen once and I won't let him do it again. Through the years I've put up with his bullying, in part to deny him the satisfaction of getting to me, but mostly to protect Helen."

"Captain, I don't know what I can do, but will you arrange for me to be relieved of my regular duties for the next two days. It's urgent that I have some time to think this through."

"I'll arrange it," said Jesik, "but I don't see it'll do much good. I think he's finally got me."

"Thank you for sharing with me, Sir. At least now I understand why you were so unnerved by my situation. Now if you'll excuse me, I've got work to do." He stood and started to leave the room. Turning, he said, "And, by the way, will you please take the advice you gave Wight and trust me that things will work out?"

"Do whatever you can, Commander. Maybe you can keep him from destroying all three of us."

When Brighton left Jesik rose and moved to his bed. He rubbed his temples, laid down and tried to fall asleep, thinking about Helen and the family they might have had together. He also thought of the child he never knew. "Why is life so unfair?" he asked aloud.

"Is that a question?" the computer responded.

"Only if you have an answer."

Once again the computer was silent.

17— SECRETS REVEALED

The next two days seemed interminable and Jesik had to constantly fight the feeling that he was in a fog. Although he was fully aware of everything going on and issued orders appropriately, he felt detached from the normal operations of the ship. He was greatly relieved when Lieutenant Commander Wight reported to duty the morning after Kensington's accusations and even more relieved that Lieutenant Commander Magill hovered nearby, in case Kevin needed support. At first, Jesik was concerned that Magill would turn on Kevin because of the unusual situation, but something had definitely changed in Magill that made him more patient and compassionate.

The most difficult challenge during the interim, was Jesik's responsibility to entertain the Captain of the Legato when he was hardly in the mood to make light conversation. When Darcy Garrard asked if he wished to invite Colonel Kensington to the dinner party, Jesik adamantly refused. *Why should he show that pompous ass any deference now?* The matter became moot, though, when Kensington showed up uninvited to the dinner and acted the role of a perfectly charming host. At first Jesik fumed, but then surrendered to his presence, actually grateful that he was there to carry the conversation. There was no reason Captain Garrard should be aware of Allegro's problem. Besides, Kensington and Garrard made a great pair, bearing names among the very finest of Kalenden society. They also had plenty to talk about, engaging in old-fashioned men's club chatter, the kind of club Jesik would never be invited to join. At least it left Jesik the privacy his mind craved. It was obvious that Kensington relished every moment of those two days, looking forward to when he would finally drive Jesik from the only other thing he'd ever cared about, besides Helen – his service in the fleet. Victory was within Kensington's grasp and he could hardly contain himself.

* * *

As the hour approached for the inquiry, Jesik reviewed all the options and still came to the same conclusion. There was nothing he could do to avert the crisis, short of his personal resignation. He fought it for a while, but finally his mind steadied and he regained the icy calm he always felt when going into battle. It was as though his mind severed the connection to his emotions and he simply responded in the most logical way possible. He would now have to make a new life for himself outside the service and so he mentally started making the adjustment.

Wight and Magill arrived at the appointed time, but Brighton was nowhere to be found. Jesik asked Williams to hail him aboard the Legato where he'd spent the previous two days, but was told that he'd implemented a personal communications blackout. *Oh, well, there's not much he can really do or say, anyway,* Jesik thought. Of course Kensington showed up precisely on time and entered the room confidently.

"And where is Commander Brighton?"

"Incommunicado." Jesik said, pointedly leaving off the word "Sir."

"It makes no difference, anyway. Shall we proceed?" The three officers present assented and Jesik initiated a recording device. It was absolutely essential that he have a personal copy of the proceedings so that he could hold Kensington accountable if he ever went against their agreement and revealed anything about either Brighton or Wight. He'd been blindsided too often to accept another double-cross.

"Well, Captain, I believe you understand the agreement I proposed. For the record I have agreed to allow Commander Brighton and Lieutenant Wight to resign their commissions privately if you will accept full responsibility for their actions as Captain of this ship. In turn, you will tender your resignation, acknowledging your combined misdeeds participating in and allowing the Morality Laws of Kalenden to be violated. Is this your understanding?"

"It is."

"Then I will need your decision, so that Fleet Command can immediately turn command of the Allegro over to Captain Garrard. His First Officer will assume command of Legato, which will transport the three of you back to Keswick, where you will formally be mustered out of the service."

Jesik's eyes flared. "You better not have spoken to Garrard about this! That would violate the second part of our agreement."

Kensington replied in a patronizing voice, "No Captain, I have not spoken to Garrard, although he should actually have received command of Allegro when it was first commissioned. Your role in the Cambriol incident was as overblown politically as the recent Shuttle Competition furor. I'm pleased that he's here to receive what's rightfully his. As to the so-called 'second part' of the agreement, please tell me exactly what you mean."

Jesik cleared his throat and spoke very clearly and calmly. "The terms you negotiated for my officers include a restriction on your part from ever revealing the nature of their violations to any outside party. You are doing this for the good of the Fleet and to prevent private misdeeds from being made public in a Courts Martial and bring discredit to the service. Should you violate this agreement, you will be personally liable for a breach of military protocol, subject to censure and further discipline."

Kensington frowned before replying. "I hardly think you're in a position to dictate terms, Captain Jesik, but you are right when you say that it's in the best interest of the Fleet that these illicit actions be concealed. Therefore, let the record show that I agree to these terms." Kensington's nostrils flared. "Now, hurry up and give me your decision."

Jesik leaned forward and picked up the electronic pen lying on the desk in front of him. Kensington smiled as he scanned the screen that presented itself to Jesik, and then watched impatiently as Jesik read through the pages before leaning over to sign.

Wight spoke up. "Please, Captain, let me to go to trial. It's not fair that you lose your commission because of my actions."

Jesik smiled at him. "It doesn't matter if you go to trial or not. Either way, Colonel Kensington will bring action against me. Isn't that right, Colonel?"

Kensington smirked.

"Besides, I've learned a lot about myself in the past few days." He glanced at Kensington, then returned his gaze to Wight. "For example, for the past twenty years I've gone out of my way to accommodate the Colonel for fear that he'd cause me trouble in my career. I thought it my destiny to command a starship and that if I ever lost that, I'd lose everything. But, it's not true. I should have known that all along, but it wasn't until now that I realized my personal worth has little to do with whether I'm a fleet officer or not. Instead, it has everything to do with what kind of people who value my association."

Turning to Kensington, he added, "And if that's the criteria for success, then I can go into private service or change careers completely and it doesn't matter."

Kensington was about to say something snide, but Jesik cut him off by reaching for the pen again. With only a moment's hesitation, he signed the document.

"Very good!" Kensington smiled as he picked up the paper. "Now we can get past this sentimental rubbish and I can bring discipline to this ship."

"The document still needs your signature, Colonel, binding you to your part of the agreement. Without it, the document is null and void."

"I suppose I must," sniffed Kensington. Reaching into his pocket for a pair of half-rim reading glasses, he put the document on the table and picked up the pen that would seal the agreement.

"It's a shame that Brighton and this young degenerate are getting off without public disclosure. It would do the populace good to see what happens when people violate morality laws. But getting rid of you, Jesik, makes it a good deal at any cost." Looking up, he added, "And about your speech, you don't need to worry that the fleet will miss you either." He smiled again and was about to sign his name when Brighton walked in. Seeing the document in front of Kensington, Brighton pressed a button on his personal digital assistant that erased everything on the paper.

"What's the meaning of this?" Kensington roared. "Restore this document immediately or I'll have you arrested."

Fixing his gaze firmly on Kensington, Brighton replied, "I'm afraid you're getting ahead of yourself, Colonel. This proceeding isn't over yet, so it's premature to sign documents."

"The decision has been made Commander and you'll be the next one to sign papers."

It was then that everyone noticed a beautiful, athletic looking woman who entered shortly after Brighton. She carried a baby in her arms. Instinctively Jesik, Magill and Wight rose from their seats.

"Captain Jesik, gentlemen, I'd like you to meet my wife, the former Sondra Vivendel of Tatrius, as well our son. According to Tatrius tradition, he is yet to be named." Brighton beamed as Sondra stepped forward and met each of the members.

"It's well and good, Commander, that you have finally accepted responsibility for your act. But, it hardly changes the outcome of our earlier discussion."

"But it does, Colonel. Sondra and I were married nearly a year ago when I went to Stirium to meet with her privately. That was well within the time allowed for an officer to marry an expectant intended spouse without facing any legal consequences or censure."

Kensington roiled as he examined the papers Brighton placed in front of him. Looking up, he said, "And why didn't you make us aware of this earlier, Commander, and save us all a great deal of trouble."

"It's my opinion, Sir, that my private life is no one's affair but mine. Until you opened this inquiry, no other officer in the fleet had troubled themselves with the issue. But, since you made it official, I'm complying with the requirement to show proof of marriage."

Kensington's face flushed, but he maintained his resolve to not lose control of the situation. "My congratulations, Commander. It's unfortunate you'll be leaving the fleet to care for your wife and child. Or do you plan to leave them to their own devices, once this inquiry is over?" He flashed a disingenuous smile towards Sondra.

"Actually, neither Sir. I plan to have Sondra and our child join us aboard the ship."

"Impossible. No one brings their spouse on a deep-space voyage."

"With due respect, it resurrects an ancient English practice from the days of sailing vessels in which officers often brought their spouses with them on distant voyages. It's also allowed in the Kalenden Fleet Code. We plan to have the stewards clean up the nursery provided on all starships since the Earth migration and actually put it to the use for the purpose to which it's intended."

Brighton turned to Sondra with obvious affection and added, "In this case it's also a benefit for the fleet. She's a skilled ceramics and alloy engineer who can assume part-time employment to keep her skills alive. It's already been cleared with Fleet Personnel." He handed Kensington another set of papers.

"I can see that you were the perfect First Officer for Jesik – obstinate and unconventional. Well, no matter. The other issue still remains, so Captain Jesik will be leaving the military shortly, anyway. I will excuse you and your wife while Jesik completes this paperwork. Now, restore the document immediately!" Kensington turned as if to dismiss Brighton.

"I have additional responsibilities here, Sir. I'll now say goodbye to my wife for a time, as I will be assuming command of this proceeding. You will please take a seat and respond to series of questions I am required to pose to you and Lieutenant Commander Wight when we continue."

"What?" Kensington bellowed. "How dare you show such impudence! You better change your attitude this instant, or you'll face a Courts Martial for insubordination."

Jesik spoke up quickly, "Commander, don't forget yourself. Colonel Kensington is in control of this tribunal."

"Fortunately, that's no longer true, Captain. I've received orders from Fleet Command to take charge of this proceeding – not the ship, for you are still Captain – but of the proceedings. As soon as I see my wife safely escorted to our quarters, I'll explain. In the meantime, everyone stay here. To observe proper military protocol, I have also stationed two armed guards at the door."

"I will not hear of this!" Kensington shouted.

Brighton turned and eyed Kensington with a cold stare. "You will sit down, Colonel, or I will have you arrested. What is it to be?"

Kensington moved as if to strike, but thought better of it and sat down heavily. He glowered at Brighton through smoldering eyes. "You will pay dearly for this Commander! More dearly than you can imagine."

Brighton chose not to reply, but instead, took his wife by the arm and walked her to the door where one of the stewards was waiting to escort her to their quarters. Before leaving, she turned and smiled at Jesik, Magill and Wight. It was a warm and tolerant smile that indicated she was on their side. Even though he couldn't imagine why, Jesik now felt more hopeful. When the door closed, Brighton stepped to the head of the conference table, took out a second recording device, placed it squarely on the table and turned to face the group.

"Gentlemen, I realize my behavior is extraordinary and deserves an explanation. When I'm done, you'll understand why I have assumed command of this proceeding, as well as the legal authority for my doing so. Some ten years ago I was an Ensign on temporary assignment at Fleet Headquarters. While walking down the hall one day, I was approached by a senior officer who ordered me to step into a side room, such as what happened to Lieutenant Commander Magill two days ago. When the officer found out I would be at headquarters for at least the next six months, he told me I was to be given a new assignment as member of the Control Board for Morals and Sobriety. Naturally I asked him why he chose me. He replied that the rules of the Council required the membership of a junior military officer to represent their interests in any proceedings and since the board met infrequently, I was as well-suited as anyone else. The reason they didn't go through a formal vetting process is that they had a case that needed hearing that very day and couldn't form a quorum unless they added someone to the board immediately. Thus, I became a member of the committee."

"Very interesting," said Kensington, "But what has that got to do with us?"

"Just this, Colonel. Since that initial assignment, I have never relinquished my membership on the board. As I've moved up in rank, I've acceded to the corresponding spot on the board. Generally we meet only once a year, when I'm on Kalenden, to review the six or seven complaints that have been logged during the previous twelve months. So, it's never been a burden to participate. I actually came to look forward to the meetings, since I enjoy the company of the other members of the board. Occasionally, I have to join a video conference if something urgent comes up while I'm in space, but as a general rule it doesn't take more than five or six days of my time each year. In recent years the Chairman of the Board has become one of my closest friends."

"Again, what does this have to do with us?"

"After you leveled your charges against Mr. Wight the other day, I moved to the Legato, where I established a secure link to the Board secretary. They activated my authority for an unrestricted search of the interstellar net, as well as calling up the records regarding the sites Kevin had visited as a lieutenant. At least two members of the board have to be logged on to the system when we go to potentially unauthorized sites, so the Chairman joined me in the search as a favor. In case you weren't aware of this, the Board for Morals and Sobriety has control over both military and civilian offenses, so any charges you might have brought against Wight would have had to go through our board before the fleet could take further action. Rather than wait for your referral, we simply assumed authority to conduct a direct investigation."

"I was not aware of your membership on the board, but it doesn't make a difference, since Captain Jesik has already agreed to terms that would preclude my bringing charges against Lieutenant Commander Wight. Therefore, your involvement is unnecessary."

"No, Sir; it is Captain Jesik's resignation that is unnecessary."

Turning to Wight, Brighton changed his tone of voice. "Kevin, this is a list of all the sites we could verify you visited. To the best of your knowledge, can you warrant that this is complete?"

As Wight scanned the document, his face flushed. Some titles were quite embarrassing. Finally he said, "Yes, Sir. These are the only sites I've ever gone to." He acted as if he wanted to say something more, but decided against it.

Brighton relaxed considerably, which flustered Kensington.

"Very well then, Lieutenant Commander Wight. The Board has officially reviewed these sites and certified that they do not violate the Morals Code." He handed an original copy of a certification document to Wight, along with forwarding electronic copies to Kensington's and Jesik's viewer screens.

"As you said earlier, these sites simply provide background information on ancient practices in our society that are still openly practiced in other places in the universe, including many of our allies. As such, they are authorized for open research, although I advise you to seek permission in advance before you search there in the future, to avoid this sort of misunderstanding."

"Thank you, Sir" Wight stammered, "I appreciate the trouble you've taken." The relief in his voice buoyed Jesik's feelings beyond measure.

"This is still a load of rubbish!" Kensington blasted. "Whether the sites are approved or not has little to do with the underlying inclinations that prompted his visits. It's clear that such attitudes are harmful to the service and, as such, this man should be mustered out!"

"Colonel Kensington," Brighton replied, "even on Kalenden one cannot be prosecuted for private thoughts. We can only react when there's a cause of action and Mr. Wight has provided none. He's broken no laws, either military or civilian, so he's entitled to his privacy."

Kensington attempted to interrupt, but Brighton cut him off. "There's nothing more to be said on this matter. From a legal standpoint, it's closed." Turning to the group he added, "And because this inquiry was conducted as a confidential investigation, you are all obligated, legally and ethically, to refrain from ever discussing this matter outside of this room. Should you communicate even the essence of this discussion to anyone else, you will be subject to military censure. Is that understood?"

"A grand way to protect your little conspiracy…"

"You may find, Colonel, that our privacy requirements are there to protect everyone." He gave Kensington a menacing glance that seemed to unnerve him.

"Well, then," said Kensington importantly, "in spite of my reservations, I'll be on my way." Turning to Jesik he added, "It seems your cadre has protected you once again, Jesik. But time will eventually reveal all your dirty secrets and you will be known for who you really are." With that Kensington stood and started towards the door.

"Not so fast, Colonel Kensington, we have another matter to settle before this inquiry is concluded. Please take your seat again."

"Commander, I've been patient with you, but I will not have you ordering me around. I am not a subject of these proceedings, so I will go whenever I damn well please."

Brighton stepped between Kensington and the door and put his hand on his sidearm. "This is an official inquiry, Colonel, conducted jointly under military and civilian authority." He reached down on the table and handed Kensington a piece of paper. "And since you are a target of the investigation, I require your participation."

"What in blazes is this?" Kensington's face reddened.

"It's a subpoena, Colonel, directing you to participate. Again, please take a chair."

Kensington's hands trembled as he fumbled through the document while attempting to take his seat.

"During the course of our investigation of Lieutenant Commander Wight, we encountered a disturbing trend in which a number of individuals were logging onto some extremely hard core pornographic sites maintained on distant planets – sites that go beyond human sexuality, employing graphic scenes of murder, torture and bondage. These are the type of sites that Kalenden laws quite rightly prohibit."

Jesik glanced up from the viewer screen listing some of the titles and noticed that Kensington had gone as white as a sheet.

"As you can see, each of these sites were visited multiple times by these individuals. Naturally, it became our responsibility to identify the offending parties and bring them to justice. What we found, however, is that all the names traced back to men who had previously retired from the service, thus making service related computers unavailable to them during the times noted. In at least one case, the officer in question had died several years before he supposedly went to these sites."

"I don't see what any of this has to do with those of us in this room…"

"Perhaps not, Colonel, but let me describe where our investigation took us. In an attempt to find a common denominator to these hits, we noted there was never a period during which any of the individuals in question were logged onto a site at the same time. That seemed strange, so we initiated a query to show the geographical location of each computer used for these visits and to then relate it to the known positions of command officers who might have been at those locations at the indicated times. The search narrowed the field to two candidates."

"Why only officers?" Magill asked.

"Because automatic filters would have blocked access to these sites for enlisted men. We knew that only someone with intelligence authority could bypass the filters without drawing attention. So, we pulled the profile on one of the men and found that during an unusually intense period of activity, he had been assigned to a project that required him to work during the specific logon times noted in the record. That left us just one name."

Brighton paused. "Of course the name on the record was no help, since we already knew the access was stolen, but the pattern of usage provided us the name of just one active officer."

The sick feeling in Jesik's stomach made it difficult for him to look up from the table. While he'd sometimes felt Kalenden laws were too restrictive of people's individual freedoms, he'd never doubted the wisdom of keeping this kind of material from the public. He'd read that on ancient Earth, even children had been exploited to fill the increasingly insatiable appetite for sexual stimulation and that people had actually been murdered in the production of sadomasochistic video images. More than one convicted felon had pointed to this material as the main contributing factor to the emotional desensitization that allowed them to inflict horrid suffering on their victims. It seemed impossible that anyone in contemporary society could actually watch material such as this.

"Colonel Kensington, would you like to add anything to the discussion at this point?"

"Why would I want to add to this discussion, it has nothing to do with me."

"Of course it has something to do with you," Brighton fixed his gaze on Kensington. "You are the officer the system identified as meeting all requirements of the search criteria."

"Which simply shows that your search methodology was flawed. There is nothing concrete to tie me to any of this and I bitterly resent the implication." Gone was his usual bombast, replaced by suppressed rage.

"You're correct, Sir, that we could not break through the encryption that would have provided us the true name of this user and we could never bring charges through merely circumstantial evidence."

Kensington seemed to relax a bit.

"But, then, we caught a break. It turns out that while most of the sites were available without charge, there was at least one where credit was required. We were able to use our security clearance to log back through the originating computers' search history, where we found the encrypted card number. The issuing company at first resisted our attempt to name the owner until we reminded them that they carried the risk of criminal charges themselves for not blocking payment to an unauthorized site."

Kensington stood abruptly. "I suppose it was my name on that credit! Well, for your information, my card was stolen and could have been used by anyone."

Brighton sat down and sighed. "Colonel, you never reported the card stolen and you've used it many times since then."

"I was unaware it was lost for a time and obviously someone else used it while out of my possession. When I got it back, I had no idea it had been used for such a purpose."

"Colonel, enough already. The card had an encrypted retina scan which the computer took automatically while you were viewing the site. The credit card vendor has absolute verification that you witnessed the site in question with your own eyes. The proof is irrefutable."

Kensington let out a strangled cry and dove at Brighton, but the Commander sidestepped, which caused Kensington to crash into the wall. The door opened when the guards heard the commotion and two guards rushed in to subdue Kensington. After a few moments of struggle, Brighton asked if Kensington would like to know his alternatives. Picking himself up he finally settled back into his seat. Brighton handed Magill a weapon set to stun force and asked him to keep it trained on the Colonel in case he lost control again.

"Colonel, up to now I've brought no formal charges against you. Nor have you confessed to any crime. You are, of course, entitled to legal representation in a Courts Martial. In spite of your current assignment, these incursions into forbidden territories took place while you were an active military officer, so the Army can claim jurisdiction."

Brighton paused, awaited a response from Kensington, but the Colonel sat stiffly in his chair as if he didn't understand what had been said.

"You have a choice, Sir. If you sign this letter of resignation, from both the military and your diplomatic assignment, along with a second document that requires you to submit to a formal psychological reprogramming sequence, no formal charges will be brought against you. These accommodations are made in recognition of the negative effect your arrest would have on your family, the military and the diplomatic corps."

"Yes, we wouldn't want to embarrass any of those august groups, would we?" replied Kensington.

"Colonel, the main person we want to avoid embarrassing is you. That's why the choice is entirely up to you. I have Lieutenant Commander Magill as an impartial witness that I am not asking you to sign under duress."

"And what additional requirements are included in these documents?"

"First, that you surrender, forever, your authority to use the interstellar net for anything but financial transactions and electronic messages. Second, that you submit to periodical psychological reviews to confirm that you have not acted on any impulses created by your viewing of forbidden material. And third, that you never reveal anything you have heard or seen about my personal situation or that of Lieutenant Commander Wight and Captain Jesik. If you violate any of these terms, the protection afforded by this agreement will terminate immediately and you will be arrested and brought to a public trial where all your activities will be revealed. You will be monitored electronically to detect any breach of the agreement."

"So you think you've got me, Commander. Well, I don't think so! You've forgotten that I'm the charge d' affairs to Alturus. I suspect the Prime Minister will not be at all pleased to have me disappear suddenly. That would be too great a public embarrassment. So, in spite of any supposed difficulties in my personal viewing, I will not resign."

"Did I mention, Sir, that the Chairman of the Council Control Board for Morals and Sobriety is Prime Minister Larimore's eldest son? Naturally, before we decided to offer this plea bargain, we discussed it with the Prime Minister. He has agreed to accept your resignation. Publicly he'll express regrets that your personal health has forced you to take this action and wish you well in your recovery. Kalenden's privacy laws will prevent any disclosure of the health issues he refers to, so as you can see, Colonel, sometimes privacy protection is indeed an important part of doing what's right for an individual."

Kensington looked around with malevolence. Jesik felt the hatred that had driven him all those years with new recognition that it was fueled by the insipid things he'd viewed. He finally understood that there was nothing he could have done to appease Kensington. It also explained how Kensington had discovered Wight's wanderings through cyberspace. He undoubtedly used the computer on many occasions to try to find like-minded individuals and a random search turned up Wight's name. Kensington's high level clearance, stolen from a dead man, allowed him to build a record he hoped to use to destroy Wight and Jesik.

An angry growl brought Jesik's thoughts back to the proceeding. He watched as Kensington picked up the electronic pen and angrily attacked the piece of paper with his signature. That initiated an automatic computer sequence that instantly sealed the record, securing it so that only a member on the Quadrant Council Control Board for Morals and Sobriety could open it in the future. It also ensured that any public utterances of the items or individuals mentioned in the document would be reviewed for compliance with the secrecy agreement Kensington had agreed to. If he directly or indirectly produced a leak, the computer would automatically open the file and bring formal charges. Kensington had effectively signed away his room to maneuver.

"Now am I free to go?" he asked Brighton icily.

"You are free to return to your cabin to prepare for your transfer to the Legato. The Prime Minister will communicate to Captain Garrard the need to return you to Keswick, where you will be transferred to the next available ship destined for Kalenden. While you will not be a prisoner, he will make it clear to the Captain that you will not enjoy full liberty and that he is to enforce your return home."

Kensington stood, shook his head, and then turned to Kevin. "Just think, Mr. Wight, my bad habits on the interstellar net started much like yours – doing 'research.' Why, in time you could become just like me, facing a group like this. Wouldn't your mother love that!" Jesik stood, ready to block Kensington before he could reveal his personal knowledge of Kevin's mother, but Kensington saw him and backed off.

"And as for you, Jesik, I suspect you'll long bear the scars of our initial encounter. I'd hoped for more, but I'll just have to be content with what you've already lost." His sneer was intended to infuriate Jesik, but it only added to the pity he felt. Kensington left the room, accompanied down the corridor by the guards.

As the doors closed, Jesik and Brighton sat down in their chairs. No one said anything, too stunned by their reversals of fortune.

Finally, Lieutenant Commander Magill inquired, "How'd you figure all this out in just two days, Commander? I find it remarkable what you accomplished. And how can any one person nurture such hatred that he would try to harm others in such a vicious way?"

Brighton chewed his lip for a moment.

"I'll never be able to answer your second question, Commander. It makes no sense to me. As to the first, my motivation was simply to save Kevin from a fate he didn't deserve. I knew what it felt like to be on the receiving end of Kensington's wrath, but at least I was prepared. Kevin has never experienced that kind of malice, and should not have had to face it." He turned to Kevin and added. "Mr. Wight, have you thought about what you'll do now?"

"I don't know, Sir. I'm very confused."

"I know the feelings you have are considered unnatural on Kalenden and to act on them would be illegal. But there are places in the system that holds the opposite view, good places with decent people. Perhaps, even Earth. You should go there to explore for yourself what you feel. There may be someone special with whom you can share your life."

Wight didn't say anything, so Jesik added, "Or, perhaps you can discover a way to sort out your thoughts in our own system. There are coun-

selors who will treat you with consideration and in confidence. I think it's
long overdue that we address this issue as a society." He searched Wight's
face for how to proceed, but saw only confusion. "In any event, there's no
hurry. We still need your service here."

"You mean you'd allow me to serve, knowing my struggles?"

"As long as your performance remains unaffected."

"But, what about the effect on the ship's morale if someone should find
out or guess? What would it do to you?" Wight was obviously trying to
think through all the potential ramifications.

Jesik really didn't want this discussion, because it was so unfamiliar.
But, that's what leadership was all about, so he had to respond.

"In the first place, no one need ever know, unless you decide to share
it. None of us will break the confidentiality of this proceeding. Then if you
feel you want to open your thoughts to another person and it gets spread
around, I'll deal with the ship's morale. That's my job. My concern is the
effect it would have on you. As Commander Brighton indicated, there are
other planets in our area of space that are very open to people's natural
expression of their nature. I think you'd find our crew far more understanding than you might expect."

Wight shook his head in unbelief.

As he watched Kevin trying to sort it all our, Jesik found his own opinions were softening. "You are a man of integrity, Mr. Wight, so I have
no reservation asking you to stay aboard this ship as an active member of
the crew for as long as you like. Mr. Brighton, Mr. Magill, what are your
thoughts?" Both nodded their assent.

Finally, Wight looked up and explained, "The truth is I don't know
what I'll do in the long run. I've spent so many years being afraid that
I simply don't know what to think. Right now I'm trying to understand
how mistaken I was about what would happen if this became known. In
my imagination I thought everyone would see me as Colonel Kensington
did, loathsome and contemptible. Yet, the three of you have done everything possible to reassure and protect me. I guess I wasn't prepared for that.
Thank you."

Jesik stood and extended his hand to Wight. "You have plenty of time
to decide what to do next – that is, after after you help pilot us to Alturus.
Right now that's your most important responsibility."

Turning to Lieutenant Commander Magill, he related, "I'll discuss
with the Prime Minister what to do in Colonel Kensington's absence. My
suspicion is that he'll not want to delay our initial contact with Alturus

while waiting for another civilian representative to be appointed. So, he's likely to ask me to serve as a military liaison. If so, I would like you to serve as my attaché. Do you object to that?"

Magill answered that he did not and stood to leave, then decided to add his thoughts. "Captain Jesik, Mr. Brighton, I want you to know that I consider it an honor to have participated in these events. I've learned more about integrity and loyalty in the past two days than in all the classes I've ever attended. Thank you for protecting Commander Wight." Then, turning to Kevin he said, "How about a game of racquetball before lunch." Wight smiled, nodded, and the two left the room.

When they were alone, Jesik turned to Brighton and asked, "How can I ever thank you, Tom? You found a way to elude the disasters threatening to swamp me. I can't believe my change in fortune."

Brighton returned the smile and said, "Kensington was right when he said that all secrets will be revealed. He just didn't know it applied to him." They laughed and Brighton said, seriously, "I should have told you about Sondra earlier than today, but the truth is that you came down on me so hard in our initial conversation that it irritated me to the point where I didn't want to involve you. Now I realize you were trying to protect me because of your own experience. I'm sorry."

"No need to be sorry. After all, I didn't choose to let you in on the reasons for my panic. Still, I'm glad to hear you married her. A child deserves a mother and a father who love each other. I hope you do love her."

"Very much – in fact I can't believe my good fortune in finding such a woman to spend my life with."

"May I ask what changed your mind?"

"I don't think my mind ever did change, really. I just finally accepted what I knew to be right all along. I grew up as an orphan and would never intentionally do that to my own child. Plus, when I returned to Sondra on Stirium, I realized the reason I was attracted to her in the first place was that she had all the personal characteristics I wanted in a woman. After I looked past her physical attributes, it was easy to fall in love again."

"That's what I don't understand—Sondra is a strikingly beautiful woman. I can't see any reason not to be attracted to her."

Brighton laughed. "It's all in one's expectations, I guess. I'd always pictured the woman of my dreams as a petite young thing – frail and hopelessly dependent on my strength. Yet, when I stopped and thought about it, I don't like that kind of woman in real life. I enjoy the company of people who are self-willed and independent. And I also realized that I had never felt such a physical attraction as I did for Sondra, which is what brought about our child in the first place. So I'm past all that now and glad for the chance to spend my life with someone as wonderful and capable as her. It's exciting to face the future with a partner."

Jesik congratulated him on his good fortune. "After you and your family have a chance to settle in will you join me for dinner and an evening together so I can get to know Sondra? Perhaps after we're underway to Alturus."

Brighton agreed and stood to leave. Jesik startled even himself by suddenly stepping forward and embracing his First Officer. It was the first time in his life he'd ever done such a thing, but somehow it seemed appropriate. What started out as perhaps the worst day of his life was ending as one of the best.

18— UPHEAVAL ON ALTURUS

Jesik found he thoroughly enjoyed Sondra Vivendel's company. She was down to earth and not easily impressed. It came from the Tatrions' natural skepticism of ritual and tradition. They were a pragmatic society who prospered in the shadow of their two idealistic neighbors, Alturus and Kalenden, by adapting the varying social customs of the neighboring star systems. Kalenden was more isolated, so had been unusually successful in holding onto their founding ideals, both positive and negative, while Tatrius was far more tolerant of social differences. Jesik found her viewpoints refreshing, even though it startled many of his officers. At any rate, Sondra was a delightful addition to the ship's company and her baby could turn otherwise macho spacemen into baby-talking older brothers whenever she met them in the galley or recreational areas. Far from having a negative impact on morale, her presence brought new life to the ship as she assumed the role of mother for many of the young men who were fresh out of the academies.

Jesik's predictions about the Prime Minister had also proven correct. In their first face-to-face discussion, he asked Jesik to assume the role of military Charge d' Affairs and accepted Magill as his designated attaché. Although he was dubious about his effectiveness as a diplomat, in many ways his new status would simplify his meetings on Alturus, since he would have official recognition at even the highest governing levels. He'd had a number of discussions with the PM and other cabinet ministers since then, to fully brief him on all matters related to Alturus and Keswick. The interaction had even changed his perceptions of politicians. He'd always viewed them as mostly self-serving egoists, but now he recognized it took pretty strong egos to deal with the many conflicts and demands placed on a government and his respect for their leadership had increased significantly.

In the first few weeks since entering the Alturian airspace, Wight seemed remarkably bright and cheerful. But, of late he'd gone quiet again, although it hadn't interfered with his work. Jesik felt it inappropriate to approach him directly, so found an occasion to visit privately with Lieutenant Commander Magill. After some small chat, he asked how Wight was doing.

"I think he's okay. Having finished the map of the Keswick asteroid belt, he is busy improving our maps of the Alturian archipelago. I know that project is taking up most of his time, but I also think he's brooding a bit."

Jesik let Magill sit quietly with his thoughts for a few moments.

"Does it bother you that Commander Wight may think of you or other crewmembers in a sexual way?"

Magill looked up, surprised. "I thought it would when I first heard about what was going on and it made me self-conscious. But when you get to know him, he's a regular guy." Magill took a long sip of his drink. "I mean, I interact with women all the time and it doesn't mean anything, even if there is an attraction. I suppose it's more difficult for Kevin since he can't ever show any interest, even if he feels it."

Jesik marveled at the maturity of Magill's response.

"I only ask because I'm worried about what might happen if any of this becomes known to the crew."

"I think you're right to worry, for they won't take the time try to understand. I can see them turning on him as a group, which would ruin him emotionally because he's so aware of what a scandal would do to his mother." He looked up and smiled. "But, remember, Captain, he's dealt with this a lot longer than we have and knows the stakes very well. I don't think there's anything to worry about, as long as we stay quiet. My biggest worry is what it means for him to live such an important part of his life in silence."

Jesik hadn't thought of it that way and it sobered him. He had a keen interest in Kevin's future, but didn't know what else to do right now. "Let's change the subject, hoping this will work itself out. I'd like to review the names of the Alturian diplomatic staff and to rehearse the proper etiquette when we meet them." Magill's experience on Keswick proved helpful and after practicing the formal greetings required in their first introduction, Jesik couldn't help but laugh. "We make quite a pair – two minor military officers from second and third-class families hobnobbing with the aristocracy of Alturus."

"Aristocracy, nothing, we'll be meeting royalty!" responded Magill. "If my mom could see me now, she'd be proud beyond words and my dad would be whispering 'Don't let them intimidate you, Sean, you're just as good as they are.' I believe he actually thinks we're better."

"My dad, too. More than anything, he wanted me to make it to the top of the military ladder just to prove that ability matters more than heredity." He looked down at his glass wistfully. "It was only after the triumph at Cambriol that I figured out that Dad was wrong."

"May I ask what you mean by that, Sir?"

Jesik looked up and smiled. "Dad passed away a month after the honors ceremony where the old Lentissimo made its final descent into the star. It was the proudest moment of his life and he died secure in the knowledge that we'd really shown them something. But in the long run, it's the Kensingtons of the world who get invited to join the best clubs. So, it didn't really change things at all."

Magill took this as an invitation to disagree and pointed out that they were Ambassadors to Alturus and that even when Kensington had the title, Jesik had the access. He argued that that alone should show that merit mattered more than form.

Jesik countered with only mild resistance, for he actually believed that Kalenden society was changing a bit. Just not as fast as he hoped for when he was young. *But why put a damper on Magill's youthful enthusiasm?* So, they continued discussing the politics of PM Larimore and the subtle changes he was making in the bureaucracy in order to make it more open to lower-class families.

Eventually Jesik threw up his arms and said, "Alright, alright, I surrender, Commander. But I never thought I'd go up against you as defender of the government."

Magill laughed easily. He and Jesik had really come to like each other. "It's a surprise to me, too, Sir. I guess it's better to feel hopeful after all these years, rather than cynical. Maybe the Keswick action is just what's needed to move things along."

"I think that's a worthy subject of a final toast. Then I need to go to bed."

As they separated late that night, Jesik felt more relaxed about his upcoming diplomatic responsibilities, knowing Magill would be at his side.

* * *

Having traversed more than a month through Alturian space in Vortex drive, they were just three weeks away from the planet when Lieutenant

Williams received an urgent hail for Jesik from Colonel Wilkerson on Keswick. It was on an ultra-secure channel, so he asked to have it transferred to his day cabin.

"I don't know why, Captain, but you and Lieutenant Commander Magill have been asked to join a three-way conference call tomorrow morning at 09:00. They've arranged redundant Esper teams to broadcast. It will include Prime Minister Larimore, the Prime Minister of Alturus, John Lansing and myself. A member of the Alturian Royal Family may also participate. May I tell them you're available?"

"Of course. Any idea at all what it's for, Mr. Wilkerson?"

"It appears that the rebel movement on Alturus is growing rapidly and has started agitating in public in some of the rural towns. So far, there are no reports of violence, but it's difficult to imagine that won't happen soon. Maybe that's what it's about. At any rate, I understand we'll have to start the conference by renewing our individual Oath of Confidentiality."

"A great time to be the lone Kalenden battleship in Alturian space. Well, we'll just have to wait and see what's up. Will it be alright if I include Commander Brighton?" Wilkerson assented.

"How's Colonel Kensington doing?"

Wilkerson gave Jesik a searching glance. "I don't know what happened out there, but Kensington is like a caged animal. One moment he's pacing with a flushed face, clenching and unclenching his fists and the next he's morose and blubbery, talking about how much the fleet meant to him. We've kept him isolated from the regular troops, but it's tough to even be around him." He waited expectantly.

"I'm sorry to hear that. Of course I'm not at liberty to discuss the medical condition that prompted his resignation, but do your best to treat him with kindness. No, even more important, show him the kind of superficial respect he so craves. I'm afraid that without consolation, he can have some real emotional problems." Jesik looked at Wilkerson reflectively. "I appreciate what you're doing to help him."

"No problem. It shows just how naïve I was as a young officer. I thought our job was to fight wars and preserve the peace. Instead, I'm a full-time diplomat and part-time orderly. At least it makes for an interesting life."

To maintain consistency throughout a fleet scattered over more than a hundred million kilometers, all meetings were scheduled according to "Fleet Time" (abbreviated FT) which corresponded to Fleet Headquarters on Manhattan Island on Kalenden. To the best of their abilities, ships in space kept their sleep/wake cycle in concert with this reference. It only became an issue when they entered orbit around a distant planet and had to accommodate local time in their communications with that surface. At their present location, deep in Alturian space, 09:00 Fleet Time meant that Jesik and the others had time to enjoy a normal night's sleep, have breakfast and check on the ship's scheduling before assembling in the Captain's private conference room. Lieutenant Williams indicated that the first ten secure links had been established and that he would notify them when the conference links were complete.

At 08:50 Williams signaled that the connection was secure and the sounds of participants in the other conference centers filled the overhead speakers. At precisely 09:00 FT, Admiral Rameira on Alturus stepped in front of the camera and called the conference to order. A quick roll call was conducted, which indicated all parties were present on Keswick and Kalenden, where Commodore Park and General Josephs joined PM James Larimore.

Admiral Rameira cleared his throat and said, "Gentlemen, it's now my privilege to introduce to you the Prime Minister of Alturus, Mrs. Katherine Richards. This will be the first time in over two hundred years, the Prime Ministers of all three governments are meeting together in a face-to-face discussion. PM Richards…"

The surprise on everyone's faces was obvious. In those two hundred years there had never been a woman Prime Minister on either Keswick or Kalenden and since there had been no contact, no one thought about the Alturian Prime Minister. PM Richards obviously saw their bewilderment, but chose not to address it. Handsome, but not beautiful, she was in her late forties, with mid-length hair and deep brown eyes. She wore a crisp business suit with very modest jewelry. Her gaze was riveting as she turned from monitor to monitor to size up the people to whom she was speaking and it was obvious by the confidence in her voice that leadership did not intimidate her.

"Gentlemen, thank you for joining us on such short notice. I'll get right to the point. The Keswick Rebellion has created problems here on Alturus. The monarchy is strong and well regarded, but the bureaucracy is inefficient. Class distinction has been grating on our second and third-class families, just as it did on Keswick. My conversations with those who served in the Keswick campaign lead me to believe that there is also some feeling between the classes, even on Kalenden. Of course none of you have any reason to help us. After all, your societies were also born out of rebellion against monarchies. Still, an open revolt here will destabilize all three systems. Plus, there are those of us who believe the ancient animosities should be set aside so that our systems can once again become friends." She looked into the cameras, earnestly, as she said, "We have missed much, here on Alturus, because our pride drove you from our brotherhood."

Jesik shared Brighton and Magill's sharp intake of breath. The one thing their history lessons had been clear on was that the Alturian Monarchy had been ruthless in squelching dissent and had refused every offered olive branch that might have held the families together. In the end, armed rebellion and exile was the only course. No apologies had been issued either, which is why Kalenden and Alturus had remained silent toward each other all these years. A statement like hers had to have the blessing of the monarchy, which meant a real olive branch was being offered.

"That's a remarkable thing to say," said PM Larimore from Kalenden. "We, too, have felt that it's often lonely in our distant corner of space. We welcome the chance to re-establish a dialogue."

There was momentary silence on the channel. None of this had directly applied to the Allegro, so Jesik refrained from making any comment.

John Lansing interrupted the silence. "Our situation was similar to that on Alturus. Although former comrades of mine destroyed much with the murder of the Royal Family, they have all been executed as it was not our intent to harm the royals, but rather to open the government to talented people, regardless of class. Now, we're starting from a zero baseline to establish a democratic government." He paused, as if pondering how best to continue. For a first meeting like this, everyone was being unusually candid. Jesik liked it. Whatever the current problem was on Alturus, it would take honesty like this for these disparate groups to cooperate.

Lansing resumed. "Mrs. Richards, if you are extending an invitation for us to enjoy a legitimate relationship with Alturus, we are pleased. Our greatest fear, however, is that you will gain our confidence, then use your force to invade us on the pretext of reestablishing royal rule. You should know that we will resist such an effort with everything at our disposal."

"So much for a goodwill gesture," Brighton muttered, making sure the mute button was pushed on his communications panel.

Instead of reacting with hostility, PM Richards replied simply, "It is your rebellion that is the cause of our current distress. Our fear is a mirror image of yours, Mr. Lansing, that you will attempt to export your rebellion to our shores. But with that said, perhaps I may explain our current problem, as well as the proposed solution."

Lansing nodded affirmatively, indicating he understood the danger the Alturians faced.

"We felt the stress of class distinction long before the Keswick rebellion. For fifteen to twenty years, it was the policy of the government to open social institutions to participation by an ever-broader segment of society. All this was done with the tacit agreement of the Royal Family. They have also included second and third-class families in their social events. In spite of what we consider great progress, the second and third-class families continue to feel oppressed and excluded. Yet, when we commission polls to see what they propose, there's virtual unanimity that the Royal Family should stay at the core of our society. In other words, everyone here wants it both ways – more open and accepting, while maintaining the dignity that comes through monarchy. Unfortunately, this sends a mixed message that makes it difficult for certain segments of the population to see progress. Hence, our current difficulties."

Richards leaned to Rameira and whispered. He then acknowledged her and stepped out of the field of vision. She glanced down at her notes, obviously concerned that she proceed in just the right way.

"Gentlemen, I must now ask something that our limited exposure to one another does not really justify. If circumstances allowed, I would propose the following only after several years of face-to-face meetings in which our governments gained one another's confidence and our people became used to open dialogue. But events are moving too quickly for such a leisurely approach."

She studied each face, intently. "All I ask of you is that if you choose not to help us, you keep this conversation confidential. To fail to do so can unleash horrors on Alturian society that are unthinkable. I'm speaking of a civil war of such a magnitude that it would totally eclipse the suffering that has recently been felt on Keswick."

She swallowed hard, as though she was envisioning the warfare that would ensue if she was unsuccessful. "If you choose not to listen to what I propose, then please indicate so now so that we can disconnect. If you will listen – and mind you, I'm not asking for your advanced agreement – I ask that you each restate your own planet's confidentiality oath."

Larimore took the lead, asking the men on the Allegro and Wilkerson on Keswick to join those on Kalenden as they recited the oath. Lansing also swore his own private oath. It was quite risky for him, since he might gain intelligence that could be used against him in the future. But his acceptation was without hesitation.

Richards relaxed noticeably. She then put the matter on the table. "Thank you and here's what's happening on our planet. We find the rebel

alliance has grown much faster than we anticipated and that it is well organized enough to undertake guerilla activities. It's our belief that in just
months it will be strong enough to seriously threaten the government. My
military advisers indicate we have more than enough automated weapons
to squelch the rebellion, even if members of the military turn against us.
So, in effect, we can destroy enough of our own people that they cannot
succeed. Some advisers have even suggested we take pre-emptive action
against the rebels now, while they're not fully organized. I've indicated I'm
not willing to do that. Of course, I can't make such a statement without
the authority of the monarchy, so I'm telling each of you and particularly
you, Mr. Lansing, that the Alturian monarchy is committed to opening our
society and instituting broad government reforms."

"I appreciate that, Mrs. Richards and I want you to know that we are
doing nothing to stoke the fires of your rebellion. We have our hands full
sorting out our own fate."

"I'm glad to hear that. Thank you. Still, there may be those on your
planet who support our rebel movement. If such a connection was ever
established our military will undoubtedly move to unseat the current
government with the intent of ultimately dominating both Keswick and
Alturus. Then, the fear you mentioned earlier, may become very real."

Again she paused, waiting for one of the others to pick up where this
would take them. PM Larimore broke the silence this time. "Of course we
on Kalenden will not allow that to happen. Beyond the orchidite mines,
we've spent billions of common currency to protect our borders and will
not see a planetoid as close as Keswick fall under Alturian domination. So,
unfortunately, we will be drawn into a war we do not want, but that we will
feel compelled to wage."

A feeling of dread seeped through the Esper links as the enormity of the
conversation sunk in. Full-scale war was possible in as soon as two months.
For societies which had avoided war for such a prolonged period of time, it
was overwhelming to think of their people being exposed to such a meaningless waste of lives and resources. And yet, it was beginning to appear
unavoidable.

"Perhaps a recognition of the danger is our best hope to avoid it," Lansing said. "What can we do to prevent this?"

"Our Royal Family has met privately with the leaders of the rebel
movement and they have indicated that what is desired is there be an absolutely irrefutable acknowledgement of the value and character of the second
and third-class families. To avoid an overthrow, the rebels believe what is

needed is change in the monarchy itself, one that will infuse lower-class blood into the monarchy, establishing, once and for all, that we are all equal. It's a difficult request that we have resisted. But now we see no other way."

Jesik was fascinated, but could see no reason for it to affect either Keswick or Alturus, other than to keep their politics at home. Prime Minister Larimore must have been thinking the same thing, for he interjected, "That's a significant change, but why does it affect us?"

"It actually affects Kalenden more than Keswick, although we hope it will give the rebel government on Keswick the cover they need to keep their more militant groups out of our affairs. What the Alturian rebel movement calls for is a marriage of the Crown Princess to an individual with pure royal blood on his maternal side, but second or third-class blood on his paternal side. It's believed this will provide the groom with the confidence of royals, aristocrats and commoners. He can then represent all our people. Although in the first generation the royal line would clearly be predominant, in time the lineage would equalize and one day the monarchy would assume the embodiment of the best of our entire society. It's a bold plan that we believe has real merit."

"So," Jesik interrupted for the first time, "you will give your people the token they need to believe in your sincerity."

"Precisely." PM Richards smiled. "We believe the substance is in place, but the rebels doubt its reality. This is the most dramatic way we can signal how serious we are."

Everyone paused to consider the impact. It was truly historic in that the course of an entire civilization was about to change by design of those leaders responsible for it. There were few examples in history where a hereditary monarchy voluntarily surrendered its authority to the common people.

"Again, Prime Minster, how does this affect those of us on Kalenden?"

"Thank you, Mr. Larimore, for bringing me back to the point. I'm a bit nervous, because the plan affects one of your citizens directly. We've conducted a genetic scan of our entire population and found the individual we seek doesn't exist. There's not one person on Alturus with the desired bloodlines. Through the years, our royals have occasionally had children with commoners and the rebels indicate they will not accept any person with royal blood on both sides, no matter how remote. They figure that can become an excuse for future royals to indicate the royal line was actually preserved. No, they insist on someone who is strictly second-class via the father and strictly royal on the mother's side. We've tried to get them to compromise on this, but to no avail."

Now, everyone was intrigued to find out how the Alturians hope was to be found on Kalenden. PM Richards continued. "We'd almost despaired of using this to avoid conflict, until our genetic scanners indicated the desired match had been found – and quite by accident. You see, during the recent Keswick campaign we rendered assistance to a number of Kalenden injured, which naturally brought us into contact with their genetic material, which was automatically sequenced. When the system flagged a match, we delved into the history of the individual to be certain we had the correct lineage and that the bloodlines were indeed pure. Our tests prove a confidence level of ninety-eight positive. Kalenden has also collaborated with us and verified our findings, per a special protocol previously authorized by PM Larimore."

"So, what you need now is to contact our citizen and seek his permission for direct genetic testing?" Larimore said.

"I'm afraid it's much more than that, Mr. Larimore. With your planet's confirmation, we already know he meets the criterion. What we need is to seek out your citizen and ask if he will be willing to consider a marriage to our Crown Princess. On Alturus that would not be an issue, since it would be considered a duty of citizenship. But, it's my understanding that you have no arranged marriages in your system."

Larimore smiled. "It's true we have no formally arranged marriages, although many leading families do everything in their power to see that a certain social status is maintained."

"I'm sure you can relate to that," Brighton whispered to Jesik.

"So, if you'll tell us who our potential royal citizen is, we'll arrange to contact him and inquire."

"Perhaps I can have our chief geneticist indicate the lines." A new face stepped into the Alturian viewing field.

"The first check is on the maternal side, since that's how royalty is distinguished from aristocracy." By the tone of his voice it appeared that the geneticist was not a fan of openness between classes. "Once that's cleared, then the father's line is searched. In this case, the normal protocol was modified to search for a second or third-class family without royalty mixed in. Of course it's irrelevant if second and third-class blood is mixed, since either would disqualify a person for inclusion in the aristocracy. In this case, the mother's blood line showed a clear connection through the Wentworths, with no corruption by non-royal lines. From our records, the woman is a Helen Wentworth, a widow in the capitol city of Kalenden."

Jesik instinctively blurted out "No," as his stomach twisted. Unfortunately, he said it loud enough that his monitor took control and his image moved to center screen.

"Is something the matter, Captain?" PM Larimore asked him.

Jesik struggled for breath. "I don't know if there is, Sir, but I'd like this conversation to be private between you and the Alturians. I think it's very important."

Unconsciously, he rose from his chair, his face flushed.

"I'm afraid the conversation must include you, Captain Jesik," PM Richards said gently, but perhaps you should be the one to continue the story."

With those words, everyone turned to look at Jesik, who had slumped back into his chair. It was the old nightmare again. Would it never leave him alone? How could this be possible?

"Captain," PM Larimore said, "do you need time to compose yourself?"

Jesik looked at a camera, his face ashen. He sat on his hands to control their trembling.

"No, Sir, I believe I can proceed. If this is going where I think it is, I must now open a very old part of my life. Helen Wentworth is now Helen Wight, which is also a first-class name." He swallowed hard. "But, as a young woman she had an illegitimate child."

His face clouded up. "My child. Her father suppressed the incident and the child was given up for adoption. I very much wanted to marry her, but Kalenden society is not so different than Alturian, in that first-class families don't want their children to mix with seconds, in spite of propaganda to the contrary." He looked around the table for a moment in an attempt to suppress the rising tide of bitterness he felt. "Helen eventually succumbed to her father's coercion and married into a first-class family." He then added, "Then she and her first-class husband became parents of one of my officers, Kevin Wight. Obviously he's not the child you seek, because he enjoys a first-class heritage through both sides."

Jesik's pause was used as an opportunity for the geneticist to continue.

"Captain Jesik is correct in thinking he's the father of the individual. As it turns out, Captain, you have absolutely pure second-class blood lines, extending clear back to the Earth Migration. Thus, your liaison with Mrs. Wight produced a child with precisely the bloodlines the Alturian government desires."

"But, I have no knowledge of my child," Jesik said. "All that was denied to me."

"Then, we are in a position to help you find him," PM Richards said softly.

"I'm not sure I want to know," said Jesik. "He's grown up with no knowledge of me, so I'm not sure if it's right that his world gets complicated by learning he has two, living, natural parents. Maybe he doesn't even know he's adopted."

Prime Minister Larimore was reading a piece of paper transferred to him by a separate Esper link. He looked up at Jesik and said, "Captain, I hold the name of your son and it's clear that he's aware of his adopted status. But, you're correct that he has no knowledge of you or Mrs. Wight being his biological parents. Perhaps you'd like me to share this with you, offline?"

PM Richards interrupted. "Gentlemen, we would normally offer time for Captain Jesik to deal with this. Unfortunately, though, we have very little of that commodity. It will be days before we can re-establish a link as complicated as this. Although I have no legal authority in this matter, I implore you to use this link to finish this."

Jesik indicated it was all right to proceed as he was curious to learn about his child. But, mostly, he was ashamed. He should have insisted Helen marry him and as awful as it would have been then, he should have never surrendered to Kensington's blackmail. Now, their child was to find the truth in the glare of the public spotlight. *How can I explain my motives in abandoning the child? How can I understand it myself? The only answer I have is that it was Helen's choice. One that I've regretted every day of my life.*

"PM Larimore, perhaps you can announce who the individual is."

"Perhaps I don't need to. Captain, do you have any idea who your son is?"

"Of course not, why would I?" He glanced up at Sean Magill and at the same moment, recognition came. The likeness of their countenance was striking. A shudder ran down his spine that turned his legs into jelly. *Who else but Magill had been injured on Keswick whose treatment required genetic analysis?*

Jesik struggled for breath and must have blanched. It took Magill a moment after he saw the utter shock on Jesik's face, and then he flushed as his eyes grew wide. He choked back a sound in the back of his throat and turned to the cameras defiantly.

"If you think you're going to tell me that I'm the one…" his voice trailed off. "My parents are Robert and Sharon Magill. That's it. I'm from a third-class family, not a royal."

He looked at over Jesik, desperate. "It's not that I wouldn't be proud to be your son, Sir, but the Magills are my parents." He pushed his chair back from the conference table as Jesik lowered his eyes to give Magill lots of room.

No one was saying anything, so Brighton spoke up for the first time. "Prime Minister, is Lieutenant Commander Magill the individual?"

PM Larimore answered. "Yes, Commander, the record match has been verified while we've been speaking. Sean Magill is the genetic child of Pietr Jesik and Helen Carlisle. There's no question about it."

There was a long, drawn out, silence across more than fifty light years. Finally, Jesik spoke quietly.

"Commander, no matter what else is said here today, you must know, absolutely, that the Magills are, indeed, your parents. They are the ones who reared you and sustained you. No one will ever take their place. Neither Helen nor I will even try." He placed his hands on the table, trembling. Brighton saw that his eyes had a faraway look. Eventually Jesik continued, his eyes down on the table. "I always dreamed of the moment I learned if I had a son or daughter. I always wondered what I'd say – how sorry I am that I was unable to stop the adoption? How much I wish I could have been part of my child's life? How deeply I loved his mother? I wanted to say I hoped he had a good life growing up, in spite of what had happened, how frustrating it was to be a second-class person, unable to stand up for my rights. But, mostly, I wanted my child to know how much I missed not having him in my life."

He looked up and found Magill staring at him.

"The one thing I never thought about was how I'd feel about that person—I was so concerned with what they would think of me. I never imagined I'd already know my son and how proud I'd feel to be his father. In the entire universe, there's no one I could desire to be related to more than you. Without knowing anything of our relationship, I've come to regard you as one of the finest men I've ever known..." His voice trailed off and he dropped his eyes again.

A few moments later Magill spoke. "I always wondered, too. I figured I'd be angry at my biological father, demanding to know how he could abandon me. But, mostly hoping there was a good reason for what happened and that he really loved me, but that something had gone horribly wrong. I wanted to feel that I was wanted."

Jesik held his position. Because he was mature in so many ways it was difficult to remember that Magill was still in his early twenties. After a few moments, Sean stood and moved uncertainly towards Jesik. Then acting on a simultaneous impulse they embraced.

"I'm proud to have you as my father, Sir." Magill whispered. "In fact, there have been times when I secretly imagined you were. Clear back on Cambriol, I thought how great it would be to have someone like you to be proud of." They hugged again.

PM Lansing cleared his throat.

"I hate to interrupt." His image took over of the central monitor. "Let me be the first to congratulate both of you on this remarkable discovery. I can't imagine two better men to show the universe why class distinction is meaningless. Together you'll do more to break down prejudice than anything we could have hoped for in our rebellion." There was a murmur of assent from the other stations. "But, I believe that there's still some unfinished business regarding the Alturian Royalty and their needs."

At that, Magill turned furiously toward the screen.

"You can stop right now, Mr. Lansing. I'm a freeborn citizen of Kalenden and as such will not submit to an arranged marriage. I think such traditions are archaic and humiliating and I will not be the one to provide window dressing for an obsolete tradition."

Jesik stood silently at his side. This battle was Sean's to fight, although Jesik stood ready to back him, whatever course he chose.

"Commander," PM Larimore said, "you are under no obligation to do anything. Yet, you show remarkable skill in understanding the political ramifications of the unrest in our three systems. Perhaps you will consider meeting the Crown Princess, to see if feelings can develop. Whether just or not, the decision you make can affect the lives of millions of people, which places responsibility on you."

"But, I didn't ask for any responsibility! I didn't ask for any of this!"

"Unfortunately, that's usually the case for those who are thrust into a position of leadership. Fate makes demands."

"But, how can I stand for something I don't believe in? I detest monarchies and social classes. Now, because I have certain bloodlines, I'm to become its champion?"

PM Richards responded. "You will become the champion of second and third-class people. Changes will come to our systems, that much is certain. But, helter-skelter change leads to chaos, rather than progress. Perhaps this elevation of your status will give you the chance to make a real difference among our population and help them make an orderly transition." She looked at him searchingly, then added, "As one who distinguished himself as a hero on Keswick and by your exploits on Cambriol, you are in a unique position to influence the citizens of all three planets."

Magill looked desperate. The simple truth was that he should do as they ask. It's as if fate had been preparing him for this moment. Yet, how could he?

"But, people who marry should love each other and there isn't room in my heart to do that right now?"

"Do you already love someone else?"

Magill looked at PM Richards. "I don't want to talk about it."

"But, we need you to talk about it. We need to know what opportunities exist. May I ask who this person is you care about?"

Magill felt hollow inside. How could he open his deepest feelings to all these people? But, their need was urgent. Finally he said, "It's not that I wouldn't love to shout her name aloud to everyone, but I've never even told her the depth of my feelings. So, how can I tell you before I tell her?" Then, quietly, "I don't even know if she loves me. She probably hasn't even thought about it."

General Josephs on Kalenden interrupted. He'd kept his peace through all of this. But, he was not a sensitive man and in his estimation, the time for sensitivity had already passed.

"Lieutenant Commander, get a hold of yourself and tell us who she is. Then decide if you're willing to consider the need of the Alturians. Thinking about it won't improve the situation. It's time for you to take hold and react to your new situation."

Magill looked up, angry. "Very well, Sir. Her name is Captain Tara Carling, an Alturian I met on Keswick. I hoped to find her during our assignment on Alturus and tell her how I feel. I even hoped we might receive permission to be married, if she feels about me as I feel about her. But now, I suppose, I'll never have that opportunity, since it conflicts with the needs of the Alturian Royal Family."

Magill failed to notice that PM Richards had settled back in her seat, quite comfortably, and when she spoke, her voice had lost its edge.

"You say the woman you care for is Captain Carling?"

"Yes."

"Then perhaps you'd like to know what she thinks of our proposal."

Magill looked up sharply. "What has Tara got to do with this?"

At that, Tara Carling appeared on the screen as PM Richards said, "Gentlemen, may I introduce Crown Princess Isabec Carlisle. Princess, this young man has just expressed his interest in Captain Carling."

Magill's legs went weak and Jesik quickly shoved a chair under him. It was Magill's turn to struggle for breath. This was certainly proving to be the most perplexing day of his life.

The Princess smiled broadly. "I think it impudent that a lowly Lieutenant from Kalenden could think himself of interest to a Captain from Alturus."

Magill smoldered. Recovering his breath, he shot back, "I think it's despicable that an officer would shield her true identity from someone whose confidence she thought to obtain."

"Please, Commander," said the Alturian Prime Minister, "the Princess occasionally takes on a pseudonym when she wishes to mix with the people. This particular Princess has proven to be a genuine headache for the government in that she demanded to serve in the Alturian armed forces so that she could learn, first hand, how her people feel, as well as share in their sacrifices." The Prime Minister turned to Isabec and added, "With all due respect, Ma'am."

Magill flashed, "I'm sure this second-class royal from Kalenden holds little interest for the Princess, so your proposal for an arranged marriage will fail anyway."

"Just a moment, Commander," Isabec declared, "we already know your feelings in the matter. All that's left to learn is about my feelings." Turning to PM Richards she said, "And what are the ramifications if I'm not interested in marriage at this time?"

Magill scowled for a moment, then broke into a grin and sat back in his chair, and put his hands behind his head.

"And just what are you laughing at?" Isabec asked.

"Why Princess, we all know I have a choice in this matter, because I come from the open society of Kalenden. But, the Prime Minister has already explained that for royalty, this marriage is a duty! So, no matter what your feelings are, you have to proceed!" He finished the sentence with triumph in his voice.

Now it was Isabec's turn to blush. Then she burst out laughing.

"So it appears that the Commander seems to have taken this hand. Still, I've never been one to complete a duty for its own sake. If this young man wishes to pursue my affections, perhaps I'll be open to private conversations later. But, I must admit, he does have a certain charm, in spite of being a bit too serious in his politics." She sighed. "I'm afraid my future may be filled with endless nights talking about water districts, union practices and the oppression of business owners. However, he did indicate his intention of proposing to Tara Carling and I can speak on her behalf, saying that such a proposal would be accepted with love and joy!" She smiled and melted Magill's heart.

The crisis was over. Even Brighton, a staunch, avowed agnostic agreed that fate, or God, or something had worked miraculously today to bring all these people together. The call ended on an upbeat note, with permission to announce a royal courtship five days hence.

Magill asked how the people would feel about the Crown Princess marrying an illegitimate child as the people on Kalenden viewed it as serious flaw, but the folks on Alturus simply laughed it off as adding to the legitimacy of Magill's connection to the aristocracy. While common people looked down upon such moral laxness, they wouldn't blame Magill. With everyone in agreement, the only item left was coordinating the time of the announcement. Enough time was needed for Jesik and Magill to convey the information to Helen Wight and the Magills and for the three governments to prepare their people for the change in relationship between the two star systems and Keswick. More than 200 years of silence was about to yield to a flood of new dialogue.

* * *

After the conference ended, Brighton offered Jesik and Magill his sincere congratulations on their reunion. As he left Jesik's room, he wondered aloud why he hadn't seen the resemblance between them before. Once noticed, it was truly remarkable.

When they were left alone, an embarrassed silence hung heavy in the air. Finally, Jesik spoke. "So, Lieutenant, how do we proceed from here?"

Magill became thoughtful. "First of all, I'd like you to call me Sean once in awhile – not while I'm on duty, but I'd like to hear my first name."

"I'd like that too, Sean." It sounded far more natural than Jesik had expected.

"Next, I'd like to know about my mother. What does she look like, how does her voice sound and what are her interests?" He looked at Jesik and added, "She must be quite remarkable to have won your heart so completely."

"Remarkable is not enough to describe Helen Wight. What does she look like..." his voice trailed off as he sought for the best words. Then, sudden recognition lit up his face. "The best way to discover what your mother looks like, is to study the face of your brother."

"What?" Magill responded. "My brother?"

"Kevin Wight—he's your half brother. You share a mother"

"I have a brother!"

"Yes," Jesik laughed. "You know how deep his eyes are – the darkest blue?"

"Yes."

"Well, that's how your mother's eyes are. She has the same refined facial features and grace of movement. I thought she was like the most perfectly sculpted china doll, with the fairest skin I'd ever seen. Kevin inherited most of his looks from her. It's probably the reason I've enjoyed having him on the ship. He reminds me of her." Then Jesik looked at Magill and said quite seriously, "I'm afraid that you inherited more of your looks from me."

Magill laughed. "That's okay, I'm used to this face and it really isn't that bad – particularly since I'm not as refined and genteel as Kevin. Your looks suit my personality better."

Jesik continued. "Yet, in spite of her beauty, Helen wasn't fragile. We loved to play tennis and she had a fierce serve. At first, when she was just learning the game, I held back to let her win once in awhile. It infuriated her when she realized that. From then on, she attacked the ball ferociously and I found it hard to stay with her."

He paused as memories flooded back to him. Magill watched, intently, trying to sort through the conflicting emotions he felt. He'd been quite angry at the fact that his natural parents had abandoned him. Now, as he saw the deep emotion his biological father exhibited, he felt empathy.

"I hate to open old wounds, Sir, but can you tell me what happened between you and my mother?"

Having spent over two decades concealing the incident, even from his own thoughts when possible, Jesik decided this boy deserved to know everything. Even about Kensington. So he told him the whole story from beginning to end. When he was done, Magill was able to accept his apology and recognized that Jesik had suffered as much as he.

"How are you going to tell Mrs. Wight?"

"I'd like you to join me, if you will. I haven't spoken to her in more than twenty years and again contacting her is very frightening. It's not right that her private life will be made public, but if the plan for stabilizing Alturus is to work, it's vital that your lineage be established. A more immediate problem is when do we tell Kevin? He probably has no inkling his mother has another child. And with what he's been through, who knows his reaction."

After discussing for awhile longer, they decided the best approach was to talk to Helen Wight first and have her decide how to tell Kevin. Jesik contacted Prime Minister Larimore, who offered to initiate the discussion with Helen so that she wouldn't be taken completely by surprise. During his call he related the needs of the Alturian monarchy and their discovery of a suitable groom for their Princess, as well as Jesik's involvement. Also that he had already met their son and was prepared to introduce her to him if she wished.

The Prime Minister called Jesik back and reported that Helen had taken the news with real grace and expressed that she was fully prepared to deal with the social consequences of the revelation of her out-of-wedlock child. She added that she was happy to have the chance to speak with "Pietr" again and looked forward to their conversation. Jesik's heart leapt and his smile betrayed his joy.

"I'd call her immediately, if I were you," Larimore said. "In spite of the confidentiality oaths, this is the greatest event of the century and won't be kept quiet for long."

"Thank you, Sir, for everything. I'll invite Lieutenant Commander Magill to join me now."

The call was more delightful than Jesik hoped for. Helen had grown even more beautiful with age and her smile still left him weak. But, her carefree attitude of youth had been replaced by a more serious tone that spoke of great disappointments. After chatting with Sean and offering to either visit his parents at their home or invite them to hers, she expressed the deep regret she'd felt at losing him. No matter what his feelings were before the call, it was impossible not to be charmed after talking with her.

When their conversation reached its natural conclusion, Magill was wise enough to excuse himself so that Jesik and Helen could talk privately. As he turned to leave, he smiled as he saw how completely engrossed the Captain was in the video image that hovered before him. It pleased him to think his natural parents were still in love.

* * *

"What the blazes is wrong with you?"

"What?" Magill looked up startled. He'd nearly run over Eaves in the corridor.

"I've never seen you smile like that," said. "It's not natural for you to smile. What's going on?"

Magill laughed. "I'd tell you if I could, and it'll knock your socks off when I do. Unfortunately, it's top secret and Security would have to cut out your vocal chords – not that that would be so bad – but it would complicate things. So, sorry, you'll have to wait a few days."

"Oh, man," Eaves said, "you politicians drive ordinary people crazy. I think your medication has gone from your feet to your head."

"Care for a game of handball?" Magill said cheerfully.

"Yeah, right. Handball with an invalid."

"I have a wheelchair and you've got a mouth. Let's see which one's more effective."

Several hours later, back at the main communications console, Lieutenant Williams muttered to himself, "They could pay for a new starship with the amount of money they've spent on high-security Esper links on this voyage. Jesik's been talking for over two hours. What the devil's happening?"

His muttering was interrupted by a sharp, "Kindly keep your concerns for fleet finances to yourself, Mr. Williams!"

"Aye, Mr. Brighton. Aye, Sir."

19 — THE DISTANT SOUNDS OF TRIUMPH

"You wanted to see me, Sir?" Wight appeared very nervous.

"Yes, Lieutenant, please come in." After inviting Wight to sit, Jesik offered him a drink, which had the unintended consequence of making him even more nervous.

"Lieutenant Wight, I've been asked by the Prime Minister to establish a communications link for you to speak to your mother. There's going to be an important public announcement in the next few days for which you need preparation."

The color drained out of Kevin's face and Jesik immediately recognized his mistake.

"No, no, Kevin. It has nothing to do with you or our conversations with Colonel Kensington. You needn't worry about that." Wight relaxed slightly.

Jesik went on to explain the Alturian situation and its potential solution, without indicating who the new Prince Consort was to be. Of course it left Wight confused, but Jesik felt it only right that Helen finish the explanation. So, he activated the communications console, then excused himself while Kevin and his mother talked. After twenty minutes, he knocked on the door and was invited back in. It was clear that Helen had been crying, but her expression conveyed more relief than distress. Wight terminated the call and turned to Jesik.

"Even though my mother never said anything, I always felt that there was a deep sorrow in her life. Now, I understand what it was and why."

There was an extended period of silence.

"My father loved me and tried to spend as much time with me as possible, before he died, but he was awfully busy at his cabinet responsibilities…" Wight dropped his gaze for a moment, then looked up again. "I knew my parents were never close and I often envied my friends whose parents were so happy with each other. It was awfully lonesome." He stopped talking again.

"How do you feel about learning you have a brother?"

Kevin brightened considerably. "I always wanted one. The house was so big and it was mostly my dad's government associates who dropped by. I wish I could have grown up with someone else to talk to."

Jesik's heart ached. "Well, it seems like you and Lieutenant Commander Magill have grown to like each other."

"He's a great guy and I don't know what I would have done when Colonel Kensington threatened me, if Sean hadn't been there to talk to." Kevin smiled the same smile that Jesik had fallen in love with twenty-five years earlier. "You must be very proud to learn that he's your son."

"I never imagined how remarkable it would feel. I'm also proud that you're related to me, if only through my son. I've often felt lonely, too, and it seems that I'm finally being compensated for what I lost."

Kevin smiled again and thanked Jesik for his kindness.

After Kevin departed, Jesik laid back in bed and considered the changes that had occurred in the last twenty-four hours. He hoped that these good feelings would hold together once the glare of the public spotlight fell on his new found family.

* * *

By the time the public announcement was made through a simulcast on Alturus, Keswick and Kalenden, the Magills had been told what was coming. As predicted, Sean's father told him to stand up bravely for "his" people. His mother became a friend of Helen Wight and they decided it would be best to meet the reporters at the Magill home. This pleased PM Larimore and other members of the cabinet immensely, as it sent the precise message they hoped about class unity. It also helped that the Wight name was important enough that the expected furor didn't materialize over Sean Magill's birth. The upper class wisely chose to keep reservations to themselves and most of them actually relished the thought that the Alturian Royalty had been humbled enough to turn to Kalenden for help. The ancient rejection was more palatable now.

Meanwhile, the story of tragic love finally reunited, played wonderfully to the second and third-classes. In the days that followed, there were some columnists who expressed the sentiment that Kalenden society should be ashamed for creating a culture where two young people in love would be kept apart by social prejudice. Fortunately, no mention was made of Kensington's involvement.

Mostly, though, the people on Kalenden and Keswick were caught up in the excitement of a royal courtship. The promise of pageantry captured the public's imagination and reporters quickly figured out that they had a treasure trove of opportunity as they updated daily on what had occurred on Alturus over the past two hundred years. It was also a good time to be an Esper, since the new openness enabled families long separated, to contact one another. The queues for basic twenty-minute links quickly overwhelmed the system and even the upper class had to enter a lottery and await their turn for communication links.

The reaction on Keswick, however, was bittersweet. With the death of their own monarchy, many felt regret. The more radical elements of the rebels were also disappointed, as this union was likely to defuse their hopes of sweeping reform for the entire system. But the press acted responsibly, providing great insight to the advantages of having two stable neighbors. That appealed to the pragmatists in the crowd, while the promise of the Royal marriage being carried on live video links helped shake off the torpor of the Loyalists as they frantically prepared for the events on Alturus. Great parties were planned for the official announcement, with huge video screens set up in public places as well as private residences. The pain of the rebellion subsided and Jesik and Magill were instant heroes of the lower-classes and their second-class credentials were replayed endlessly on the broadcasting channels. Their role in supporting the Loyalists during the rebellion was downplayed, while their courage and dash on both Cambriol and in helping establish the UCG was projected as proof of the innate ability of the common people. Lansing commented to Wilkerson that the fuss was just what the planetoid needed to shake off the bitterness and bring people together.

Meanwhile on Alturus, the news was unbelievably popular. At first the aristocracy was standoffish, but when they saw the monarchy supported it, there was no choice but to fall in line. The lower-classes accepted this as a way to avoid armed rebellion and embraced the wedding with open arms. The rebel movement evaporated as everyone prepared for the grand, official announcement.

The palace was decorated in royal banners and a receiving platform built outside the royal gardens where the Courtship Ceremony traditionally took place. Since it occurred but once in every generation, it was the equivalent of every national holiday rolled into one event and the people celebrated jubilantly.

The preparations took place while the Allegro was locked in vortex drive, so the crew only caught snippets and fragments of the happenings. Magill had become an instant celebrity onboard, eclipsing even Eaves in popularity. It was embarrassing to Magill and to Jesik, but the excitement was obviously heartfelt and a source of pride for the entire ship.

"So, you finally have an audience," said Eaves, half-jokingly.

"Apparently. And for the first time in my life, I don't know what to say."

"Your job is to say as little as possible and avoid controversy, which will be interesting."

"I thought so, too," said Magill, "but Tara – I mean Isabec – says she wants me to be active in public life. Apparently the Alturian Royalty is quite different than the ancient Earth monarchies, in that they're deeply involved in government. It's obvious I have a lot to learn about protocol and I hope I don't embarrass her. I'm not worried about meeting with government ministers, but I'll have to meet with aristocrats and members of the Royal Family and, as you know, I have no idea how to circulate in high society. I hate the thought of it."

Eaves turned and looked directly at Magill. "Sean, for once I'm going to be serious, so prepare yourself."

Magill took him at his word and looked at him intently.

"Sean, this is what you were born for. From the first moment I met you at the Academy and saw you ranting about how stuck up we were I knew you were destined to do great things. Don't ask me how I knew, I just did. And now you have to face up to your destiny. All the upper class people you talk about are just like those at the Academy. Most of them are scared silly that they'll fall into royal disfavor or make a stupid mistake that embarrasses their family. So they act like snobs to protect themselves. Just remember that they're people, just like you, and you'll get along fine. Meanwhile, it's about time the second and third-class families get the recognition they deserve. You'll be the best thing that ever happens to them."

"Thanks. It's all pretty scary right now, but I'll figure it out."

"At least you get Isabec in the deal. She's got to be the most practical royal anyone can imagine. I watched the way she bathed your legs while you were still unconscious. Nothing personal, my friend, but they sure looked and smelled awful from the burns. But that didn't slow her down for a second. And she took good care of my arm, even though there was blood everywhere. She's really remarkable and you're damned lucky."

"Indeed she is and so am I." Magill smiled. "To think she loves me. Wow! The kid from Kalenden makes it big!"

"Of course there's also the business about you being Jesik's son. That, too, is pretty amazing stuff."

"That was the biggest shock of all."

"I mean, you'd think he could have done so much better." Eaves tried to look thoughtful.

"Ah," said Magill. "Done being serious, are we?"

"No, completely serious." Eaves looked at him, innocently.

"Okay, buddy, do you want a chance to redeem yourself at handball?"

Eaves darkened. "I'm not sure. It's pretty humiliating losing to a guy in a wheelchair. I've got a reputation, too, you know."

"We'll keep this to ourselves. It wouldn't make any sense revealing the weaknesses of my best man, would it – the hero of Cambriol and all that? People need to hang onto their illusions."

"Thanks. But I'd fasten your wheelchair seatbelt if I was you. I'm desperate for revenge."

* * *

When the Allegro decelerated, to more easily maneuver through the Alturian system, they found the place in chaos, with hundreds of craft vying for position in orbit. Still, Lieutenant Commander Wight maneuvered through the traffic effortlessly. He'd been in great spirits since learning that Magill was his half-brother and they spent many hours together, playing sports or just talking. Sean had talked to him about moving to Alturus, where he was told social attitudes weren't as restrictive as on Kalenden, and Kevin was giving it serious thought.

The crew was fascinated to finally see the fabled planet of Alturus. It was larger than Kalenden and the population ten times as great. The ship had been increasing the artificial gravity slowly over the course of the voyage so that people could get used to it. In the first week after their arrival, Jesik was under constant pressure to meet with trade representatives and government officials, participate in the rehearsal for the Announcement Ceremony, and respond to the media. On his trips to the surface, it was obvious that Alturus was older than Keswick and Kalenden. Even though they shared a common language, the local dialect was often difficult to follow, so he had to give each conversation close attention or he could miss important parts.

It also turned out that on Alturus, the Courtship Announcement was almost equal to the wedding itself, since it signaled the onset of six months of celebrations, leading up to the actual ceremony. That ensured time for

vendors to get their commemorative books, plates, and coffee cup hold-
ers printed and distributed before the wedding. The Announcement itself
would be made from the Grand Balcony of the Imperial Palace, with the
King and Queen personally accepting Magill's proposal of marriage. Princess Isabec made it clear that traditional protocol would be modified so that
after her father accepted Magill's entreaty, he would then ask her directly.
Jesik liked that change and thought it to be the right way to get their marriage off on a good footing. Magill would then announce that Eaves and
Wight would serve as his best men.

After the rehearsal, with less than twenty-four hours to go, Wight, Brighton, Eaves and Jesik returned to the Allegro to assist in final preparations for the
laser show the ship would perform once the Announcement was official. Amazingly, the Alturians had never learned to adapt their ship's lasers for an upper
atmosphere display, so this promised to be the Kalendens' way of announcing
their presence and showing their renewed friendship with Alturus. It was essential, therefore, that the display proceed without any problems.

Jesik had been rehearsing his lines for the ceremony where he would
announce his approval for Sean to enter into the marriage. It was a protocol insisted upon by the Kalenden Quadrant Council to make sure that,
in the goodwill flowing all around, there was no actual reunion of the two
systems. Politics were still important.

"But I think it should be the Magill's who stand as your parents at
the actual wedding," Jesik had said, "with Helen and me at least one pace
behind." Sean had nodded and that's how it was to be. But since neither the
Magills or Helen could arrive in time for the Announcement Ceremony, it
fell to Jesik to carry the honors.

* * *

"Sir, there's a small fighter making an unusual approach to the planet."
"Can you identify it, Mr. Gentry?"
"No, Sir. It's an odd design – nothing resembling either Alturian or
Keswickian."
"What makes its approach unusual?"
"It's much more shallow than usual and at an extremely high speed."
"It's definitely unexpected," Wight exclaimed, "look how many fighters
the Alturians have scrambled to intercept it."
Jesik laid his paper down and studied the screen, now alive with ani-
mated images. At least ten high-speed fighters raced from an orbiting plat-
form directly for the small ship that headed towards the planet.

Brighton asked Gentry, "At that speed, won't it burn up in the atmosphere?"

"Yes, Sir. That's what I don't understand." Then Gentry gasped, "Wait a minute, he's not heading for the atmosphere, he's headed straight for that abandoned alinite freighter."

Jesik studied the screen and said, "At that speed he'll crash into it." He watched the Alturian fighters launch some twenty missiles, but knew they'd be too late to stop the spacecraft before it collided with the freighter. About twenty seconds later a large flash on the main screen proved the two ships had collided.

All other activity on the bridge ceased and everyone studied the monitors. The Alturian fighters broke off frantically just before they collided with the freighter. Then the automatic alarm system sounded.

"Sir, we have an urgent communication from the planet surface."

"Captain Jesik of Allegro, can you verify the angle of the collision – you're in the best position for an aerial view."

"Feed those coordinates to the surface," Jesik ordered Wight.

"Oh, no!" said Wight said. "The collision has changed the angle of orbit on the freighter. It's going to crash into the atmosphere, now."

"Why is that significant?" asked Jesik.

Wight ran some quick computations. "Sir, having an alinite hull, the ship will not burn up in the atmosphere and if my calculations are correct, the wreckage will hit the planet with the force of a small asteroid. The debris field will include the Palace in Capitol City and cause an instant fireball from the impact. If the pieces are large enough, it will have the same impact as a forty or fifty megaton nuclear explosion. The dust cloud alone could change the atmosphere for a decade or longer."

"Ground zero is where the people are gathered for the ceremony," said Brighton. "Obviously, this is a terrorist attack and the rebels knew exactly when and where to hit the ship to cause the greatest damage."

Jesik turned to Weapons, just as the Alturian command interrupted again.

"Captain, the coordinates you gave us have confirmed our concerns."

"The freighter will not break up in the atmosphere," Jesik added.

"Yes. How did you know that?"

"Our analysis shows the debris field will shatter Capitol City. Unless you can find a way to destroy the freighter, you'll need to evacuate the city at once."

There was silence on the other end. Then Admiral Rameira spoke.

"I'm afraid there's no safe way to destroy it, Captain. The debris will land in less than six hours and we can't mobilize the people fast enough. It looks like we're to be victims of a suicide attack."

Jesik turned to Gentry, who said, "We finally found a match for the fighter, Captain. It's a Keswick rebel ship, lightly disguised, similar to the one that attacked the Allegro shuttle during the Manhattan Trials."

"What can we do to help, Admiral? We'll be glad to shoot at it, if you like."

"That's the problem, Jesik, even if we break it up with weapons the debris pieces will still be large enough to incinerate most of the city. Plus, our atmosphere is quite different than yours and any explosions from above the spacecraft in the upper atmosphere could ignite an ozone fire that would be deadly to the entire planet. We're running our alternatives, but frankly there aren't many choices."

Jesik looked at the bridge crew. "Gentlemen, I need ideas, right away!"

Answers flew at him, but all were discarded because they would make matters worse, not better. Finally, Kevin Wight spoke up. "Perhaps we could dispatch a shuttle to work its way under the alinite freighter and change its angle of descent."

"That's a good idea," Brighton said quickly, "but there's no way to control it and the shuttle would be driven down with the freighter."

"Why not remote control?" Jesik demanded.

"We'd lose communication with the shuttle when it passed under the freighter and the maneuvers are too complicated to run as a pre-programmed sequence."

"Okay, so that's out," said Jesik. "What else is available?" From the corner of his eye he saw Eaves and Carter replace Wight and the navigator. "We have about ten minutes to come up with something," No one had any workable ideas, however, so he reestablished his link with Rameira.

"Admiral, we don't have any viable alternatives. What have you come up with?"

"Nothing, I'm afraid. As a last resort we'll fire laser cannons from the planet surface in the hope that we can soften the ship and burn larger chunks off before it gets through the atmosphere. Meanwhile, we've put the entire planet on alert and ordered the Royal Family into underground bunkers, where they may be safe. But, who knows?"

"Yes, who knows?" thought Jesik forlornly. "It seems that no matter what lengths reasonable people go to in order to avoid war, there are always fanatics who'll do whatever is necessary to thwart their efforts."

"Admiral Rameira, we are at your disposal and will assist any way we can. Please let us know how to help."

"Thank you, Captain. Once the damage is known, my immediate concern will be to relieve the millions of citizens who will have the dubious distinction of surviving the blast. It goes without saying that the entire planet will be affected for years." He broke the communications link.

Jesik stared at the screen, motionless. *The most powerless feeling one can have is to watch helplessly as a horror unfolds before your eyes.* No one on the bridge wanted to watch the freighter enter the atmosphere, but they couldn't take their eyes off the screen. The drama was being relayed throughout the ship, where everyone halted in disbelief. The celebration they had been anticipating moments before, had now turned into a vicious terrorist attack that was about to destroy at least a third of the inhabitable surface of the planet.

"Sir, we've launched a shuttlecraft?" said Gentry, as much a question as a statement.

"What? I authorized no shuttle. This certainly isn't the time for anyone to leave the ship!" He spoke into the ship's communication array, demanding the shuttle pilot identify himself. There was no response.

"Wait a minute," said Eaves, "That's not an ordinary shuttle. It's the Captain's personal launch."

Jesik again demanded to know who was piloting the shuttle, but no one could answer, including those in the shuttle bay.

Finally, a nervous voice came over the public address system. "Sir, Lieutenant Commander Wight told us you had authorized the launch personally, so we checked the shuttle out on his authority."

"Wight?" Jesik turned to Brighton.

"He's going to maneuver under the ship to change its angle of descent, Sir."

"Mr. Wight," Jesik called out in an all frequencies hail. "Return to the Allegro immediately. That's an order!" Still, there was silence.

Jesik was so frightened he was angry. "Commander Wight, answer immediately or I'll have your shuttle disabled by laser fire." The instrument panel lit up to show an incoming response.

"Captain, I'm almost there. Please don't stop me. We both know this is the only hope for the planet."

"But, Commander, there's no way out once you're under the freighter. The friction of the atmosphere will hold you hostage."

"I know that, Sir." There was silence on the line for a few moments.

"Captain, please tell my mother how much I love her. And tell Sean that having him as my brother was the greatest thing ever to happen to me." He paused for a moment. "Actually, the second greatest thing. The best was the chance to serve with you. Thank you."

Jesik looked on helplessly as the shuttle disappeared under the alinite freighter, from which a sudden, brilliant flume erupted.

"He's got to give it full power for at least 180 seconds," said Carter, "or he won't alter the angle enough to make a difference."

Everyone watched mesmerized as the seconds clicked off. At 160 seconds the ship started to flame as it entered the upper atmosphere. Still, the exhaust flume continued to flare until 190 seconds. Then there was a bright flash from under the ship, indicating that the shuttle had burned up in the atmosphere.

"He's gone," said Eaves quietly.

"Oh, Kevin," Jesik whispered. "There had to be another way."

After a few moments of silence, Brighton spoke again. "What about the alinite ship?"

Carter quickly ran numbers, ran them a second time and then announced, "The ship's attitude has changed significantly – it looks like it will bounce off the atmosphere and exit to space. Mr. Wight's calculations were perfect."

No one on the bridge made a sound, which amplified the ambient noises from the instruments and engines. Moments ticked by in silence until the overhead speakers came to life in a burst of static from the ground. Cheering could be heard distinctly in the background. "I don't know what you folks did up there Captain, but you managed to save the planet. Congratulations and thank you!" The voice of PM Richards was jubilant and her face on the monitor exuded the joy and gratitude she and everyone in the Alturus Control Room felt.

Jesik wanted to respond, but couldn't find the words. It was then that the Prime Minister noticed what was happening. "Something's wrong, Captain, what is it?"

Jesik tried to speak, but the lump in his throat hurt too much.

Brighton intervened. "One of our bridge officers came up with the action that caused the change in the freighter's entry pattern. Unfortunately, he sacrificed his own life to accomplish it. We're all trying to absorb what's happened."

Richards was obviously distressed. "I'm sorry to hear of your loss. May I ask the name of your valiant crew member?"

"Kevin Wight," Brighton replied.

"You mean Lieutenant Commander Magill's younger brother?"

"Yes, ma'am."

"I see." She shook her head. "Gentlemen, I know you feel his loss keenly. But, his sacrifice saved millions of lives. This date will become an annual memorial for Kevin Wight on Alturus and its colonies. The memory of this will live forever. In the meantime, please accept our deepest condolences – and our most profound gratitude." Out of respect, PM Richard broke the connection and silence returned to the bridge.

Jesik stood, unsteadily. "Tom, do you think you could ..." his voice trailed off.

"Of course, Sir. Captain leaving the bridge!"

Everyone turned and saluted, but none looked at him directly. Even a Captain was entitled to privacy at such a moment.

20— THE QUADRANTS UNITED

It seemed impossible that six months had passed since the gray day when Kevin Wight took matters into his own hands. So much had happened since then. The Announcement of Courtship had occurred, a day later than planned, but cheering was muted and the colors were intentionally dulled as a sign of respect. There had also been more than 100 million e-mails from both the Alturian and Kalenden quadrants expressing sympathy for the Allegro's loss and emphasizing support for the Alturian government. The rebel movement had effectively been decimated by the double impact of introducing second-class blood into the Royal Family and the shock and outrage over the terrorist's attack.

The rebel's assault nearly de-stabilized the government on Keswick, but Lansing managed to avoid catastrophe by tracking down the terrorists who had furnished the ships for the two attacks on Kalenden and Alturus. The people responsible were well-entrenched into the general population, but his anti-espionage unit managed to turn one member against the rest of the group. Based on this intelligence the Coalition troops surrounded the compound where the main group was. When the terrorists discovered their presence they launched a vicious counterattack. The bloody fight left more than a dozen government troops dead or wounded. Over one hundred extremists also perished. The surviving captives committed suicide with cyanide pills. It was gruesome and Lansing used all his persuasive powers to calm the population and build a consensus for the reforms that were now starting to take effect. He managed, through personal force of will, to keep the coalition together, too. Still, the pace of reform had slowed, with the Loyalist Party standing a better chance to pick up a near-majority in the upcoming elections.

The most significant change in Jesik's life came in a coded message from Wilkerson that reported Kensington had taken his own life. He hanged himself using cords from his mattress hem. There was no suicide note, which was not what would be expected from Kensington, but Jesik didn't push Wilkerson for more details. Apparently the news that Wight had been elevated to hero status was just too much for him. In spite of everything that had transpired between them, Jesik felt sorrow for the life that Kensington had lived. He was aware that hatred was what robbed the man of his freedom. Whatever drove Kensington to his death, it was to Jesik's relief not to have to again protect himself from the Colonel's wrath.

"I never understood his motives," Brighton had said when Jesik told him of the suicide. "Why nurture a grudge for so many years?"

Jesik shook his head. "I never did understand him. The best I can come up with is that he had a particular way of viewing the world that to him seemed right. And my involvement with Helen went against that. I became the person-ification of what he thought was going wrong in the world, and so he wanted to destroy me."

"Instead it destroyed him."

Jesik nodded. "That's usually the way it is when hate takes over."

With only a few weeks before the royal wedding, Jesik was also pleased that the feelings between Sean and Isabec proved to be true love. They relished each other's company and enjoyed light-hearted banter that made their relationship fun as well as romantic. Jesik found that he loved being the father of an adult child and thoroughly enjoyed his conversations with the young couple. He also found Isabec's parents articulate, well-informed and together they caught up on the two centuries of isolation. There were dozens of parties to attend, public ceremonies and introductions and a number of memorial services for Kevin. In what was apparently one of the most notable changes in Alturian public life, distant relatives of Jesik and Magill were invited to the royal functions, even though they were from second-class families. This received much recogni-tion on public video, with commentators reflecting on how polished Jesik and Magill comported themselves with even the most illustrious of Alturian society.

When the Magills arrived, Jesik backed off and made sure that they assumed their proper place as Sean's parents. Lieutenant Commander Magill was obvi-ously grateful to have them there, but the military had given him something in common with Jesik, something he didn't share with the Magills, so Jesik enjoyed a special relationship with his son. The Magills were less comfortable in the public spotlight, but the Royal Family was gracious and kind, shielding them as much as possible from scrutiny. All-in-all, things worked out well and Jesik expressed appreciation to these two good people who had accepted the opportunity to raise his son.

His first meeting with Helen Wight didn't go as well as he'd hoped for. While extremely gracious and composed in public, she was tentative and standoffish during their private time together. She was reluctant to talk about Kevin, even though Jesik ached to tell her what a great young man she bore.

Two nights before the wedding, Jesik and Helen were having a quiet dinner to prepare themselves for the press of public affairs that would soon engulf them. A knock came on their door. It was Tom and Sondra Brighton.

"Mind if we come in for a few moments?"

"Not at all. Please join us for dessert." Jesik was actually relieved to have them join in conversation. He stepped to the food panel and requested two additional hot fudge sundaes.

"So, Captain Brighton, how does it feel to have your own ship? Are you finding your bearings on the Legato?"

"I think I am, Sir. I enjoy being able to think strategically, rather than focusing on schedules and daily operations. But there are times when the personnel issues are overwhelming. I don't know how you kept track of everything."

"The better part of wisdom is to know what to keep track of and what to delegate. All you're really responsible for are the important decisions and making sure those who are assigned to carry out orders are doing so." Brighton nodded assent.

They chatted on about the service for awhile and particularly on Brighton's promotion.

"Captain, I hope this isn't an untimely request, but you quoted a poem at Kevin Wight's memorial service. The lines continue to run through my head and I wonder if I might have a copy of the original?"

Helen looked up and said, "You spoke at Kevin's service?"

Jesik flushed a bit, "I thought you'd seen it. It was broadcast in all three systems and as Kevin's Captain, it was my responsibility to preside."

"Please recite the poem for me?"

"It's an old earth poem written by Emily Dickinson. She'd been to a Veteran's Day parade and wanted to convey the idea that as great as their sacrifice was, it couldn't compare to those who pay the ultimate price in behalf of others.

> Success is counted sweetest
> By those who ne'er succeed
> To comprehend a nectar
> Requires sorest need.

Not one of all the purple host
Who took the flag today
Can tell the definition so clear of victory
As he defeated, dying, on whose forbidden ear
The distant sounds of triumph
Bursts agonized and clear.

— Emily Dickinson"

Helen looked thoughtful. "So, was Kevin all alone when he died?"

"Not for very long. And he spoke to us until the last moments."

"Did the other men like Kevin?"

"Very much," Brighton interjected. "He was a person who could brighten a room with his laugh and make you feel like your comments were the most important that he had ever heard. I think if you were to ask around the bridge, everyone would say he had the amazing ability to make each of us feel important."

"I'm glad," she said softly, "he was often lonesome at home. I hoped he found happiness in the service." Turning to Jesik she added, "I know from his letters that he thought the world of you, Pietr."

"And that's how I thought of him. He was an outstanding officer and friend." What more could he say?

"Which brings us to our main reason for dropping by," said Brighton, trying to lighten the moment. "Sondra?"

"Yes, well, on my home planet, Tatrius, it is traditional that parents wait at least six months to a year before naming a child. It's our belief that we should get to know the child before making such an important decision as to how they will be known throughout their life." She paused expectantly. "Tom and I would like your permission to name our son Kevin Pietr Brighton."

Jesik blushed. "I'd be honored. Truly honored. Both to have your son bear my name and to share that honor with Kevin."

"Of course I'd be proud as well, to have your son carry Kevin's name," Helen said. "And while I understand that many children are being given his name since his death gained so much attention, we in this room will know that it is your son who will most remind us of him. Thank you."

Brighton and Sondra smiled and excused themselves. Jesik marveled at how much depth Tom had gained since his marriage. He'd always been an excellent officer, but now was an excellent man. He would be the kind of father every child deserved. After the door closed and Jesik and Helen were alone, he said, "Would you like to talk more about Kevin?"

She looked up, anxiously.

"No, thank you. I'm not ready yet."

"Then perhaps we should talk about our boy, Sean. He's an outstanding young man as well. Many of his mannerisms remind me of you."

"But, he looks and acts like you – decisive and strong."

"Improved by your sensitivity and concern."

Tears appeared in her eyes. "Oh, Pietr, I failed both of them, don't you see."

"You did what was forced on you."

"No, I was too weak to stand up to my father. We should have raised Sean together. After I married Richard Wight I was also too weak to insist we move to a neighborhood where Kevin wouldn't be so isolated. Kevin's father was concerned only about our social standing and children bothered him. So we rarely had any youngsters over for Kevin to play with. I was lonesome too." Helen put her face in her hands and started crying. Jesik moved to comfort her, but she stiffened at his approach and immediately wiped her eyes. "I'm sorry, Pietr, I shouldn't have. I think it would be better if I returned to my room now." She stood to leave.

"May I escort you?"

"No, thank you. I know my way. And thank you for a pleasant evening. I'm glad the Brightons stopped by; it seems like they'll be wonderful parents."

Back in control, she was again the perfect hostess. She moved to the door and out into the darkened corridor, leaving Jesik alone—again. Her isolation had made her a recluse and the light that once shone from her eyes was gone.

* * *

As the magical day approached, the wedding party assembled for the traditional rehearsal and wedding dinner. "Well-orchestrated pandemonium," one participant noted, with video crews from every star system and sector angling for the best position to capture the couple as they emerged from the temple. According to ancient tradition, the ceremony itself was private, with just family and closest friends. But after the couple emerges, they were to board a small, open, air shuttle to float down the main boulevard of the Capitol City to the great plaza, where the craft would rise to officially greet the assembled crowd as husband and wife, the Crown Princess and. in this case, her Consort. The title was unusual and followed an earlier conversation between Isabec and Sean. "While it's tradition to wait until after my accession to the throne to declare my husband a consort, my father and I feel that doing so immediately will show the monarchy's resolve to include you as royalty in spite of your mixed bloodlines. Is that alright with you," Isabec asked Sean. "We're going to be married forever, so why wait?" Sean agreed, overwhelmed by all that was happening. The announcement was to be a surprise to the crowd.

At the appointed time in the rehearsal dinner each parent was allowed to stand and offer a toast or remembrance of the couple, which led to some amusing stories and sentimental recollections. Then it was time for the Best Man's toast, and Travis Eaves's rose to his feet, coughed to clear his throat, and then said, "Perhaps you'll join me in a toast to the fortunate couple."

"To a life of endless surprises,
To a life of sorrows shared,
To a life of meaningful service,
To children, carefully reared,
To laugh and love each other,
Best friends in all the worlds,
That in the end the memories,
Will be worthy and complete,
From an old friend who will always cherish you,
Best wishes and healthy feet"

The crowd applauded their approval and then Sean laughed as he looked down at his feet. He'd had the first of three scheduled surgeries and even though he'd taken the prescribed anti-radiation medicine, the exposure to his feet had caused the bones to deteriorate to the point where the surgeons had to go in and scrape each surface smooth and clean. That was followed by a series of injections with synthetic marrow that, in time, would provide the strength needed to sustain the weight of his body. Next was to reconstruct the tendons and muscles and finally graft skin from his thighs to replace the tissue that refused to heal. It would be easier to accept prosthetic feet, or a cadaver transplant, but the Alturians had an almost-mystical attachment to the natural body that made them fight long after Kalenden medics would have given up. His doctors took him on as their chance to make an offering to he who would stand at the side of their monarch. Thus, they treated his feet with reverence. He endured the pain, hopeful that one day he could fully use his legs again. In the meantime, he'd been fitted with special braces that attached to his calves and thighs in such a way that he could stand with his feet suspended a few centimeters off the ground. The braces were painful and took getting used to, but eventually he learned to balance on them. Unfortunately, though, they were only practical for standing, not walking and so he was fine with Travis wheeling him down the corridors until the moment of the actual ceremony, where he would stand briefly, then kneel at an altar to take Isabec as his wife.

"Who would have thought I could write poetry," said Eaves.

"I liked the part about the old friend who will cherish me," Magill responded, "I'm more surprised that you can be sentimental than that you can write poetry. Will you read that again,?" Everyone laughed.

Then Jesik stood. "All I can add is that it's been my privilege to know Sean as an officer, before I knew him as my son. He's a superlative person in both roles and our systems will be well served to enjoy his service as a diplomat and adviser. Congratulations, Sean. And may God grant you and Princess Isabec long life and good fortune."

His words were greeted with the traditional "Here, here!"

Finally, the King rose, mindful that every word spoken this night would be repeated by the servants and most likely appear in the morning editions of the paper.

"It's been too long that there's been a division among our many families. While it's appropriate to distinguish people by roles, so that each can perform his or her life's work with excellence, it's simply wrong to do so exclusively by virtue of birth. In this young man, whom I have come to love and respect, we have hope of reconciliation. Sean, you are taking the one thing in the universe, aside from my wife, that I truly value. Please treat her well, placing the needs of your family ahead of even the needs of our system. Only when your family is right, will you be able to offer great service to others."

Turning to his daughter he said, "Isabec, Sean's a good man. Don't try to run over him, as is so often your wont. He and I have talked privately and he knows he doesn't have to take it." She looked up at her father with a scowl, but quickly changed it to a mischievous smile. "Love him forever, as deeply as I know you do now and I have no worries for your future." Then, picking up his glass he said, "A toast to the royal heirs." And on that, the evening adjourned.

The ceremony, the next day, was elegantly simple and they were pleased that their most important moment when they accepted each other as husband and wife, was held away from the glare of the spotlight.

When they exited the temple, things were no longer quiet. The welcoming they received moving toward the Plaza was spectacular, with more than 100,000 people lining the way and billions more viewing from all corners of the adjacent universe. The wedding party floated down the main concourse on an open reviewing platform until they reached the historic center of the plaza, which tradition held was the place of the first landing of the original Earth settlers.

At the conclusion of the wedding ceremony, Travis Eaves slipped away from the main party and led an honor guard of six Allegro fighters in a dramatic fly-over, dipping their wings in honor of the royal couple on the first pass. On the return pass, just as they reached the reviewing stand, Eaves peeled off and disappeared as an honor to the sacrifice made by the new Prince's younger brother. That one did Jesik in, for Kevin's death would forever remain an open wound.

As the platform rose so that the couple could address their subjects, Eaves managed to slip aboard at the last moment, to help Sean stand at the appropriate time.

"Where did you hide your fighter to get here so fast?" Jesik whispered.

"In the lily pond over there," said Eaves triumphantly. "It'll be hard to clean, but no one will ever suspect."

The Crown Princess stepped to the microphone and spoke with sincerity about her love of the people and her hopes for a new and greater unity among all the descendents of Earth (a nice way to include Keswick and Kalenden). She also spoke of her love for her husband and the great regard she had for both his natural and adoptive families.

Then Sean stood, a bit awkwardly, and stepped to the podium. The crowd quieted, some hoping he'd do well, others convinced he'd show the folly of mixing classes, for everyone had a stake in his performance.

It was like his dreams, except that there were a lot more people than even his vivid imagination had conjured up. Tradition required that he say something non-controversial. Instead, he decided to be himself and let his story convey his feelings. It didn't take more than five minutes.

"As a boy I grew up with an attitude that life was unfair and that the unofficial aristocracy of my planet would always work to keep the lower-classes down. The best entertainment we had was when my friends and I could beat-up an upper class kid if we found him alone. It was exhilarating to feel the power that came from anger and resentment. In a way, it also freed us from responsibility for our own lives, because we could blame someone else. Then fate intervened to help me find my way out of prejudice. Without my seeking it, I was accepted to an upper class academy – a concession to the lower-classes that I desperately wanted to avoid. But, my mother insisted." He turned and smiled at Candace Magill, who glowed in return. "And so, off I went. But, things didn't change when I arrived there, because I believe you always find what you're looking for and I wanted to see arrogant snobs. So, that's what I saw. My grudge grew deeper. I was a pain to be around, mostly because I was in so much pain. I felt embarrassed, out of place and wanted to make it their fault I felt that way. I hated them, maybe because I hated myself. But, then one of those spoiled kids decided to make me his project and instead became my friend. You've all heard of the Cambriol incident. The reason we could do that was because I'd come to realize that Travis and the others were just like my third-class friends, just as trustworthy, just as loyal and just as smart. They had their own prejudices, but not because of class. They just didn't like people who talked more than they performed."

"At any rate, I learned that everything I believed about the upper class was wrong, at least for some of them. You shouldn't make generalizations about individuals. We're all people. We all have something to offer and we all have something we need."

He paused to catch his breath.

"In my heart I'm a member of the third-class, the solid part of our population that does the work of our civilization. But, it turns out that my only connection to that class is through my adoption by the Magills. It's quite a thing to realize my bloodline descended from royalty. But, I don't feel like I'm royal – I don't even really know what it means to be royal. Instead, it feels like the real adoption that took place is that I was adopted by the upper class – first by Travis Eaves, and later, by my natural father. He was kind to me long before we knew of our relationship. Now I've been accepted into this Royal Family with open arms. And even though it doesn't feel natural, it feels good. All these people accommodated me even before my true genealogy was known. The Princess won my heart during the Keswick Campaign when she didn't ignore me because I was third-class. She simply saw me for who I am and helped when I was in trouble. That gives me hope that the frustrations some of you feel can be overcome." He took a deep breath.

"Monarchy can be a great institution, because it provides continuity over time and gives us each a common point of reference. A good monarch provides us a reason to feel proud of who we are. Their love of system and their people, inspires us to do our very best. Democracy, on the other hand, empowers all its citizens to provide the very best they can to their society. Rank and privilege are earned by accomplishment and the entire society prospers. Perhaps the best government is one that combines both elements. I believe that's what we can accomplish now." He looked at his bride with pride.

"I think some people feel I agreed to this marriage to satisfy the needs of a hereditary unity. If our marriage accomplishes that, it will be worthwhile. But the truth is that I married Princess Isabec because I love her. Long before I knew she was royal, I found she is smart, shrewd and skilled. More than that, she cares as deeply as any person can. The most frightening part is that had I known she was royal, I likely would have spurned her, because of my old prejudices. But now that I know her, I know that if she is what it means to be royal, then that's wonderful. It's something we can all be proud of, because she represents the best in what it means to be human. I plan to spend the rest of my life with her. I hope you'll come to trust us and that together we can serve this planet in a way that allows all its people to reach their full potential."

He coughed, then cleared his throat.

"The great challenge of our day is to unify all the classes. I believe I'm proof that we can. I'm an adopted son of the third-class, a paternal son of the second-class and a maternal heir of the royal class. Hopefully, my experience of being in all these classes can be an icon for our society. With fathers like Robert Magill and Pietr Jesik and mothers like Candace Magill and Helen Wight, I know we can find unity. So, God grant us the wisdom and courage to let go of our ancient prejudices."

He paused and swallowed, fearful that nothing he'd said made sense and that he'd embarrassed Isabec. He looked at her in panic, but her reassuring smile told him that even if he'd failed to win the crowd, she was proud. It was then that he heard the roar of approval from all sides. Travis, who'd been holding him steady, grinned broadly and turned his disabled friend to see all the people cheering. It would have been expected that the cheers would be loudest from the second and third-class members of the crowd, but it was actually the aristocracy that shouted with the most fervor. They recognized that the monarchy had been enhanced by the heartfelt words of this young man from Kalenden.

After Sean's speech, the entire wedding party moved to the front of the reviewing platform to watch the fireworks and laser display.

As they stood there, Eaves leaned over to Sean and whispered, "A fine speech by anyone's standard. But was it as good as the ones you've practiced through the years?"

"Better, because none of those included Isabec."

Eaves swept his eyes from side to side, before whispering again. "You know what the single most important responsibility of a Prince Consort is, don't you?"

Magill looked at him suspiciously.

"It's to create a suitable heir."

Magill turned with a frown, but Eaves was undeterred. "It's not bad work, I understand."

"You are one sick puppy, aren't you, Travis?"

"Just trying to be a good adviser."

"I'd stick to fighter jets, if I were you."

"At least your business partner in the enterprise is a lot better looking than Carter!"

At that, Sean cracked up.

"Alright, alright, I'll add it to my To Do List. Father an heir to the imperial throne of Alturus. Boy, that's one that's been on my Lifetime Goals list, something your average third-class boy aspires to."

Eaves turned thoughtful and whispered, "At least now they can aspire to it, thanks to you."

Both Magill and Eaves looked up, deer-in-the-headlights like, as Isabec glowered at them for talking during the ceremony. Impulsively, Sean responded by leaning over and kissing her on the cheek.

Of course that shocked her, as it was a violation of the strict rules that govern such events. She was about to say something, but apparently thought better of it, because she reached up with both her hands, placed them squarely on Sean's cheeks, and planted, on his lips one of the longest kisses ever recorded on interstellar video. He staggered back when she released him and fell into Eaves' arms, a dazed smile on his face.

Isabec simply blinked her eyes coyly and said innocently, "Sorry, but I just can't seem to resist a good-looking guy in leg braces—particularly one who can't keep his mouth shut during an ancient, solemn ceremony."

"Okay, then," said Eaves, shoving Magill back into Isabec's arms, "I can see my work here is done."

The crowd went crazy. After all, it was long odds that an arranged marriage actually included a bride and groom who liked each other.

Standing a few feet back, Jesik observed Travis, Sean, and Isabec enjoying each other's banter and a warm feeling flooded through him. He loved young people and the thought that his own son could be so happy was perhaps the best thing that had ever happened to him.

He relaxed his hands at his side so they fell open and suddenly he felt the delicate hand of Helen Wight slip into his. He turned and she smiled. She'd been watching Sean and Isabec as well. It was the first time he'd seen hope in her eyes and the first time she'd been able to show affection since her arrival at Alturus.

Maybe even the most deeply wounded heart can heal, though Jesik. Then he gave her hand a gentle squeeze and raised his other arm to wave to the crowd.

The End

ABOUT THE AUTHOR

Jerry Borrowman is an award winning author of historical fiction and co-authored biography from the late 19th and early 20th Centuries. Visit www.jerryborrowman.com to view all his books and stories. This is his fourteenth book to be published.

Made in the USA
Charleston, SC
12 April 2014